Book 7
of the
Cornish Chronicles
A New Era

The Hand that Wrote this Letter

Ann E Brockbank

The Hand that Wrote this Letter.

For Caroline

For good company and conversation over a cup of coffee.
Your visits brighten my day.

By Ann E Brockbank

Cornish Chronicles

1. A Gift from the Sea – Set between 1901 - 1902
2. Waiting for the Harvest Moon - Set between 1907-1908
3. My Song of the Sea - Set between 1911 -1912
4. The Path We Take – Set in 1912
5. The Glittering Sea - Set between 1912 – 1919
6. Our Days in the Sun – Set in 1919
7. The Hand that Wrote this Letter - Set between 1922-1923

Historical Novels

Mr de Sousa's Legacy – Set between 1938 – 1960

Contemporary Novels

The Blue Bay Café
On a Distant Shore

The Hand that Wrote this Letter.

ACKNOWLEDGMENTS

My upmost thanks go to you, Angie, for your editorial help, support, and historical guidance. You have no idea how much I appreciate your generous time, friendship, and expertise. Also, to Hazel, who helps me to polish this manuscript ready to send out to the world.

To my partner, Rob, for every single wonderful thing you do, your love and encouragement has kept me writing, and as always, your beautiful artwork adds a special quality to my novels.

To the amazing staff at Poldhu Café Cornwall - thank you for selling my novels and your continued support.

To Caroline - For good company and conversation over a cup of coffee. Your visits brighten my day. This book is dedicated to you.

To my darling late husband, Peter, you are forever in my heart.

My heartfelt gratitude goes to Sarah and Martin Caton and their lovely family for allowing me to use their beautiful home Bochym Manor as a setting for my 'Cornish Chronicles' novels.

And last, but certainly not least, my grateful thanks go to all you lovely people who buy and read my books. I so appreciate your continual support. You are all wonderful and I'm enormously privileged that you believe in me and chose my books to read. Special thanks as always goes to Kim, my friend who continually champions my books on social media so that they reach a larger audience.

ABOUT THE AUTHOR

Ann E Brockbank was born in Yorkshire but has lived in Cornwall for many years. The Hand that Wrote this Letter is Ann's tenth book and the seventh Cornish Chronicles book. Ann lives with her artist partner on the beautiful banks of the Helford River in Cornwall - an integral setting for all of her novels. Ann is currently writing her next novel. Ann loves to chat with her readers so please visit her Facebook Author page and follow her on Twitter and Instagram

Facebook: @AnnEBrockbank.Author
Twitter: @AnnEBrockbank1
Instagram: annebrockbank

The Hand that Wrote this Letter.

1
Sunday 30th April 1922

The tiny community of Polhormon, near Mullion, situated amongst lush green meadows looking down upon the majestic Poldhu Cove, consisted of the Polhormon Farmhouse - home to Farmer David Trevorrow, a jolly, but powerful ex-boxer, his wife Alice and their three sons, the Trevorrow Dairy Farm, two tied cottages and the Polhormon saddlery. It was in this saddlery, teetering on the top of a rickety ladder, that the local saddler - twenty-year-old Ben Pearson - spat off the dust and feathers falling on his face as he tried desperately to rescue his pet white dove, Amara. She had become entangled in the netting that he'd put across his skylight to stop the jackdaws from entering.

'Settle down, girl,' Ben soothed as the bird frantically flapped its wings in fright.

The ladder wobbled alarmingly as he grasped the bird a little too hard, wincing as she pecked his hand.

'Hush now,' he soothed, releasing the bird so it could fly to its favourite perch on top of the bookcase which housed a dusty collection of leather-bound books. Satisfied of a job well done, he brushed his hands together, only to feel the ladder slip from under his feet just as a waft of expensive perfume preceded a woman's voice bidding him good morning.

Down he went in the most ungainly fashion, crashing against the bookcase and landing with an almighty thud against the corner of his scrubbed oak table. The pain that shot through his back was like nothing he'd ever felt before, and in embarrassment, he tried to roll away from his unexpected visitor, releasing an involuntary groan of agony.

'Oh, good gracious me, Ben.'

Through his fug of pain, Ben looked up into those familiar beautiful, pale blue eyes of Lady Emma Dunston - the Earl and Countess de Bochym's eldest daughter.

As pleased as he was to see her, the pain coursing through his body made him feel ill, and Emma's perfume, although beautiful, was adding to his nausea.

'Goodness, Ben! I'm so sorry,' Emma cried - her face stricken with concern. 'I fear I caused this dreadful accident?'

'No, no,' he tried to protest, but his eyes rolled back in pain with the effort of speech.

'Stay still, Ben, I shall go fetch the doctor.'

'No,' his voice cracked, 'I'll be fine, I just need to get up. Argh!' But Emma had swept from his workshop, and a moment later he heard her canter away.

Drenched in perspiration, he dragged his knees towards his chest, in an agonising attempt to move himself onto all fours. The pain, initially in his back, transferred to his lower right rib, and as he shifted his weight, the rib moved with a sickening intensity.

Get up, Ben, he urged, moving tentatively towards his work chair. Amara had now perched herself on the chair back, her head tipping side to side as he crawled towards her. After several attempts, he heaved himself onto the chair, sending a prayer of thanks that his back and neck were not broken. He felt a trickle of blood running down the back of his neck, and his left-hand little finger was sticking out at an alarming angle. He was sweating profusely from the effort, but couldn't remove his jacket for the pain and had a thirst like no other from his constant shallow breathing.

The dove sat casually observing him and Ben gave her a sidelong glance. 'Don't look so innocent, Amara, look what you've done to me.'

Ben had raised Amara since she was a fledgling, found floundering at the foot of a tree with an injured wing three years ago. He brought her home, tended her and she'd since thrived and rarely left his side.

He glanced at the unfinished work on his table, from the pain he was experiencing he knew he would be incapable to complete any of it for a few days. Thankfully the eighteenth birthday present, a saddle he'd made to fit Lady Emma's new palomino horse, had been delivered to Bochym Manor yesterday in time for her party. That must have been her purpose to visit him - to thank him for it.

Ben was the only son of Sydney and Rose Pearson - Sydney being the Bochym Manor estate steward. Despite their obvious class difference, Ben, Lady Emma, her brother William - Viscount Dunston - along with the Blackthorn siblings, Zack and Agnes from Poldhu, had all played together as children in the vast grounds of the Bochym Estate.

Emma. Ben smiled at the thought of seeing her again. She'd been away almost a year at finishing school in Switzerland, and my, from what he'd seen of her through his fug of pain, a transformation had taken place. No longer was she the gangly girl with the wind in her hair and her dress soiled from hours playing in the fields and by the stream. With golden hair, pale blue eyes and porcelain skin, she was the image of her beautiful mother, Sarah Dunstan. He winced at the shooting pain in his ribs, and bemoaned the fact that she'd found him in such a state.

*

Some twenty minutes later, the clatter of hooves preceded the sound of a car driving into the yard. Voices could be heard and the doctor knocked and came through to where Ben was sitting. Emma, still stricken faced, brought up the rear.

'Oh dear, you have been in the wars,' Doctor Martin said. 'That's a nasty gash on the back of your head, and by the way you're holding yourself, you've probably broken a rib. Right, let's take a look at you. We need to remove your jacket and shirt.'

Ben glanced at Emma, and the doctor followed his gaze.

'Lady Emma, would you be so kind as to step outside while I examine Mr Pearson.'

'Oh, yes, sorry, of course.' She blushed, smiled gently at Ben, and retreated to the yard.

Once alone, the doctor checked Ben's eyes for signs of concussion and then asked him to breathe deeply as he gently felt his rib cage for damage.

'From the gasps of pain, I suspect that you've probably fractured a rib in your back and undoubtedly broken one, maybe two, of your lower right ribs,' he pronounced as he bandaged Ben's torso tightly and gave him breathing exercises to do. 'You must do them every hour – no matter how painful it is. You need to keep your lungs clear, and take gentle exercise. I suggest you sleep in a sitting position until your ribs feel more comfortable. Now, your little finger is clearly broken by the angle at which it's sitting, so brace yourself, I'm going to reset it.'

Knowing Emma was just outside, Ben forced himself to stifle a yelp as the finger was put back into position and splinted against his ring finger to keep it stable.

'You'll be in considerable pain for some days. I don't think you'll be able to work. Do you want me to inform your parents?'

'No, thank you, doctor. I'll manage fine,' he said gasping as a pain seared through his chest.

'I'll send my fee to you.'

'Thank you,' Ben said – though he could well do without the expense.

*

The doctor emerged from the gloom of the workshop, blinking in the bright April sunlight. He nodded curiously at Lady Emma who'd been waiting patiently outside – her face full of concern.

'Will he be alright, doctor?'

'In a few weeks, yes. He has several injured ribs, a broken finger, and a head injury, so he'll be out of action a while.'

'Oh, dear Lord. Please send the invoice to my father – I'll settle it with him. It was I who insisted you were called.'

'Very well, my lady. Good day to you.'

Emma waited until the doctor had driven away before knocking tentatively on the door. Popping her head into Ben's workshop, she inhaled the sweet, earthy smell of good quality leather, smiled, and asked, 'May I come back in?'

'Oh, goodness, Emma, you should not come in - I'm not properly dressed!' he said adding a groan of pain.

'Fiddlesticks. I've seen you shirtless many times when we played together near the stream on the estate.'

'We were children then! Ouch!' Ben cradled his broken ribs.

Emma noted he looked pale and sweaty, and the pad, which was bandaged to his head, showed signs of seepage already.

'Do you need to put your shirt back on? I can help you.'

'It's not proper, Emma, your papa will kill me if he finds you here alone with me – in a state of undress!'

'Then let me help you dress. Stand up.' She grabbed the rough linen shirt from the back of the chair and held it out. 'Put your arms out and I'll carefully ease it on.'

He yelped as he pushed his arms down the sleeves and as she lifted it over his head, she was close enough to feel the heat coming from him. There was a tang of sweat from his perspiring body and she was very conscious of how broad his chest was now - and how dark and glossy his chest hairs were, protruding from the bandage around his ribs.

He sat for a moment - his eyes closed until the pain subsided.

'You poor thing. I'm so very sorry,' Emma said kneeling at his feet.

He frowned. 'What have you to be sorry about, Em,' he rasped, the effort to speak causing great problems.

Emma smiled - Ben had always called her Em in private. 'Well, I obviously startled you when I came in, because you fell almost immediately.'

'Please,' he gasped, clutching his hand to his chest, 'it was not your fault – the accident was mine alone. My ladder was unsteady. I was teetering moments before, and I was losing my balance before you came in.'

'What were you doing up there? Was there something you needed from the top shelf that I can retrieve for you?'

He shook his head. 'I was rescuing Amara, she got caught in the netting over the window.' He lifted his hand to point to the skylight and took a sharp painful intake of breath.

'Bless you, Ben, to do an act of kindness and then for this to happen.'

'Em, you must get up. Your skirt will be a terrible mess kneeling on the floor like that.'

She stood up, brushing down her pale blue riding habit. 'May I sit with you a while then?'

'If you wish,' he smiled, 'but I'm poor company.'

'As I was riding here, I took a detour through the woods. Did you know that the great oak by the stream, where we used to all play as children, has been completely uprooted?'

Ben nodded, wrapped his arms around his torso to help him speak and answered, 'A terrific storm blew up a week ago - it caused chaos up and down the coast.' He paused to catch his breath. 'I lost half of the tiles from the stable roof, and the old oak was a casualty of the storm. Agnes, Zack, and I went to look at it at the weekend – it's changed the whole look of the place now.'

'We had some happy times there, didn't we?'

Ben nodded hesitantly.

'There was something about that tree that spooked you and William though, wasn't there? I remember, it was just before your sixteenth birthday and I suggested a birthday picnic there, but you both refused to go and wouldn't say why.' She tipped her head for him to explain, but Ben just smiled feebly. 'You spooked us all you know, with your caginess about it! The rest of us never felt comfortable there just in case you had seen something horrible – some ghoul or something.' Emma looked into Ben's eyes, and apart from the obvious pain he was in, she was sure there was something he was keeping from her. 'Will you ever tell us what happened?'

'Nothing happened there,' he said almost inaudibly, but Emma knew he was fibbing.

'It's hurting you to speak. Shall I put the closed sign up outside so no one else comes?'

'I suppose so, yes. I'm not going to be able to work for a while.'

*

Outside, dairymaid Merial Barnstock, her long dark hair flowing behind her, made haste up the farm track towards the Polhormon Saddlery to see Ben after her milking shift.

Merial was one of four dairymaids employed by Farmer Trevorrow, along with Susie Carne, Maria Kimbrel, and Jane Lanyon. All of them were in love with Ben Pearson, with the exception of Jane who was newly engaged to Bill Trevorrow, Farmer Trevorrow's eldest son, but that didn't stop Jane stealing the odd admiring glance at Ben whenever he stepped into the dairy to fill up his milk can.

Ben would always bid the maids a cheery, 'Hello, ladies.'

They would giggle and blush and reply in unison, 'Good morning to you too, Mr Pearson.' All except for Merial, who would trill, 'Good morning, Ben. And how are you this fine day?' The other milk maids were deeply envious that she was bold enough to engage him in conversation, but Merial believed herself to have a special relationship with him. After all, Ben had danced twice with her at last year's harvest dance, and that, as far as she was concerned, was as good as being engaged! Since the dance though, she'd visited him occasionally after milking, but though always polite he was frustratingly reticent with her. He often told her he was far too busy to speak to her. There was no way she'd give up on him though, he just needed to be worked on. He'd taken enough interest to dance with her - when nobody else would - she'd find a way of making him interested again.

Merial was twenty years old now – she needed to get settled with someone, before she became an old maid! It pained her to think that with her pretty face, long dark hair and trim figure she should have lads falling at her feet, but that was not the case. She knew the lads kept their distance from her, due in part to an incident which occurred a year or so ago between her then beau, Harry Pine, and her brothers, Bernard and Barry. Harry had enjoyed a couple of tumbles in the hay with her, but when she had asked him when they would marry, he'd laughed at her. Humiliated, she told her brothers, and the next she'd heard, Harry had been found in a ditch late one night, beaten to within an inch of his life – a beating he'd never fully recovered from. There had been a general consensus that the Barnstock brothers were the culprits, but without witnesses and Harry too frightened to come forward, nothing was ever proved.

Approaching the saddlery, the sight of a beautiful horse tethered outside the workshop slowed Merial's pace. When the saddlery door suddenly opened and an elegantly dressed woman in a riding habit emerged, Merial hid behind the gatepost. She watched the woman place the closed sign on the door, before going back in.

Tiptoeing towards the workshop, she felt a prickle of jealousy when she recognised the saddle on the horse, it was the one that Ben had been working on since

Christmas. That could only mean one thing - Lady Emma must be back!

Cursing under her breath, she knew there had been talk, rumours in fact early last year, about Ben being quite taken with Lady Emma. At the time Merial brushed the rumours aside with a derisory snort. So, what if Ben had played with the privileged children at Bochym Manor when they were younger - they were adults now, and Lady Emma was far above Ben's station in life. Nevertheless, she needed to know why they were ensconced in that workshop alone and what, exactly, they were doing.

There was a ladder in Ben's stable, which led up to the hayloft, where from a high window, you could see down into the workshop, Merial knew this, because she'd surreptitiously watched Ben occasionally from it! She decided to take a look now - just to make sure they weren't doing anything untoward.

2

With the sign on the door, Emma returned to find Ben clutching his torso to stem his pain.

'Oh, you poor thing. Let me make you some tea, or do you want something stronger?' she said, touching his shoulder gently.

'I'm fine, Em, please don't bother yourself.'

'It's really no bother.'

'A glass of water will suffice then, thank you. I have a rare thirst.'

The kitchen and living quarters were situated at the back of the workshop, partitioned by a heavy curtain to keep out the dust. It was brightly lit by a rear window, a glazed back door and the skylight above. Emma had been in here two years previously, when Ben moved into the saddlery after finishing his apprenticeship with Mr Doyle the saddle maker in Helston, so she knew her way around. Drawing two glasses of water, she put the kettle on the stove for good measure.

He drank thirstily and smiled through his pain.

'Did the doctor give you some pain relief?'

Waving the small bottle of laudanum, he nodded. 'I'm not sure if it's kicking in yet.'

'Give it time. I've put the kettle on to boil – I'm going to make you some tea.'

He made to protest, but a wave of pain engulfed him and it took all his resolve not to cry out. He swallowed hard until it passed and smiled weakly at Emma.

'Anyway, happy birthday for yesterday, Em....' Another pain caught him making him gasp.

'Ben, don't speak if it hurts.'

'But, I haven't seen you for almost a year – I want to talk to you.'

Reaching over she put her hand on his. 'Speak more softly then - it may not hurt as much.'

'Did you have a nice day yesterday?' he said almost inaudibly.

'I did, thank you.'

'Did you like the saddle?'

Emma beamed with delight. 'It's truly beautiful and fits Saffron like a glove.'

'Saffron! Ah, I wondered what you would call that beauty. She's a fine horse – I had no trouble with her while I fitted her for the saddle.'

'I absolutely love her. I've always wanted a palomino – her golden colour reminds me of saffron.'

'A beautiful horse for a beautiful lady.' Ben crinkled his nose.

Blushing at the compliment, she was saved by the kettle coming to the boil.

Automatically, Ben tried to get up to make the tea, gasped in pain and sat down again.

Emma gave him a stern look. '*I'll do it.*'

'You're a lady, I should be making tea for you!'

'And you will one day, when you feel better,' she placed a hand on his shoulder, 'now stay there.'

In his sparse kitchen, Emma searched for a teapot, unable to locate one, and not wanting to bother him, she selected two mugs to mash the tea in. While waiting for it to brew, she cast her eyes around his living quarters. It was clean and tidy, though perhaps missing the comfort of cushions on the chairs. A large bookcase, which formed part of the living quarters partition, housed many leather-bound books, some of which she too had read. There were three which had fallen to the floor when Ben fell against it. She picked them up, returning two to their places, the third, Robinson Crusoe, had been quite badly damaged. To the side of the kitchen was another curtained area which, after lifting the curtain, she found was his bedroom. His bed was unmade and there was a dent in the pillow where his head had lain. She imagined him lying there asleep and smiled to herself. Though she'd known Ben all her life, she

11

bit her lip nervously, deeply aware she was intruding on his personal space.

With the damaged book under her arm, Emma handed him the tea, which he accepted gratefully. 'This was on the floor. You must have knocked against the bookcase when you fell,' she said. 'I'm afraid the spine has broken and loosened the pages.'

Ben picked the book up with a pained look. 'Oh dear - it's my favourite book!' A sharp jab in the ribs beaded his forehead with perspiration, causing his dark blond hair to adhere to his face. 'Good grief, I've never known pain like this. Apparently I have to sleep in a sitting position until I can breathe a little easier!'

'Do you want me to sort out the pillows on your bed?'

'Oh, no!' His blue eyes widened with alarm. 'I'll manage.'

'As you wish,' she smiled, 'now, I've brought you some birthday cake - it's in my saddle bag, I'll just fetch it.'

As she unwrapped the cake, a rich aroma of brandy-soaked fruit filled the room.

'Gosh!' Ben inhaled deeply. 'Ouch! Oh, God,' he held his torso again, 'I was just going to say that looks and smells delicious.'

'It's Mrs Blair's speciality fruit cake,' she presented it to him proudly, 'apparently it's been maturing with a good dash of brandy every week since Christmas!'

As Ben took the cake from her hand, they brushed fingers, and a secret smile passed between them.

'It's so good to see you again, Em.'

Emma cupped her hand over his. 'It's so good to see you too.'

'Thank you for the postcards. Switzerland looked wonderful.'

'It's quite stunning. I wish we could have written to each other, but matron would not have allowed it, I'm afraid. I was frightened that you would forget me,' she said boldly, blushing again at her forwardness.

'Not a chance,' he said softly, thus making her smile. 'Tell me about your party?' he asked, gratefully sipping the tea.

'It would have been better if you'd been there! I was quite put out to find you missing from the guest list. William, Zack and Agnes – all the rest of the old gang were there, and so should you have been! After all, Nanny always let us have our birthday parties together when we were younger!'

'But they were not held around the Bochym dining table then!'

'Even so!'

'Em, we were lucky that your parents and Nanny gave us all free rein to play together when we were children, but things are different now we've grown up. I'm not the sort of person who is invited to dine with the Earl and Countess de Bochym.'

'Rubbish! You're as good as any other man. Besides, Uncle Justin married our housekeeper Ruby, and she happily sits around the Bochym table when they're in England. Anyway, I made my feelings very clear to Mama and Papa that I was unhappy you were excluded.'

'It doesn't matter, Em,' he said gently.

'It does to me,' she said fiercely.

'So, William came for your birthday then?'

'He did - he came down yesterday for my birthday dinner, but went back to Oxford this morning – he's busy studying. He sends his regards to you though.'

Ben smiled at this. 'He came to see me at Christmas. I must say, university has made him into a fine young gentleman.'

'Yes, it has. We're all growing up, but it's lovely that we're all still friends.'

'I hope we'll remain so,' he said seriously.

Detecting concern in his voice, Emma answered, 'You can depend on it – never doubt it. Now, shall I write to William to tell him about the demise of the oak tree?' She awaited Ben's response, but when none was forthcoming, she added, 'Do you not think he would be interested?'

'Probably not,' he answered guardedly.

Emma looked curiously at him, but he changed the subject.

'I have something for you – a present – you'll have to fetch it for me though.'

'Oh!' She shivered with delight. 'But you've already made me the saddle!'

'That was from your parents – I wanted to make you something from me. There is a hessian bag on the dresser, could you get it for me, but don't peep yet.'

Placing the bag on the table, Emma clasped her hands in excitement. 'Can I look now?'

'You can.'

Emma pulled out a beautiful ten by eight leather-bound ornate box with the letters ℰℒ𝒟 - Emma Lucinda Dunston carved onto the hide. A leather toggle fastener finished it off.

'Oh, Ben!' Emma ran her fingers over her initials and the running pattern carved into the leather along the edge of the lid. 'It's so beautiful.'

'I made it for you to keep special things in. Zack made the box for me - I just covered it.'

As she moved around the table to kiss him, he offered up his cheek, but instead she brushed her soft lips on his. 'Thank you,' she murmured looking deep into his eyes.

'Thank *you*,' he answered smiling.

*

Peering through the grimy stable window, Merial had seen enough. A curl of jealousy manifested as she watched the exchange between Ben and Lady Emma, jealousy which quickly turned into tears of frustration. To think she'd invested all this time, trying to build a relationship with Ben, only for Lady Emma to come back and spoil things, well, she would see to that! As her foot stepped off the bottom rung of the ladder, a voice behind her made her jump. Merial turned sharply to find Farmer Trevorrow's young son Jimmy watching her.

'What do you think you're doing up there?' he hissed.

'Minding my own business, as you should be.' She flounced past him.

'You don't look like you're minding your own business,' Jimmy called after her, but Merial carried on walking.

Jimmy, who often called on Ben after finishing his own chores at the dairy, to see if Ben had any odd jobs for him had seen the closed sign, but also noted the horse Ben had made the saddle for. He too knew that Lady Emma must be inside with Ben. He glanced at the ladder Merial had just descended and snorted in disdain, realising she'd been peeping on them. He'd have to come back later to tell Ben.

*

Inside, Emma and Ben were doing nothing more untoward than enjoying each other's company over a cup of tea and a slice of cake.

Despite his pain, Ben settled his adoring eyes upon Emma, knowing now after that kiss, his heart was totally and utterly lost to her. My goodness but he loved this woman - though he knew he should not. Her delicate patrician beauty was a sight to behold - she was the warmth on a sunny day, the blue in the sky and the stars at night. When she was near him, his world became alive. He'd wondered if the separation would have lessened his adoration for her. He'd tried not to think about her, for he knew loving Emma was a lost cause, but now she was back, his feelings for her were as strong as they had always been.

'So, what are your plans now you've finished school?' he asked in a hope of shaking these feelings.

'Well,' she smoothed down her skirt, 'I have the delights of the London season to look forward to, where I'll be presented to royalty!' She waved her hand with mock flourish.

'What an honour!'

'Yes,' she tipped her head, 'I'm rather looking forward to that part of it.'

'Are you not looking forward to all the balls and parties that will follow?'

'Yes, and no. I fear those balls and parties are for me to find a suitable husband,' she answered jadedly.

Feeling his heart plummet, it took all of Ben's resolve to hide his devastation, knowing there was a very high chance of him losing Emma again - and this time to another man!'

'To be truthful, Ben, I'd rather stay here, riding, walking the fields, sitting by the sea, making up my stories,' her eyes twinkled, 'and, being with you.'

He exhaled softly as a warm feeling settled in his heart. 'I'm glad to hear you're still writing your stories. No plans to follow William to Oxford then? You're clever enough!' *Oh goodness, why did he say that? He didn't want her to go away to university for three years!*

'Apparently not. William said the entrance exam would bamboozle me. I'm useless at Latin you see – in fact most languages, except French. Besides, I don't think Papa was too keen on me going anyway.'

'Never mind, you'd not be able to walk the fields, sit by the sea or find time to write if you went away again,' he added genially.

'True, but a degree perhaps would have helped me to get some of my work published.'

'Your work is good enough already, Emma. I know, I've read some of the stories you wrote before you went to Switzerland and they're excellent. I don't think you need to go and study for three years to become a published author. It *will* happen.'

'Thank you for having faith in me, Ben. That's high praise coming from you. Forgive me, but when I was waiting for the kettle to boil, I was browsing your books.

You have quite a collection there – I never knew you were so well read. It is *you* who should go to university.'

'Alas, that's something else that is not within my reach. I need to work, and work I do, or did until today!' He sighed heavily. 'I'm not one to pander to pain, but this,' he shook his head, 'this is bad. I can barely breathe without yelping. You'll think me some sort of weakling.'

'I think nothing of the sort. I think you've been very brave – having to put up with me here while I'm sure you wish me gone, so you can groan in pain to your hearts content.'

'I would never wish you gone, Em, I've missed you. I've missed us all being together,' he added for risk of sounding too familiar. 'Tell me more about your birthday dinner, you said Zack was there. How is he? I haven't seen him for a couple of weeks.'

Emma's teeth dug deep into her lower lip. 'Troubled I think.'

'Oh! Why?'

'He's coming to the end of his carpentry apprenticeship with Kit Trevellick in the summer and there was much talk last night from his pa Guy, about buying old Mr Gray's premises in Cury to set him up – perhaps making coffins. Guy made a big thing about him having his name above the door - *Mr Zackary Blackthorn – Carpenter & coffin maker.* Zack, I might add, did not seem at all enamoured with the prospect.'

'Oh dear, did you manage to speak to him about his reticence?'

'No,' she sighed, 'he seemed quite out of sorts after dinner. I'm a bit worried about him really.'

'Did he go back home to Poldhu?'

'Yes, but I got the impression that Zack didn't particularly want to go home – I think he quite likes being in Gweek at the Trevellicks.'

Ben nodded. 'Yes, I've noticed he often feels at a loose end when he's home for the weekend.

17

'Well, Ben,' Emma said getting up, 'I think I must take leave of you now. Mama and Papa have gone to Trelissick today to dine and stay overnight with the Cunliffe's, but I told the groom I would just trot around the estate, he'll be wondering where I've got to.'

'It's so lovely to have you back again,' Ben said trying to get up, only to yelp and sit back down.

'Oh, Ben,' she grasped his good hand, 'are you going to be able to manage? I could tell your parents - they could come and get you.'

'No, Em. I'll be fine,' he said dabbing the perspiration from his forehead with his sleeve.

'Goodbye then,' she said, this time kissing him on the cheek. 'And thank you again for this lovely box.'

'It was my pleasure to make it for you.' As he watched her leave, her perfume filled his senses – he was more in love with her now than he had ever been.

3

Under a bright blue Sunday sky, albeit with a chill Cornish breeze sifting off the sea, seventeen-year-old Zack Blackthorn, the only son of Guy and Ellie Blackthorn, sat quiet and forlorn on Poldhu beach, aimlessly throwing pebbles towards the water's edge. Pa's talk about buying Mr Gray's carpentry shop for him last evening, while they were celebrating Lady Emma's eighteenth birthday, still rang alarmingly in his head.

"It will be a gift that keeps on giving - for you will never be short of work - everybody dies," his pa laughed. But Zack was not laughing, all he could see before him was an unhappy, unfulfilled life making an object he found most unappealing. His thoughts turned to his siblings, Agnes, who was nineteen and had only ever wanted to work with Pa, thatching roofs, joyous in the fact that she was doing just that. And little Sophie, now fifteen and happily working alongside Ma at the Poldhu Tea Room - also fulfilling her long-time wish. Zack though, always the quieter of the three, knew what he wanted to do, but also knew it was as far out of his reach as was the moon, therefore never had the courage to state it, for it would be completely out of the question.

Their family, although they mixed regularly with the local gentry at Bochym Manor, were basically working folks, happy to do a good days work for a good pay packet. Guy had been eager for his only son to gain a profession which would see him through life, and as he had no interest in joining the family thatching business, he'd secured him an apprenticeship with his good friend, and excellent cabinet maker, Kit Trevellick in Gweek.

In truth, from an early age, Zack had felt that music moved him - it was his only passion. There were no instruments at home other than Pa's old flute, which rarely saw the light of day nowadays, Zack's love of music had come from visiting Bochym Manor as a child and hearing

Sarah – the Countess - play the piano so beautifully. Zack and Agnes, along with Ben Pearson, had enjoyed playing with the privileged Dunstan children, though when in the manor they rarely went beyond the nursery. Zack though could often hear Sarah at the piano, her music drifting melodically up from the Jacobean drawing room. Lately, now they were adults, they were included in occasional dinner parties at the manor, so Zack had the enormous pleasure of hearing Sarah play in the drawing room, rather than through a closed door. Although his carpentry apprenticeship was not exactly reaping the rewards his pa was hoping for, spending the last three years as Kit Trevellick's apprentice, and living with him, his wife Sophie, their daughter Selene and their son Christopher on Monday to Fridays, had brought him great joy. They had a piano for Selene, and more importantly a gramophone, which delighted Zack every evening after dinner when a record was played. It was as though the music spoke to him, comforting and calming him. For every piece of music he heard, his brain seemed to store it, and when music was not being readily played, he could draw on this inner store to a point where he could almost recall a whole movement. Without doubt, it relaxed, entertained, and evoked deep emotion within him. It gave him peace, caused him to reflect, brought him hope and many a smile – it also helped to lift the burden of his bleak future. He lay back on the sand with his hands behind his head and conjured up Frédéric Chopin: Prelude in E minor – a heart-wrenching, but incredibly beautiful piece of music – music which matched his mood perfectly today. It was while thinking of this piece of music that his peace was shattered by the thunder of hooves approaching him down the beach.

Zack lifted his head in alarm, and then smiled to find Lady Emma Dunstan slipping graciously from the saddle and walking up to him. Holding the horse by the reins, she sat down with Zack and looked out to sea.

'Agnes told me where you were. Are you alright, have I disturbed you?'

'No, I'm just pondering on life.'

'I'm here on a mission actually. I've just come from Ben's workshop. He's had an accident – fallen from a ladder and broken a couple of ribs. He won't let me call for his parents, but I think he might need some help, getting undressed and the like. I've made him a pot of tea, but he won't let me do anything more for him. He's been told to sleep sitting up, but he can barely move to arrange his bed, and it's really not proper for me to do such things. Are you able to go up there? You can hitch a ride on Saffron with me if you like.'

Zack grinned. 'Emma Dunstan, have you not just attended finishing school to learn the intricacies of correct upper-class behaviour? I'm sure riding around the countryside sharing a saddle with a mere carpenter is not the proper thing to do!'

'You're not a mere carpenter, you're my friend, Zack. So, it's either that or you walk!' she teased. 'Come on, give me a leg up.'

Instead of sitting side saddle, she sat astride, and held her hand out for him to mount the horse.

With a quick glance around, to see if anyone was looking, he grabbed her hand and settled behind her as they galloped up the beach towards Polhormon Saddlery.

*

Guy and Ellie Blackthorn stood at the balustrade of the Poldhu Tea Room veranda and witnessed their son beating a hasty retreat from the beach on the back of Lady Emma's horse.

'Well,' Ellie breathed, 'so much for Peter and Sarah hoping that the Swiss finishing school would erase Emma's tomboy traits and turn her into a real lady. I know Sarah was hoping that she would mix more with the company of other ladies when she returned, but she still seems to be one of the boys.'

'Just like our Agnes!' Guy agreed.

'Is it all still an innocent, albeit enduring, friendship from childhood, I wonder?' Ellie mused. 'Or should we all be worried that Lady Emma, and our son, are galloping around the countryside together?'

They both turned when their daughter Agnes walked up the veranda steps.

'I see Emma found Zack then,' she said watching the horse cantering away up the hill.

'Yes. Any idea where those two are going?' Ellie asked.

'To Ben's workshop I should think. Emma came looking for Zack because Ben has had a fall and broken a couple of ribs. She brought the doctor to see him, made him a drink, but thought Ben might need Zack's help with other things like getting undressed. Ben has to sleep sitting up, but he wouldn't let her get the bed ready for him.'

'I'm glad to hear he wouldn't, Guy breathed. 'what was she doing there anyway?'

'Visiting him, most probably,' Agnes said nonchalantly.

Guy glanced at Ellie, raised an eyebrow, and whispered, 'I don't think it's *our* son the Dunstans need worry about.'

*

Ben pulled a grin from the depths of his pain when he saw Zack enter the workshop – his dark hair wild and unkempt from the ride.

'I hear you've been doing some acrobatics. I thought you might need some help, old chap.' Zack stood, hands on hips, regarding his friend with sympathy.

Ben laughed until the pain made him wince. 'Is this Emma's doing?'

Arching his eyebrows. 'Possibly.'

'Emma is convinced I can't manage on my own.'

'And can you?'

Ben's mouth twisted. 'In truth, no. But I couldn't ask her to do certain things, as you can imagine.'

'She loves you - she'd do anything for you,' Zack added seriously.

'Oh, Zack, don't. It's tearing my heart out, she's so unattainable.'

'I know, my friend. From the talk around the dining table at Bochym last night, it seems she's to be touted around the London scene this year in search of a husband, and doesn't seem to be enamoured with the idea! Possibly because she knows where her heart lies,' he teased.

'That's not going to happen though, is it?'

'No, probably not.' Zack slumped down on the chair opposite. 'It seems neither of us are able to have what we want.'

Ben tipped his head. 'I hear from Emma that we might be neighbours if you take on old Mr Gray's coffin shop.'

Zack narrowed his eyes. 'Over my dead body.'

They exchanged a grin at the pun.

Ben ran his hand over his sweaty face. 'My God, I feel shattered – pain is exhausting.'

'Come on then, I know it's early, but let me help you get ready for bed. You'll be more comfortable there.'

Ben's skin was slick with perspiration by the time Zack undressed him. He then stacked his pillows and a couple of blankets to pad the head of the bed, so Ben could sleep in a slightly reclined sitting position. Ben felt absolutely exhausted by the time he'd settled.

'Stay awhile, will you, Zack, there is a bottle of brandy on the shelf there. Share a drink with me – for medicinal purposes. I see so little of you nowadays. Won't you consider taking on Gray's old place?'

Zack shook his head. 'Not even for you, my friend.'

*

Tomkins the groom was waiting for Emma when she cantered up the fields towards the manor.

'We were a little worried about you, my lady,' he said. 'You've been gone for some time.'

'Thank you, Tomkins, no need to worry, I've just been getting used to Saffron. She's a fine horse,' she said untying the hessian bag containing the box from the saddle.

'Yes, my lady, she is.'

David the footman opened the door for Emma and she ran upstairs to put her precious leather box in pride of place on her dressing table. She couldn't wait to show her parents.

*

After flouncing home from being caught red handed spying on Ben, Merial Barnstock sat down, disgruntled and resentful, to plot her revenge. The 1½d cost of the stamp would be worth it.

*

The next morning, Joe Treen the Bochym butler collected the bundle of letters delivered by the postman, to sort out into two piles. One for the family, which would normally be delivered on a platter at their breakfast table should they be at home, the other for the staff. He withdrew slightly at the sight of one grubby envelope addressed to *The erl is lordship'* and dropped it to one side as though not to contaminate the other letters.

The kitchen at Bochym was the usual hive of activity that morning as the staff breakfast was served. Mrs Blair the cook, and her assistant, Alice, were dishing out the food. With Theo and Lowenna Trevail - the valet and lady's maid to the Earl and Countess - away, Nanny was settling their children, Denny nine and Loveday six, at the table.

'Now eat your breakfast, or you'll be late for school,' Nanny warned.

'But it's my birthday today,' Loveday complained. 'I shouldn't have to go to school!'

'Lots of people have to go to school on their birthday, Loveday, now eat up and the sooner you go, the sooner you can come back for a birthday tea with your ma and pa.'

When Joe walked in, everyone, even the children, stood as was protocol until Joe sat down. When he did, he glanced at his wife Juliet and frowned.

'What is it?' she whispered to him.

'A strange letter has arrived for the Earl. I'm not quite sure what to do with it,' he murmured back. 'It looks a little suspect to me. Thank goodness they're from home, as it's too grubby to grace the family's breakfast table.'

*

With their parents from home, Emma breakfasted with her sixteen-year-old sister Anna.

'What time will my parents be home, Treen?' Emma asked.

'His Lordship said they would be back before luncheon.'

'What are you doing today, Emma?' Anna asked scraping butter onto her toast.

'I thought perhaps to have Saffron saddled again.' *And ride over to see Ben.*

'I wish I could go out riding. I wish I were older,' Anna bemoaned, 'I wish I was going to be presented to royalty and start my London season.'

'Your time will come, Anna,' Emma said.

'Not for two whole years though!'

Emma glanced at Anna and shot her a sympathetic smile. Emma might not be looking forward to the season away from Cornwall as Anna coveted, but at least she wasn't stuck in the stuffy schoolroom with even stuffier Miss Gilbert - the governess. Poor Anna, their lovely old governess Miss Riley had retired due to ill health when Emma went off to Switzerland, and her replacement, Miss Gilbert, was a lot sterner than their old governess had been.

'I feel for you, Anna, but time will pass, and quicker than you think. Next year you'll be in Switzerland, so that's something to look forward to.'

'It can't come soon enough.' Anna got up resignedly to present herself in the schoolroom.

4

Zack was back at Kit and Sophie Trevellick's house in Gweek that morning, having taken the early Helston wagon as far as the crossroads. After drinking copious amounts of brandy with Ben the previous evening, the brisk walk down Gweek Hill amongst the rolling countryside had helped to ease his headache. Before Zack caught the wagon that morning, he'd checked back in with Ben to help his friend get up. Ben had mentioned that the doctor was emphatic that he should not lay abed, he must get up to move about, no matter how painful it was. Apparently if he didn't try to fill his lungs with air, he was at risk of pneumonia. Poor Ben, he'd looked sickly pale when he'd got him up out of bed to get him dressed – he clearly needed more help. So, as an incentive, Zack told him, 'You know if you go to your parents' house on the Bochym Estate to stay, you'll be closer to Emma.'

It was this thought on Zack's mind when a wood splinter pierced his hand making him curse audibly.

'You alright there, Zack?' Kit asked ceasing carving his signature seahorse into the leg of the table he was making.

'Sorry for cursing,' Zack said jadedly, sucking the blood oozing from where he'd extracted the splinter.

Kit left his work, moved to Zack's side, and a quick inspection of the chair leg he'd been working on made it evident to them both that he hadn't turned the wood enough.

'I'm sorry Kit. I'm not sure I'll pass my apprenticeship. Which is a terrible thing to say after working at it for three years,' Zack sighed. 'I'll never be as good as you.'

'Don't beat yourself up, Zack – it took me years to hone my skill.'

'I don't think I have any skill to hone.' He put down the grit paper he'd been using and wrapped his handkerchief around the bloody wound.

'Your work is not that bad, Zack.'

'It's not good either, is it? It seems I'm destined to make coffins all my life.'

'Well, everyone needs a coffin!'

Zack sighed and turned away from his work.

'Look it's almost time for a break. Come on, ten minutes away and you'll feel a lot better.'

Zack's shoulders drooped - he very much doubted that he would.

They walked to the kitchen of Quay House to beg a mug of tea from Sophie who was busy baking.

Zack smiled as Kit kissed his wife on the cheek as she passed the mugs of tea over.

'May I take mine into the garden room?' Zack asked.

'Of course,' Sophie smiled, 'but Selene is having her piano lesson in the next room.'

'I don't mind. I love listening to the music.'

Settling into one of the deep cushioned chairs, Zack closed his eyes and mind to his work. Carpentry was not for him, no matter how much Kit encouraged him – he simply had no passion for it. In the past three years, he'd made a shoogly chair, a table that lost its legs as soon as it was up right, and three milking stools, which in truth, had been easy as they needed no finesse, but they had to be returned for him to polish them to a smoother finish after one of the dairymaids suffered a splinter in her derrière!

He knew Kit would award him his apprenticeship certificate out of friendship – he and his pa had been lifelong friends. The apprenticeship was a favour, because Zack could not decide on his career path after he had left school at fourteen. Zack only agreed to this apprenticeship, because it gave him another three years to sort out what he really wanted to do with his life. Now he was at the end of the apprenticeship he still couldn't decide. His father would be so angry with him – his mother, Ellie, not so much. He was in such a dilemma. It was then he heard the first tinkle of the piano keys next door and smiled. Miss Pope was at the instrument by the sound of it, for her playing was beautiful. Zack let his mind drift, enjoying the waves of notes as her fingers so elegantly played the keys. He'd heard her play this piece before, and knew it note for note, along with all the highs and lows of each part of the piece. Then the music stopped and with a shuffle of the stool, Selene must have seated herself poised and ready. For a few short notes, Zack listened and hummed along with the melodic sound, until Selene hit a wrong note, making Zack's face twitch until she found her stride again. He loved this time alone with his cup of tea, taking in the music, albeit grimacing occasionally. Selene was not a bad pianist - she just couldn't keep her mind on the job. He laughed to himself, a little like *he* could not keep his mind on *his* job. He looked up when Kit beckoned him back to work.

Zack took his mug back to the kitchen, happy in the knowledge that at his next tea break at three o clock, Sophie would set off to pick up her youngest child Christopher from school, Kit would take himself off to the quayside to work on the boat he was building, and Zack would take his place by Selene's side at the piano. Though he'd had no instruction himself, once a piece was in his head, his fingers knew what to do, and they would spend a rather happy half hour going over the piece of music Miss Cope had left her as homework. It was their little secret.

*

When the Dunstans arrived back at Bochym later that morning, and His Lordship had settled in his study, Joe Treen knocked on the study door with the letter in hand.

'Begging your pardon, my lord.'

Peter Dunstan looked up. 'Yes, Treen.'

'Another letter came for you this morning, but it's a little grubby to say the least. Also, the envelope is ill written.' He handed the platter with the letter on it.

Peter looked down on the letter, with the words, 'The erl is lordship' written in a scrawl, grimaced, but took it. 'That will be all, Treen.'

'Thank you, my lord.' Joe bowed.

Peter opened the clean letters first and frowned – one was a bill from Dr Martin in lieu of services for the treatment of Mr Ben Pearson. *Why the devil has he sent this to me?* He thought.

Opening the other letter tentatively, as though he might catch something from it, his frown deepened as he tried to decipher the almost illegible writing.

DID YOU NO LADI EMMA AS BIN WITH BEN PEARSON ALON IN IS WORKSHOP. HE GAV HER A BOX AND SHE KISD IM

Peter screwed the grubby letter up, threw it on the fire and left his study.

'Is everything alright, my lord?' Joe asked, as he wound the grandfather clock in the hall.

'Where is Lady Emma, Treen?'

'Out, my lord. She had her horse saddled.'

Peter nodded and took the stairs two at a time and entered Emma's bedroom, where the maids, Dorothy and Lucy, were cleaning the room. They stopped and bobbed a curtsy.

'Can we help you, my lord?' Dorothy asked.

Peter's eyes scanned the room until they came to the dresser and settled on an ornate box which had not been there before.

'Thank you, no. I was looking for Lady Emma,' he said, retreating.

*

Emma was Ben's third visitor of the day, Zack had been his first, and the second being Merial Barnstock, whom he'd heard knocking and calling through the locked door, but chose to stay quiet, hoping she'd go away.

Jimmy had told him last evening that he'd found Merial skulking outside the workshop yesterday when Emma had been inside with him, so she was not particularly welcome that morning - not that she ever was! More often than not, Ben would feign being too busy to stop and speak to her, in the hope that she would get the message that he was not interested in her. It didn't seem to work though, and seemed to spur her on to try everything and anything to grab his attention. She was a dreadful flirt, though Ben had never given her any encouragement - all he'd ever done was dance with her at the harvest supper. The Barnstocks, particularly the brothers Barry and Bernard, were a deeply disagreeable family, and were not the sort of people Ben had any desire to become entangled with.

He'd been relieved when the knocking ceased and Merial had gone away, because not five minutes later, Emma arrived, knocked softly on the door, and her voice, when he heard her call his name, almost melted his heart.

'I'm coming, Emma, give me a moment to get to the door,' he said.

Her smile when he opened the door was like a ray of sunshine on a grey day. Her golden hair had fallen into soft curls about her shoulders during her ride over, but her face, oh, her beautiful face, glowed with health.

'Oh, good, you're up and about!'

'Yes, thanks to Zack. Thank you for bringing him. I couldn't really have managed without him.'

'I'm glad I did now.'

She swept passed him in a fragrant cloud of perfume and he winced in pain as he inhaled the scent deeply.

'I take it Zack has gone back to Gweek now, so, will you let me tell your parents when I go back?'

'Yes, if you would. I couldn't have managed last night, or this morning, without Zack's help. Goodness, but you must think of me as a real weakling.'

'Not at all. You're clearly in pain. Can I help you get things ready before I fetch your father. I've no doubt he'll bring the cart to pick you up.'

'If you can collect a couple of books from the shelf that would be helpful.'

'What about your clothes?'

'I'll sort a few things out, don't worry. The range has gone out, so I need not worry about that either.'

Emma looked up at the dove who was fluttering her wings making the occasional feather float to the ground.

Ben too looked up. 'Amara is agitated – I think she knows something is amiss.'

'What will you do about her?'

'I'll send word down to Jimmy at the dairy, he'll come and give her some grain and keep an eye on the place for me.'

Putting the books into a bag for him, she placed her hand gently on his arm and smiled. 'I'll get your father now. A bit of tender loving parental care will not go amiss.'

'Mmm, once my ma gets me back home and starts to mother me again, I'll have a devil of a job untying those aprons strings again,' he laughed, and then clutched his sides.

'Oh, dear.' Emma kissed him lightly on the cheek. 'I'll see you when you get to Bochym.'

He stood at the door savouring her soft kiss as she galloped off, and was shocked when someone stepped into his peripheral vision. He turned as Merial, her face like thunder, appeared from the side of the saddlery. The smile dropped from his face.

'How long have you been there?' he asked sharply.

'Long enough to see that you opened your door to Lady la di da, but when I knocked only a few moments earlier you chose to ignore me.'

'I was probably busy elsewhere, and do not speak of your betters in such a fashion.'

Merial shrugged indifferently. 'She's not *my* betters!' She tipped her head. 'What's up with you anyway? You're stooped like an old man!'

'Nothing, it's nothing, now sorry, Merial, but I need you to go, and you must stop coming here – it's not proper.'

'But entertaining Lady Emma is?' she answered sarcastically.

'Goodbye, Merial,' he said firmly.

Her nostrils flared angrily, as she turned on her heel and stormed off.

*

When Rose Pearson answered the door, she quickly smoothed down her apron on sight of Lady Emma on her doorstep.

'Oh! My lady, how can I help - is all well at the house?'

'Yes, Mrs Pearson, we're all fine. It's Ben.'

'Ben!' Her face blanched.

'He had an accident yesterday - fell from a ladder and broke a couple of ribs.'

Her hands shot to her face. 'Oh, my goodness!'

'Please don't be alarmed. He's up and about, but only because Zack Blackthorn helped him last night and again this morning. Unfortunately, Zack has gone back to Gweek this morning, and Ben has realised that he can't manage without a bit of help. He's agreed that perhaps he needs to come home for a few days.'

'Oh, yes, of course he must, but, how do you know this, my lady?'

'I was there when he fell yesterday. I fetched the doctor for him. I wanted to come and tell you then, but he was adamant that he could manage and didn't want to bother anyone.'

Rose's mouth twisted. 'He can be as stubborn as a mule sometimes can our Ben!' She started to undo her apron. 'Right, I'll need to go and find Sydney.'

'Don't worry, I'll find him - I haven't unsaddled Saffron yet.'

*

33

Sydney Pearson was down in the arboretum with Papa when she found them.

After both men learned of Ben's plight, Peter said, 'You must get Lennox to take you in the car, Pearson.'

'Thank you, my lord.' He doffed his cap.

'I'll come with you, Mr Pearson.' Emma turned Saffron to follow him, but Peter stopped her with a very firm, 'No, Emma! You stay here.'

'But….' Emma looked down from the horse.

'I said no. Let Pearson sort this out. Get down from Saffron - I need to speak to you.'

Emma dismounted and watched Mr Pearson run up to arrange the car.

'Now, Emma. Would you like to tell me how you know all this about Ben?'

Emma tipped her head, puzzled at the question. 'I went to see Ben yesterday. I saw him fall, so I fetched the doctor for him, but he wouldn't let me get him any more help. When I returned today, he asked if I could fetch his father.'

Peter pursed his lips. 'That explains the doctors bill I received today then.'

'Oh, yes!' She clamped her hand to her mouth. 'I haven't seen you to tell you. I thought that it was I who had startled Ben and made him fall you see, so I told the doctor to send the bill to you. I shall pay for it out of my allowance.'

Peter folded his arms. 'I take it you went to see Ben alone?'

She frowned. 'Yes, I went to thank him for the saddle he made for my birthday, and he gave me the most beautiful leather box as a gift from him – I can't wait to show it to you.'

Peter gritted his teeth. 'Emma, it has come to my attention that there are rumours circulating in the area regarding your unchecked behaviour with Ben.'

'Unchecked behaviour!' Her face blanched. 'I've only been back in the county three days!'

'And it seems two of those days you've spent alone with a man!'

'He's not just any man – he's Ben!'

'Nevertheless, you've been seen, and Ben is still a man! You're a lady, Emma and should be sensible enough to know that you should not be alone with him now. I'm surprised Ben allowed it to happen.'

'He was hurt, Papa, when I called, but afterwards he *was* worried about me being there alone with him.'

'Well, I can credit him with some sense of what is correct then – I suppose that is something. But I'm very disappointed in your conduct.'

Emma cast her eyes downwards, it was rare for her papa to be upset with her.

'I'm really sorry, Papa, I did not mean to do anything improper. Please don't be angry with me.'

'It's alright, my darling girl, I'm not angry, but you must promise me that you will not be alone with him again.'

Emma felt her heart constrict. 'But, Papa, Ben is my friend - we grew up together!'

'Darling, and that is the optimum sentence – you grew up! It's time to put this childhood friendship behind you. Your world is about to open up. You and Ben are not children anymore, and the dynamics between you may well shift. Ben has grown into a very handsome young man, and I fear that he'll become a distraction to you. Your mama and I have spent a great deal in preparing you for this - your first London season. You're set to go into society, to be presented to royalty, and to be introduced to eligible rich young men, whom, I hope, will catch your heart, and give you the life a society lady such as you deserves. Now, Ben is going to be in close proximity to the manor for a few days, so I ask you to leave him to his parents while he is recuperating there.'

'Oh, but Papa, may I see him before we set off to London?'

'The day before, yes, as long as Mr and Mrs Pearson agrees, and there is someone there to chaperone you. But when you return from London, you must promise me that you will not see Ben alone again.'

'Yes Papa,' she answered dejectedly, as a heavy weight settled on her chest at the prospect.

5

It had been a week now since Ben had arrived on the estate, and Emma had done as her papa asked and not gone to see him. She'd secretly hoped that Ben would take some exercise in the grounds, where she could perhaps, accidently, bump into him. Surely Papa wouldn't object to that! But it was not to be, the dreadful weather had put paid to that. It had rained continuously all week, keeping most sane people indoors.

Thankfully, Emma and her mama had been incredibly busy that week, shopping and having the last fittings for all the gowns she would need to attend the society balls in London.

Emma suspected that Mama was more excited about this coming season than she was. Mama had had a very successful season twenty-two years ago. Her beauty, poise, and deportment had served her well and Grandmama Devereux had often proudly announced that Sarah had been the belle of every ball she attended. It was at her first ball after being presented, that she'd been introduced to Papa. Mama said that from that moment on, there was no other young man who could hold a candle to him and Papa told her, no other young woman could have captivated his heart like her mama had. They were engaged before their last summer ball, and married in early 1901. Now Mama was presenting her own daughter to London's elite, and was thrilled to be doing so. Emma just wished she could find the same enthusiasm.

With the majority of the preparations complete, Emma sat at her writing desk in her bedroom, a warm fire glowing in the grate, as the rain came in squalls, battering the windowpanes.

Placing her pen down on the note she'd just written, she walked to the window and folded her arms. Tomorrow she'd be allowed to see Ben - if only to say goodbye. She could hardly wait as she had missed Ben dreadfully while she had been in Switzerland, but this weeks enforced separation seemed more intense. She'd so been looking forward to spending some precious time with him before having to go away again. What bad luck that he should have injured himself like that. Still, absence makes the heart grow fonder so they say - and it was true.

Emma's Persian cat Molly jumped down from her cushioned chair, her aloofness with Emma for abandoning her for a year seemed to be waning, because she wrapped her furry body around Emma's ankles, purring to be picked up.

'I see, I'm forgiven now, am I?' She cradled the cat in her arms, feeling the content vibration of Molly's purr through her body. Her attention was caught when she saw Papa and Mr Pearson, clad in oilskins, walking up from the arboretum, having done their morning walk of the estate.

'Darling, Papa,' she murmured to herself, 'you were correct when you said the dynamics between Ben and I may shift - because they already have done!' When Emma had been sent to Switzerland just after her seventeenth birthday, her feelings for Ben had already developed into something more than friendship, and now she was back, those feelings were reciprocated - of that, she was sure. Oh, goodness! She snuggled her face into Molly's fur as her heart felt as though it would implode. How could she throw herself into this merry-go-round of the London season? She didn't want a rich husband, she just wanted to be with Ben. They fit together so well - like a hand in a glove - they always had! Ben loved books and nature, the sea, and the cliff walks, just as she did, and there had always been an easy companionship between them. She was in total awe of his skill as a saddler, as he was of the stories she wrote. He'd read everything she'd written, which up to press had been only three short stories, but nevertheless, he'd always been the one to encourage her.

Emma looked back at her writing desk and the novel she'd been working on. Her interest in writing had come about when she was twelve - helped by a friend of her parents - the author James Blackwell. He often dined at the manor when he was staying in his house at Gunwalloe, and would always gift his latest book to their library. Emma had devoured his books, and when James found out that she too had an interest in writing, he'd encouraged her. Poor James, he had sadly died of lung disease in 1919 – another victim of the Great War - having been gassed in the trenches. Everyone missed James, he'd been a kind, lovely man, but Emma missed him most of all for his help and encouragement. She always thought he might have introduced her to his publishing house one day.

*

The day before the Dunstans set off to London, Sarah spent the afternoon organising Emma's trunk, supervising Emma's temporary lady's maid, Juliet Treen in the folding of the many garments Emma was taking with her.

'I should think the season will be very busy this year, darling, especially as King George V and Queen Mary paused the Debutant Ball last year because of the coal strike. But you,' Sarah placed her hand gently on Emma's face, 'my beautiful daughter, will shine above them all. You will make Papa and I very proud, especially as you will undoubtedly attract many suitors. I may even be arranging your wedding next year!'

'Oh, Mama. I'm really not ready to settle into marriage. Would it be so bad if I didn't attract a suitor this season?'

'Darling, I know you're a little concerned about the season – it's to be expected. It's a big thing for a young lady to do. I remember feeling a little apprehensive myself, but then I met your papa, and it was all worth it.'

'You were lucky that you found each other. I should rather like to marry someone I love.'

'And you will, my darling girl, you will.'

Only if you allow me to marry the man who is residing at this moment next door in the steward's cottage!

39

'Well, darling. I think we're just about ready.' Sarah gave a satisfied look at the trunk. Papa would like us to set off at nine in the morning. Your grandparents are expecting us late afternoon. Make sure you break your fast early.'

'I will, Mama.'

At last Mama and Juliet left her alone, so she picked up the note she'd written to Ben and set off with intent across the kitchen courtyard towards the steward's cottage. If she did this in full view of everyone, no one could say she was doing anything improper.

*

In the kitchen, Mrs Blair and Alice were busy cooking, but Juliet, who had settled at the kitchen table to mend a tear in one of Lady Emma's petticoats, heard the side door close. She glanced into the courtyard, smiling to herself. She knew exactly where Lady Emma was heading to, and how much her mistress had been pining this week, having been separated from the young man in the steward's cottage.

*

Buffeted by the wind and rain, Emma stood at the Pearson's door, knowing that it was perhaps not appropriate for her to be calling on a man, but with Mrs Pearson in residence there could be no impropriety about the visit. She knocked purposefully, and as the door was opened, Emma thought Rose Pearson's smile faltered at the sight of her.

'Forgive the intrusion, Mrs Pearson, but would it be possible to see Ben? I'm leaving in the morning and would like to see that he's on the mend.'

'He is on the mend, yes, thank you for asking, but...'

'Who is it, Ma?' Ben called out from behind her.

Almost reluctantly, Rose stepped aside, glancing anxiously at the smiles exchanged between these two young people.

'Lady Emma,' Ben moved forward gingerly, 'what a lovely surprise! Come in. It's alright if Lady Emma comes in, isn't it, Ma?'

'Of course,' Rose said resignedly.

Emma stepped into the tidy, cosy cottage. The smell of beeswax confirmed that Rose spent a great deal of time on the highly polished furniture.

'Can you stay long, Lady Emma,' Ben said, grinning as he used her correct title.

'Ben, I'm sure my lady has a thousand things to do today,' Rose interjected.

'No, no,' Emma said brightly. 'Everything is packed and ready to go.'

'Well, that's settled then. Ma, could we have some tea please?'

Emma couldn't help noting Rose's stony face as Ben led her into the parlour which adjoined the kitchen and offered her a seat.

'I must say, Ben. A mothers love was just what you needed – you look so much better than last I saw you.'

Ben laughed. 'She's doted on me - continuously.'

'As all mothers should,' Rose called out from the kitchen.

'And very grateful I am too,' he shouted and then lowered his voice and smiled gently at Emma. 'I can breathe now without yelping. I felt such a baby in front of you last week, but in truth I've never felt pain like it.'

'I thought you were very brave to try and look after yourself.'

Rose came in and placed a tray of crockery on the table, before returning to the kitchen.

'It's lovely to see you, Em,' he whispered, 'I was beginning to fear that I wouldn't see you again until after the summer.'

'I was desperate to see you too,' she whispered, 'but… well, Papa does not think it's appropriate for us to be so alone.'

Ben nodded. 'My parent's sentiments too, I'm afraid.'

They exchanged a look that left neither in doubt they would defy any sanctions their parents might try to put in place.

'I wanted to give you this.' She surreptitiously handed him the note which he pushed deep into his pocket. 'When do you expect to go home?'

'Next week. I can manage most things myself now, and much as it is lovely to be fussed over, I'm rather looking forward to going home. I'm not sure how much work I can do though.'

'Mama was very impressed by the box you made for me. She thinks you're very talented, and you know she has an eye for quality craftmanship! Perhaps you can make some more things like that to sell, just to tide you over.'

'I'm honoured that your mama thinks that. Then perhaps I *will* see if my talent extends to more smaller things, until I'm able to get back to making saddles.' Ben glanced through to where his mother was brewing the tea. 'I shall miss you, Em.'

'And I you,' she said in earnest. 'I'll write to you, telling you all about my presentation.'

'I'd like that.'

She put her hands over his. 'And perhaps these talented hands of yours, might put pen to paper to write back to me?'

'I would be honoured to be able to write to you, of course, but what will your parents say?' he whispered.

'I'll say the letters are from Agnes - they won't ask to read them. Mama and Papa know we all keep in touch.'

'I wouldn't put Agnes as much of a letter writer,' Ben said, in between Rose's journey to and from the kitchen.

'Oh, she wrote the odd letter to me when I was in Switzerland, and kept me up to date about what you were doing.'

'Did she now?' He raised a mischievous eyebrow.

'I wanted to know if you'd forgotten about me.'

His eyes twinkled. 'Not a chance, Em.'

Emma felt a tingle run down her back, but the spell was broken when the teapot was brought in.

'So, you're off to London then, my lady?' Rose said sitting down with them.

'I am, yes.'

'To be presented to royalty, Mrs Blair tells me!'

'Yes – I'm rather looking forward to that.'

'I'm sure you'll find a wonderful husband while you're there. That's what the London season is for, isn't it?'

'It is, but I'm not looking for a husband just yet.'

'Ah, we'll see, won't we, Ben? Lady Emma will no doubt catch the eye of some lucky gentleman, and then we will have a wedding to look forward to.'

Emma shot a fleeting glance at Ben who had lowered his eyes to take a sip of tea.

'Will you be away all summer, my lady?' Rose asked.

'Lord, but I hope not,' Emma laughed, 'London is a hot smelly place in mid-summer. I much prefer to be with my friends down here, and of course enjoy the beautiful coast and countryside. London is fine for a few weeks, but Cornwall, and *all* it has to offer, will no doubt beckon me home.'

Emma saw Ben smile into his teacup.

The threesome spent a pleasant quarter of an hour together and when there seemed no chance of being left alone again, Emma reluctantly took her leave.

'Have a wonderful time, Lady Emma,' Ben said.

'Thank you, I will. You take great care of yourself now. No falling off any ladders again rescuing doves.'

'I'll try my best.'

Rose Pearson tutted behind them. 'He'd do well to get rid of that silly bird,' she muttered, 'he could have broken his neck!'

'She's my pet, Ma,' Ben answered, making Rose tut again.

'I hope the weather improves, Ben so you can get out and about before you leave the estate?'

'Well, come rain or shine, I'm going to take a walk down to the arboretum each morning from now on. Perhaps I shall see you as you leave tomorrow morning.'

Emma smiled brightly. 'Perhaps. We will leave at nine in the morning.'

Emma heard Rose give an anxious sigh behind them, so she bid them both goodbye.

Ben stood at the door until Emma had gone through the gate, he smiled and waved as she skirted the fence towards the kitchen courtyard, and she saw him mouth the words 'goodbye' a moment before she stepped out of sight.

*

Rose Pearson fiddled nervously with her apron as she anxiously watched the subtle intimate exchange between Lady Emma and her son. It was all very well to be so close when they were children, but this, this was clearly developing into something more than childhood friendship! Lady Emma was far out of Ben's league - she was about to be presented to royalty! Rose knew little about the debutantes, except that they would attend many balls during the London season, where His Lord and Her Ladyship would expect her to find a suitable rich husband. Hadn't the Earl, told her husband Sydney, exactly that. So, when Lady Emma brought home a fiancé, what would Ben do then? It would only mean heartbreak for him. Oh, how she wished she could have nipped this in the bud before it had gone this far.

When Ben returned indoors, Rose collected the tea tray and stood for a moment with the tray in hand.

Ben tipped his head waiting for her to say something.

'Be careful there, Ben,' she said softly.

His eyes clouded. 'What do you mean?'

'You know what I mean,' she said sternly. 'Just be careful.' As she turned to walk out of the room, she feared the warning was too late.

*

Later that night, in the privacy of his old bedroom, Ben opened the note from Emma.

Dearest Ben.

I have missed you terribly this week, and I am so sorry I am going away again.

Wait for me will you? I shall wait for you. x

I shall wait forever, Em,' he whispered holding the note to his heart.

6

There was a flurry of activity in Bochym Manor that morning. The family had breakfasted early and Theo Trevail, having seen to His Lordship, was now helping David the footman load the trunks onto the back of the car under the supervision of Joe Treen. Lowenna Trevail, Sarah's Lady's maid, was saying a tearful goodbye to her children Denny and Loveday, who were to be given over to the loving care of the Bochym Nanny for the duration of the London season. Whereas the parting almost broke Lowenna's heart, the children were excited at the prospect - Nanny always spoiled them to death!

Emma was the first to come downstairs, and kissed her sister, Anna, warmly on her tear-stained cheek.

'Don't cry, Anna,' Emma said sympathetically.

'It's not fair.' Anna stamped her foot in frustration. 'You get new dresses and get to go to parties and have all the fun, while I have to stay home with stuffy Miss Gilbert, who wouldn't know what fun was if it hit her in the face!'

'You're time will come,' Emma soothed.

'But a whole summer without you,' Anna wailed.

'Hush now, Anna,' Emma whispered. 'I've no intention of staying in London all summer.'

'Oh, really!' Anna's face brightened.

Emma put her finger to her lips, and as she did, she noticed Ben standing by the stable wall. So, he *had* come out to see her off, her note hadn't frightened him off.

Sarah and Peter stepped out of the manor and ushered Emma into the car, but before she did, Emma stole another look at Ben. Thankfully, he'd kept his distance so her parents hadn't seen him. Ben raised his hand in farewell, and Emma's spirits lifted, making her smile to herself many times during the journey to the Devon residence of her maternal grandparents Charles and Patricia Devereux.

*

Dropping his hand to his side, Ben sighed, as the car drove off down the driveway. When he turned, he saw his parents watching him in disapproval. Fortunately, he was saved from any comment, when Mr Lennox the chauffeur pulled up to take Nanny and the children to school, and Loveday came running up to Ben with open arms.

'Ben!' She squealed in delight.

'Whoa there, Princess,' Ben said, fearful of his ribs.

'Loveday, be careful!' Nanny shouted. 'Ben has hurt his ribs, so he can't hug you today.'

'Oh!' Her face fell. 'What have you done?'

'I fell off a ladder,' he said crouching down to her level.

'What were you doing?'

'I was climbing too high on it.'

Loveday folded her arms. 'That was silly.'

'Yes it was. Now, come on, Nanny and Denny are waiting for you in the car.'

She wrapped her arms around his neck, making him wince slightly. 'Bye, bye, Ben. Don't climb any more ladders.'

'I promise I won't.'

He watched her get in and waved her goodbye. Everybody loved Loveday - she was just the sweetest little girl.

*

The Devereux estate was slightly larger than the Bochym estate, sitting in acres of prime Devon agricultural land.

The estate was managed by Charles Devereux, his estate manager, and a land agent. Charles had never forgiven his son, Justin, for shirking his duties after university and not staying on to manage the estate – wanting instead a life as an artist! He'd swanned off to Italy to live and granted, he'd become a renowned artist both in Italy and England, but this did not cut any mustard with Charles. As far as he was concerned, artists were wastrels, something Justin himself proved to him. Justin had come home to England briefly in 1912 and promptly got himself attached to some gold digger, as Charles called Ruby, who used to be the Dunstan's housekeeper! Even though that had been ten years ago, and Ruby and Justin were very happily married, Charles still hoped the idiot would come to his senses, divorce his low-born wife, come back from Italy, take up his position on the estate, and perhaps marry someone young and more suitable, who might produce an heir!

Relations between Charles and his daughter, Sarah, had also been strained over the last ten years. As far as Charles was concerned, it was her fault for letting such a match between her housekeeper and her brother happen, and endorsing it!

Sarah had never had a good relationship with her father. They were civil to each other, but they would never be close, she was her mother's child and always would be. Therefore, when Sarah and Peter arrived with Emma, they found that Charles had taken himself up to London to his club for the duration of their stay. This suited all parties.

After taking refreshments, the group settled into their rooms. They were staying only one night and travelling on to London the next day.

It was while Peter was taking a quick afternoon nap after the drive, that Sarah went in search of her mother. She found her in the drawing room, reading one of the many books she devoured over the year.

'My darling girl, have you settled in? Come, sit with me, and tell me all about the preparations you've been making. Gosh it only seems like a couple of years when we were preparing you for your grand entrance into society – and what an entrance you had! Is Emma looking forward to it? She seemed a little out of sorts when she arrived.'

'Yes, Emma seems to be euphoric for a while and then plunge into, well, I can only call it melancholia. She did not want to leave Cornwall for some reason – I think she misses her friends. Mama, please could you speak to her, she seems so indifferent to the coming season. I don't understand it, I couldn't wait for mine.'

Patricia Devereux smiled gently. 'I remember it well. You couldn't wait to grow up, and when you finally hit the London scene, you were the belle of every ball. Tell her to come and see me.'

'Thank you, Mama.'

*

Emma was about to go out into the gardens when her mama told her that Grandmama wanted to see her in the drawing room.

Emma loved Grandmama Devereux much more than Grandmama Dunstan who thankfully resided with Aunt Carole in France for most of the time. Grandmama Devereux was always one to hold her arms out for a hug, and always had snippets of wisdom which she had offered up to Emma while she was growing up.

'Come sit with me, my darling girl.'

Emma dutifully sat down – knowing exactly why she'd been summoned.

'Now my dear. What are you looking forward to the most about this coming season?'

'Going back home to Bochym as soon as possible.'

'Don't be facetious, Emma. I don't think you understand what a privilege it is to be presented, and attend all the parties which follow.'

'Sorry, Grandmama. I am looking forward to being presented. It's just…that, oh, goodness, I really don't want to be touted around to find a suitable husband.'

'It's not all about finding a husband. A ball is a ball - a time to dance and enjoy yourself. It's a time to dress up and meet different people. Yes, there will undoubtedly be suitors - and many of them. It's your time to shine and make your parents, myself, and your grandpapa proud. Your parents have done a wonderful job bringing you up. You've had freedom to run free as a child and encouraged to befriend children less fortunate than yourself, which will stand you in good stead as you grow older. But there comes a time when you need to slip back into the sphere in which you belong. It's time to leave all childish things behind and show society what a marvellous job your parents have done, and what a remarkable young woman you've become. And really, my darling girl, what is wrong with attracting the attention of a handsome suitor?'

Emma said nothing, but her mouth twitched.

'Do you not want to marry?'

'Eventually, yes, but not yet.'

'It's important you do well in your first season, Emma. You may miss the opportunity to attract a rich husband with this attitude, what then?'

'I shall marry a poor man who allows me to be who I want to be,' she answered softly.

Patricia raised an eyebrow. 'Ah, do I detect a certain someone has caught your attention.'

'No!' she answered rather too quickly.

Patricia took a sip of tea and observed her from over the edge of the teacup.

'I want to live a little, Grandmama. I want to be back in Cornwall again – I missed it so much when I was away in Switzerland. I want to write novels and enjoy not being told what to do by a governess for once. If I attract a rich man, a wedding will soon follow and my husband will expect me to do as I'm told. He'll expect me to be a docile wife, sitting in my fine drawing room, playing bridge, and entertaining people to whom I have no affinity.'

'So, I take it you're planning to do everything in your power to dissuade suitors.'

Emma lowered her eyes.

'That would be a very rude thing to do, you know! Don't think that you can be rude to anyone and escape being disliked for it. Any rudeness you display will bar you from many social occasions in the future.'

Emma lifted her eyes to her grandmama.

'I'm going to give you some advice, Emma, and you're to take heed of it. Whenever you're out in public, at any of these parties, your fundamental duty in commonest civility is to overcome your impulse to deter the attentions of anyone. You must always behave as a grown-up person, and a well-bred grown-up person at that! You will be courteous to everyone you meet. You must always look directly and attentively at the person speaking to you, and offer up your hand as though you're happy to meet them. You must always smile and say, "How do you do." The impression you make with that person may easily gain or lose a friend for life. It takes years to build a reputation and a few seconds to ruin it. I would have thought finishing school would have taught you all these things.'

'They did, Grandmama,' Emma said meekly.

'Then I want to hear no more of your reluctance to throw yourself wholeheartedly into this season - you might even enjoy it!' Patricia stood up, and Emma, realising that she was being dismissed, got up too. Before she reached the door, Patricia added, 'You know, I fear you seemed to have picked up some of your Uncle Justin's genes. He went his own way too and it has split this family forever. Don't do that to your parents. I implore you, my darling granddaughter, to only do what makes your parents proud - you owe it to them. And you know, I'm sure there is a future husband out there that would gladly agree to *all* your wishes, just so that he has you on his arm. Now, off you go, I shall expect you to be the belle of every ball.'

Emma walked back to her grandmama and kissed her soft cheek. 'Thank you, I will do my best.'

'Just always do the right thing, and you will make us all proud.'

7

Zack Blackthorn was home for the weekend and had called into the saddlery en route, to check on how Ben was fairing - only to find it closed!

'He's staying with his ma and pa,' a voice behind him spoke, as Zack peered through the window for any sign of him.

Zack turned and smiled at young Jimmy Trevorrow.

'I'm looking after the place for him, and feeding Amara,' Jimmy said pulling a handful of grain from his pocket to show him.

'Thank you, Jimmy. I'll go and see him there then.'

'Tell him to hurry back, won't you?' he said scuffing his worn shoes on the gravel path.

'Are you missing your wage?'

'Yes, I don't earn much at The Old Inn collecting glasses. I like this job. Ben's kind to me, not like Mr Blake the innkeeper – the miserable old beggar. Keeps clipping me around the earhole he does.'

Zack smiled. 'I'll tell Ben to hurry up and mend his broken bones then.'

'Ta,' Jimmy said unlocking the workshop door to feed the dove.

*

When Jimmy returned to the dairy, Merial was standing by the door, arms folded, watching him.

'Where has Ben been all week?'

Jimmy ignored her as he walked past.

'It's rude to ignore someone who has spoken to you.'

'And it's rude to spy on people, like you were doing the other day.'

'I was just making sure Ben was alright! I could see he'd closed the workshop for some reason.'

'A likely story. I told Ben, you know - he knows what you were doing.'

She blanched. 'You might regret that, Jimmy Trevorrow. I might just tell my brothers that you've been telling tales about me.'

'And I might just have to tell my pa to dismiss you for threatening me,' Jimmy snarled.

*

Zack found Ben in low spirits, so enticed him out for a walk in the fresh air.

His ma pursed her lips. 'Now, don't be long, Ben. Dinner will be on the table at noon.'

'Yes, Ma,' he answered jadedly.

'What's amiss?' Zack asked.

'Oh, this and that.' Ben plunged his hands deep into the pockets of his trousers. 'Emma's gone away to London, for God knows how long,' his eyes cut to Zack's, 'and I fear she'll come back with a rich fiancé in tow.'

Zack tipped his head. 'I don't think that's likely, do you?'

'No, it's not what either of us wants, but it is what is expected of her, so *Ma* keeps reminding me.'

'I don't think you've anything to worry about, my friend,' he put his hand on Ben's shoulder. 'I'll tell you what though, I wish I could go to London.'

Ben stopped walking. 'Don't you leave me as well. What the hell do you want to go to London for anyway?'

'For a better life – one away from the inevitable one awaiting me – making coffins!'

'What would you do in London?'

'Don't laugh, but I would rather like to be a pianist.'

Ben did laugh. 'Don't you have to play the piano first?'

'I can, and quite well, I believe.'

'Oh!' Ben was astonished. 'You've never said any of this before to me, have you been having lessons then?'

'No, I've just sort of picked it up over the last three years at Kit's house. I mention it now because it's all I can think about.'

'Well, I'm impressed. I don't have a musical bone in my body. I take it you haven't broached this desire to be a pianist with your pa.'

Zack rolled his eyes. 'What do you think? Pa is hell bent on me having a skill where I can actually make something, and earn a living.'

'I highly recommend it,' Ben grinned, 'making things people want will keep the wolves from the door, you know!'

'I know,' Zack said gloomily. They stopped at the boating lake, where they had all played as children.

'We're a right couple of miseries, aren't we? It seems neither of us can have what we want.'

'Oh, I don't know, Ben. I think Emma will find her way back to you very soon.'

Ben's mouth tightened. 'Even if she does, what can I offer a woman like that?'

'What you've always offered her - undying love and companionship.'

'My God, do I wear my heart on my sleeve so that it's evident to all?'

'It's always been apparent to Agnes and me – probably William too if the truth were told.'

'I think it's apparent to our parents too. Emma's father has told her she shouldn't be with me alone, and my parents have warned me off any attachment to Emma.'

Zack shook his head. 'And we thought being grown up would give us the power to do as we please. It seems we're always to be conscious of what our elders expect of us. You know, when Emma gets back, you can always call on either me or Agnes to pretend to chaperone you two, so you can spend some time together.'

'Thank you, my friend. I know we shouldn't, and we're probably on the road to nowhere, but……'

'No buts, if we can help, we will.' He grinned. 'Oh, by the way, Jimmy wants you back in the saddlery. It was he who told me where you were.'

'I want to be back there too. Ma has been wonderful looking after me, but she's starting to treat me like a child again. So, I shall be back in the saddlery by your next visit home.'

'Good, I'll come and spend some more time with you. It's strange, but I feel very displaced back at Poldhu. I miss being at Kit and Sophie's house. I feel I can be myself there, without judgment. At home, Pa continually keeps me busy. I don't mind doing my share of work to help out, but it's as though he thinks because I'm an apprentice I don't do a proper days work, but I do! I might not be as good as Kit, and I never will be, but I do work hard.'

'I know you do, Zack, and that box you made for me to cover in leather for Emma's birthday was fantastic. She loved it.'

Zack's shoulders drooped. 'She loved what *you* did to it. I just made the box – like the coffin boxes Pa wants me to make.'

'Well, Zack, thanks for coming to cheer me up,' Ben laughed, as he gave him a slap on the back.

'I'm sorry, my friend.'

'Don't be, I'm jesting. What are friends for, if not to exchange moans with each other?'

*

At Poldhu, after Ellie Blackthorn had closed her tearoom for the day, and the family settled down around the kitchen table, Ellie was sifting through the post which had been delivered too late for her to read that morning.

'Oh! Well, I never,' she declared as she read one of her letters.

Everyone looked in her direction.

'It's from Jessie!'

Guy grunted, as he always did when Jessie's name was mentioned, and Ellie shot him a hard stare.

Guy had never forgiven his sister-in-law, Jessie, for taking off ten years ago with Daniel Chandler or her 'fancy man' as Guy always called him. Granted it was only days after Jessie's husband, Silas - Guy's brother - had been killed, but no amount of reasoning with him that Jessie had been estranged from Silas for months beforehand, could sway him otherwise. Therefore, Jessie had never been back to visit Poldhu Cove.

'What does Aunt Jessie say, Ma?' Zack asked.

'They're just getting ready to go on tour to Norway with Daniel's orchestra, would you believe. They'll be gone for three months and then she says they're planning a trip down to Cornwall in August!' Ellie looked up from the letter. 'It's the tenth anniversary of her first baby's death, and they would like to visit the grave.'

Guy placed his hands firmly on the table top to ease himself up. 'They're not staying here,' he said grumpily.

'I'm sure they will have made their own arrangements,' Ellie said curtly. In the twenty years she had been married to Guy, it pained her that the only cross words they shared was when Jessie and Daniel were discussed. Oh, but how Ellie missed Jessie, besides being her sister-in-law, she'd been her best friend. They had always kept in touch via letter these last ten years, but it wasn't the same as seeing someone face to face.

'Well, I for one would very much like to see Aunt Jessie again,' Zack said defiantly.

Guy narrowed his eyes and parried, 'That's because you were only eight when she left, you can't possibly understand the hurt she caused here.'

Ellie took a large intake of breath, she wanted to say so much in Jessie's defence but it would only cause bad feeling, and she didn't want that in the household, so she did as she always had when this argument came up, she held her tongue.

'I'm going out to look at a job,' Guy said. 'Zack, don't sit about all day, there is a pile of willow in the yard to make up into spurs.'

'It's his day off, Guy,' Ellie said in Zack's defence.

'I don't get a day off – jobs don't do themselves you know.' He put on his hat and left the house.

'Grumpy old devil,' Ellie uttered, and reached out to her son. 'Don't take it to heart, he's just taking his frustration out on you because he knows he's wrong. The mention of your aunt Jessie always stirs up old bones.

'I think it's more than that,' Zack said softly. 'I'm a real disappointment to Pa, aren't I?'

'Of course not. I think he worries that you won't settle into anything. Thatching is in his blood, and I don't think he can understand why it isn't in yours, like it is in Agnes's. He'll be fine once you're your own man, working for yourself and earning a proper wage. It will be up to you then, and nobody else, as to whether you make a go of it.'

'What? Making coffins for a living!' he said chasing a piece of sugar around the table top.

'If it's not what you want, Zack, then work towards what you do want.'

'I wish you meant that, Ma.'

'I do, my sweet boy, I do. Whatever you decide to do, I'll back you one hundred percent.'

'What if I was to move away?'

'*Move away!*' Ellie clutched her chest. 'Well, my heart would be very sore.' She must have seen the disappointment in his eyes because she added, 'but Zack, if you need to fly the nest, then fly you must.'

'But Pa is adamant that he's going to purchase old Mr Gray's coffin shop for me!'

'And you definitely don't want that?'

'I don't!'

'Then leave it with me. I'll talk him out of it.'

'Would you, Ma. Would you really do that for me?'

Ellie got up and brushed Zack's soft dark hair back from his face. 'I'd do anything to make my handsome boy happy - you know that.'

Zack hugged her as though his life depended on it.

*

With a bundle of willow under his arm and a sack to put the finished spurs in, Zack walked down to sit on the dark rocks at the right-hand side of Poldhu Cove. The tide was as far out as it could possibly go, and after the inclement weather of the past week, the sun was out and the sea was a luminous turquoise. He gazed into the bright blue sky as the seabirds cried on high, and the sand martins swooped and dived overhead, feeding their young nesting in the soft cliffs. He sighed contentedly - whereas the piano at Kit and Sophie's house was his happy place there - here on the rocks at Poldhu, where he had grown and played as a child, was a place of serene comfort. He began the process of bending and twisting the willows into spurs – something he could do in his sleep. As his fingers worked, the sound of the sea was almost like music to him, and made-up tunes began to flood his mind. If only he could read and write music – perhaps he could compose his own pieces. Oh, how he envied Aunt Jessie and Daniel, travelling the world, and Daniel doing what he loved to do. Even the fact that they had young children did not hold them back. *Well, Zack,* he mused, *if Ma has given you her blessing, it's down to you to make things happen.* First though, he must complete his apprenticeship, it was only fair to Kit after he had spent so long teaching him carpentry.

*

When the letters arrived at Bochym that morning, Joe Treen sorted them out, smiling when he saw one addressed to him by the hand he knew well.

When Juliet noted his delight, she gave her husband a questioning look.

'It's a letter from Jessie, by the look of it,' he said to her.

'Oh, that's nice for you,' Juliet answered, trying to hold a smile on her face. Jessie Chandler, or Blackthorn, as she'd once been, had been Joe's first love. He'd met her when she worked at Bochym Manor as a maid and he was a footman over twenty years ago. She'd left service to help run the Poldhu Tea Room with Ellie Blackthorn, and though Jessie had always remained very good friends with Joe, the love Joe had felt for her was unrequited. It didn't stop Joe holding a candle for her though, and he had done until he met and married Juliet nearly ten years ago. It still gave Juliet's heart a little uneasy pang though, to see Joe's face light at the prospect that Jessie had thought about him enough to write to him.

Thankfully, he never kept the letters secret, so it was later that day that she learned that Jessie, her husband Daniel, and their three children were coming for a fleeting visit in August to commemorate the tenth anniversary of the death of their first baby, buried in Cury Churchyard. Juliet had never met Jessie before, and if the truth were known, she'd rather not meet her nemesis now. She was very much afraid that Joe would look at Jessie and her happy little family and would realise how inadequate his life was with herself?

*

When Zack was back at Kit and Sophie's house on Monday, he told them about the letter his Ma had got from his Aunt Jessie and how his father had reacted.

'Yes, I received a letter from Jessie too. I'm afraid your pa took Silas's death very hard,' Sophie said gently. 'I think he always felt that Jessie's departure was a little too swift after what had happened. Poor Jessie though, she'd had a terrible time that year, hadn't she Kit? I didn't blame her one little bit for grasping happiness with Daniel. Gosh, but I can hardly believe it's ten years since she lost that baby.'

'I hope I see her when she comes,' Zack sighed. 'The anniversary is on Sunday the 6th of August, but I fear she may stay away from the tearoom because of Pa. I miss Aunt Jessie – I still remember how lovely she was.'

'She certainly doted on you as children. Ellie told me you were all devastated when Jessie went away. But don't worry about not seeing her. The 6th of August is Bochym Manor's garden party and we're all going, so I shall write to

Sarah Dunston and ask her to extend the invitation to Jessie and Daniel.'

8

On a bright, sunny May morning, the day arrived for Emma to be presented to King George V and Queen Mary. She was rather excited at this prospect! Dressed in a pure white gown of silk georgette with a long white train, her hair was piled atop of her head and was finished off with a white ostrich feather headdress. Sarah stood back and smiled at her daughter with love.

'You're going to make us so proud, Emma. Now, I hope you had a good breakfast.'

'I did, Mama.'

'Good, because by the time you're presented you will have been in the queue for a very long time. I remember it well - I thought I would faint with hunger by the time I got to the throne room. I have to admit to you, my darling, this will be a day of very long waits, but it will all be worth it.'

A car had been sent to collect them from their London residence, and they now sat in a long train of vehicles, awaiting to enter the gates of Buckingham Palace. Emma was astounded at how many people lined the Mall to watch the debutantes go past.

'You see, Emma. Never forget how privileged you are to get this honour. Many young women would love the chance to dress up and meet royalty, but instead they have to stand in line and watch others do it. So, wave back to them, my dear,' Sarah instructed.

Finally, after what seemed like an age, they entered the gates of Buckingham Palace. One by one, the cars drew into the quadrangle of the inner courtyard towards The Grand Entrance where they alighted the car, and entered the West Wing which took them to the Grand Hall.

'This place is called the Marble Hall,' Sarah whispered, 'because of its fabulous marble columns.'

The chatter from the excited girls increased in volume, and though several mothers tried to hush them, they could not be silenced completely. With their bouquet of flowers in hand, the young ladies, and their chaperones, eagerly began to climb the ornate golden Grand Staircase to the first floor. At the top of the stairs, Peter left Sarah and Emma, to join the other fathers and family members, who would be waiting in The Throne Room. The ladies thus began the enduring and painfully slow process of the long queue towards the King and Queen.

*

It was almost two hours before Emma and Sarah reached the door of The Green Drawing Room - the antechamber to The Throne Room, but they had admired many portraits adorning the gallery wall as they moved along at a snail's pace.

Emma's new shoes pinched alarmingly, and she longed to kick them off and bury her feet into the lavish carpet, but protocol would not allow it! Sarah started to tire and several times she sat down with the other mothers to take a break. Emma was famished, as Mama had warned her she would be, and she longed for a drink of cool water. To keep her mind off her discomfort, she thought of Ben and the times they had played down by the boating lake at Bochym. Emma was a girl of nature, and without doubt, she would struggle to settle into a life of parlour teas and entertaining. She grimaced as the pain in her feet increased, and tried to imagine the cool water of the lake washing over her hot tired feet. Those heady days of punting on the lake made her smile, their childish carefree laughter drifting on the summer air. Emma had been given the freedom to play on Poldhu beach with Agnes and Zack, where Ben, and her brother William, had taught her to swim in the sea. Thoughts flooded into her mind, of riding out with Mama in the Cornish countryside, on Timmy her favourite pony, before the authorities came to take all the equines from the manor for the war effort. Emma had only been ten at that time, and the fate of Timmy still cut her to the core. The thought of Saffron her new horse, gave her a warm glow, and she longed to climb onto the saddle which Ben had so lovingly made. Sighing heavily, she wondered how long it would be before she could persuade Mama to allow them to return to Cornwall so she could ride Saffron again. Alas though, no sooner was a girl 'out' into society, than the many dances and other soirees would begin. Ben, Cornwall, and Saffron would all have to wait.

Sarah joined Emma again, pulling her from her reverie, and suddenly the girlish chattering ceased, as the girls entered into The Green Drawing Room. This room was as beautiful and ornate as all the other rooms they had entered and exited, though this one calmed the nerves and gave the occupants something new to look at. This had been the favourite room for Queen Victoria and Prince Albert and they had adorned it with their collection of watercolour paintings and Sevres porcelain.

'Stand up straight, darling, we're almost there now,' Sarah whispered as she handed over the card to the speaker of the room, who announced, 'The Countess de Bochym, presenting Lady Emma Dunstan.'

Emma felt a flutter in her stomach as they stepped into the Throne Room, as her eyes observed the opulence of the gold and deep cerise coloured walls. The floor was covered in a soft pile dark red carpet, and glittering cut glass chandeliers dripped from the ceiling. There, set against a backdrop of deepest red velvet, were the thrones where the King and Queen were sitting.

A card was taken again from Sarah and passed to the speaker of the room, and the door keeper held his arm across them so that they could not proceed until their names were called.

'The Countess de Bochym, presenting Lady Emma Dunstan,' the speaker said, and Emma felt every nerve ending tingle as she walked slowly towards the King and Queen. Curtseying low, first to the King, Emma moved sideways and curtseyed again to the Queen before she and

Sarah stepped away backwards, to let the next young lady be presented.

When they joined Peter in the reception room, he looked ecstatic. 'Well done, darling,' he kissed Emma on the cheek, 'you both looked stunningly beautiful there.'

'Thank you, Papa,' Emma said eyeing the buffet table eagerly. 'Can we eat something now?'

Peter laughed heartily. 'That's my girl.'

*

About the time Emma was enjoying the delights of the buffet table at the Buckingham Palace reception, Ben was settling back into his workshop - away from his doting ma – bless her. As thankful as he was of his ma's help these last two weeks, he was desperate to be back in his own home - with his own things around him. In his bag, he found Ma had packed a loaf of bread and a can of stew so that he didn't have to bother cooking. He'd warm that on the range later.

'Shall I light the range, son?'

Though Ben knew lighting it would be no mean feat - as he couldn't lean forward without wincing with pain, he said, 'No, Pa, let me manage it in my own time.' He didn't want Pa to see that every time he moved, his rib moved too, making him gasp audibly, he'd have him straight back into the car and back to Bochym.

Once Pa had reluctantly left him, not entirely convinced his son would be able to cope, Ben relaxed and walked to the door with a very happy dove on his shoulder. Stepping into the brilliant sunshine, he savoured the warm breeze on his face - Summer was on its way. He walked as far as the gate and leant heavily against it to look down the Polhormon path to Poldhu Cove. The sea in the far distance was calm, sunlight peeped periodically through the racing clouds, as seagulls drifted on the breeze. He closed his eyes and breathed in the warm salty air. Bochym Manor estate was marvellous, but the sight of the sea was like life-giving elixir.

The Hand that Wrote this Letter.

*

Jimmy Trevorrow was sweeping out the shippen after milking that afternoon when he heard the dairymaids gossiping that Ben was back in his workshop. Apparently they'd seen the Bochym car drop him off earlier. Jimmy could hear Merial spouting her rubbish about being Ben's sweetheart, and that she was going straight to the saddlery after milking to see if she could offer to *do* anything for him. Jimmy cringed at the inference - Ben would not welcome her visit.

*

Merial could hardly keep her mind on the job of milking, twice the cow had mooed angrily and kicked at her bucket when Merial had been too heavy handed with her teat. She knew Farmer Trevorrow was watching her - he was always watching her - hoping to catch her doing some misdeed, no doubt, in order to dismiss her. Merial was already in the bad books for being late to milking that day. She'd been shopping for her ma at Helston market, and the wagon back from Helston had been late getting into Mullion, meaning she'd had to carry her shopping bags up to the dairy instead of dropping them off at home. Conscious that she should get the shopping home as soon as she'd finished milking, but having heard that Lady Emma had gone up to London to be presented to royalty and to possibly find a rich husband, Merial wasn't going to miss a chance of trying to win Ben back.

*

Once the cows had been turned back out into the fields, Jimmy watched with dismay as Merial skipped across the meadow in the direction of the saddlery.

'Jimmy, that floor won't sweep itself you know,' his pa chided. 'What's amiss, lad?'

Jimmy nodded towards the saddlery. 'Ben has come home today, and Merial's gone to see him.'

'I wish I was rid of that damn woman – she's nothing but bad news,' David Trevorrow breathed. 'I was a fool to take her on - knowing who her brothers were and what they did to poor Harry Pike.'

'Why *did* you take her on, Pa?'

'Oh, I don't know, I suppose I don't rightly care for the saying *sins of the fathers,* or in this case the *sins of the brothers.* I didn't want to tar her with the same brush. I thought to give her a chance, to see if she was different, but she's a lazy milkmaid, does more gossiping than work, and she's selective which cows she milks, she only likes the docile ones!' He tutted and shook his head. 'Ben needs to give her a wide berth.'

'He does, he sends her away whenever she turns up, but she persists in going. Oh, my, God!' Jimmy's jaw dropped when he saw Bernard Barnstock, Merial's elder brother, walk past the dairy in hot pursuit of Merial.

'Now what's up?'

'Look, Pa! Now her mad brother is heading to the saddlery.' Jimmy shot an anxious look at him. 'Ben won't be fit enough to deal with Bernard – he's still recovering from his broken ribs.'

'Come on then, son. Put your broom down, we'll go and pay Ben a visit,' he winked,' just to see how he is.'

*

Ben was sweating profusely from rib pain when the fire in the range finally took light, he'd just knelt back to gather his breath when a sharp knock came at the door and Merial stepped inside.

'Oh, you *are* back! Susie Carne thought she'd seen a car pull up,' Merial said gaily. 'Can I help you with anything, do you need a hand to get up?' She walked towards him, but he put his hand up to halt her.

'I'm fine, Merial, thank you.'

'But you look like you're struggling down there on your knees.' She began to advance again and this time grabbed his arm.

'No, I said *no!* Thank you. I can manage very well, and I'd like some time to myself.' He tried to shake her off his arm. 'So, if you'll close the door on your way out please.' The last thing he needed was for one of her mad brothers to find her alone in here with him, but before he could make her leave the workshop, he heard a voice that chilled his spine.

'Merial, where the hell are you, woman?' Bernard yelled from the yard.

'In here,' she trilled.

Ben felt every nerve ending prickle. He'd had dealings with Bernard at school, and in normal circumstances could hold his own against him, but injured as he was, he was not so sure he'd come out favourably this time.

Bernard burst through the door and scowled at Ben on his knees and his sister holding onto his arm.

'Oh, yeah, what's happening here then?' Bernard growled.

'I was just giving him a hand up,' Merial said.

'What the hell was he doing at your feet? And why are you here alone with him? He'd better be proposing to you while he's down there.'

Ben mustered all his strength to get up off his knees, shirking Merial's unwanted help.

'I was lighting the range, that's all,' Ben said, brushing the dust from the knees of his trousers.

Bernard narrowed his eyes. 'A likely story.' He scowled at Merial. 'You, get yourself home. Ma is bleating that she needs the shopping you did for her.'

'Bye, Ben. I'll see you very soon.' Merial gave a little wave as she left the workshop.

Bernard snorted before turning his gaze to Ben. 'Now then, what are your intentions towards my sister?'

Ben held onto the back of the chair to steady himself. 'I've absolutely no intentions towards your sister.'

'Oh, yeah! So, you think you can mess about with her without consequences, do you?'

Ben ground his teeth angrily. 'There has been no messing about - as you call it.'

'She was in here alone with you.'

'*She came uninvited!*'

Bernard snarled, 'You've compromised her reputation by having her here alone!'

Ben laughed sardonically. 'I think Merial compromised her reputation long before she presented herself here - and *you* know it!' As soon as the words left his lips, Ben braced himself for a fight - and fight he would, for he'd not be accused of something he hadn't done!

'What did you say?' Bernard roared, grabbing Ben by the throat, and slamming him towards the lit range.

Amara, had flown up to the top of the bookcase flapping its wings in fright, sending a flurry of white feathers floating down.

Though the force of the knock left him in sheer agony, Ben reached for the poker from its stand and held it aloft. 'You heard what I said. Now get out of my workshop and keep your sister away from me. I've absolutely no interest in her at all.'

'Oh, yeah, not good enough for you, is she?'

'That's about the measure of it, yes,' Ben said, the sweat from holding the poker aloft, coupled with the heat from the range, trickled down his back.

'Got your sights set a bit higher have you?' Bernard curled his lips. 'A certain lady from the big house I hear?'

'Get out.'

'You'll be sorry you led my sister along then. Don't think you're going to have a happy outcome from this.'

'I said, get out!'

The sound of footsteps halted the argument and David and Jimmy Trevorrow entered the workshop.

'Hey, what's going on here then?' David shouted.

Bernard quickly released his grip on Ben. David Trevorrow, a mountain of a man, had been a prize boxer in his day, and nobody could beat him in a fight.

'Just a warning, for him to do right by my sister,' Bernard growled.

'I've no interest in your sister,' Ben shouted. 'I don't want her here, so tell her to keep away. It's all in her silly head.'

'Why you…..' Bernard clenched his fist.

'Hey.' David stepped forward. 'It's true what Ben says. Merial has practically thrown herself at him. Now if I find you threatening my friend here again, where there has been no cause to, Merial will find herself out of a job. So, get out.'

Once Bernard was through the door, David slammed it shut after him, and only then did Ben allow himself a painful cry, as he dropped the poker and cradled his ribs to ease the terrible pain.

'Are you alright, Ben?' David helped him to his seat.

'Thank you, yes. I'd have come out of that a lot worse if you hadn't turned up.'

'You need to log his threats at the police station – just in case,' David said cautiously. 'Can we do anything for you before we go?'

'No, thank you again.'

'Let me know if Merial visits again. I've no qualms about dismissing her. I've maids a plenty wanting her job.' He patted Ben on the back. 'Will you be able to work properly with your injuries?'

'I can do smaller things to tide me over, but I'll need Jimmy's help to carry the hides to the cutting table. So, Jimmy, if you want, you can come see me after milking tomorrow.'

'Yes please.' Jimmy grinned.

9

The morning after Emma had been presented, invitations to teas, dinners, and glittering balls, came aplenty, and so the merry-go-round of dances and introductions to eligible bachelors began.

Peter had agreed to stay in London after the presentation, so was able to accompany Emma and Sarah to the first of these social engagements, and as was customary at the first ball the debutantes attended, all the young ladies wore their white dresses and ostrich feather headdresses again.

The ballroom was a lavish room covered with beautiful gilded plasterwork and hung with glittering crystal chandeliers. Awaiting in the side-lines amongst the eligible bachelors were Lord Hugh and Lady Elizabeth Montague, and their handsome son Viscount Henry Montague.

'Anyone take your eye, Henry?' Hugh Montague asked as he sipped champagne.

Henry yawned and took a jaded glance around the ballroom. 'No, Father.'

'You need to settle down soon, my boy, you're twenty-one now.'

Henry stifled another yawn, as his eyes scanned the other handsome bachelors - marrying was the last thing on his mind.

'I need you to choose well. Choose someone with a father I can do business with. You know the criteria.'

'And what about my happiness?' Henry said, turning his attention to the sea of white dresses and ostrich feathers.

'Choose well, my boy and your happiness will be complete.'

Henry rolled his eyes – he very much doubted that.

'I mean it, Henry. If you don't marry this year – I shall disinherit you and your brother Charles will take your place as my heir. I'll not put up with your idle playboy attitude much longer. You *will* settle down!'

The speakers voice started to announce the next batch of newly presented ladies and Henry's ears pricked up.

'The Earl and Countess de Bochym and Lady Emma Dunstan,' the speaker called.

'Here we go, my boy,' Hugh Montague said eagerly, 'take a look at Lady Emma, she's grown into an absolute beauty and the image of her mother.'

Lady Elizabeth Montague peered derisively down her hooked nose at Lady Emma. 'Beauty isn't everything, Hughie.'

Hugh gave a sidelong glance at his wife, who, he believed, must have been last in the queue when God gave out looks, and shuddered at her visible facial hair. 'Certainly not in your case,' he muttered.

'What, what was that?' she frowned.

'Nothing, dear. Now, Henry, you can do no better than Lady Emma. An alliance between our families wouldn't go amiss either. Lord Dunstan and I know each other well. We've had business dealings over the years, but an alliance there would bring so many opportunities. So, go on, be quick sharp about it and mark her card, for she is without doubt the belle of the ball. Go on,' Hugh pushed him, 'make yourself known to her.'

Henry gave Lady Emma a cool once over, sighed wearily, and set off towards the Dunstan party. If he had to choose a wife - and it seemed to be the thing expected of him – it might as well be someone ravishing to show off with.'

*

Now the excitement of being presented was over, Emma, if she were being honest, would rather have gone back home than entertain young men hopeful of becoming her husband. Royal Ascot in June held no appeal to her either, she would rather be riding Saffron, than watching racehorses being beaten with a whip to reach the finishing post. Perhaps after the Chelsea Flower show later that month, which her mama was so looking forward to, she might be able to persuade her into going back home.

Emma shifted uncomfortably - her feet still hurt in her new shoes, even though Lowenna had tried to stretch them for the last few days. Unfortunately, her discomfort was evident on her face.

'Emma darling, stop scowling, it doesn't become you.'

'It's my feet, Mama, my shoes pinch terribly. If I'm to attend these balls, I shall need a more comfortable pair of shoes!'

Despite her grandmama's words about how important it was for her to be sociable at all times, the thought of eager young men, baying for her attention, all with hot sweaty palms leaching through her silk gloves, made her grimace.

Emma looked up as a young gentleman approached to greet her.

'This is Viscount Henry Montague,' her mama informed her.

Henry bowed first to Peter and Sarah, asked after their health and then turned to Emma to bow low. 'You look radiant, Lady Emma.'

Emma smiled at the tall handsome young man before her as his dark hair flopped slightly over his right eye. 'Thank you, Lord Henry.'

'It's a pleasure to meet you. I met your brother, William, briefly a few years back. I must say, good looks run in your family.'

Emma laughed softly. 'Thank you again for the compliment. I'm not sure William ever mentioned you to me.'

Henry gave a half smile. 'So,' he said, changing the subject, 'how did you like being presented to the King and Queen then?'

'It was everything I hoped it would be, thank you.'

'So, now you're out in society, you will set many hearts a racing, you do know that don't you?'

'You're too kind.'

'May I be the first to mark your dance card today?'

'Thank you, I'd like that.' Though her feet disagreed.

He bowed again and disappeared into the crowd.

Emma's dance card was filling up by the time Henry made his way back to her for the first dance. It felt strange being in the arms of a man. At finishing school, she'd only ever partnered another girl as they learned the dances, and very much hoped she'd remember not to take the lead!

The first dance was a foxtrot and Henry was a capable dancer, making Emma feel safe in his arms.

'Speaking of William, how is he nowadays?' Henry asked casually.

'He's busy at Oxford,' she answered, feeling quite disconcerted at having to speak while trying desperately to remember the steps of the dance.

'Oh, I see, what is he reading?'

'Politics and economics, in readiness to help Papa with the Bochym Estate,' she said stepping on his shiny shoe.

'How droll,' he answered, choosing to ignore her misstep.

Emma frowned. 'He's loving it actually. Why did you not go up to Oxford?'

'No need, Father will teach me all I need to know about estate management and business. Anyway, I'm rather enjoying myself at the moment. I'm done with education!'

'You're lucky to have the choice. I would give anything to join William there after this season.'

Henry gave a short derisive snort, pulled her closer, so she moved in unison with his body making the dancing smoother.

Emma narrowed her eyes. 'You don't agree with women going to university!'

'I don't disagree with it, but someone like you won't need to further your education.'

'Someone like me!' She almost halted the dance.

'Yes, you know, its normally the blue stocking brigade – the horsey looking ones, who have no chance of finding a husband, who go. You, my dear, will have no problem on that score, in fact, I might just claim you for myself.'

'Well for your information, I'd rather go to Oxford and read literature then get married.'

'I think our fathers might think differently about that. Besides if you become my wife,' his eyes glistened mischievously, 'we have a wonderful library at Montague Hall, with fine works of literature, so you'll be able to read to your heart's desire.'

'We have a fine library at Bochym Manor, thank you. Besides, I wanted to study to become a writer,' she said adamantly.

'I'm sure if there is a writer inside you, you do not need three years at a stuffy university to get words down on paper. My dear, become my wife, and you'll have all the time you need to write your stories. I can offer you a good life you know. Look around you, can you see anyone else who would make a better husband than I?'

Emma frowned at his conceitedness. 'I told you - I am not looking for a husband.'

'Oh, are you,' he raised an inquisitive eyebrow, 'you know, leaning towards a more unconventional type of relationship?'

'Pardon?' She blanched. 'No, absolutely not! What a thing to say.'

'Then I shall do my upmost to sway you from your reluctance to allow me to woo you.' He grinned as the music stopped and walked her back to her parents.

'Henry has turned out rather handsome, don't you think, my dear?' Sarah whispered to her daughter.

Emma had to admit, he *was* one of the most handsome men in the room – if not the most conceited.

'Well done, darling. Your Papa was very pleased that you took your first dance with him. He and Lord Montague have known each other for many years.

Emma smiled warmly, glad at least that she was making Papa happy.

*

It was to be the next ball Emma attended – the one before Papa made his return home to Cornwall, that Henry once again, marked Emma's dance card first.

'So, my pretty one, have you considered your options yet?'

'I'm considering no one at the moment. I'm not looking for a husband.'

'Are you not bored with these balls? Because I am. But attend them I must until I find a wife – Father insists. He rather hopes - as I do - that it will be you I choose.'

'But I…'

'I know, you don't want to marry yet. If the truth be known, neither do I - yet. I've other things to do before I settle down, but Father insists I make a match this summer. So, I have a proposition to put to you. Why not agree to me as a serious suitor and we can both get off this merry-go-round.'

Emma took a deep breath. 'But I….'

'I know, you've told me many times now, but, and here is the best thing, if we declare to each other, we both take ourselves off the wedding market, as we'll have been seen to have made our choices. We can go back to doing whatever we would rather be doing. Our fathers will be happy, they will do business together or whatever, and when we simply drift apart, it will be amicable on both sides. What do you say, eh?'

Emma frowned. It would be a way out she supposed. 'Let me think about it.'

'Oh, Lord, are you going to make me attend another one of these dreadful balls while you think about it? Your dance card is full for this ball.'

'It's a big decision.'

'But the right one for both of us,' he pressed.

'Let me think on it,' she said seriously.

Henry led Emma back to her parents. 'Your beautiful daughter,' he said, bowing low to them. 'A more dazzling jewel is nowhere to be seen on this dance floor. I'm bereft that her dance card is full for the rest of the evening.'

Emma watched her mama's eyes glisten with delight at his words.

'Until the next ball, my lady.' He gave Emma a half smile.

'Well, Emma. I think Lord Henry is in earnest about you.'

'Yes Papa.' Emma narrowed her eyes as she watched Henry making his way across the dance floor, so sure of himself, so handsome, but yet so underhand.'

'You could do a lot worse, you know,' Papa said, nodding to her next dance partner who was approaching to take her hand. He was a tall, thin man, with a sharp nose, a supercilious smile, and very hot hands. Henry's words, *"Why not agree to me as a serious suitor and we can both get off this merry-go-round,"* came back to her with a vengeance as her partner's damp hands leached through her silk gloves.

Perhaps she would take Henry up on his offer.

*

On the morning of the 20th of May, there was a flurry of cleaning going on in Bochym Manor as His Lordship was due to come home. Nanny felt a little easier that morning, knowing that Theo Trevail would be back too. Theo and Lowenna's children, Loveday in particular, were clearly missing their parents. They'd been no trouble at all – so well brought up were they, but Loveday's teacher at school had voiced some concerns about Loveday.

'She's a very lazy little girl,' the teacher stated.

'Loveday! Lazy!' Nanny had questioned with a frown - the girl was like a whirling dervish normally.

'She has no concentration, and often falls asleep during my reading lessons,' the teacher continued.

Perhaps your lessons are boring, Nanny thought to herself, but instead replied, 'Perhaps the school room is too warm.'

The teacher folded her arms. 'No other child falls asleep during my lesson! I suggest you put her to bed earlier.'

Nanny felt her hackles rise at this slur on her care of the children.

'Those children are in bed before seven every evening, I'll have you know!'

'Well, she's certainly not getting enough sleep,' teacher said with a nod.

After that conversation, Nanny had kept her off school for a few days, thinking Loveday was coming down with something, and yes, she was a little lethargic, but Nanny put that down to either her missing her parents, or perhaps a summer cold. Hopefully when Theo came back, she would perk up a little more.

10

On the 25th of May, Sarah and Emma were to attend the Chelsea Flower show. Although always a lovely event, Emma couldn't help thinking about what, and who, she was missing in Cornwall. So it was with delight, a letter from Ben came for her that morning. As promised, Emma had written to tell him all about her presentation and had been longing for a reply from him. Fortunately, Mama had not yet joined her for breakfast, so was able to read it in peace.

My dear, Emma.

As promised, the hand that wrote this letter, put down the needle from my leather work to put pen to paper. Emma smiled at the way he'd started his letter, and would use it to start all correspondence with him from now on.

I want to thank you for your lovely letter about being presented to the King and Queen, The way you described everything, made it all sound so wonderful and I felt as though I was there with you.

The days are growing longer now, early summer is here! I took a walk up to Poldhu Head last week and the grassy cliffs below The Poldhu Hotel are awash with the purple haze of bluebells. Pink thrift is also in abundance, I enclosed one for you, so that you don't miss them this year, and I found at least two orchids growing wild which of course, I left alone.

Emma studied the pink thrift, smiling at his thoughtfulness.

We've had a good dry spring, and the sea is calm at the moment, a pellucid blue. It's so clear you can see the sandy sea bed. I long to be fit enough to swim in the sea again. There are weaver fish about though, and I watched another chap having to be helped out of the water up to the tearoom to beg a bowl of hot water for his foot. I've had one of those stings once and they're painful for many days.

My ribs are healing and I returned to the saddlery a week after you left, so, the hand that wrote this letter is back doing what it does best, passing needles between two pieces of hide. While it was difficult for me to do heavy work such as saddles, I did, diversify as you suggested, to making money pouches, wallets, hand, and saddlebags, which, to my amazement, people have bought from me. I should break a few more bones – it's good for business - I jest of course. Speaking of the fall, as a precaution, I have taken down the netting to the skylight, so Amara will not get caught in it again.

I'll finish my letter now. I'm sure you have better things to do than read about all the menial things I've been up to.

Enjoy yourself, but don't forget about us down here in Cornwall. Take care. Ben.

Emma was folding the letter back into its envelope when Mama swept into the breakfast room. Mama normally breakfasted in bed, but with Papa back in Cornwall she chose instead to join her daughter in the mornings.

'Who is your letter from?' Sarah asked pouring a coffee.

'Agnes,' Emma lied, 'telling me about the flowers blooming on the coast.'

'How lovely, that is nice of her. It's funny, I always think of her as a tomboy due to the job she does, she never struck me as one to wander the coast path taking in the delights of the flowers.'

Emma smiled, popping the letter into her pocket before Mama could see who it was really from.

'Do you think Agnes and Jake Treen will ever marry? I know Elise is despairing of ever arranging a wedding for her daughter. I think she's looking forward to becoming a granny.'

Emma smiled at Mama's insistence at calling Ellie by her proper name of Elise.

'I can't think of Ellie as a granny. As for Agnes, I don't know, perhaps she's married to her work - thatching. You know it was the only thing she dreamed of doing when she was little, and now her dream has come true, she is keen to hold onto it. She believes that if she marries and starts a family, her pa will not let her scramble about a rooftop, when she has little ones depending on her.'

'I feel sorry for Jake then – he's courted her for a long time now.'

'To be truthful, so do I. Juliet told me before we left for London that Jake confided in his brother Joe that he is getting restless waiting for her – she won't even get engaged to him! Jake is worried though, if he breaks his relationship with Agnes and finds someone new, he might find it difficult for them all to work together, and he'll have to leave and find employment elsewhere.'

'Gosh, that is a dilemma. You must be happy that settling down with a husband will be so much easier for you.'

'Quite,' Emma answered noncommittally.

*

In Cornwall, it was quite by chance that Kit Trevellick found out that Zack had been helping Selene with her piano lessons. Kit, as he always did in the afternoons, had been working on his boat Harvest Moon II which was moored at the quay at the top of the Helford River. It was a replica of the first boat he'd built, but which had been raised to the ground in an arson attack.

Kit was rarely clumsy with his tools, but this particular day he had not been concentrating and had caught his hand with a chisel. Wrapping his handkerchief around the wound, he walked back up to Quay House and was greeted with the most beautiful piano music. Glancing first at the gramophone, Kit found there was no record on the turntable, and realised the music was coming from his own music room. It crossed his mind that Selene had become extremely proficient with the instrument, and felt an overwhelming sense of pride for his beautiful and talented daughter, but with the blood running down his arm, tending the wound was his first priority. Minutes later and with the wound cleaned and the blood stemmed with a gauze bandage, Kit could still hear Selene playing the piano, and breezed into the music room to congratulate her, stopping dead in his tracks when he saw who was playing.

'Zack!' Kit said in astonishment.

Zack blanched at being found out and stood up. 'I'm really sorry, Kit, I was….'

'You were playing the piano,' Kit said, stating the obvious.

'Yes.' Zack hung his head guiltily.

'Don't be angry with him, Papa,' Selene pleaded, 'Zack has been helping me with my lessons.'

'I'm not angry, I'm astonished, Zack. I didn't know you could play.'

Zack cleared his throat. 'Neither did I until Miss Cope started to come and give Selene lessons.'

'So…has she been teaching you too?' Kit asked, puzzled though as to how she could have taught him, the lessons were in the morning when Zack was working in the carpentry shop with him.

Zack shook his head. 'I just listened when I was taking a tea break. I sort of picked it up from there.'

Kit's mouth dropped. 'And you have never played before you came here?'

With another shake of the head, Zack answered, 'We don't have a piano at home.'

'Well, as I say, I'm astonished.' Kit raked his hand through his hair. 'So, I take it you help Selene in the afternoon, whilst I'm at the boat, and Sophie is out collecting Christopher from school?'

'I'm sorry, Kit, really I am.'

'Don't apologise, Zack, you play magnificently. You play like a professional.'

Zack gave an embarrassed smile.

'He's helped me an awful lot too, Papa,' Selene said winding her arm through Kit's arm.

'Your parents will be so proud of you!' Kit said.

Zack started to wring his hands. 'They don't know I can play.'

'Why ever not?'

'Pa already thinks I'm not pulling my weight to become the carpenter he wants me to be. If he knows I've been spending half an hour a day playing the piano, instead of getting on with my apprenticeship, he'll be really angry with me. Please don't tell him.'

'Of course, I won't, if you don't want me to, but Zack, you have a real talent there.'

'Thank you, Kit, thank you for being so understanding.'

'Would you play for us later when Sophie is home? I want her to hear you too.'

Zack visibly relaxed as he nodded enthusiastically.

'Tonight then, you can play for us all after supper. Now, get back to that workshop before the boss catches you.' Kit grinned and slapped him playfully on the back.

*

After a glorious day at the Chelsea Flower show, Emma and Sarah returned home, joyous and smelling as fragrant as the flower pavilions. At dinner that night, after exhausting all conversation about what delights they had experienced that day, Emma watched her mama fall quiet and thoughtful - undoubtedly missing her own flower borders at Bochym. This gave Emma hope that Mama was feeling suitably homesick to want to soon head back to Cornwall.

They both retired to their beds early that night, but sleep was not on Emma's mind. She was itching to write back to Ben, having carried his letter in her bag all day so as to keep him close.

Dipping her pen in her ink, she smiled as she wrote,

My dearest, Ben.
The hand that wrote this letter..................................

*

At Polhormon saddlery two days later, the postman took a sniff of the letter, raised an eyebrow, and handed it to Ben with a smile. Before Ben even looked at the handwriting on the envelope, the delicate perfume Emma wore filled his senses, and a happy sensation filled his heart. He opened the letter, smiling at the way she had started it.

My dearest, Ben.

The hand that wrote this letter, longs to hold your hand. I have danced with many young men over the past weeks, but no one can make my fingers tingle as your touch does. I read your letter this morning and it made the distance between us close. You made me remember where my heart truly belongs..........

Footsteps halted his enjoyment of the letter as Jimmy Trevorrow knocked and stepped through into the workshop, sniffing the air.

'Blimey, what are you wearing? He moved to sniff Ben and stepped back, 'are you going soft or something?'

Ben folded the letter into the pocket of his shirt to read later, and clipped Jimmy around the ear for his cheek, but for the rest of the day, until he could read the rest of her letter, Emma's beautiful perfume delicately teased his nostrils.

*

Emma received a letter at the breakfast table in early June, immediately recognising the handwriting on the envelope.

'Another letter?' Sarah asked.

Emma nodded placing the envelope in her pocket. 'From Agnes. I'll read it after breakfast.'

'I'm astonished. I never thought of Agnes a woman of letters.'

'I've been telling her all about the dances and teas we've been attending.'

'And she's interested in all that?' Sarah asked, not entirely convinced.

'Apparently.' Emma felt her cheeks pink slightly at the lie.

'Well don't be too long reading it, we're having luncheon with Lady Goodman and we'll need to take a cab right across London to her residence.'

Emma nodded, finished her breakfast, and in the privacy of her room, slit open the envelope.

My dearest, Emma.

The hand that wrote this letter! The opening to your letter to me made me smile when you mimicked the words I wrote. So, we'll make it a rule now, to always start our letters as such. So, here goes…..

The hand that wrote this letter is very much missing opening the door of my workshop to you. In fact, every part of me is missing you, and I long for you to come back. You said in your last letter that you might try to persuade your mama to return to Cornwall in June – I do hope so. You're missing our lovely summer here and I know how much you love this time of year.

Chelsea Flower show sounded wonderful. I should very much like to attend it one day – I do love flowers. Your letter made me smile in more ways than one. I could detect the fragrance of your perfume on the pages – so too could young Jimmy, who now thinks I have taken to wearing cologne – my reputation as a working man is thoroughly shot!

I'm back working on my saddles now. I can lift things a little easier with the help of my cheeky assistant, so life is back on track.

Agnes and Zack send their love to you. Did you know, Zack can play the piano now? He plays like a professional, apparently! Kit and Sophie Trevellick have him playing every evening now - who would have thought it? Having told you that, Zack is keeping this information secret from his pa, who, he thinks, will not look favourably on this, so if when you get back and you see Guy over the summer, it's best not to say anything to him.

I shall close this letter now. Forgive me if the pages are infused with the smell of leather, hopefully the pressed Chamomile flower will mask it.

I hope to see you soon. Ben.

11

In London, Emma and her mama had attended so many parties, afternoon teas, smart cocktail parties and openings to new cabaret shows, they were both really quite exhausted. As they breakfasted in their London residence, more invitations came through on the silver platter.

'Most of these today are for the summer balls in the country houses of our friends,' Sarah said passing the invitations to Emma.

'Do we have to attend them all? It will mean an awful lot of travelling around the country.'

'We perhaps need to attend at least two of them, and of course we shall have to host our own for you, my darling.'

Emma clasped her hands. 'Well, at my ball, I want my real friends there, not just socialites.'

Sarah nodded. 'You're right, I should think Cornwall will be a long way for most people to travel to, so of course you can have your friends there.'

'Ben too, this time. I didn't like how he was left out of my birthday party.'

'Oh, darling, are you sure? Do you not think that Ben would be out of his depth in such an occasion.'

'No, I don't! We've been friends for many years. You entertain many people who are not from our sphere – Guy, Ellie, Kit, and Sophie to name but a few. Ben is no different, and to be honest, if Ben isn't invited this time, I don't want a ball at all!'

Sarah cupped her hand over her daughter's. 'Your loyalty to your friend does you justice, my darling, of course Ben will be invited.'

'Thank you, Mama.' Emma sat back satisfied, but the thought of Ben, made her feel overwhelmingly homesick.

'Mama, can we go home?'

Sarah sipped her tea. 'Are you weary of London already?'

'Yes, the weather is turning very hot here and I long to feel a cool Cornish breeze on my face. I've no interest in attending the racing at Ascot or Goodwood, nor do I want to attend Cowes regatta in August.'

Sarah laughed lightly. 'I don't know why I'm surprised - you always were a girl of nature. You can take the girl out of Cornwall, but you can never take Cornwall out of the girl!'

'True, but you must be missing Papa too, he's been gone almost a month now. And your garden, it will be in full bloom now and Mr Hubbard the gardener will be missing your help in the flower borders.'

Sarah held her hand to her chest. 'I admit, I am missing it, but it's important that we are here. This is your year.'

'I would rather be in Cornwall.'

'Well, I suppose we are close to securing a husband for you with Henry. Lord Montague has written to your papa to tell him that Henry has made quite clear his intentions towards you – your papa is pleased about that.'

Emma smiled weakly, she just hoped that this false alliance she and Henry had agreed on would not backfire, and that Henry would keep his promise and not pursue her beyond this season.

'Then let's go home, Mama.'

'Well now you mention it, I think Lowenna is keen to go home too. Little Loveday seems to be pining for her. It's strange, she's normally such a robust little girl. Very well, It will give me more time to organise the ball, and of course we have the garden party too.'

'I'm surprised you're doing both the garden party and my ball within a week of each other!'

'Well, I don't like to let everyone down. The workers from the villages enjoy the garden party on our estate.'

'See, Mama, you're just like me, loyal to your countrymen - no matter what class.'

*

It was midsummers day - Ben had almost recovered from his accident, albeit his broken rib still gave him some pain.

Ben had woken with the dawn that morning with an effervescent feeling that something good was going to happen - though he knew not what. He walked out into the morning sunshine to enjoy a fine vista of the sea at Poldhu Cove while he drank his mug of tea. It was a good quarter of an hour walk to the cove, and before his accident, Ben would walk down to the sea to swim, either first thing in the morning, or after a day's work hunched over a saddle. Today was a perfect Cornish day, warm winds, blue sky, and a sparkling ocean beckoning him. He just hoped that his rib would allow him to swim.

With a towel over his shoulder and Amara flying overhead, he set off to Poldhu Cove. As usual, as Ben entered the water, Amara settled on the roof of the tearoom, knowing she would get scraps thrown up to her.

The sea was invigoratingly cold, and almost took Ben's breath away, but it felt so good to be back swimming. Walking back up the beach afterwards, the cold swim had done nothing to tamper the strange feeling he still had – something was definitely going to happen today! It wasn't a worrying feeling – it was clearly something good. It was the sort of feeling a child gets on Christmas morning before retrieving a juicy orange or a wooden toy from a Christmas stocking.

He waved to Guy Blackwell and Agnes, who along with Jake Treen and Ryan Penrose were loading thatch onto their wagon. Guy and Ryan's wives, Ellie and Betsy, were handing out their lunches.

'You're in for a busy day at the tearoom with weather like this,' Ben commented to Ellie as she and Betsy waved the wagon off.

Ellie smiled. 'It's always a busy day at the tearoom now that summer is upon us. I swear as the years go by, this little cove gets busier. Are you joining us tonight on the beach for our midsummer party?'

'I will. Thank you, Ellie.'

By the time Ben had climbed the hill and turned into Polhormon Lane, rivers of perspiration were trickling down his back and the cool invigorating swim was just a distant memory. As he approached Polhormon Farm to collect a can of milk from the dairy, he passed Farmer Trevorrow's four dairymaids walking across the lush green field towards the waiting cows, three legged stools in hand. In unison they placed their stools down, wiped the udders clean of mud and settled their pails in readiness. They turned their faces sideways to rest their heads on the cows flank, trapping their tails to avoid getting whipped in the face by them! They had not seen Ben, which was a good thing, as he didn't want to attract Merial's attention, and so he was able to watch this perfect vision of country life for a few moments until David Trevorrow approached him.

'Morning, Ben.'

'And a good morning to you too, David.'

All the dairymaids raised their head to see who Farmer Trevorrow was speaking to, so with his cover blown, he shouted over to them, 'Morning ladies.'

'Good morning, Mr Pearson,' they all said in unison – all except Merial who shouted, 'Good morning, Ben.'

'Merial, get on with your work,' David cautioned, to which she huffed and dropped her head back to her cow.

'Have you had any more trouble from her?' he whispered to Ben, who shook his head. 'Good, let me know if you do.'

*

With his can of milk swinging in one hand and his towel slung over his other shoulder, Ben was making his way back to the saddlery when he heard the thunder of hooves behind him.

'Ben!' Emma shouted joyously as she rode up to him.

He turned, and suddenly felt lit within. Now he knew why his body felt alive today. The connection they had – had always had – must have been triggered by her return.

He didn't know she was back, but something in his subconscious had been aware of it.

'Ah, so the debutante returns from London.'

'As you see, we came home yesterday.' She smiled brilliantly. 'Help me down will you?' He quickly put down his can of milk as she unhooked her leg from the pommel. Holding his hands aloft, she slipped gently down into them. He unashamedly tightened his hold on her waist as he gently lowered her to the ground. His senses picked up the delicate fragrance of her perfume, and he kept his hold on her for a few moments longer than was appropriate - but she seemed not to mind at all.

*

Merial had stopped milking when she had seen the familiar horse gallop past the dairy, en route to the saddlery. She stood to get a better view, upsetting the cow she was milking. Scowling, she watched Ben help Lady Emma from the horse – and there in broad daylight, he held her far longer than was appropriate for a man to hold a lady. So much for the letter she'd sent to the Earl - that had been a waste of 1½d!

Thankfully, none of the other dairymaids had noticed Ben with Lady Emma, otherwise Merial would have looked like a fool, especially as she'd made a big thing about being Ben's sweetheart in front of them! Well, she thumped her hands on her hips, nobody got away with making her look a fool!

'Merial, get back to work,' Farmer Trevorrow barked.

Sitting back on the stool, she grabbed the udders roughly, the cow protested and whipped its tail into her eye, making her squeal.

'Merial, I won't tell you again,' Farmer Trevorrow shouted.

*

Oblivious to being watched, Ben picked up his can of milk and walked with Emma to the workshop.

'I feel I should bow low to you now you've been presented to royalty, my lady.'

Emma giggled and slapped him playfully.

'So,' he asked tentatively, 'did you attract many suitors then?' He felt his heart constrict at the question.

She shrugged. 'A few. My determination to parry any marital advances, was thwarted when Grandmama Devereux warned me against my rebellion.'

Conscious of keeping the apprehension from his voice, he asked, 'So, is there a potential husband on the horizon?'

'One has declared, yes.' She frowned.

'Oh! And?'

'And nothing. I'm hoping that now I've come home he'll find someone else.'

Ben tipped his head. 'Will your parents not expect an engagement to follow?'

'They might, but I'm decided,' she cut her eyes to meet his, 'I'll not find the husband I want at society parties. They're full of young men of wealth who are all just looking for someone with a decent marriage settlement.' She rolled her eyes. 'They're looking for ladies whose fathers get on with each other, and can form some sort of business arrangement that makes them both money after the nuptials. I don't want that. I want someone who will love me, not for my money and position, but for me! Someone to romance me, not just pay attention to me for a couple of dances.' She blinked several times before she said the next thing. 'I need someone who will love me forever, and not someone who will settle me in my own parlour while he goes off to entertain his mistress.'

'Not all men are like that,' Ben said gently.

'They seemed to be in my circle of friends. I think I was the only one at finishing school whose parents still loved each other. Lots of the other girls knew that their fathers had a mistress, and that their mothers did not seem to care.' She leant against the saddlery door and turned her face to the sunshine. 'I want a husband who will walk hand in hand with me through a summer meadow. Someone I can speak to on an equal footing. Someone whose face lights up when he sees me.' She turned to look directly at Ben. 'I need someone who understands me, who will let me be who I want to be.'

'Someone like me?' The words tumbled out of his mouth before he could stop them.

Emma smiled. 'Someone exactly like you, Ben.'

Ben's mouth curled into a smile. 'Oh, Em, if only.'

They stood together for several moments – words said, could not now be unsaid.

To break the silence, he lifted the milk can. 'I have milk. I can make you some tea if you wish.'

'I wish I could, but I told them at home that I wouldn't be long. I just wanted to come and say hello, to see for myself how well you've mended.'

'As you see, I'm almost healed now. The rib has set, so the pain has lessened. Jimmy has been a godsend helping me.'

'Good.' Emma reached to gently touch his face, sending shock waves through his body. He cupped his hand over hers and they smiled at each other through the pain of not being free to love each other.

'I'm so glad you're back, Em.'

'I missed you too,' she said, softly kissing him on his cheek.

He walked her horse to the mounting steps and helped her up, marvelling at how magnificent and beautiful she was on her horse. 'You really are a sight for sore eyes, Em.'

Discarding her glove, she kissed her fingers, and pressed it to his lips before she gathered the reins ready to set off.

'There's a midsummer party on Poldhu beach tonight – might you be able to come?' he said in earnest.

'Wild horses won't keep me away.' She blew him another kiss and cantered off towards Bochym.

'Emma, my Emma,' he breathed, 'you're like the sun to my moon – we only briefly meet, and like the sun and moon we seem to light each other's life for such a finite time. Then all too soon, you have to go back to your own life, and my poor soul is once again unsettled and my heart breaks a little each day at the loss of you.'

12

Emma felt as though she was walking on air when she dismounted from Saffron for the groom to take her. It was as clear as day that Ben loved her as much as she loved him. Now she was back, she would try to see as much of him as propriety would allow - starting with this evening at the midsummer party on the beach. She headed off to the gardens where she found her mama knee deep in deadheading flowers.

Sarah listened to the request, stood up and brushed the soil from her skirt.

'Oh, darling, it would be quite inappropriate for you to go, now you're almost engaged to Henry.'

'But why? I always go to the midsummer gathering at Poldhu when I'm home!'

'Things are different now – there is a certain etiquette to adhere to.'

'Then I've a mind to refuse Henry if I'm going to be so restricted in my movements,' she said crossly.

'Emma, it's essential that your good reputation remains so.'

'But, Mama, these are my friends! *Your* friends as well! Ellie and Guy will look out for me!' Emma could see her mama was faltering, so added, 'Why don't you and Papa come too?'

'I'm sorry, darling, we're to dine at Trevarno with Matthew and Hillary Bickford tonight.'

Emma sighed in hopeless frustration.

Sarah reached out to her sympathetically. 'Well, perhaps…'

Emma looked up hopefully as her mama tapped her lip thoughtfully.

'I understand the Treens have the evening off, and that they asked to borrow the pony trap to go to Poldhu. I'll ask if you can go with them – that way you'll have a chaperone.'

Emma could hardly contain herself. 'Oh, thank you, Mama.'

'You must thank the Treens if they agree. After all, it *is* their evening off!'

*

Merial Barnstock stood in front of her pitted mirror in her best Sunday dress. She'd been gutting fish in the backyard with her mother that afternoon and knew the reek of mackerel was still evident on her, so she dabbed on some cheap scent to mask the smell. She too was heading to Poldhu Cove that evening, for she knew Ben would be there – he never missed the midsummer beach supper. A beach party was probably no place for Lady Emma now, so the chances were that she'd find Ben in need of some company. It was on an occasion such as this, albeit a harvest supper, that Ben, loosened with a few glasses of cider, had danced with her twice last year when he had seen her sitting all alone. He might wish to do so again if he found her sitting on the beach all alone tonight.

*

Bernard Barnstock sniffed the air as Merial swept through the room on her way out.

'Hey,' he grabbed her by the arm, 'you smell like a cheap brothel?'

'Well, you'd know what that smelt like, wouldn't you?' she sniped.

He twisted the skin on her arm until she squealed.

'Where are you going? If you're meeting Pearson, there had better be a wedding ring on your finger afore harvest this year. You told us he was going to marry you after last year's harvest! We could do with one less mouth to feed.'

'Ben has been busy,' she countered.

'Not too busy to mess about with my sister though, is he? You tell him, he'd better start arranging a wedding or we'll do for him.'

Merial grimaced as she wrenched her arm from Bernard's grip.

*

In the Montague's estate in Devon, Henry Montague felt very pleased with himself. With his duty done towards Lady Emma, she and her mother had returned to Cornwall and there was now no reason for him to attend any more of those silly balls in London.

'Well done, my boy, for making your intensions clear to the girl. Lady Emma is perfect for you,' his father said to him over dinner that evening.

'Thank you, Father,' he said trying not to sound too jaded.

'Ah! Do I detect that you're missing the beautiful Lady Emma already?'

Henry smiled and lifted his glass of claret. *I don't think so.*

'So, when are we to announce an engagement then?'

Henry felt a prickle of irritation. 'No rush, Father,' he said nonchalantly.

'Of course, there is a rush. You saw the girl - she'll be snapped up by another if you don't make it official?'

'The Dunstans have returned to Cornwall. She's hardly going to find another rich husband down there. Anyway, Lady Emma won't accept another,' he said confidently.

'How can you be so sure?'

'She told me - she wants only me.'

'Well then, get her married and into your bed – you might as well have some fun with her, before she goes off you.'

'As I say. There is no rush. We're both young and would like a bit of time to get to know each other more.'

'I'm warning you, Henry, I expect to do some good business with Dunstan, I don't want any complications along the way from you two.'

'Hughie let's not talk business around the dining table,' Elizabeth Montague said, 'let the young people have some time – it's a big step, marriage. I'd like to get to know

Emma more, if she is to become our daughter in law. Shall I invite them to stay, Henry?'

'No!' Henry said. 'I believe Lady Emma wanted to spend the summer in Cornwall. They're to hold a summer ball in August. We can see them then.'

'Nonsense, we need to see them before then – seal the deal as it were,' his father said, beckoning the footman to fill his glass. 'I've a mind to call a business meeting with Dunstan in the next couple of weeks, so you can see your intended then.'

Henry's smile did not reach his eyes. The last time he went to Bochym Manor, he'd had his nose broken by some ruffian from the village – it quite detracted from the fun he'd been having there. Still, he'd go, and if he ever saw that bastard ruffian again, he'd make him pay, because he still couldn't breathe properly through one nostril!

When Henry retired to his bedroom that night, his valet began to undress him.

'I think I may have got myself into a bit of a pickle?'

'My lord?' his valet asked as he undid Henry's cufflinks.

'My father wants me to marry Lady Emma Dunstan.'

'I see!'

'I may have to do it.' He looked directly into his valet's eyes, 'for propriety's sake, you understand.'

'Indeed, my lord.' The valet laid the cufflinks on the dressing table and returned to his task.

'It won't make a blind bit of difference, you know.'

The valet unbuttoned Henry's shirt and smiled.

'How long can you stay?' Henry asked.

'I've said my goodnights to the butler and downstairs staff.'

'Good,' Henry said, and kissed him.

*

A hundred and fifty miles away, in Cornwall, Henry was the last person on Emma's mind. She was sat on the beach, wrapped up warm from the chill off the sea, despite it being midsummer, with the only man she wanted to be next to - Ben. They sat as near to each other as was decent, knowing that many people were watching. It was a jolly group to watch the summer solstice with. Betsy and Ryan Penrose sat with Ellie and Guy and their collective brood of children. Tobias and Meg Williams had joined them too. Agnes, and Jake Treen settled next to Emma and Ben, and Joe and Juliet Treen sat close by, but far enough away to give the young ones some freedom. There was a great fire roaring on the beach, built far enough away from the dry marram grass of the dunes. A couple on a fiddle and accordion played tunes to dance to. Ellie and Betsy had made pasties for everyone and copious amounts of cider was consumed as they watched the sunset, which was always magnificent at Poldhu this time of year. Later in the summer the sun would set over Land's End, but this evening it dipped its fiery ball into the inky blue sea, casting a rosy glow on the faces watching. It was as though you could almost hear it hiss, as it disappeared, leaving a red gold slit across the evening sky before nightfall began to drift across the clifftops.

*

Merial was marching angrily back up the hill to Mullion, having just seen Ben and Lady Emma laughing together on a rug on the beach! Yet again her efforts of winning Ben back had been thwarted by *that* woman, well, she'd show Lady Emma what she thought of her.

*

As clouds of midges danced in the twilight, the fire on the beach collapsed into a pile of grey ash, and people began to move, stretching the stiffness out of their joints.

'When can I see you again?' Ben whispered to Emma.

'Since my debut, I'm not meant to go out riding without a groom to accompany me, so I shall have to walk to meet you whenever I can get away.'

'Don't be getting into trouble, Em.'

'I'll just say I'm taking a walk in the gardens to write, but I'll slip away over the fields to come and see you as often as possible. I'd like to spend some time with you - like we used to.'

'I'd like that too, Em, but I think we both know things are not the same now, we're not children anymore.'

'More is the pity - I miss the freedom of that time.'

They both turned as Agnes approached them – wearing a knowing smile. 'The barometer is set fair for the next few days, so we're going over to Church Cove on Sunday, if you two want to join us. Zack will be home, so it'll almost be like old times.'

'I'd love to come,' Emma enthused, 'what about you, Ben?' she asked hopefully.

'I wouldn't miss it for the world. Are we taking a picnic?'

'Yes, and we can swim too if it's still calm. We'll set off from here at ten.'

Ben turned and gently brushed his fingers against Emma's hand. 'I'll see you on Sunday then.'

'It can't come soon enough,' she whispered.

*

When everyone stood up to go home, Ben walked with Emma to their pony trap, but when they came within a couple of yards of it, they found the pony agitated, and the air filled with the stench of rotting fish.

'Oh, my goodness!' Joe said, cupping his hand to his mouth. The seats were swimming in fish guts. 'Whoever would have done this?'

Guy, Ellie, and the others came over to take a look, all stepping back in disgust.

'Good grief!' Guy said, 'we can swill it down, but you can't get in it tonight. Ellie, take the ladies to our house for a few minutes. Joe, Jake, Ryan, can you help me to swill it down? Joe, we'll stable the pony here for the night and I'll drive you all home in the wagon. Someone can come and pick the pony trap up tomorrow, when it might smell a bit sweeter.'

Joe ran his hands through his hair. 'Thank you, Guy.'

'Who the hell would do this?' Guy asked, as they ferried buckets of water to throw over the trap.

Ben didn't say anything, but he had a very good idea.

13

Peter and Sarah had not been at all keen to let Emma go on this picnic, raising the question again as to whether it was right for her to be doing such things now she was almost engaged to Henry.

'Mama, Papa, I long to be with my friends again,' Emma pleaded, 'I've been away from them for so long. I wish now that Henry hadn't declared himself to me, if I'm to be so restricted in my movements because of him.'

'We're only concerned for your reputation, Emma,' Sarah said, touching her gently on the arm.

'Please, let me enjoy this summer in Cornwall – It may be my last *if* I'm to be married.' Emma crossed her fingers behind her back for more than one reason.

Sarah looked at Peter who nodded resignedly. 'Very well you can go to the picnic.'

'Thank you,' she said, kissing both of them on the cheek. 'Could someone drive me down to Poldhu in the car – there is still a whiff of fish guts in the trap.'

Peter furrowed his brow. 'It is beyond me why anyone would do such a thing to our pony trap – we have no gripe with anyone that I know of!'

'There are some strange people about,' Emma suggested.

'All the more reason for you not to go galloping around the countryside alone now you're back home,' Peter answered. 'So, I reiterate, you must always take a groom with you from now on.'

Emma blanched, it felt like she'd climbed one hurdle only to be faced with another. 'But, Papa, I like to ride out on my own. I like to find secluded spots to sit and write. I can't concentrate if I have a groom in tow.'

'It's for your own safety, Emma,' Sarah said gently.

'I've spent my whole life riding these grounds, playing on the coast path and beach with my friends, and I have never come to any harm!'

'I told you the other day, Emma, things have changed since your debut,' Sarah reminded her.

'I don't want to feel the shackles and chains of being a debutante. I want to write books – you know I do! I want to have freedom and time to hone my craft. Please, please, let me have my freedom.'

'Emma…' Peter started, but Sarah put her hand on Peter's arm to stop his protest.

'Your father and I will give it some thought,' she said.

*

On Sunday morning, Ben packed a bag with his swimming attire, a towel, a flask of cider and an assortment of cheese and ham sandwiches. He had no doubt that Emma would bring with her one of Mrs Blair's famous picnic baskets, and Ellie would have packed Agnes with enough food to feed an army, but he still felt he should make a contribution.

He walked out of the workshop into the bright sunlight with Amara flying out with him. She settled on the gate post while Ben turned his face to the sun. Summer made his heart sing, he defied anyone to feel blue on such a day. He locked the door and slung the bag over his shoulder, and a frisson ran through his body, knowing he would be spending a whole day with Emma, albeit with four other people. They were all friends together though, and shared a close bond that few could break into – with the exception of Jake Treen – Agnes's long time and very patient beau.

By the time they walked over from Poldhu, the service in Winwaloe Church that morning had finished, so Church Cove, Gunwalloe was deserted but for a man walking his dog.

They were hot after their walk and Amara flew into the shade of the trees in the churchyard as soon as they settled. The men took themselves off to the rocks to the left of the cove to change into their swimming attire, while

Agnes and Emma took it in turns to hold a towel up so they too could change.

They were all good swimmers, but with the tide being well in, there was a ledge of soft shingle where the waves broke which were buffeting the girls, so Jake held onto Agnes's hand and Ben took Emma's until they negotiated calmer waters.

'William would have loved this,' Ben said, as he was swimming alongside Emma. 'When is he coming home?'

'I don't think he is. Papa got a letter from him to say he was going to tour Europe with some friends for the summer and asked if he could meet us in Italy in August when we go to Uncle Justin's villa in Tuscany.'

'So, you're leaving me again, are you?' Ben pulled a sad face.

'I know, I'm sorry, but we'll have the whole summer before that.'

'Promise?'

'Cross my heart. I pleaded with Mama and Papa to let me have my freedom this summer and they have agreed, albeit reluctantly. They've also given me the use of the Dower Lodge as a writers retreat on rainy days.'

'Splendid. You do know I'm away most of next week, don't you? I'm visiting a horse fair in St Austell, so that should give you time to write to your hearts content.'

'There is always something separating us,' she said as her teeth chattered.

'We'll make plenty of time to be together. Come on, you're cold. I'll race you back to shore.'

They quickly changed into dry clothes, and with the June sun warming their chilled skin, they lay their rug on the beach with a checked tablecloth on top and opened the delights of their picnics. Amara, eyeing the food, flew down, knowing there were treats in store for her. Mrs Blair, as always, had excelled herself, including a Victoria sponge cake, pork pies, cheeses, and pickles in the basket. Ellie too had packed Agnes with pasties, scones, and jam.

Ben looked at the splendid fare before him and thought of his rough made ham and cheese sandwiches with dismay.

'Come on Ben, what delights have you brought,' Zack grinned.

'Nothing as fine as all this,' he mused tipping them out onto the tablecloth.

'Oh! Cheese and ham doorstep sandwiches! My favourite!' Emma said reaching for one, making everyone laugh.

Zack grinned. 'I see being presented to royalty hasn't curbed your appetite for good wholesome food, Emma.'

'Not in the least. I'm so tired of cucumber sandwiches,' she said, lifting the bread to spread a dollop of pickle on the filling before devouring it with various happy sounds.

Ben watched her with delight. 'That's my girl.'

Amara, satisfied with tiny morsels of bread, flew back to the shade. After eating their fill, everyone lay on the beach in the sunshine, except for Emma, who, to avert the wrath of her mama for tanning her English rose complexion, was laid under the shade of a parasol. Ben was close beside her, as was Zack.

Agnes, who could sleep on a washing line if needed, was gently snoring in the sun, much to the amusement of everyone else.

'How is the piano playing going,' Ben whispered to Zack.

Emma sat up on her elbows to hear his answer. 'Oh yes, pray tell,' she asked.

Ben gave a guilty smile. 'I hope you don't mind, but I shared your secret with Emma in our correspondence while she was in London.'

'I don't mind at all,' Zack grinned. 'Just don't say anything to Pa, I might get into trouble for wasting precious carpentry time.'

Agnes grunted and began to snore louder, until Jake pushed her gently onto her side, rolling his eyes as he did so.

'So, how is it going?' Ben whispered again.

'I appear to be improving with every day that passes. Kit and Sophie know about me playing, Kit caught me one day, but instead of being cross with me, he's had me playing for them most evenings now.'

'Well, at least you have an outlet for your music. Perhaps they might know someone who can help you to become a pianist.'

Zack shrugged. 'I think it's a pipe dream.'

'That's very defeatist. Don't give up, Zack,' Ben answered.

'And don't you two give up on each other either,' Zack winked at them both. 'You were made for each other.'

Emma lifted her eyes to Ben and gave a weak smile. Whether they were made for each other or not, finding a way of being together was going to prove very tricky.

'Oh, look! Isn't that the Bochym pony trap coming over the track from Cury?' Ben said recognising the piebald pony.

Emma sat up and shifted a little away from Ben. Shading her eyes with her hand, she said, 'It looks like Theo and Lowenna with the children.'

Tying the pony to the church gatepost in the shade, the Travails gathered their things and started to walk down the beach. It was Loveday who spotted Ben first, and squealed with delight as she made for him.

With open arms, Ben greeted the little girl. 'Hello, Princess,' he said as she wrapped her arms around his neck.

'Is there no girl you don't attract?' Zack said wryly.

Lowenna rushed up to them in a fluster,' I'm so sorry, I couldn't stop her,' she halted when she saw that Emma was in the party. 'Begging your pardon, my lady. We didn't mean to intrude.'

'You're not. It's a free beach, you're all welcome. We may even have some cake left if you'd like to join us,' Emma said lifting the basket lid.

'Oh, no,' Lowenna shook her head, 'thank you, my lady, but we've brought a picnic. We thought to bring the children for some sea air. Loveday has been a little out of sorts while we've been away.'

Ben pulled Loveday's arms from his neck, and held her at arm's length. 'Oh, dear, what's the matter with you?'

Loveday shrugged her shoulders. 'I don't know.'

'We think she just doesn't like going to school,' Theo whispered.

Ben nodded – he knew that feeling well.

'Is Amara with you, Ben?' Loveday asked.

'She is - she's sitting in the tree up there, see. Come on, I'll get her down for you.' Ben walked a little way from where they were sitting, and the dove, thinking it was time to go, flew down to settle on his shoulder.

Kneeling down so Loveday could stroke Amara's neck, the little girl sighed. 'I wish she would sit on my shoulder like that.'

'Let's see, shall we.' Ben put his finger under Amara's feet and tried to place her on Loveday's shoulder, but the dove flew off back to the tree.'

Loveday's mouth turned downwards. 'Doesn't she like me?'

'She does like you, but she's more used to me.'

When they joined the others, Lowenna shook her head. 'My daughter is besotted with you, you know that! It's always, Ben this, and Ben that, when is Ben coming to see his ma and pa, and will Ben come to see us too. I truly think you're her favourite person by the way she has perked up.'

'He has a way with the ladies,' Zack joked.

Ben rolled his eyes. 'She is a lovely little girl. I hope I have a daughter like her one day,' he said, glancing surreptitiously at Emma.

'Come on,' Lowenna said, steering Loveday and Denny away from them. 'Let's leave Lady Emma and everyone to their picnic.'

*

A week later, Joe Treen had returned with his brother Jake from visiting their parents in Falmouth, which was a good two hours and two bus rides away. They were only able to make the trip if His Lord and Her Ladyship were away from home at the weekend, as Jake only got weekends off.

It was later that evening when Joe and Juliet were getting ready for bed before Juliet had a chance to enquire as to how his parents were.

'They're in good health, thank you. They send their regards and were sorry you couldn't come, but I told them you were tasked to stay here to look out for Lady Emma while her parents were from home. Speaking of Lady Emma,' Joe added as he climbed into his side of the bed, 'Jake said something, that perhaps he should have kept to himself.'

'Oh?' Juliet turned. 'And are you going to keep this snippet of information to yourself?'

'Well, I know if I tell you, it will go no further, and I've warned Jake not to say anything to anyone else about it.'

'Now you have me intrigued,' she said patting the covers flat around her.

'Jake overheard Zack speaking to Lady Emma and Ben Pearson on the beach last Sunday. Zack was saying to them that they were not to give up, and that they were made for each other! What do you make of that?'

Juliet fell silent and Joe turned to her. 'Do you know something about them?'

'I do know they're sweet on each other, yes.'

'Oh, good Lord!' Joe gasped.

'What? Why shouldn't they be together if they love each other?'

'Oh, Juliet! You know it's not as easy as that.'

'Why? Ruby married Her Ladyship's brother!'

'This is different. Lady Emma has been brought up for bigger and better things than Ben Pearson. By all accounts there has been a promise of an engagement between Lady Emma and Lord Montague's son Henry.'

'Well, she won't be happy about that! She loves Ben!'

Joe looked at his wife in alarm. 'Juliet, you must promise me not to do anything to help Lady Emma act irresponsibly.'

Juliet folded her hands on her lap.

'You haven't already, have you?'

'No,' she said quickly – hiding the fact that she was telling a great big lie. Only that morning, she'd walked down to Polhormon Saddlery with a note from her mistress.

'Good. I hope I can rely on your good sense not to. It could cause a great deal of trouble.'

Juliet bit down on her lip and kept silent.

Presently Joe said, 'I remember the Montagues son, do you? He came with his father a few years back and got into a scrape with a ruffian from the village – made a real mess of him he did – never did get to the bottom of what happened. All I remember was Master William getting into real trouble for running off and leaving Henry to his assailant.'

'I do remember the incident, yes. William was really subdued for the rest of the school holiday,' Juliet answered. 'Anyway, changing the subject, has Jake got any closer to securing Agnes's hand in marriage?'

'No, he's been very patient, but I fear he'll give up on her if she doesn't make her mind up soon.'

Joe put his lamp off and shuffled down under the bedclothes, Juliet leant over and gave him a chaste kiss on his cheek, turned over and put her lamp off. As always when they settled down to sleep, she heard Joe sigh deeply, and felt a great pang of sadness, not only for Jake, but for Joe too – who also had the patience of a saint. Joe had been married to her for ten years and because Juliet had suffered abuse from the hand of her evil stepfather, Joe had been more patient with her than any man should have had to be. He was truly a saint!'

14

The note that had been delivered by Juliet that day to the saddlery, gave instructions of where Ben could meet Emma in secret the next day. With her parents from home until later that afternoon, it was easier for Emma to slip away, pretending to Joe that she would be writing in the lodge.

They met by the stream which meandered its way down Poldhu Valley. It was just a short walk from the saddlery, and one Ben took regularly. It was a slightly longer walk for Emma from Bochym, but they both knew it was quite a secluded spot.

He was waiting for her as she made her way through the glade and led her to where he had laid a blanket.

'How was your horse fair?' she asked as she sat down.

'Very lucrative. I've several orders for saddles, and I've completely sold out of bridles, wallets, and purses.'

'Good, you'll soon be a rich man.'

'I'm already a rich man because of the friendship I have with you, Em.' His eyes sparkled as she smiled happily back at him. 'I have bread and cheese and a flask of water - refreshments fit for my lady.'

The stream beside them was crystal clear as it trickled over stones worn round and shiny by the constant flow. Without any awkwardness of being alone with Ben, Emma lay down on the rug, sighing happily under the dappled light of the great ash tree – its leaves shivering in the soft breeze.

Ben loved her ease of being with him – nothing had changed from when they had been little.

'Lay down with me,' Emma said patting the rug. Once he was beside her she smiled contentedly. 'Oh, how I longed for this when I was caged up in London.'

'I'd like a chance to go one day,' Ben said, knowing it would never happen.

'Would you?'

'Of course. I'd like to see Buckingham Palace where the King and Queen live. I might even like to go to the theatre. I've only ever seen the travelling shows which put on a performance in a soggy field or a stuffy barn.'

'The theatre smells strange in London – I think it's the grease paint they use – it's really rather overpowering if you're too near the front, but otherwise it's a joyous evening out.'

'What else did you do there?'

'We met up with the Bickfords, from Trevarno? We dined at a very swanky restaurant called the Criterion, I must say Hillary Bickford is a hoot, and insisted we visit the club they inhabit afterwards. So, we experienced the delights of The Lotus Club, though I don't think it was to Mama and Papa's tastes – they play something called Jazz.'

'Did you like it?'

'I can't decide, some of it is nice, yes, but sometimes it's as though the musicians are all playing from a different song sheet – it's an attack on the ears. It's a real eye opener though, people seemed to be so free up there. Women and men drinking in the same establishment, dancing dances I didn't even recognise. It's very different from the formal balls Mama and I had to attend.'

'I'm glad you weren't gone all summer.'

'I had no intention of staying away. I missed Cornwall too much, and you.'

Ben felt his tummy flip as she turned to look at him.

'I missed you too, Em, more than I can say.'

Emma folded her arms behind her head. 'Once someone had declared an interest in me, and Papa approved, I took it as a chance to ask Mama if we could come home. We still have a couple of balls to attend in the country, and Mama is holding one for me in August. That one I *am* looking forward to, because I've insisted you are to be a guest.'

'Me!' Ben sat up on his elbows.

'Zack and Agnes will be there, and so should you – we're all friends together. I shall expect you to mark my dance card.'

'Then I shall probably disappoint you and make a fool of myself. I can do a reel and a ceilidh, but ballroom dancing – I think that is out of my comfort zone.'

'Then I shall have to teach you to waltz.'

'So, do I now have to duel this other man who has declared his heart to you?'

Emma laughed. 'I shouldn't think so.'

'Who is he anyway?'

'He's called Henry,' she answered without delight, 'he's Lord Montgomery's son.'

Ben picked a blade of grass and threw it. 'I think I've heard of the family,' he answered gloomily.

Emma sat up. 'Hey, don't worry, nothing will come of it.'

Ben too sat up and looked questioningly at her. 'What do you mean?'

'Henry no more wants me as a wife, than I want him as a husband. He has no desire to leave his bachelor days behind. He knew that Papa was pushing for me to make a match with a potential husband with whose family he could do business with, and Henry's father was keen for Henry to settle down, so, we hatched a plan together. This attachment we formed stops all other declarations coming our way. It will melt away into the ether, and will be forgotten at the end of the season - you'll see.'

'I should think your papa will not be too pleased if Henry reneges on his promise, especially if they have done business on the strength of it,' he answered tremulously.

'Don't worry, Ben. As I say, we've decided to just let it run for a while. There is no formal engagement between us, we will just announce a change of heart.'

'And then you will have to start the whole process again next year. Your parents will want you settled and settled well.'

'I shall do everything in my power not to go to London for a second season. I'm not ready to leave all I love here,' she said meaningfully.

He turned and looked deep into her eyes. 'I'm not ready to lose you either.'

'You will never lose me, Ben.'

Biting down on his lip, he sincerely hope not.

*

In the dairy, Merial was keen to finish milking for that day. From where she'd been sitting on her stool in the middle of the field milking her quota of cows, she had seen Ben heading off alone into the thicket of trees which led to the glade by the stream. He was obviously going to spend a lazy afternoon there, so perhaps she might just stumble upon him. Farmer Trevorrow might have warned her to stay away from the saddlery, but if she were to come across Ben in the countryside, nobody could object to that, could they?

*

In the warmth of the day, after eating their fill, and feeding tasty morsels to Amara who had flown down from the tree as they ate their picnic, they laid back down in quiet companionship. Emma felt at peace with the world and it was times like this she found inspiration for her writing. Reaching for her notebook, she rested her head on her bag and began to make notes in her beautiful handwriting.

Ben turned to watch her write, and she looked down at him with love. He did not ask what she wrote, he just let her write. Eventually he stifled a yawn, smiled sleepily, and his eyes fluttered until they closed.

Emma lowered her pen to observe him. It was such an intimate thing to see someone fall asleep. She'd watched her young sister fall asleep of course, but this was different, this was Ben, and she had never thought she would see a man asleep until she married, but here he was, relaxed, breathing deeply, his face slack and his lips parted slightly. Quite unexpectedly, his arm wound its way across her tummy to rest languidly. The weight of it on her body thrilled her, especially as his hand twitched, making his fingers involuntarily pull at the material of her dress.

Observing his throat from the open neck of his shirt - free from his neckerchief, his skin glistened with the heat of the day. Only pure willpower kept her from reaching down to touch his skin. She loved this man who had grown up with her - who had played in the stream with her, built dams and dreams, as they negotiated their way through their youth. Ben truly was the only man she wanted to marry, but if she knew her Papa, she was very much afraid she would have a battle on her hands for her wish to come true.

As a blackbird filled the valley with its song, the heat of the day, the bees buzzing on the wild flowers, and the gentle trickle of the stream soon blurred Emma's senses, and she too closed her eyes to the music of the countryside and slept beside the man she loved.

*

Jimmy Trevorrow watched curiously, as Merial turned right out of the dairy farm lane instead of left to go home. He knew exactly where she was heading - and who she'd find when she got there. He himself had taken a walk to the stream earlier, only to back track his footsteps when he saw Ben with Lady Emma. If Merial were to find them together alone, she could make some serious trouble for them.

'Jimmy, where are you going – tea will be on the table in ten minutes,' his father barked.

'I'll be back in five,' he answered as he headed off to where he knew Ben would be.

Thankfully Merial was slightly off course, giving time for Jimmy to skirt the top end of the woods to come to where Ben and Lady Emma were. They were laying on a rug, quite motionless, so he knew he must do something to alert them. Cupping his hand to his mouth he made the bird call which he knew would alert Ben.

*

Ben woke with a start, realising the compromising position he was in with Emma, he pulled his arm from her tummy.

'What is it, what's the matter?' Emma's eyes snapped open.

'Someone must be coming. I'm sure Jimmy has just given me a sign.'

Emma got up and brushed down her skirt. 'Jimmy! Does he know we're here?'

'He must do – it was definitely him. 'Jimmy,' he called out softly.

'Someone is coming, Ben.' Jimmy appeared from within the thicket of trees.

'Where?'

'Up the stream path.'

Emma gathered the rug, as Ben put the remnants of their picnic into his bag.

'I'll head them off. You take that path.' Jimmy pointed up stream.

'Thanks, Jimmy,' Ben said, grabbing Emma's hand to pull her away into the canopy of green.

*

By the time Merial had got to the clearing, all she found was a flattened piece of grass and Jimmy dangling his feet in the stream. Knowing that Jimmy had been sweeping the shippen when she left the dairy, and that now he was here, she had an inkling that she'd been had.

*

Emma and Ben ran to the edge of the woods, and stood breathlessly for a few seconds, until reluctantly they had to part ways.

'I had a lovely time, Ben.'

'So did I. Forgive me though for falling asleep.' He grinned.

'I think it's lovely that we can relax together and not need to constantly chatter.'

'When can we do it again?' he asked in earnest.

'I don't want to be taking you from your work all the time.'

'You're a wonderful diversion from my work, Em. I love spending time with you. Besides, I can make the time up in the evenings.'

'Well, Mama and I are going to Gloucestershire for a ball the day after tomorrow, but we'll be back on Thursday. Is there somewhere I can leave a message for you so we can arrange another day out? I don't want to compromise Juliet by sending her with notes to you.'

'There is somewhere, yes - the stile by the barley field, you know the one which borders the drive?'

She nodded.

'There are a couple of loose stones next to the bottom step on the field side, if you move them, there is an open shelf between the stones. Leave a message there for me, I'll pick it up early Friday morning and leave you a return message.'

*

On Friday next, there were letters for three members of the Dunstan family waiting, but not all were brought on a platter to the breakfast table.

Sarah and Emma had returned the day before, from a grand ball in Gloucestershire, and Sarah was up early to breakfast in the dining room, so that she could go out to help Mr Hubbard in the garden.

Sarah's letter was from Sophie Trevellick.

'How wonderful! Sophie writes to tell me that Daniel and Jessie Chandler are coming down on August the 5th, and staying the night in Helston. They're coming for a quick visit to the grave of their first baby, it being the tenth anniversary of her death on the Sunday. Sophie asks if I could invite them to the garden party, so that she and Kit can meet up with them. Well,' Sarah put down the letter,' I think we can do better than that. I shall invite them to stay here and extend the invitation for a week so they can come to Emma's ball. Goodness, but we haven't seen Daniel for years and,' she looked up at the butler, 'Jessie was a good friend of yours, Treen, wasn't she?'

'Yes, she was, my lady.'

'That will be nice for you to catch up with her then, if they agree.'

Joe nodded, trying to suppress a smile.

'You do remember that Guy and Daniel parted on unfriendly terms, don't you, darling?' Peter warned.

'Well, it's time this silly feud was over. Elise has missed Jessie – they were good friends, but Guy has kept them apart all these years. Who is your letter from, Peter?'

'Lord Montgomery. He wants to visit, talk business, and he's bringing Henry.'

'When are they coming?'

'Next Friday. He asks if they can stay the weekend, to give Emma and Henry some time together.'

'That would be a good idea. Henry is such a steady man, and very handsome. Emma has chosen well. Oh, but do you remember, Henry got a bloody nose from someone from the village last time he was here - poor lad?'

'I do, thankfully it hasn't put him off in his quest to woo Emma. I'll phone Lord Montague after breakfast. Shall we tell Emma, or shall we keep it a surprise?'

Sarah raised an eyebrow. 'You'll be hard pushed to keep any surprises in this house!'

'Oh, I don't know,' Peter folded his paper. 'Treen, can this visit be kept secret from Emma, and could you tell Juliet not to say anything?'

'Of course, my lord. Leave it with me.'

'Just tell Mrs Johnson to prepare rooms for two guests and a servant,' Sarah said, 'I'll come and see Mrs Blair about the meals.'

'Very good, my lady.'

'Where is Emma, anyway, Treen?' Peter asked.

'I believe she went to the garden to write, my lord.'

'Ah, the secret novel she is meant to be writing?' Peter mused.

'Actually, darling, she really is writing a novel! I read a little of it last week – it's really very good. Do you know anyone in the publishing business we could send it to?'

Peter tapped his chin thoughtfully. 'The only person we knew who had anything to do with publishing, was James Blackwell – God rest his soul.'

'Speaking of James, his widow Jenna, who is now married to Lyndon FitzSimmons, may still be in contact with his publisher. I shall invite them to the garden party too, as their friends Matthew and Hillary Bickford will be coming.'

'Good idea. But don't tell Emma, she will get her hopes up. I understand most manuscripts never get published.'

15

Emma was not in the garden writing. After retrieving a letter from Ben from the stile hidey hole, she'd set off along the edge of the barley field to meet him in his workshop - dodging the muddy puddles as she ran. Despite it being high summer, a short sharp storm had whipped up during the week, leaving the barley lying flat in the field and the farmers praying for a change in the inclement weather.

At the workshop door she knocked softly before entering, marvelling at the way Ben's eyes lit when she walked in. There was nothing more welcoming than seeing someone's face brighten when you entered a room.

'Emma! Hello, come in.' Ben smiled brilliantly. 'Just give me a moment, I need to finish this off.'

She took off her coat, walked around the workshop for a moment, and then moved to watch him working - his strong hands so nimbly threading two needles simultaneously through the leather. Very gently her hand moved across the saddle towards his hands, stopping him from working.

'These hands,' she said curling her delicate fingers around them, 'they make beautiful things.'

Exhaling slowly, he let his needles rest, curled his hand around hers and pulled her hand to his lips to kiss it. His blue eyes sparkled as he held her hand to his mouth, reached out with the other hand, and gently caressed her face. 'These hands like to touch beautiful things too,' he whispered.

A frisson of pleasure made Emma step closer. She rested her head against him as he very gently gathered her into a tender embrace.

'Oh, Em, my Em, why are you so out of my reach?' he murmured.

Turning her face up to his, she whispered, 'I'm right here, Ben.'

His eyes were suddenly serious and he stepped away from her – the spell broken.

'Let me make us some tea,' he said moving swiftly away.

*

Back at Bochym Manor, Joe beckoned Juliet into his office to share the news about Her Ladyship inviting Jessie and her family to come and stay for a week in August.

'I didn't want to say anything to the others until Jessie confirms they will come,' he said excitably.

'Oh!' Juliet said, 'That will be nice for you.'

He held her by the arms. 'And for you too. I can introduce you to her – for you never got to meet her.'

'Yes, that would be nice,' she said tremulously, secretly hoping that Jessie would not come.

A sudden downpour diverted their attention as the guttering overflowed splattering water down the office window.

'Is Lady Emma still out?'

'I don't know,' Juliet answered. 'I think so.'

Joe looked at her questioningly. 'You told me she'd gone out to the garden to write.'

'Yes, that is what she said.'

'Then she is going to get very wet!'

'Perhaps she's taken herself off to the Dower Lodge – she sometimes does,' Juliet offered.

Joe glanced at the key rack – the Dower Lodge key was still there.

'Juliet,' he said seriously, 'is Lady Emma somewhere she should not be?'

'I don't know.'

Seeing the muscles in Juliet's jaw tighten, he asked, 'Is she with Ben?'

Juliet shook her head. 'I, I don't know.'

Joe frowned. 'Well, I think you do know more than you're telling me. Listen, you must steer her away from this – no good can come from it - for Lady Emma - and for you for that matter. If you were found to be aiding and abetting her, your job may be on the line.'

'I truly don't know anything, Joe. I don't know where she is today, I just know she was excitable when I helped dress her this morning.'

'Oh, Lord!' He ran his hand through his hair and then quickly flattened it down again. 'You had better be ready to see to her when she does come in – she'll be like a drowned rat.'

Juliet gave a half smile. 'I don't think Lady Emma could ever resemble a drowned rat, Joe.'

'Don't be facetious, Juliet, this is serious.'

*

While Emma settled herself at the table, Ben put the kettle on the stove. He closed his eyes and leant against the sink. *Oh, Ben, Ben, what are you doing?* Their moment of intimacy brought feelings for her to the forefront, and he was not sure he could contain them. Certainly, if he had not moved away when he did, he would have embarrassed them both. He shook his head. This relationship, though endorsed by their close friends, could only lead to heartbreak for both of them.

He returned to Emma and sat down. Besides the drumming of the rain on the workshop roof, there was a marked silence as they sat opposite each other, nursing a mug of tea.

'Have I displeased you?' Emma asked presently.

'My, God, no, never think that.'

'Tell me what is wrong then?'

His lips tried to form the words and he shook his head. 'It's this, us!' He saw the sadness in her eyes, 'It's wrong for me to hold you - for us to be so close. We should not be so alone together. Your papa would kill me if he found out. I would hate for him to lose his trust in me - and he clearly trusts me to behave accordingly with you. If we were found out, he would take you away from me. You would be persuaded to marry someone more suitable, and

I would lose you forever. I can't lose you, Em – my heart would be broken.'

This declaration, until now had gone unspoken, hung like a weight around their young shoulders.

'I have no intention of marrying anyone else, Ben, nor do I intend to break your heart. It's you, I want. Zack was right, we were made for each other. I love you, Ben.'

'It goes without saying that I love you too, but Em…'

She reached out her hand to his and he curled his fingers around it.

'Oh, Em, If you were a milkmaid working down the road, there would be no problem. I would marry you in a heartbeat, but…. you're not. You're Lady Emma Lucinda Dunstan, and so far out of my reach that you may as well live on the moon!'

'And yet, our hands are entwined,' she answered softly.

He glanced down as his fingers tightened around hers. The very touch of her skin roused such desire within him. 'Your papa will skin me alive if he learns of this.'

'Most probably, after he's skinned *me* alive,' she answered seriously.

'We jest, but Em, we both know I'm not what your parents' want for you. You deserve so much more than I can give you. I have nothing to offer you. I cannot keep you in the manner you have been accustomed. I've no money to speak of, only a business that barely sustains my needs. You can see how I live. I can't expect you to cook, clean and launder my clothes – this life is not for you.'

'There is nothing I need more, than to be loved by you, Ben.'

He pressed a kiss into the cup of her hand. Keeping hold of her, he got up from his seat, and a moment later they were stood together, close enough to feel the heat from their bodies. He gathered both her hands and brought them to his lips.

'Emma, my Emma. I won't be enough for you.'

She turned her face up to his. 'You will, Ben. I'm prepared to give everything up for you.'

That was it, their destiny was sealed. He cupped her beautiful face in his hands and kissed her tenderly on the lips.

*

As soon as there was a lull in the weather, Emma and Ben decided that it would be best if she returned home - otherwise they would wonder where she'd been in this downpour.

'I'll walk with you to the stile,' Ben said, cupping her face in his hands again to kiss her. Boundaries had definitely been crossed that morning and his heart was utterly lost to her. 'Don't forget, Zack has booked a table at the Poldhu Tea Room for us next Saturday, for my birthday.'

'I won't.' She sighed as she leant against his chest – her arms wrapped around him. 'I don't want to leave you, Ben, because I'm not sure if I'll see you before then, I shall be really busy this week. Mama has the garden party to organise for the 6th of August and then my ball the week after, on the 11th and I've promised to help her.'

'Don't worry, I shall be busy too,' he nodded towards the saddle, 'the client is expecting it before the end of the month, so that works out well. Come, my love, let's dash before the next downpour hits us.'

*

Sydney Pearson was checking the Cornish hedges around the barley field when he spotted his son walking up the fields with Lady Emma. Keeping out of view, he watched them say their goodbyes, and though there was no visible show of intimacy, Sydney was not stupid. He knew how Ben felt about Lady Emma, and the very fact that she kept sneaking off to see him, would suggest the feeling was mutual. He felt the familiar niggle of worry whenever he saw them together. If Ben were to do anything inappropriate with Lady Emma, his job here as estate manager would be in serious jeopardy. He and Rose could find themselves without employment or a home, should the Earl blame him for his son's actions. He watched until Lady Emma climbed the stile - her beautiful voice singing a happy song as she went, and Sydney had to swallow down the lump forming in his throat.

*

It was Friday – Ben's birthday. Emma had just finished wrapping his present with the familiar feeling of butterflies in her stomach at the thought of seeing him again. She and Mama had been very busy the past few days, so she had seen nothing of Ben other than a quick wave to him while she was out riding with Mama.

Emma had been so looking forward to this weekend. She planned to see Ben today to give him his present, then tomorrow they would all have tea at Poldhu, and then no doubt they'd spend Sunday swimming at the beach if the weather stayed fine.

'Good morning,' Emma said cheerily as she walked into the breakfast room. 'Oh, hello, Mama, what a nice surprise. You normally breakfast in your room!'

'I've been out riding early – it's going to be a busy weekend.'

'For me too!' Emma smiled, as she lay her napkin on her lap.

'But, Emma, don't go too far, darling, we have guests arriving today, and I would like you to be here.'

'Why, who's coming?'

'Just some guests.'

'But it's Ben's birthday today – I have a present for him.'

'What did you buy him?' Peter asked.

'Mr Rogers from the bookshop in Helston has managed to find a beautiful copy of Ben's favourite book, Robinson Crusoe. When Ben fell from that ladder in April, he knocked a few books off the bookcase. His copy of Robinson Crusoe was badly damaged – the spine was cracked open and all the pages fell out. I think he'll rather like the copy I found him. I can't wait to give it to him.'

'Then you must leave it at the Pearson's house. I have no doubt he will be visiting them today,' Sarah said.

'Yes, but I should have liked to take it to him, just to see his face when he opened it.'

'Your Mama needs you here, darling,' Peter reiterated.

Her shoulders dropped - she knew it was fruitless arguing if Papa had spoken. *Who were these people anyway that were going to keep her restricted today.*

*

After questioning Juliet as to who was coming, Emma was none the wiser, other than they were due around about midday. She glanced at her clock - it was five to eleven, It was only just over a fifteen-minute walk to Ben's workshop - she could be there and back within the hour. So, with his present tucked under her arm, she stole out of the laundry door, skirted the stables, and climbed the stile before anyone knew she had gone.

By the time the clock had struck a quarter past eleven, Emma was in Ben's arms, and to her delight, he loved the book she'd given him.

'I can't stay long. Mama has some visitors coming and she needs me to help with them – I know not why.'

'I'll walk back with you then because Ma and Pa are expecting me at midday. First though, I shall steal a birthday kiss from my beautiful Emma.'

He gathered her into his arms, and his kisses, so warm and passionate, almost melted Emma's heart. She never wanted their lips to part.

'Well, Em, I can safely say you're the best birthday present any man could wish for.'

*

They were walking happily up the barley field, when Ben felt Emma's step falter, he turned and saw her face blanch.

'What's the matter?'

'Henry is here,' she hissed, 'look, he's stood at the stile waiting. What on earth is *he* doing here?' Then it dawned on her. 'Oh, goodness, the Montagues must be the guests I was told about.'

Ben felt his heart plummet, and consciously moved away from Emma, as Henry climbed the stile in the most ungainly fashion to approach them.

'Well, this is nice. I come all this way to see my intended, to find she is walking out with another man!' Henry's eyes locked on Ben with disdain.

'This is my friend Ben Pearson.'

As Henry looked derisively down his nose at him, Ben felt a strange, visceral feeling about this man - and he wasn't sure if it were just to do with him claiming Emma for his own.

'What are you doing here, Henry? I wasn't aware *you* were coming.'

'Come, darling, that's no way to greet your future husband. Thank you... *Ben*,' he sneered, 'I'll escort Emma from here.' He pulled Emma to one side and dismissed Ben with a flick of his hand.

'I hope you have a lovely birthday tea, Ben. Give my regards to your parents,' Emma called after him.

Ben nodded, unable to trust himself to speak – having been well and truly put in his place. He set off towards the stile, pulling on all his reserves not to look back at Emma.

*

Watching Ben leave so dejectedly, Emma felt a similar feeling in the pit of her stomach. Turning to Henry, the smirk on his face made her face flush with anger.

'How dare you dismiss my friend as though he was an irritating fly.'

'He *was* an irritating fly! Seems to me I've a rival in your affections.'

'Ben is a good friend of mine - nothing else,' she lied. 'Anyway, what *are* you doing here? And stop referring to me as your intended – that's not what we agreed.'

Henry grabbed Emma's wrist, pinching the delicate skin there. 'Just remember, this situation was to get us both off that merry-go-round of the London season. It's still only half way through though, I could throw you over now, and you would have to step back on it.'

Emma shrugged his hand away indignantly.

'So, keep away from *Ben,* or else. I'll not have you humiliate me with some low born, while we're under this pretence. You can beggar yourself at his door once I've made the decision to break with you – and not before.'

16

The Pearson's kitchen was small and warm, with a table at the centre, which stood upon large stone flags. His ma and pa greeted Ben with a chorus of 'Happy Birthday,' but still reeling from the altercation with Henry, it failed to raise a smile. Deeply unsettled, he took his seat at the table, his stomach churning, as to why Henry had turned up unannounced and the pain of having to leave Emma with him.

'Ta da!' His mother presented him with cake.

'Thank you, Ma,' he said, uninterested in sampling it.

She tipped her head. 'Well, I was hoping that would raise a smile, because you've had a face like a wet weekend since you stepped through the door.'

'Sorry, Ma.'

'Come on then, tuck in.' She gestured to the plate of sandwiches.

Ben took an egg sandwich, but his mouth was so dry if felt as though he was eating grit paper.

'Looks like there will be a wedding on the cards at the big house,' his ma said, pouring the tea. 'Viscount Henry Montague has arrived today, and your pa says His Lordship is hoping for an announcement soon. Didn't he, Sydney?'

Ben felt a surge of panic rise at the very thought.

Sydney glanced at his son. 'Don't look so downhearted, lad. I know you like Lady Emma, but you know it can be no more than that. She's destined for a rich husband - make no mistake on that.'

'Aye and the sooner the better,' his mother said tartly.

Ben stood up, almost upsetting his cup. 'Has it not occurred to you that she might not want a rich husband?'

Rose Penrose's mouth pinched and her eyebrows knitted with disapproval. 'Whether she wants one or not – it's her destiny. Both your pa and I can see how this ridiculous infatuation you have with her is stopping you from finding a nice girl to settle down with. Lady Emma has been clearly stringing you along until someone more suitable came along – and now someone has, and you'll have to get used to it! Now sit down and eat some cake.'

'Thank you, but this conversation has made me lose my appetite.' He scraped his chair back on the stone floor and picked up his coat.

'Where are you going?' his ma cried.

'Home.'

'But it's your birthday!' she called out, as he closed the door.

*

When Henry and Emma walked into the drawing room together, Emma noted her parents looked very cross with her.

'Emma, darling, where on earth were you? I said we had guests coming.'

'I'm sorry, Mama, I just went out for some air.' Emma heard Henry snort beside her and her hatred for him intensified. 'You didn't say who was coming, Mama.'

'Well, it was meant to be a surprise for you. Still, at least you found each other. Isn't this nice for Lord Montague and Henry to visit?'

Emma smiled weakly, but as she walked past the window towards the sofas, a figure climbing the stile into the barley field caught her eye. *Ben! Where on earth was he going? He was supposed to be having a birthday tea with his parents!* She glanced at Henry who had followed her gaze, and a curl of resentment rose in her when she saw his lip curl in amusement.

'Lord Montague and Henry are staying until Sunday, so it should give you two young people some time together,' Sarah said. 'After luncheon, you can show Henry around the gardens. Lord Montague has some business to attend to with your papa.'

If Emma's stomach could have plummeted any further - it would have done. What on earth was she going to do about the birthday tea arranged at Poldhu with Zack, Agnes and Ben? For sure, spending time with Henry was the absolute last thing she wanted to do!

*

There was a clear, angry silence between Emma and Henry as they walked down the garden.

'I hate gardens,' Henry said.

'Well, I love them,' Emma answered tersely.

'You might like the gardens surrounding our pile in Devon then.'

'I've no intention of coming to see them,' Emma said flopping down on one of the garden benches. 'Henry, why are you here? This was not part of the plan.'

'My father wanted to do some business with your father, and he thought it would be good for us to get to know each other better,' he said flatly.

'Henry, you and I both know that we have no need to get to know each other better. You could have refused.'

'I could have, but I wanted to see the old place again. Thought I might bump into William - is he not home?'

'No, he's travelling in Europe.'

'Pity. Will he be home for your ball?'

'No, we're to meet him a week after the ball in Italy, when we visit my Uncle Justin.'

'Late summer in Italy, eh? That sounds temptingly good.'

'Yes, it does,' Emma said cautiously – *but don't think you are coming with us!* 'So, what do you want to do? Do you ride?'

'No.'

'Walk?'

'No.'

'What do you like?'

'Clubs, Jazz - I like to have fun.'

'Do you help to run the estate with your father?'

'We employ people to do that.'

'But do you not take any interest in it?'

'Why should I?'

'I should think that if you inherit, you will need to know. That's why William is studying, so that he can help to run this estate in a way that it stays financially secure. It's his future.'

Henry laughed derisively.

Emma pursed her lips. 'It's quite boring being idle, you know. Everyone benefits from some direction in their life.'

'I'm not bored doing the things I like to do. So, this so-called friend of yours, Bill…'

'Ben,' she corrected.

'You say he's your friend.' It was a leading question.

'Ben is *our* friend. We all grew up together - William, Zack, Agnes, and me.'

'Who are these people – Zack and Agnes - where do they reside?'

'Poldhu. Agnes is a thatcher like her father. Zack is a carpenter.'

'My, my, what strange people you associate with. Commoners, all of them!'

'What a snobbish thing to say, Henry. I'm glad I'm not marrying you, if that is the attitude you take towards people not of your class.'

'They're not of *your* class either, Emma.'

'Lady Emma, if you don't mind.'

'And do these commoners call you Lady Emma?'

'My *friends* don't have to.'

Henry raised an eyebrow. 'Am I not a friend?'

'No, especially after the way you treated Ben earlier.'

'I took an instant dislike to him!'

'I think the feeling was reciprocated,' she said dryly.

Henry laughed. 'I won't lose any sleep over that. So, what does this *Ben* do?'

'He's a saddler – a master in leathercraft.'

Henry snorted derisively.

'He is renowned in the county.'

'Is he now? Well, I think I've seen enough of the garden. If you'll excuse me, I've a letter to write.'

*

Once upstairs, Henry sat at the writing desk, drumming his fingers for a moment. He'd never got a clear view of the lad who had beaten him up – he'd been too busy covering his face with his hands to stem the blows raining down on him. But after the enlightening conversation with *Lady* Emma, Henry had a very good chance of finding out. He stood and rang for his valet.

'How far away from me are you?'

'In the attic, my lord – a floor up from here.'

'Will you be able to visit tonight?'

'Of course!'

'Good. First though I want you to do something for me. I need you to find out downstairs where the best man who does leathercraft is – tell them you have a belt that needs repairing or something.'

A quarter of an hour later, with directions to Polhormon Saddlery, Henry took the car to make a visit.

*

Ben was busy with the saddle he'd been working on – he needed something to settle his mind – for it was in turmoil. He should not have walked out on his parents like that - it had been incredibly rude. He'd have to go and apologise later. For now, though, he needed something to occupy him.

He looked up when he heard a car draw up and a few moments later, his breath caught as a very unwelcome visitor stepped through his door.

Ben eyed Henry cautiously as he stood and surveyed his workshop. 'Can I help you?' Ben said, settling his needles on the saddle.

'I thought I'd come and see for myself just what it is about you that fascinates Lady Emma.' He folded his arms and gave Ben a derisory once over. 'Frankly, I can see no attraction.'

131

Ben tamped down his rising anger. 'If you're not here to order anything, perhaps you should leave. Some of us have work to do.'

Henry sniggered. 'How droll it must be for you to have to return to your working-class roots now you're a man. It seems to me that you were given privileges far, far, above your station as a boy. Privileges you seem to be taking liberties with now.'

Anger was beginning to give way to contempt, but Ben remained silent. He didn't want to make any trouble for Emma.

Amara started to flutter her wings as she sat up high on the bookcase – she could always sense when there was an air of unpleasantness in the room.

Henry looked up. 'Where is a gun when you need it.' He turned his attention back to Ben. 'Stay away from Lady Emma if you know what's good for you. You're tarnishing her reputation.'

'I think you need to leave now,' Ben said.

Being an athletically lean muscular man, who kept himself in peak physical condition, and being a good six inches taller than Henry, when Ben stood up to him, Henry's demeanour changed.

Henry gave Ben another scornful look, turned, feigned he had a shotgun in his hand and pointed it at Amara. 'Bang!' he said loudly, to which the bird lifted from its perch, promptly leaving a calling card on Henry's jacket, before fluttering back to settle his feathers. 'Why you filthy…' Henry looked around for something to throw at the bird, picked up a carving knife from the table and took aim, but Ben was quick and caught him by the arm.

'Drop it.' Ben squeezed Henry's arm until the knife clattered to the floor. 'Now, get out,' he said shoving him towards the door.

'You'll be sorry, Pearson,' Henry uttered as he stormed out of the workshop.

Amara flew down to settle on Ben's shoulder. 'Good work, clever girl,' he said as she rubbed her head against his cheek. 'Although I think we've made an enemy there.' A thought that made him very uneasy.

*

Emma was quite put out that Juliet had known Henry was coming today and had failed to tell her when questioned earlier.

'I'm sorry, my lady. I was under strict instructions to keep the visit a secret.'

'Well, I'm disappointed in you, Juliet. I thought we had a better relationship than that.'

'I'm sorry, my lady, truly I am. I was between the devil and the deep blue sea. It was either your wrath, or Mr Treen's.'

Emma glanced at Juliet's stricken face. 'I'm sorry, Juliet. I should not take it out on you – you've been very good to me. I'm just so angry that Henry is here.'

'So, is it not true that you might be getting engaged soon to Mr Montague?'

'Over my dead body - but you haven't heard that from me.'

'Heard what, my lady.' Juliet smiled.

As she helped Emma dress for dinner, Juliet said, 'There is something I think you should know, my lady.'

Emma looked up at her through the mirror.

'Mr Montague's valet was asking this afternoon where the nearest leathercraft workshop was. David, the footman gave him directions for Polhormon saddlery.'

Emma put her hand to her throat. 'What did he want that for, I wonder?'

'I don't know, but Joe said Mr Montague took his father's car shortly afterwards.'

Emma stopped fastening her earrings and dropped her hands to her lap. 'Oh, goodness! Do you think he went to see Ben?'

'Well, my lady, when Mr Montague came back, his valet had to try and get bird muck off Mr Montague's jacket lapel.'

Emma felt her stomach plummet - that must have been Amara – but she only messed in the workshop if something had upset her.

'I'm sorry, my lady, perhaps I shouldn't have told you - Joe said not to tell you, but…'

'No, thank you Juliet, you were right to tell me. I just hope all is well with Ben.'

'Yes, my lady, so do I.'

*

At dinner that night, Emma was seated beside Henry and his father, but Sarah, observing her daughter throughout the meal, noted an air of unease between the two young people. There was little or no conversation between her and Henry, other than when Emma answered any questions directed towards her. Henry, of course, was full of himself, as was his father – the business he had come to see Peter about must have gone well. Sarah had a very grave feeling that perhaps she and Peter were wrong to push these young people together like this. Looking at them, away from the bright lights of London, they didn't seem at all suited.

'So, what did you two do this afternoon?' Lord Montague asked Emma and Henry.

Henry smiled. 'After Lady Emma so kindly took me for a turn around the garden, I went for a drive to see the sights – you know the sort of places that Lady Emma is so keen on visiting.' He cut a glance to Emma, which, Sarah noted, made Emma uneasy.

'You should have gone with him, Emma,' Peter said.

'Henry didn't tell me he was going - he said he was going in to write a letter,' Emma said stiffly in her defence.

'Just wanted to check out the lie of the land on your own, eh, my boy,' his father guffawed.

'Did you go to the beach?' Sarah asked.

'Along with other places I know Emma frequents. I wanted to know what places excite her, so to speak.' He glanced again at Emma, who blanched.

'So, you two lovebirds, when are we going to have an announcement?' Lord Montague said, holding his glass aloft.

Emma's eyes widened, so Sarah interjected, 'Oh, I don't think there is any rush.' As she spoke, Emma visibly relaxed.

'Well, these things need to be settled. We don't want their feelings to wain for each other, now do we?' Lord Montague chortled.

'I think that is a good enough reason to wait,' Sarah said, dabbing her mouth with her napkin. 'It would be far too late if they found they no longer wanted each other, once they had made it down the aisle.'

'But it's a perfect match,' Lord Montague announced. 'The moment I saw your beautiful daughter, I said to Henry, now, there is the wife for you. You'll do no better than her. Snap her up, I told him. Didn't I, my boy?'

'Yes, father.' Henry smiled.

'And of course, a union between the lineage of our ancient families can only strengthen us all, and will be beneficial for all concerned, eh, Dunstan?' He winked.

Peter raised his glass to Lord Montague, but when Sarah glanced at Emma, she wore nothing but a blank expression.

'That's all very well, Lord Montague, but there is a matter of love,' Sarah said.

He guffawed again. 'An overrated emotion if you ask me. There was never any of this romantic nonsense between myself and my wife, Lady Montague, and we've had one of the most successful marriages,' he boasted.

Emma put down her cutlery – her appetite clearly waning.

'Well, this is where we shall differ,' Sarah answered him. 'Love in a marriage is the most important element, and I shall not allow any son or daughter of mine to marry until I know they are completely and utterly happy with their intended.'

Sarah was aware of furtive glances between Peter and Lord Montague, and wondered just what business these two were plotting on the strength of this potential marriage.

'And I'm sure they will be very happy together, once they've got to know each other better,' Peter said jovially. 'After all there must be some spark between them - they both agreed to be taken off the marriage market!'

Emma reached for her glass of wine and took a great gulp.

Sarah smiled. 'As I say, there is no rush to set a date. I insist they wait, until they know they're right for each other.'

It did not escape Sarah's notice that Lord Montague's nostrils flared alarmingly.

17

At breakfast the next morning, Emma and Sarah were up before the others.

'What do you and Henry plan to do today, Emma?'

'I'm sorry, Mama, but I have plans of my own today. Agnes, Jake, Zack and I are meeting Ben at the tearoom for his birthday.'

'Then you must take Henry along with you – he's come all this way to see you.'

'No, Mama, I can't!' she argued quite forcefully.

'What can't you do?' Peter asked as he walked into the breakfast room with Henry and Lord Montague.

'Emma has plans today to attend a birthday party at the tearoom at Poldhu, and I suggested that Henry should perhaps join them.'

'But I'm afraid that will not be possible, Papa,' Emma smiled amiably at Henry and his father. 'The table we booked is for five people. It's been planned for some time.' Emma tried without success to keep the anxiety from her voice.

'Emma darling,' Sarah said calmly, 'Elise will find another chair for Henry.'

'Of course, she will,' Peter interjected as he helped himself to breakfast. 'You'd like to go for tea at the beach, wouldn't you, Henry?'

'It will be the highlight of my stay,' Henry said flatly.

'Good chap, but first, your father and I would like to go over a few things with you after breakfast.'

Emma gritted her teeth, torn now. If she decided not to go to Poldhu, Ben would be unhappy for her to miss it - and so would she be. But if she did go and take Henry with her, Ben would not be at all happy, and it was his birthday! She had to think of something quickly.

*

The table was booked at Poldhu for two, so after luncheon, Emma retired to her bedroom feigning a headache. She sent down for a headache draft, which she poured into the poor unsuspecting aspidistra plant, and at one o clock, she rang for Juliet.

'I'm going out for a ride to clear my head,' she told Juliet, as she helped her on with her riding habit. She thought it best not to tell Juliet where she was really going, so that she wouldn't have to lie for her.

'Yes, my lady. It's a shame you're not feeling well. I know you were looking forward to the birthday party.'

Emma just smiled and nodded - the least said the better. 'I'm going out the back way through the laundry. I'll saddle Saffron myself, so don't tell anyone I've gone unless they ask.'

'Very well, my lady.'

*

Ben had resigned himself to the fact that Emma would not come to tea, so was astonished when he saw her galloping across the dunes on horseback. After settling Saffron, she walked up the tearoom veranda steps, smiled at Ben, and his heart melted at the sight of her.

'I didn't think you would come,' he whispered.

'I had a terrible job getting away. I was told to bring Henry with me, but I stole away. They think I'm in my bedroom nursing a headache.' She sat down and said, 'I wasn't going to miss your birthday party though, was I?'

'Oh, Em, I hope you don't get in trouble on my account,' he said, delighted and concerned in equal measure.

'You're worth it, Ben,' she grinned, 'where are the others?'

'They're on their way.'

'Ben, I'm sorry about yesterday. Henry was very rude to you.'

Ben hummed. 'I admit, he did rattle me - I won't lie. So much so, I took it out on my poor parents.'

'Oh, no! I thought I saw you walking back down the barley field yesterday lunchtime. What happened?'

'Oh,' he shook his head, 'they were going on and on, about you marrying Henry.'

'Well, I'm not! I'm going to marry you one day.' She touched his sleeve and gave him a smile that made his skin tingle.

'Do you know Henry paid me a visit yesterday?'

Emma pursed her lips. 'I guessed as much from what he inferred last night at dinner. What did he say?'

'He warned me off you.'

Emma clenched her teeth. 'He has no right to say such things.'

'He believes he does, Emma. Are you sure, this pretence of a match is two sided.'

'Absolutely! He has no wish to marry me, nor would I want to marry such a hateful man.'

Ben felt himself relax, and then smiled. 'Amara made her feelings known to him – she pooped on his jacket.'

Emma giggled. 'I heard that his valet had the devil of a job getting it out. Good for Amara. I shall bring her a piece of apple next time I visit.'

'How long is he staying, Em, and what is he here for?'

'Just some hair-brained idea of our fathers that we should get to know each other. But frankly, Ben, we can't stand the sight of each other.'

'I shall be glad when he's gone,' Ben breathed.

'You and me both. Oh, look! The others are coming now.'

*

Lord Montague had gone upstairs for a lie down, and Peter was attending to some estate business in his study when he heard someone knocking billiard balls about. He found Henry in the library playing billiards alone.

'I thought you'd gone to Poldhu with Emma?'

'Cancelled, I'm afraid. Lady Emma retired to her room with a headache after luncheon.' Henry's raised eyebrows indicated to Peter that he did not believe Emma's story.

'I see.' Peter nodded. 'I'll leave you to your game.'

Leaving the library, Peter took to the stairs and knocked on Emma's bedroom door. When no one answered, he opened the door, to find the room empty. *What the devil was Emma playing at?* Peter strode meaningfully into the kitchen to the shuffle of chairs being pushed back, as everyone present either bowed or curtseyed to him.

'Can I help, my lord?' Joe asked.

'Sorry to disturb you all,' Peter said, searching the assembled staff for Treen's wife. 'Ah, Juliet. Where is Lady Emma?'

'She said she was going out for a ride to clear her headache, my lord.'

'When was this?'

'About half an hour ago, my lord,' Juliet said vaguely.

'Very well.' Peter turned to leave, unaware that Joe and Juliet were exchanging furtive glances.

*

When Emma returned, she brushed Saffron down, apologised to the groom for stealing away without telling him, then entered the house the way she left – hoping that no one had missed her. She had barely put her foot on the stairs when Joe Treen cleared his throat behind her.

She turned and smiled at him. 'Yes, Treen, what is it?'

'His Lordship would like a word with you in his study.'

'Oh!' Emma's shoulders drooped – she'd been found out! As she knocked and walked into the study, Papa looked more cross with her than he had ever looked before.

'Where have you been?' Peter asked, barely keeping his anger under control.

'Out riding, to clear my headache.'

'To Poldhu?'

Emma hesitated, knowing she could not lie. Ellie would tell Papa if he asked her.

'Emma!'

'Yes, Papa, by the time I rode down the valley, I felt better, so I joined the others for tea.'

Peter clasped his hands behind his back and paced the room slowly.

'I don't believe you had a headache, Emma. I think you deliberately left Henry here to go to that party on your own - and don't try to deny it. Your Mama knows of your little outing too, but I said I would deal with it.'

Emma lowered her eyes.

'We have covered your tracks, Emma, but I have to tell you, I think what you did today was the height of rudeness. I'm ashamed of you.'

Emma lifted her eyes to face his disapproval. 'But Papa, you brought Henry here without telling me. I had my weekend planned, things *I* wanted to do with *my* friends.'

'Henry wants to marry you, Emma. He came all this way to see you, but you have continuously failed to engage with him. You could have taken him with you!' he said sternly.

'No, Papa I could not! Did you not see the look on Henry's face when you asked him if he would like to go to tea – he could hardly hide his disdain. Henry doesn't like Ben!'

'Henry doesn't know Ben!' Peter countered.

'Yes he does! He met him yesterday, and was incredibly rude to him!' She decided to omit the part about Henry's visit to Ben yesterday afternoon - for obvious reasons.

'He probably sees Ben as a rival - and I'm not surprised - you are so in each other's pockets.' He laughed sharply. 'Not that I believe there is any relevance in that, of course. But you can't go running around the countryside with another man! No decent man would stand for that! This is no way to act with someone who may become your future husband, Emma. Now go to your room and change, it's nearly time for tea and you had better squeeze another slice of cake in, for Henry's sake. Do *not* let me down again.'

'Yes, Papa. Sorry, Papa.'

*

The next morning, while Emma was waving her unwelcome guests off from the front door of Bochym Manor with a sigh of relief, Sophie and Kit Trevellick had just returned home to Quay House in Gweek, having just spent the previous night with the Bickfords at the Trevarno Estate.

They were sorting through the mail that had arrived the previous day over a cup of coffee, and to Sophie's delight, she found a letter from Jessie Chandler.

'Listen to this, Kit. It seems Jessie and Daniel are extending their visit to Cornwall. They are to come down on Friday the 4th of August now, and Sarah has invited them to stay at the manor, so that they can also attend the garden party on the 6th and Emma's ball on the 11th! So, we will have a chance to really catch up with them.' She put the letter down on the breakfast table.

Kit smiled as he drained his cup. 'You know, I'd rather like Daniel to hear Zack playing. Could you write back and ask them to drop by for luncheon before they make their way to Bochym on the 4th?'

Sophie smiled. 'What have you in mind?'

'I know it's wrong of me, but I feel that someone with some real knowledge of music should hear what Zack does. He has a rare talent, but I'm not sure Guy will see it. He is so set on Zack making a career in carpentry, but personally, even though I've trained Zack myself, I think if someone doesn't help him to become a pianist, his real and rare talent will be wasted.'

Sophie raised an eyebrow. 'You're dicing with fire - Guy won't like it.'

'I know, but I think we should give Zack all the help we can.'

'If the Chandlers agree, shall we tell Zack they are coming? I know he was excited to hear his aunt Jessie would be visiting Cornwall again, though he was worried she might not come near Poldhu - knowing Guy's prejudice against her and Daniel. Zack was always a favourite with Jessie.'

'No, we'll keep it secret. It'll be a nice surprise for him, and he can have her all to himself for a couple of hours.'

*

Once Henry had left, Emma had to practically plead with her papa to allow her to spend the day at Poldhu Cove with the others – he was still quite angry with her.

'You should be made to stay here, Emma,' Peter said forcefully, 'especially after the disgraceful way you treated Henry yesterday.'

Emma felt a swelling of emotion in her throat – Papa had never been so angry with her before.

'Peter, darling,' Sarah intervened, 'we did rather spring this visit on Emma – and we were not aware she had a birthday weekend planned, otherwise we could have delayed their visit by a week. All this could have been avoided if we had just involved her in our plans.'

'You two are ganging up on me, I can see that!' He folded his arms. 'Oh, very well, go to the beach,' Peter said resignedly. 'But Emma, when Henry comes again, you must be more attentive towards him. Right, I shall be in my study if anyone needs me.'

Emma sighed with relief – the battle was won – the war might prove more difficult.

18

The next morning, Joe Treen closed the door of the Jacobean drawing room after being summoned by Her Ladyship. He paused for a moment at the foot of the stairs - his mind a whirl with a myriad of emotions.

'Are you quite well, Mr Treen?' the housekeeper asked.

'Yes, thank you, Mrs Johnson.' He smiled and walked past her. Composing himself before he entered the kitchen, he lifted his chin to address Mrs Blair the cook. 'A date for the diary, Mrs Blair.'

Cook put down the whisk she was beating eggs with, wiped her hands on her teacloth and reached for her well-thumbed diary. With pen poised she smiled at Joe.

'We have Mr and Mrs Daniel Chandler, their three children and their nanny coming to stay on Friday 4th August - and staying until Sunday the 12th.'

'Lordy me, if that isn't the busiest week in the year – what with the garden party on the 6th and Lady Emma's ball on the 11th!'

'I'm sure it's nothing you can't handle, Mrs Blair.'

With a snort she wrote the dates down, then paused and looked up at Joe. 'Mr and Mrs Daniel Chandler!'

'Yes.'

'Jessie!'

'Yes, Mrs Blair.'

In unison, Mrs Blair's nostrils flared at the mention of her name and Juliet looked up from her sewing.

Mrs Blair snapped the diary shut, put it back on the shelf and began to beat the hell out of the eggs.

Joe glanced at Juliet. 'I'll be in my office,' he said to no one in particular.

When he'd gone, Juliet put down her sewing and asked, 'Do you not care for Mrs Chandler, Mrs Blair?'

'I do not care for how she snared her husband!' Cook sniffed haughtily.

Joe unexpectedly returned to collect some papers he'd left behind and stopped short when he heard Cook's denouncement.

'And I do not care for your attitude towards Mrs Chandler, nor will I tolerate any unpleasantness from you towards her for the duration of their stay. Do I make myself clear, Mrs Blair?'

Cook, taken aback by the reprimand, replied, 'Yes, Mr Treen.'

'Good.' Joe swiped the papers from the table and marched back out of the kitchen.

Juliet glanced at Cook, whose cheeks had pinked with humiliation, and she felt her own heart implode. Joe's uncharacteristic rebuke in Jessie's defence, made Juliet suspect that he still had very powerful feelings for her.

'I'm just going to get some air, Mrs Blair,' Juliet said. Leaving her sewing on the table, she took herself off for a walk to settle her mind.

*

Joe sat at his desk, leaned back on his leather chair, and gazed out of the window at the washing blowing on the line. So, Jessie was coming to stay - and for a whole week! His thoughts took him back many years. They had worked together, when he was a mere footman, and Jessie a maid. They had shared a nice friendship, and it was no secret that Joe had loved her, unfortunately when she left service to work with Ellie Blackthorn at the tearoom, Silas Blackthorn had turned her head, and that put paid to Joe's hopes. Joe watched Jessie marry him, witnessing her dismay when their marriage turned sour. Then with envy he watched as Jessie found solace in Daniel Chandler's arms, going on to marry him when she was free of Silas. After all these years, how would it be for him to see her again? Would old feelings surface? They'd exchanged several letters since she'd left Cornwall, so he knew about her three children, and though Joe was happy with Juliet, he always wondered what life would have been like for him if Jessie had chosen him. He would certainly have been a father by now! His shoulders drooped at the thought. He and Juliet had not, and never would be, blessed with children. Juliet's previous troubles involving her salacious stepfather, marred their shared intimacy. As much as they loved each other, and as kind and gentle as Joe had been on their wedding night, Juliet had found it too much of an ordeal, so he had never pressed her again. They were good friends and companions to each other - it was a relationship of gentle consideration. He had settled for the life of a celibate husband, but he'd very much liked to have been a father.

*

A whole week had passed since the birthday weekend. Emma had been kept busy with the upcoming garden party and the ball, so had been unable to see Ben. Invitations to the ball had gone out that week, and arrangements had been made with nearby Bonython Manor to accommodate the many guests.

'May I take Ben's invitation down to him, Mama,' Emma asked.

'Yes, you may. We've made arrangements for Zack and Ben to be fitted with evening suits from Thomas' Tailors and Outfitters, in Coinage Street, Helston. They can both pick them up on the day of the ball – everything is paid for.'

'Oh, thank you.' Emma flung her arms around her mama's neck and kissed her on her cheek.

'I want you to have the best ball, Emma – you deserve it.'

Emma could hardly contain her excitement. 'I'll go now and tell Ben,' she said, scooping up his invitation.

'Oh, and Emma. The Montagues are coming down for the garden party as well as the ball.'

Emma felt her stomach drop. 'They're not staying all week are they?'

'No, darling. It will just be for the night.'

*

After falling into Ben's welcoming arms and sharing a loving kiss, Emma handed him the invitation.

'Gosh,' he said delighted, 'thank you, but what on earth will I wear?'

'Ah, that is the next surprise.' She handed him the address of the outfitters in Helston, 'It's all arranged for you and Zack to get fitted out.'

'Goodness, pinch me, for I don't recognise myself anymore. I thought I was a lowly saddler, but here I am, with an invitation to a ball, and I'm to be suited and booted! Thank you, Emma. Thank you for everything.'

'It might just be one of the last balls we attend, because I've made my mind up,' Emma said seriously, 'once this season is over, and Henry and I go our separate ways, I shall tell my parents that I want to marry you.'

Ben took Emma's hands in his. 'Oh, Em, they won't like it. What if they forbid you to see me again?'

'Then we'll elope. I told you, Ben, I'm prepared to give up everything for you. We may have to move away from here though. Are you prepared to give up this place and start over somewhere else, if we have to?'

'I am.' Ben brought her hands to his lips and kissed them.

Seeing the worry etched deep into his face, she kissed him passionately on the lips. 'All will be well, Ben.'

*

On August 4th, Jessie and Daniel Chandler were nearing Truro, and though they were dropping in on Kit and Sophie Trevellick in Gweek first, Jessie was slightly nervous about the onward journey to Bochym Manor, where they were to stay for a week.

Confident that Sarah and Peter would welcome her into their home as equals – that was their nature - it was the staff who concerned Jessie the most, though there were only a few people left there with whom she once worked with. Poor Thomas, the footman, had been killed in the war. Her good friend, Betsy was married now and working as tearoom assistant at Poldhu. Mary the assistant cook had also married and left and of course Mrs Saunders – Ruby the housekeeper - had married Sarah's brother and now lived and worked in Italy. Dorothy was still there, so Joe Treen had written to tell her, and so too was Mrs Blair – the formidable cook whom Jessie knew looked unfavourably on her for committing adultery all those years ago. Thankfully, Joe would be there to smooth any obstacles which might arise, as he was a stalwart of the manor, and it was he in particular who she was longing to see again.

Lovely Joe - they had been such good friends for many years and had corresponded regularly. Jessie had always known how Joe had felt about her, and she'd worried that he would never marry because of it. To her delight and relief though, he did find someone to love - a soul mate in his wife Juliet, and Jessie was keen to meet her. It was just such a shame they hadn't been blessed with children though – Joe would have made a wonderful father.

As Jessie watched the familiar Cornish countryside go by, she smiled to herself. Now here she was back in Cornwall - the wife of a gentleman - and a gentleman Daniel truly was. Daniel had given her a life she thought was so out of reach during her loveless marriage to Silas Blackthorn. Yes, her affair with Daniel had been deeply frowned on by many, namely her ex-brother-in-law Guy Blackthorn, but there were equally as many who understood her reasons. Silas had not been looked on favourably by a lot of people – and then he had died – killed in fact, but she didn't want to dig all that up again. That was all ten years ago, but all the old fears about that time were fighting their way to the forefront of her mind, and she hoped they would not mar this visit.

Life had truly been wonderful with Daniel. As soon as she left Cornwall with him, and despite her low birth, Jessie had quickly fitted into society life as though she was born to it. Now, the mother of three wonderful children, the wife of an acclaimed musician, owner of two houses, one on the Devon coast and one in London - they lived a sublime life. They had travelled the world together until the war started, then had hunkered down in Devon to start a family, praying that Daniel would not be called up. He was, of course. He was conscripted in 1916 as an officer, but had thankfully made it through the latter part of the war physically unscathed, but along with everyone else who had been part of that long bloody battle, he struggled mentally with the horrors he had seen.

Jessie jumped slightly when Daniel reached over and cupped his hand over hers.

'I know exactly what you've been thinking – it's written all over your face. Everything will be fine, sweetheart.' He squeezed her hand.

*

Zack knew Kit and Sophie had visitors coming, but knew not who, and to his delight Kit had specifically asked him if he could play for them just as soon as they arrived.

'Of course, I will. I'm honoured to be asked.'

'It will just be a little light music to welcome our guests in through the door and then we will all join together for a luncheon.'

Zack was in his element, and as soon as the car pulled into the drive, Kit gave Zack the cue for him to start playing the piano, which he did with relish.

*

Kit and Sophie ran out to the drive to welcome the Chandlers, one and all, into their home.

'Jessie!' Sophie flung her arms around her.

Kit reached out his hand to shake Daniel's. 'Welcome back to Cornwall, my friend – it's been too long.'

'It has indeed. May I present our children, Stella, Marina, and this is James,' he nodded to the sleeping child in a young girl's arms. 'Oh, and this is Nanny Charlotte.'

'Welcome to all of you,' Sophie said. 'Come, and we'll have a cup of tea before I serve luncheon.'

Everyone was shown into the large airy front room which had a wonderful vista down the Helford River. They had only been seated a few seconds before Daniel asked, 'Is that a gramophone record playing or is someone playing in the house, Kit?'

Kit smiled to himself. 'It's Zack Blackthorn playing.'

'Ellie and Guy's son!' Jessie asked astonished.

'Yes, and he hasn't had a lesson in his life, but he can just about play anything, once he has listened to it.'

With his interest piqued, Daniel asked tentatively, 'Is he making a career in music?'

'Alas, no! He lives and works here while he completes his cabinetmaker apprenticeship,' Kit said helping to bring in the tea trays.

'I see. How is that going?'

Kit chewed at his lip. 'He's good, and makes a thorough job of whatever I task him to do, but....'

'His heart isn't in it,' Sophie interjected. 'You remember Zack as a child, Jessie. He was always the sweet, quiet boy - I don't think carpentry is really his calling.'

'But music clearly is!' Daniel said.

'Yes, but for a man like Zack, who comes from a thatching family, Guy expects him to carry on with a craft as such.'

'That would be such a waste,' Daniel breathed.

Jessie touched Daniel's hand. 'What are you thinking, darling?'

'I'm remembering the passion I had for music, starting when I was very young.' He glanced at Kit and Sophie, 'Fortunately, my parents saw that I had a calling to do the arts and I was lucky to be sent to The Royal College of Music. It's one of the world's great conservatoires, training gifted musicians from all over the world for international careers as performers, conductors, and composers.'

Zack finished one piece and began another melodic tune.

'He'll play like that for hours if we let him,' Kit said. 'He entertains us every evening. Zack was one of the reasons I asked you here first. I'd like your opinion on whether to speak to Guy about him taking this further.'

'He is remarkable, simply remarkable. Does Guy not know then?'

Kit shook his head. 'Zack won't let me tell him. He's frightened he'll be angry that he's spent his time playing the piano, instead of buckling down to his cabinetmaker apprenticeship.'

'May we go in and see him, I know Jessie is keen to see her nephew again, aren't you, darling?'

'Be our guest.' Kit gestured to the door.

*

Zack stopped playing and turned on the piano stool when he heard someone come into the room, and for a moment he could not believe his eyes.

'Aunt Jessie, is that really you?' He rushed to her and wrapped his arms around her with warmth, feeling the years of separation peel away.

'My goodness, Zack, look how you've grown? You're a fine, handsome man now – you were just a little boy the last time I saw you,' Jessie said with tears in her eyes. 'We were just admiring the way you were playing.'

'Oh!' Abashed, he cleared his throat awkwardly. 'I was just tinkling the ivories, as they say.'

'Zack, may I introduce my husband Daniel Chandler, and our children, Stella, Marina and James.' She nodded to the sleeping child, now in Daniel's arms.

Zack reached out to shake Daniel's free hand. 'Ah, so you're the one responsible for stealing my beloved aunt away from me, are you?' he joked.

'Guilty as charged.' Daniel smiled. 'Zack, I have to say, you play magnificently.'

Zack blushed. 'Thank you.'

'You have a rare talent. Kit said you haven't had lessons, is that true?' Daniel asked.

'Not a one,' Zack replied. 'The piano teacher comes in to teach Kit and Sophie's daughter, Selene, every week, and I just listen to them while I'm working next door. I help her out when she struggles with the notes.'

'I don't understand,' Daniel said aghast, 'are you just listening to the music and then copying it?'

'Yes, I suppose I am.'

'And can you play anything you hear – say if I put a record on the gramophone, could you copy it?'

'Short pieces, yes, longer ones I have to listen a couple of times.'

'Then you *do* have a rare talent. Have you thought about taking it further?'

'Further?' Zack's eyes widened with interest.

'Studying it, so that you can play in an orchestra.'

'Daniel is a cello player with the Royal Philharmonic Orchestra,' Jessie explained.

Zack smiled, but shook his head. 'I'd love to, but I'm destined to be a carpenter.'

'You don't have to follow that path - you could come to London and study music. Believe me, I know talent when I hear it.'

'Kit says Guy doesn't know, has Ellie heard you play?' Jessie asked.

'No.'

Daniel's eyes cut to Jessie, and she knew what he was thinking, Guy would not take too kindly to Daniel putting his suggestion that Zack should down tools and carve a different career for himself.

'How long are you staying – are you going to see Ma at Poldhu?' Zack asked.

'Of course, I can't wait to see her again. We're staying at Bochym Manor for a week.'

Kit and Sophie had now joined them and Sophie said, 'Play us something else, Zack and then we can all have a spot of luncheon afterwards.'

Zack sat back down and put his slender fingers to the keys.

'Do you not play from a music sheet?' Daniel asked confused.

Zack shook his head. 'I can't read music.'

'Well then, you *are* truly remarkable.'

19

When Jessie and Daniel arrived at Bochym, Joe Treen stood at the front door along with David the footman, as Sarah and Peter welcomed them. Joe felt his heart accelerate as David stepped forward to open the door for the arrivals.

Jessie, dressed in a pale green drop-waisted suit, her hat at a jaunty angle - the epitome of a fashionable woman of the era - graciously took David's hand to alight. Daniel followed and allowed his three children and their nanny to spill out after him.

As Jessie stood and straightened her dress, she locked eyes first with Joe, beaming a smile at him, and then walked towards Sarah who took her warmly into her arms.

'Have you had a good journey?'

'We have. We stopped at Gweek for a couple of hours to have luncheon with Kit and Sophie. It's so good to see you once again, Lady Sarah.'

'No need for formality, Jessie. We're all friends here.'

Peter stepped forward, kissed Jessie on the cheek and offered Daniel a firm handshake. 'Welcome back to Cornwall. Come, we'll get you settled into your rooms and have tea shortly.'

While Nanny, stood back with the children, Daniel put his hand to the small of Jessie's back to guide her through the front door of the manor – and past the brass knocker she'd once used elbow grease on, to make it shine.

'Hello, Joe,' she said warmly. 'We'll catch up soon, I promise.'

They were ushered through the library and out to the main staircase, while Joe led Nanny and Jessie's children through the housekeeper's room towards the back stairs up to the nursery.

*

After tea, Jessie and Daniel retired to the Blue Room they had been allocated, and were admiring the magnificent view of the gardens from the window.

'I cannot believe I'm staying here as a guest – I've cleaned this room more times than I've had hot dinners,' she mused.

'As my wife, this is where you belong now.' Daniel curled his arms around her waist.

She leant back into him with a sigh. 'My life has been blessed since you stepped into it.'

'As has mine, my love.'

She circled round in his arms and they kissed like young lovers.

'So, is this room haunted then?' he gave a wry smile.

'It's had its moments – but they are all friendly ghosts, and I'll look after you,' she teased.

A knock came at the door. 'Come in,' Jessie said, not moving from the circle of Daniel's arms.

'Oh, I do beg your pardon, I didn't mean to disturb you,' Juliet said, flushing up to the roots of her hair.

'You're not,' Jessie said, kissing Daniel and gently parting from his embrace.

'The children are in the nursery, and your nanny says they're asking for you, Ma'am.'

Thank you….?'

'Juliet, Ma'am.'

'Oh, Juliet - Joe's wife!' Jessie reached for Juliet's hands. 'I'm so happy to meet you at last. Joe has told me much about you. I can see he has been very fortunate in his choice of wife.'

'Thank you, Ma'am. That is kind of you to say.'

'We'll catch up later, if that's alright?'

'Of course, Ma'am.' Juliet looked quite nonplussed at the idea.

*

Jessie went in search of her children and knowing this house like the back of her hand, made straight for the nursery. Her three children were just finishing their supper, along with two other children, who were being overseen by the Bochym Nanny and Nanny Charlotte.

James, Jessie's youngest reached out his arms for Jessie to pick him up, which she did.

'Gosh, you've both got your hands full in here. So, who are these two,' Jessie smiled at the other two children present.

'These are the Travail's children, Ma'am - the valet and lady's maid's youngsters,' Nanny answered. 'This is Denny who is nine, and six-year-old Loveday.'

'How lovely. Denny is the same age as Marina, and Loveday is a year older than Stella, so they'll have some nice friends to play with!'

'We're just about to run the baths for the children.' The Bochym Nanny said as she started to clear the plates onto a tray.

'Would you like me to take the trays back to the kitchen then?' Jessie offered.

'Don't worry about the trays, Ma'am, I've just rung for someone to take them away. In fact, here is someone now.'

Jessie turned to find Joe at the door with Dorothy in tow.

'Hello, Joe.' Jessie kissed him warmly on the cheek. 'Oh, and Dorothy too, she hugged her old friend. 'Congratulations on your marriage to David. I believe we met him when he helped us in with our luggage.'

'That was him, yes.' Dorothy beamed.

'He is very handsome.'

'That he is,' Dorothy nodded as she picked up the tray, leaving with a broad smile on her face.

'I would very much like to take the children to see Mrs Blair, so they can thank her for supper,' Jessie said. 'Could you possibly hold James for a moment, Joe, while I help Stella on with her shoes. The nannies are going to run them a bath.'

Jessie handed three-year-old James to Joe, unaware of the numerous emotions he was experiencing - none more so than the touch of Jessie's lips on his cheek. He shrugged the boy into a more comfortable position and the little lad smiled at Joe.

'Come on, Stella, Marina,' Jessie beckoned. She reached for James from Joe's arms, but Joe pulled away slightly.

'I'll carry him down the stairs if you wish.'

'Thank you, Joe.'

As they walked into the kitchen, both Mrs Blair and Juliet stopped what they were doing and both wore a shocked frown for very different reasons.

'Good evening, Mrs Blair,' Jessie said brightly.

Mrs Blair's nostrils flared momentarily until she noted Joe holding one of Jessie's children in his arms. 'Evening,' she answered with little warmth.

'What do you want to say to Mrs Blair?' Jessie looked down at the children.

'Thank you for a delicious supper, Mrs Blair,' Marina said.

'Yes, thank you very much, it was yummy,' Stella joined in, sporting a gap tooth smile.

'James?'

'Thank you,' he said before turning his attention back to Joe.

Momentarily taken aback, Mrs Blair said, 'Oh, well, I see. Thank you for coming to see me,' she answered, wiping her dry hands down her apron. 'Now, I must get on,' she added, busily stirring a pot on the stove.

Just as they were all walking out of the kitchen, Mrs Blair said, 'Mrs Chandler, would the children like a glass of warm milk and a biscuit?'

'Would you, children?' Jessie asked.

'Oh, yes please, Mrs Blair,' the two girls answered.

'That would be lovely, Mrs Blair, thank you,' Jessie said. 'Please, call me Jessie though – we've known each other a long time,' she added.

'Yes, yes we have,' Mrs Blair coloured up. 'I'll send someone up with the milk shortly.'

As Jessie turned again to leave the kitchen, Mrs Blair spoke again, 'Jessie?'

Jessie turned and smiled. 'You have three beautiful children – they're a credit to you.'

'Thank you, Mrs Blair.' Jessie smiled – a truce had been called.

*

Juliet watched as Joe ushered Jessie and the two girls up the back stairs. The boy in his arms had wrapped his arms around Joe's neck, and her heart constricted to see Joe's arms tighten around the child, before he followed Jessie up the stairs. Mrs Blair was watching her when she tore her gaze away.

'It's a crying shame, you and Mr Treen never had children. He's a natural with that boy,' she said to Juliet.

'Yes, Mrs Blair,' Juliet answered, feeling herself tearing up. 'Excuse me.' She got up and walked out of the kitchen with no idea where she was going.

*

It was an intimate dinner that evening - just Jessie, Daniel, Peter, Sarah, Emma and Anna and there was much talk of the coming garden party, and of course the ball in honour of Emma.

'You must be very excited, Emma,' Jessie asked.

'Yes, it's the one ball I've been looking forward to, and we've attended a few this summer, haven't we, Mama?'

'Yes, I'm glad I only have one more daughter to bring out into society,' Sarah glanced at Peter, who raised his glass.

'Did you enjoy your London season, Mrs Chandler?' Emma asked in all innocence. 'Is that where you met Mr Chandler?'

Jessie laughed lightly. 'No, Emma. I had a very ordinary upbringing. In fact, I was a maid here for many years before going to work with Ellie Blackthorn.'

'Oh!' Emma looked to her mama, who nodded confirmation.

'I met Daniel on the dunes at Poldhu – we both have a passion for swimming in the sea,' she added with a smile.

'Gosh, so you escaped service, and married a gentleman!'

'I did.' Jessie glanced at Daniel with love.

'How romantic,' Emma breathed.

'Emma has had a very successful season,' Peter announced. 'She has caught the eye of a certain young gentleman, haven't you, darling?'

'Yes, Papa,' Emma answered with a smile, that Jessie noted did not reach her eyes.

'He's a young gentleman called Henry Montague – the son of an old associate of mine. So, if anything comes of it, and I sincerely hope it does for my darling girl, at least we know the family well.'

Emma, Jessie thought, didn't look at all enamoured with the prospect.

'It's a shame you won't see William while you're here, Jessie,' Sarah said, 'he would have been ten when you left. He's at Oxford in his second year, but has gone off to Italy. We're to meet him when we stay at my brother and Ruby's villa there – you remember Ruby, don't you?'

'I do. She was like a mother to the maids here. Have they had children?'

'No, I don't think they will either – they have been married a while now.'

'That's a shame.'

'Yes, but they're both very busy with their art.'

Jessie glanced at Joe who was presiding over the dinner with David. He had lowered his eyes at the talk of children and she wished she hadn't mentioned it now.

'You know, Jessie,' Sarah said, 'I do believe that this is the first time we have sat around a table together since our little trip to London in 1911!'

'I believe it is. What a wonderful trip that was,' Jessie answered.

Peter tipped his head. 'You two went to London in 1911!'

'We did.' Sarah and Jessie exchanged a secret smile.

'Forgive me, but were you not still married to Silas then, Jessie?' Peter asked.

'I was,' she answered with a roll of her eyes.

'I'm surprised he let you go - he was rather a...'

'Possessive husband,' Jessie interjected. 'Yes he was. He was working away, so I did not tell him, though when he found out, there was hell to pay!' She shuddered at the thought. 'It was worth the wrath though. Sarah asked me to accompany her - I believe Lowenna was unwell at the time.'

'Oh, you went in the capacity of lady's maid?'

'On the pretence of.' Sarah lifted her glass to Jessie. 'We had a jolly old-time shopping, and then we went to see Daniel play in the Albert Hall.'

'Ah yes, I remember now,' Peter said, 'though I had no idea you had taken Jessie. The secrets women keep, eh Daniel?'

'Well, at the time, it was best to keep things quiet,' Jessie answered.

Peter nodded, remembering Silas's character. 'So, you all had dinner together?'

'We did, with James Blackwell - God rest his soul,' Daniel said sadly.

'Yes, terrible shame to have lost him.'

'So, Daniel,' Sarah said brightly, 'Did I bring you and Jessie together then?'

'You certainly helped that evening.' Daniel shot a loving look at Jessie. 'If you remember, you encouraged Jessie to dance with me. I'd been in love with Jessie since the first moment I saw her running into the sea one evening at Poldhu. It was while we were dancing that I told her.'

'Now that *is* romantic,' Sarah clasped her hands together.

Jessie smiled, but noted Emma's pained expression at the mention of romance.

'We have a lot to thank, both you, and James Blackwell for our union.'

Everyone raised their glasses to that.

'We called our son after James. He was born just a few months after James died. It felt the right thing to do.'

'I'm sure he would be delighted to hear that,' Peter said.

'Tell me, what happened to James's young widow? We have quite lost track of things, what with being away on tour. Is she still at Loe House?' Daniel asked.

Jessie felt a warm feeling, at the mention of the house - it was there they had consummated their love on New Year's Day 1912.

'Jenna Blackwell remarried at Christmas 1919,' Sarah answered. 'She married Lyndon FitzSimmons – a good friend of Matthew Bickford. They have a son, Linton.'

'A happy outcome for her then too.' Daniel raised his glass.

They kept the house on, but they live on the Trevarno Estate in Helston. Loe House is still utilised by them for weekend getaways, and James's London friends use it whenever they come down to stay – they call themselves the Sundowners! You'll no doubt meet Jenna and Lyndon, they're coming to the garden party, and again next Friday for Emma's ball.

Daniel smiled. 'We shall look forward to meeting them on both occasions.'

'Now,' Peter said, putting his napkin on the table, 'I think we should leave the servants to clear the table. Shall we go through to the drawing room?'

As they poured themselves a drink, they settled on the sofas while Sarah played for them for a few minutes. An appreciative round of applause followed.

'Perhaps you will accompany me on the cello tomorrow night, Daniel?' Sarah asked. 'We're hosting a dinner for Emma's young man Henry and his parents – Lord and Lady Montague. They're only staying one night, so they can attend my garden party the next day.'

'I would be honoured, Sarah.'

'We shall look forward to meeting the young man who has stolen Emma's heart.' Jessie smiled at Emma, noting that her return smile bordered on a grimace. Jessie turned to Sarah. 'Daniel and I rarely entertain on a grand scale, but if we do, or we're invited somewhere for a formal dinner, I employ the services of a hairdresser. Is there anywhere in Helston you recommend, Sarah?'

'No need to go anywhere. Juliet will see to you. She is acting lady's maid to Emma at the moment until we see her safely married off.'

'I don't want to make extra work for anyone.'

'I'm sure Juliet will be happy to help. She normally does if we have guests who come without their maid.'

'You must tell me more about Henry, Emma,' Jessie enquired, but Emma looked stricken at the thought.

'Forgive me, Mrs Chandler, may we speak another time. I have a sudden headache.'

'Of course,' Jessie smiled. 'We'll catch up later.'

'Excuse me everyone. It's been nice meeting you, Mr Chandler, Mrs Chandler,' Emma said as she made her hurried departure.

20

Once the breakfast room was cleared the next morning, Joe stood at the window and watched Jessie and Daniel walk hand in hand down the front path to the garden. At the gate to the garden, Daniel opened it, and as Jessie walked through, he kissed her. Joe dropped his chin to his chest. Jessie and Daniel had been married two years longer than he and Juliet – yet their love was still fresh and new. How he wished for intimate love like that. *Enough, of those thoughts, Joe.* He brushed his hands down his jacket as though to dust the thoughts away.

*

As Joe walked out of the breakfast room, Juliet, who had been in the library opposite, stepped out from behind the curtains, where she'd hidden when she'd seen her husband so engrossed in watching his old sweetheart. Juliet too had seen the intimate kiss – their open gesture of love - and felt the terrible pang of guilt she carried always at the way she'd subjected Joe to a life of celibacy.

*

Walking around the garden, taking in the fine display of blooms in the borders, Jessie and Daniel passed through the avenue of lime trees, stopping a while at the memorial to Thomas, the footman who had died during the war in tragic circumstances.

'Dear Thomas, he was the kindest of men, but a terrible tease to us maids. 'He married Mary - the kitchen maid in the end. Do you remember him, Daniel?'

'I do, yes.'

Jessie smiled. 'He was a good friend and colleague. Rest in peace, dear friend.' She kissed her fingers and touched the memorial plaque.

'What happened to Mary, his poor wife, is she still here?'

'No, Sarah tells me she fell in love and married a gentlemen called Gabriel who came to restore the plasterwork in the French drawing room a couple of years ago. He was a widower with a small son. Sarah said they welcomed a daughter into their fold in January, so a happy ending. As they walked back up the garden, Jessie said, 'I'll be interested in meeting this Henry Montague.'

'Oh?'

'I get the strangest feeling that Emma is not at all enamoured with him.'

'How do you know? You've not seen them together yet.'

'Call it intuition.'

'Ah, the famous intuition rears its head again,' he joked.

'Don't mock, I've never been wrong.'

'I seem to remember you and Ellie shared this strange intuition.'

'We did.'

'I wonder if she knows we're dropping in on her today.'

'Without doubt. She knows we're here at Bochym, so she'll be expecting us.'

*

At the Poldhu Tea Room, Ellie Blackthorn was busy filling a teapot from the hot water geyser, when a sudden visceral feeling told her something very close to her heart was in the near vicinity.

'Are you well, Ellie?' Betsy asked, noting her friend's consternation, as she made her way to the back kitchen with a tray of dirty dishes.

'Yes, I…Betsy, can you take over behind the counter a moment?'

'Of course.'

As Ellie walked to the door, she wondered who, or what, was drawing her to the veranda. She glanced to her right, smiling at her customers, and then felt the pull on her heartstrings, because there at the far end of the veranda, was someone she had not seen for over ten years.

'Jessie!' she cried.

Jessie beamed, and opened her arms to embrace Ellie. 'I knew you'd sense I was here, that's why I didn't come in. We haven't lost that perception, have we?'

'Apparently not! I just felt that someone I loved was close by. Where is Daniel - is he with you?'

'He is, yes, and the children. He took them to the water's edge while I had my reunion with you.'

'Goodness, Jessie, but it's so good to see you again.' Ellie held her at arm's length, admiring her beautiful outfit of a white lace dress with a mint green satin over jacket. 'Look at you - you look like you've stepped out of Vogue, and you look very happy.'

'I am, Ellie – I'm truly blessed. You look wonderful too – you do not age!'

Ellie batted the compliment away with a smile. 'So, you're staying at Bochym for the whole week!'

'We are, for the garden party and Emma's ball now. We only initially planned a quick visit to see Cordelia's grave – to mark the tenth anniversary of losing her.'

'Ten years - it's gone in a flash,' Ellie breathed, 'what a time that was!'

Jessie nodded, remembering, not only the loss of her baby, but the violent death of her estranged husband Silas which followed at the hand of a crazed gunman.

'How is Guy?' Jessie asked tentatively.

'He's fine. We're all looking forward to the ball – it should be a very fine affair, we've never been to one before,' Ellie said, excitedly.

'It will be so lovely for us all to be together – I'm so looking forward to seeing my nieces again.'

'And they're excited to see their aunt Jessie again too.'

'We've already met Zack. We dropped in on Kit and Sophie, and were reunited with him there. He's grown into a fine young man.'

'He has.' Ellie smiled proudly.

'Ellie?' Jessie's eyes dimmed. 'How will Guy be with us at these social events - I take it we've never been forgiven?'

Ellie shrugged. 'Who knows. He doesn't speak of that time. Silas's death hit him very hard. I know he never wants to read your letters - so perhaps not. But you have just as much right to be at these occasions as anyone. Look, sorry, Jessie, I must get back, I'll send Betsy out to take your order, she'll be tickled pink when she sees you. Oh, and look, here is someone else who will be happy to see you.'

Jessie smiled to see her old friends Tobias and Meg Williams, as they came walking up the beach, chatting animatedly to Daniel and the children. After a noisy reunion, they all settled down to one of Ellie's famous cream teas.

'I shall have to remember where I am when I put the jam and cream on. We do it differently in Devon you know,' Daniel teased.

'No, you do it *wrong* in Devon,' Tobias joked. 'Woe betide, Daniel Chandler, if you do not put jam on first, we'll hound you back out of Cornwall before you've unpacked.'

*

Later that evening, Juliet's fingers trembled as she dressed Jessie's hair - this was the woman her husband coveted.

'Are you alright, Juliet? You look a little tentative,' Jessie said softly.

Juliet forced a smile. 'I always am when I'm faced with a new head of hair.'

'Well, it's always a treat for me to have my hair done. I normally wear it up in a chignon, like I used to do when I was working here or at the tearoom. There is something so relaxing about someone else doing your hair though.'

'I wouldn't know, Ma'am.'

'I'll tell you what, Juliet, I'll do yours one day, shall I? It's a long time since I acted as a lady's maid, but I could give it a go, if you would like?'

'Me, Ma'am? Oh, I don't know about that.'

'Please, Juliet call me Jessie. I don't give myself airs and graces. It will be nice to spend a little bit of time with you – getting to know you. We have a lot in common, you and I!' she smiled at her.

Juliet glanced at Jessie through the mirror, but said nothing.

'We've both been maids here at Bochym, and we both care deeply for Joe.'

Juliet's head dropped, and she returned to her task of piling Jessie's long auburn curls onto the top of her head.

'Oh, no, Juliet,' Jessie put her hand on Juliet's, 'I don't mean anything by that. I'm not about to steal Joe from you,' she laughed softly. 'I love him very much - as a friend, but I'm very happily married to Daniel.'

'Yes, Ma…Jessie,' she corrected herself, 'that's quite evident.'

'I hope you and Joe are as happy.' Jessie added with warmth,' I'm sure you were just what he was waiting for.'

Juliet could not look Jessie in the eye.

'I'd like us to be friends. Betsy told me lots about you in her letters to me when you and she were working together here.'

Juliet blanched and asked tremulously, 'What sort of things?' Thinking Betsy might have told Jessie about her past troubles with her hateful stepfather.

'She told me about how she valued you as a friend after I left Cornwall, and about the love and knowledge of flowers you and Joe share. She told me how Joe fell completely and utterly in love with you - almost as soon as you arrived here. I was overjoyed to hear that Joe had married you, and that he had found his soul mate at last.'

'I think…..'

'You think what, Juliet?'

'Nothing, it's nothing.'

Jessie tipped her head questioningly.

'I think he'd have rather married you – he would have been a father then – but with me, well, it's not to be – there will be no babies.'

'Oh, my dear, I'm sorry,' Jessie reached out for her hand, 'don't give up hope though. Sometimes little miracles happen. Sophie Trevellick went many years before Selene was born!'

Juliet nodded sorrowfully – knowing full well there would be no little miracles.

'Well, I must say, Juliet,' Jessie said turning to check her hair in the mirror, 'My hair has never looked lovelier, thank you.'

'It's my pleasure. Would you like me to come back later to help you undress?'

'No, Daniel will help me do that.' She smiled knowingly.

As Juliet turned to leave, Jessie said, 'Joe loves you very much, Juliet. He wrote to me just after he had married you to say how lucky he was to have found you.'

Juliet nodded and left the room. Outside in the corridor, she stood for a moment and looked skywards. *Oh, Lord, but I don't deserve Joe.*

*

Emma was in a heightened state of excitement at the coming week. First the garden party tomorrow, and then the ball. Both days she could openly be with Ben, and Henry could do nothing about it. Emma had secured a pass for Ben to attend the family champagne buffet. Everyone else who attended the garden party had to bring their own picnic, though tea and cordial was supplied. Emma loved the fact that her parents felt Ben was worthy of joining them at these occasions – it gave her hope that when she finally told them she was in love with Ben, and wanted to marry him, they would see that he could easily fit into their social circle. Her stomach gave a flip at the thought of marrying Ben. They would both speak to her parents about their wedding plans, just as soon as she returned from Italy, which was only a few short weeks away. It was a holiday she was not particularly looking forward to though, as it meant she would be separated from Ben for three whole weeks!

As Juliet helped her to dress for dinner, Emma glanced around the lavish surroundings she had been brought up with. If her parents did not look favourably on their union, she would have to leave all this behind. It also struck her that she would have to get used to dressing herself when she became Ben's wife. In fact, she would have to get used to things being very different from the way she lived now. It would all be worth it, to be able to be with the man she truly loved though. She tried to imagine herself living in the saddlers shop – she would have to make it a little more homely – better bedding, good rugs, and more comfortable seating. She relished cooking dinner together with him – though she could only cook the basics Mrs Blair had instructed her in. Thankfully, Ben could cook, so they wouldn't initially starve. A quick glance at her hands reminded her that they had never laundered anything in her life, and her hands would very soon resemble Izzy the laundry maid's red chapped hands. All this she would endure for Ben though.

Emma was wearing a sleeveless gown of deep navy satin and lace, which complemented her complexion. As Juliet placed a diamond clasp to hold back her hair, Emma glanced at Juliet through the dressing table mirror.

'Thank you, Juliet. That is lovely,' she said pulling on her long black satin gloves, 'I shall not be needing you after dinner, so you're free to go to bed.'

'Oh! Very well, my lady. I shall drop by to see if your gloves need laundering.'

'If you must.'

Juliet frowned. 'Have I displeased you in anyway, my lady?'

'Oh, no, of course not. I just think I can manage on my own.'

A knock came at the bedroom door and her mama walked in. 'Henry and his parents are here, Emma.'

The happiness Emma had felt a few moments before, vanished in an instant.

'Hurry now and finish getting ready. You must come down to keep Henry company.'

When her mother had gone, Emma glanced at Juliet, and then turned to the mirror to observe the disappointment etched on her face. Sighing wearily, she reluctantly made her way down the stairs to see Henry.

*

At dinner that night, Jessie and Daniel spoke about their reunion with all their friends and how wonderful it had been.

'Did you see Guy?' Sarah asked tentatively.

'No, but we understand he'll be here for the garden party tomorrow, so, we'll see him then.' Jessie raised an eyebrow, but did not elaborate more on the enduring estrangement with Guy, as there were other guests around the table that night.

Jessie observed Lady Elizabeth Montague, and thought that although she was personable, she seemed to be devoid of any female traits, which probably accounted for the unfortunate facial hair she sported on her upper lip, along with the various tufts on her chin. Fortunately, she seemed to have a shared interest in horticulture with Sarah, so she was not short of conversation. Lord Montague, a portly, ruddy faced man, had, Jessie decided, an air of supremacy, which bordered on boorishness. Throughout the evening, Jessie watched with interest, the interaction between Henry and Emma - her perception that Emma was not entirely enamoured with her beau, seemed to bear some relevance. For a couple to be interested in each other, as Peter stated, Emma seemed quite put out that Henry was here at all!

'I understand you and Mrs Chandler are planning on staying until after Lady Emma's ball,' Lady Montague spoke directly to Daniel. 'Do you have plans for the week?'

'Yes, my lady. Jessie has never seen St Michael's Mount, so we're going down there on Monday. We enjoy walking the coast and swimming, so we'll most likely be doing a little of both.'

'Swimming? In the sea! Is it not freezing?' She asked astonished.

Daniel laughed. 'We're used to it. We live for part of the year on the Devon coast and regularly take to the sea with the children.'

'Good grief, you must all be mad!' she said, turning rudely away from him to speak to Peter.

*

After dinner, they retired to the drawing room and as Sarah played the piano, accompanied by Daniel on Sarah's cello, Henry took a seat beside Emma.

'I trust that saddler has heeded my warning to keep his distance from you.'

'Yes I heard about your visit. I know not what gave you the right to do that. You have no authority over who I can and cannot see,' she said through gritted teeth.

He snorted derisively. 'I most certainly do. It's all part of our deal. To all intents and purposes, we are meant to act like we are about to become engaged. I don't expect my intended to be galivanting around the countryside with the local riff raff.'

Emma seethed in silence. She regretted the deal with every waking moment. She fully intended to break the deal herself after her ball – to do it before that would open the door for other eager suitors to declare themselves to her.

'Well, it won't be for much longer, Henry.'

He gave a short, sharp, snort, but before he could say more, Lady Montague asked, 'What are you two so secretive about?'

'Just making plans,' Henry answered.

Lady Montague clasped her large hands together. 'How lovely. I said right from the start that you two were made for each other.'

Henry beamed, but Emma could only muster a feeble smile, and when she looked, she was sure Jessie had seen the insincerity in it.

21

The day of the garden party dawned bright and sunny, and Jessie lay in Daniel's arms thinking about their little daughter Cordelia - as she always did, on the anniversary of the birth and death of their firstborn. Although ten years had passed, the pain and suffering of that day still tore at her heart. After breakfast, they would all set off to Cury Churchyard to visit Cordelia's grave. Jessie felt Daniel's arms tighten around her, and she knew what he was thinking too.

*

Although extremely busy with the garden party later that day, Sarah had gathered flowers from the garden to give to Jessie and Daniel for the grave. At the churchyard they found Cordelia's grave well-tended. Betsy had promised Jessie she would tend it, and though Betsy had three children of her own, tend it she had.

Jessie and Daniel's other children stood back, unsure of how to react to their long dead sister's grave. They knew about her, and remembered her each night in their prayers before bed, but the little ones struggled to understand why she was here - so far away.

Kneeling by the lichen encrusted headstone, Jessie arranged the flowers in a jar. She read the inscription, and her breath caught with a sob, as she ran her fingers across Cordelia's name. Daniel held her in his arms and they both shed silent tears for the baby born out of their love, and snatched so quickly from them. Wiping the tears, Daniel encouraged each of the children to lay the flower they'd been given on the mound.

'Will Cordelia be cold in the ground, Mama?' Stella asked.

'No darling. Only her bones lie there. Cordelia is here,' she touched her own heart and Daniel's. 'This is where she'll always be, warm and safe with her mama and papa.'

*

At Bochym Manor, Emma had spent the morning busying herself with the garden party - mostly to keep away from Henry.

The garden party was for everyone in the vicinity to enjoy. Everyone was encouraged to bring a picnic and enjoy the beautiful grounds of the manor. There was a marquee erected just to the right of the front garden, where people could get a cup of tea or a glass of cordial. For the VIP guests, they would be given a blue paper pass to enjoy the champagne buffet in the French drawing room.

Emma, dressed in a white voile drop-waisted dress with a pale blue cardigan around her shoulders, completed the ensemble with a wide brimmed white hat, which she kept having to hold onto due to the gusty warm breeze. Keeping her eyes peeled for the arrival of Ben, when she saw him she was at his side in an instant, tucking a blue pass into Ben's top pocket.

'You're my guest now. Come and have something to eat and a glass of champagne,' she laughed, pulling him through the front door of the manor.

*

The fragrance of the many vases of flowers hit Ben's senses and he was transported to another world in here. Whereas everyone milling about in the gardens were dressed in their Sunday best, here, everyone was dressed in their finery, and he felt slightly underdressed, even though he wore his best shirt and jacket.

'Here.' Emma passed a glass of sparkling champagne to him, which when he took a sip made him sneeze.

She giggled. 'The bubbles always make me sneeze too. Just a moment, I'll go and find Zack and Agnes, and then we can all take some food out to the front garden.'

Emma went off, leaving Ben to peruse the buffet table, which was groaning with cake, delicate sandwiches, fruit, and fancies.

'I do believe you're in the wrong place,' Henry sneered as he sidled up to him. 'The riff raff stay the other side of the front gate.'

Ben turned his back on Henry and glanced around for Emma.

'Don't turn your back on me when I'm speaking to you,' Henry hissed.

'I wasn't aware you were addressing me.' Ben being a good six inches taller, glanced down his nose at Henry.

'Well, I can't see anyone else here in workmen's clothes!' He flicked Ben's jacket lapel.

Ben could feel his blood boil, but Henry was saved from an expletive when Peter walked up to them.

'Ah, it's good to see you two are getting to know each other now. Ben is one of Emma's oldest friends, Henry - they grew up together, running wild around the estate, didn't you, son?' Peter patted Ben's shoulder.

'Yes, my lord.' Ben's anger abated, happy to be so singled out.

Henry rolled his eyes. 'Goodness, what an unusual upbringing Lady Emma has had – to mix classes and sexes I mean,' Henry answered as his eyes travelled the length of Ben's attire.

'Class does not come into it, Henry. We're all the same, except some of us are lucky enough to be more well-appointed.'

'Well, let's hope she has tamed her wild ways now.' He tipped his head and wrinkled his nose. 'No one likes tomboy traits in a young woman.'

'I can assure you - Lady Emma is every bit a lady, Henry. Have no worries on that score,' Peter answered placing a hand on Henry's shoulder.

'Excuse me, my lord,' Henry said, 'I need some air, I feel slightly nauseous, there appears to be an unpleasant aroma in here.' He cut his eyes towards Ben, gave Peter a curt bow and left.

Peter sniffed the air. 'I can only smell flowers, can you? Perhaps Henry has an aversion to them.'

Or me, Ben mused.

They both turned as Emma approached them with Zack and Agnes in tow.

'Come, Ben. I have us all together now, let's fill our plates.' She led him to the buffet table.

'Henry has just stepped outside, Emma – the flowers seemed to be bothering him,' Peter said. 'Perhaps you could ask him to join your picnic.'

'Yes, Papa,' Emma answered joylessly.

When they all settled on a rug on the front lawn with their picnic, Henry was fortunately nowhere to be seen. It was a glorious day, if not a little breezy, and periodically unsecured hats took off, accompanied by roars of laughter as people scurried to catch them.

No sooner had they sat down, than Loveday Trevail spotted Ben, and slipping away from Nanny's, not so watchful eye, left her new playmates, the Trelissick children, and ran over to him.

'Hello, Ben,' Loveday said excitedly.

Ben laughed heartily as the child wrapped her arms around Ben's neck.

'Hello, Princess.'

Loveday turned and then curtsied to Emma. 'Hello, Lady Emma, Zack, Agnes,' she said shyly. 'Can I sit with you, Ben?'

'You can for a moment, but I think Nanny is looking for you.'

'You look very pretty in your dress, Lady Emma, are you the bride?'

Emma laughed. 'No, Loveday. Nobody is getting married today – it's just a garden party.'

'Oh, well, when you do get married, Lady Emma, can I be your bridesmaid, and have a lovely dress to wear like yours? I've never been a bridesmaid.' She sighed.

Emma looked up at Ben and smiled secretly. 'Of course, you can. Oh, look! Nanny is here now.

'I'm very sorry, my lady,' Nanny apologised.

'It's fine, Nanny,' Emma smiled warmly.

'Loveday, I think your playmates are missing you,' Ben said to her.

Loveday nodded, then turned to Nanny. 'I'm going to be Lady Emma's bridesmaid, Nanny,' she said skipping away, turning to wave as she left.

Emma shrugged when the others gave her an amused look. 'Well, what was I supposed to say, and she *is* the most adorable little girl, with the sweetest nature. Anyway, when I do get married,' she glanced at Ben, 'she'll make a wonderful bridesmaid.'

Ben cupped his knee with is hands. 'I have to agree with Emma,' he said sharing a not-so-secret smile with her, 'I hope I have a daughter one day – as sweet as Loveday.'

'Are you two planning something?' Zack whispered to Ben.

Ben touched his finger to his lip. 'What about you, Agnes, no sign of marriage for you and Jake yet?'

'Nope!' she said adamantly. 'I'm not ready to give up my job yet, not even to produce the sweetest of daughters like Loveday, and don't give Jake any ideas – it's bad enough holding him at bay at the moment.'

'He won't wait forever, you know!'

'I know,' she said sadly.

'Where is he anyway?' Zack looked around.

'He'll be along soon enough. So, stop your talk about marriage please.' Agnes folded her arms.

*

Henry, obscured by a copper beech tree, watched with cool reserve as Emma and her *common* friends emerged from the manor, plates laden with food, laughing as they made their way to the front lawn to eat their picnic.

Henry studied with interest the other man in the party – Zack, he understood he was called. Emma had told him both Zack and Ben were William's best friends while they were growing up. Henry glanced between the two men - he knew the beating he'd taken had been at the hands of one of William's friends - but which one of these bastards was it? Henry had been too preoccupied, when the attack on him happened - the heavy punches administered that day, rendered it impossible for Henry to get a good look at the assailant, but by the stature of these two men, Henry was bloody sure it wasn't that Zack fellow!

He turned, aware of someone standing nearby - a young woman clearly in an agitated state. Henry followed her gaze, which had settled on the occupants of the picnic on the front lawn, this piqued his interest. Curious as to why this was causing her distress, Henry addressed her.

'Are you quite well, Miss?'

Merial gave him a sharp look, sniffed back the tears, and returned her gaze back to the front lawn.

'Has someone upset you?' he asked.

'Aye, Ben Pearson.'

'Oh! How so?'

'He's meant to be my sweetheart – danced with me he did last harvest – twice! But Lady Emma has stolen him from me.'

Henry narrowed his eyes. 'So, you think Pearson and Lady Emma are sweethearts, do you?'

Merial gritted her teeth. 'I know they are!'

'Hey, what's going on here!' A voice hollered in Henry's ear, and a rough hand clasped his sleeve.

Henry turned indignantly and found himself staring into the glowering angry eyes of a brutish chap, with an equally disagreeable chap standing next to him.

'Unhand me, or I'll have you thrown out,' Henry warned.

Realising Henry was one of the toffs, Bernard quickly stepped back and growled, 'What are you doing with my sister? You better not be propositioning her.'

'I can assure you - *I am not!*' Henry sneered.

'Good, 'cause she's spoken for.'

'Yes she was telling me. Alas, the man in question seems to be otherwise engaged.' Henry nodded towards Ben.

They all observed the group on a blanket on the lawn. They were all laughing merrily at something.

'Look how Ben is looking at Lady Emma,' Merial cried and stormed away.

'I'll bloody do for him if he's taking our sister for a ride,' Bernard snarled.

'Well, that's what it looks like from here,' Henry said coolly. 'Perhaps someone needs to teach him a lesson.'

Bernard turned to Henry. 'What's it matter to you who my sister grieves for anyway, eh?'

'It matters because your sister's sweetheart is *coveting* my soon to be wife!'

'Ah, I see!' Bernard bared his green, rotting teeth. 'Perhaps he does need a lesson taught then.'

'And are you the man to do it?' Henry questioned.

Bernard took in Henry's expensive attire. 'I might be - for a price.'

Henry gave him a sidelong glance and nodded.

'Ask for me at The Old Inn in Mullion - should you decide a lesson needs teaching.' Bernard said, as he touched his hat and walked away.

*

Lord and Lady Montague had found seats near a table on the front lawn to observe the goings on at the garden party. The look of disdain on their faces, clearly revealing what they felt about sharing the gardens with what they called 'the great unwashed.'

'Good lord, Hughie. Whatever are the Dunstan's thinking – to allow these sorts to wander about the grounds. I hope they've hidden the silver – if any of this lot find their way into the house they'll clear it in seconds. Apparently it's not a one off – they've done it for years.' She pursed her lips. 'Where is Henry anyway? I don't like the fact that Lady Emma is neglecting him – I mean look at her! Sitting there. Laughing and speaking with people who are clearly not of her class – look at their clothes, Hughie.'

Hugh grimaced. 'Dunstan tells me, that lot are her childhood friends. Two of them are from a thatching family, and the other man is the son of his estate steward, would you believe!'

'Good lord, Hughie, I hope she isn't going to try and invite all and sundry from the village into our home if Henry marries her.'

'When - not if!' Hugh said confidently. 'And no, she won't. I'm sure you'll teach her the error of her ways when we get her there, my dear.'

22

Guy and Ellie were talking to Kit and Sophie when Jessie and Daniel came into the French drawing room for some refreshments. Guy suddenly stopped talking, making the others follow his gaze. The room was busy so Jessie and Daniel hadn't seen them at first, but when they did, Jessie waved at Ellie, and with plates piled with food they set off towards them as everyone else in the group held their breath.

'Hello everyone,' Jessie smiled, glancing at Guy who was studiously looking elsewhere before excusing himself to leave the room.

Ellie grimaced at his departure. 'I'm sorry,' she said to Jessie and Daniel.

'Don't apologise, Ellie. We did come over without invitation,' Daniel answered.

'You shouldn't need an invitation to come and speak to friends,' Ellie countered.

'Ah, well, he'll no doubt come around when he's ready,' Daniel said, then seeing the raised eyebrows, added, 'Perhaps.'

'Ellie. Daniel wants to talk to you about Zack,' Jessie said.

'Zack! Why, what has he done?'

'Nothing bad.' Daniel smiled, and cleared his throat. 'You do not know it, but he has become an accomplished pianist.'

'A what?' Ellie said astonished.

Daniel nodded. 'I've heard him play, and he's outstanding.'

'Our, Zack!' she looked puzzled, 'are you sure?'

'Quite sure.'

'But he's never shown any signs of being musical except for the odd song he used to sing to himself.'

'Well, I think he has a remarkable talent. Some people are just born with it. They have an ear for music that can

181

take years for normal people to perfect. I'm going to get him to play next week at the ball. I want you and Guy to hear him.'

Ellie's face blanched. 'And then what?'

'And then, I should very much like to put a proposition to you both.'

'Oh dear,' Ellie's hand flew to her face, 'I'm not sure Guy will hear you. You know how he feels about you.'

'I think when he hears Zack play, he'll understand that I only have Zack's interest at heart. If you could keep it a surprise for now though.'

'Of course, I wouldn't dare broach the subject.'

Daniel smiled. 'Now, Ellie, we are aware that our presence here is keeping Guy away from his family. We'll come and see you again at the tearoom this week.'

*

As the afternoon drew on, Sarah took the opportunity to join Matthew and Hillary Bickford, who were seated at a table with Lyndon and Jenna FitzSimmons, at the opposite side of the lawn from Emma and her friends.

Jenna Fitzsimmons was cradling Linton, her young son sleeping on her lap. She looked up and smiled at Sarah. 'What a lovely day for a garden party. Thank you for inviting us. I shall walk around once this little fellow has woken up,' she said.

'He's a fine young man,' Sarah said, 'the image of his handsome father.' Sarah glanced at Lyndon, who smiled proudly back at her.

'We have another one on the way in January,' Jenna said happily.

'Congratulations,' Sarah said warmly. 'May I ask, Jenna, are you still in touch with James's publisher?'

'I am, yes. James left a couple of unfinished manuscripts and several short stories that he never published, so I'm working with him on that. Why, are you thinking of taking up the pen?'

'Alas, not me, but our daughter Emma - she seems to have a talent for writing novels. James used to give her advice, and I wondered if you could speak to James's publisher about her.'

Jenna raised an eyebrow. 'I take it you think they are good enough?'

'Well, I suspect I'm biased, but I do read a great deal of novels, and I think she has a real talent for telling a story.'

'Well then, that's good enough for me. If she is prepared to send some of her writing over to me, I shall gladly show James's publisher.'

'Thank you. It may be some time though, what with the ball next week and then we're in Italy for three weeks with Justin and Ruby.'

'Oh, how lovely! Please send our regards to them both. We had the most glorious holiday there with them in 1919, didn't we Lyndon?'

'Glorious.'

'I must say, Sarah, Emma looks very happy with her beau – they look so well matched.' She nodded to where Emma sat with Ben and the others.

Sarah followed Jenna's gaze. 'Oh, goodness, no. That isn't Emma's beau – that's our estate steward's son, Ben. He grew up playing with William and Emma and has stayed firm friends. I'm so sorry, this is very remiss of me, I must introduce you to Henry. Now where is he?'

*

At four o clock, after a very successful day, everyone began to make their way home.

When Ben bid goodbye to Emma, he whispered, 'I love you.'

'I love you too,' she said, 'I'm bereft at our parting.'

Ben left her and had only just reached the stile when he heard his name called. He turned to find his father walking up to him. 'Hello, Pa.'

'Had a nice day, have you, son?'

'Yes, Emma got me a pass for the VIP room. I'm rather merry on champagne,' he grinned.

Sydney took a great intake of breath. 'Don't let a taste of the highlife turn your head, my boy. Remember who you are.'

'I know exactly who I am, Pa. I was enjoying an afternoon with the friends I grew up with!' he said ardently.

Sydney's mouth tightened. 'That may be, but you're too familiar with Lady Emma – you're not children anymore.'

'I don't know what you're talking about,' Ben said, knowing guilt was written all over his face. 'Emma is my friend – she's always been my friend.'

'She's more than that though, isn't she? We were watching you, your ma and I today, so too was Henry Montague – the man she is supposed to be getting engaged to. He didn't look at all pleased that you took all Lady Emma's attention.'

Ben gazed into the distance – he did not want this conversation.

'This *friendship* with Lady Emma…'

Ben's eyes cut to his father and waited.

'You must end it.'

'I love her, Pa.'

'She's not for you, my son – she is destined for a better man than you.'

'That's debatable as to whom is the better man!'

'Ben, for God's sake.'

'She is the only woman I will ever love, Pa.'

'You say that now, but you're young. Your whole life is in front of you. Someone will come along to sweep you off your feet.'

'Alas!' he smiled, 'that happened to me a long while ago. I know where my heart lies!'

'She's too young to understand the serious consequences of this relationship. You are older, it is for you to halt this now before too much damage is done.'

Ben slowly shook his head.

Sydney sighed in exasperation. 'You must give up this folly, Ben - for it is a folly. This friendship can go no further, you must understand that. Your actions are making mine and your ma's position here untenable too. Think on that.' He turned and marched away.

*

While Ben was arguing with his pa, Sarah, Peter, and Emma, were seeing the Montague's off, and Emma was just wishing they would hurry up and go.

Sarah stepped forward to kiss Henry on the cheek. 'I hope you and Emma snatched some time together, Henry. I'm afraid I kept her very busy this morning, and she had all her friends with her this afternoon. I do hope you joined them for part of the time.'

Henry gave a stiff smile. 'I was fine, Lady Sarah. I was busy talking to His Lordship and enjoying the day spent in your glorious garden.'

'We'll make sure you and Emma spend some quality time together next week at her ball,' Peter said, shaking his hand.

'I hope very much to do that, my lord.'

If Emma wasn't mistaken, Papa and Henry exchanged a knowing smile.

'Lady Emma.' Henry beckoned her forward and kissed her hand. 'Until next week,' he said giving a small bow and added with a whisper, 'And I *will* have you all to myself.'

Emma very much felt that it was an order rather than a statement.

When the Montague's car had disappeared from sight, Sarah turned to Emma. 'Please come with me to my parlour, will you?'

'Yes, Mama,' she answered, unsure of her mama's tone.

In Sarah's sumptuous parlour, Emma was invited to sit.

'Jenna FitzSimmons congratulated me today. She commented that you looked well matched – with *Ben!*'

Emma was unsure how to reply to this – it was too soon to declare her interest in Ben, so she remained silent.

'If Jenna could see that you were intimate with Ben – others would have seen it too.'

'I wasn't intimate with him!'

'Emma, you had your heads together chatting most of the afternoon.'

'That is what we do when we're together.'

'But in doing so you neglected Henry, again.'

'Henry doesn't like my friends, Mama. He's made that quite plain.'

'You will have to make allowances for him, if you are to become engaged, Emma. It's all very well having childhood friendships, but there is a time when you have to forge a different life for yourself. Very soon, you will have your own drawing room and your own collection of new friends and acquaintances. I left behind many of my friends to come and live here with your papa, but I made the most wonderful friendships with people down here, and you will too, wherever you live with your husband. Now, please, I ask you, to tread more carefully in future.'

'Yes, Mama,' she said with crossed fingers.

*

Later that evening, Sarah sat at her dressing table, working some hand cream into her skin. When Peter came in, he took off his dressing gown and kissed her on the neck.

'Well done for today, my darling – another triumph.'

Sarah smiled. 'Peter, are you sure Henry is the right man for Emma?'

'Why, are you having doubts about Henry?'

'I'm not sure of him yet, and to be honest, I don't think Emma is either.'

'Good Lord, I hope you're wrong. The Montagues are very keen on the union, as am I.' He put out his light and settled down.

Keen or not, Sarah needed to know if Emma was entirely happy with Henry before she gave her blessing.

*

After being dismissed again the previous night from helping Lady Emma to undress, Juliet's fears that she'd done something to upset her, came to fruition when Juliet knocked on Emma's door to wake and dress her that next morning. Not only did she find the bedroom vacant, but that Emma had bathed and dressed herself, and had made her own bed!

*

Emma had been in an effervescent mood since saying goodbye to Ben yesterday, so much so she was up and about bright and early that morning - hardly able to wait to see Ben again. The glances they had exchanged yesterday about Loveday being a bridesmaid, and how Ben wanted a daughter like her, only added to her delight that she and Ben wanted the same things.

Emma decided that now the Montagues had gone, she may as well start as she meant to go on, and so she had risen early to dress herself. Her hair had been the most problematic part of her toilet, so she brushed it back loosely and tied it with a ribbon.

Glancing at the clock as it struck seven - it was too soon to go to Ben, so she slipped out of the kitchen side door to go and saddle Saffron for a trot around the estate. Jessie, Daniel, and the children, she knew were setting off for St Michael's Mount later that morning - taking with them Denny and Loveday Trevail. Papa had business in Truro that morning, and Mama had a luncheon appointment at Bonython Manor. So, just as soon as they had all gone their separate ways, Emma planned to take a walk down to Ben's workshop.

*

Downstairs, Joe Treen came out of his office and found a very distressed Juliet standing outside the laundry.

'My love, whatever is ailing you?'

Juliet's watery eyes met her husband's. Oh, Joe,' she said, bursting into tears.

'Goodness me. Come in to the office.' He put a protective arm around her shoulders, led her through and held a chair out for her. Juliet sat down, laid her head on her arms, and sobbed brokenheartedly.

Kneeling by her side, Joe was at a loss as to what was wrong. Juliet's distress was such that it rendered her unable to speak for a couple of minutes. Eventually she lifted her head, her handkerchief soaked in tears clutched in her fist. He took his own handkerchief from his pocket, pushed it into her hand and she blew noisily on it.

'Can you tell me what the matter is, my love?'

'I think I've displeased Lady Emma,' she wailed.

'Why, has she said something?'

'No, but she did not want me to undress her last night, or the night before, and this morning she was gone before I got to her - and she'd made her own bed!' She dropped her head into her hands and sobbed again.

'This is for the housekeeper to deal with, so I'll get Molly Johnson to speak to Lady Emma. If there is a problem, and I don't believe for one moment that there is, Molly will get to the bottom of it.'

'Oh, Joe, I feel like my life is falling apart.'

'Because of this!' Joe asked astonished.

'No,' she lowered her eyes, 'not just this!'

Joe got off his knees and pulled his chair around his desk so he could sit opposite her. 'What then? Tell me what else is bothering you?'

She lifted her head and sniffed back the tears. 'I'm so sorry, I've been such a disappointment to you.'

Joe laughed, and then furrowed his brow. 'Whatever makes you say something like that?'

'I'm sorry I haven't been as intimate with you as a wife should have been.'

'Oh, Juliet. We've been through this, and I've told you over and over, it doesn't matter. All that matters is that you feel comfortable with me.'

'But I've denied you the chance to be a father!'

For a moment Joe hesitated in his answer, causing Juliet's tears to begin again.

'I've seen you watching Jessie and Daniel together. I saw the look of longing on your face when you held her son in your arms.'

Joe lowered his eyes.

'As I said - I feel I've been a disappointment to you.'

Joe smiled softly. 'Granted, I do envy the way Jessie is with Daniel – they look like newlyweds.'

'Even as newlyweds we were never that loving.'

'Well, you had been through a terrible time, Juliet. All I've ever wanted, was for you to feel safe with me.'

'I do love you, Joe.'

'I know, my love, I know.' He put his hand to her damp cheek.

'You deserve better – you deserve to be loved by someone like Jessie. Not someone as cold-hearted as I.'

'Darling, Juliet. You have never been cold-hearted.'

'I feel it, when I turn away from you in bed.'

Joe gathered her into his arms. 'I understand why you must turn away from me – it's too traumatic for you - I know that. I always said that I would never press you to make love, and I never will.'

'But it's wrong, Joe, and I want to make things right for you - for us.' She pulled away from his embrace. 'Can we try again?'

Joe gasped. 'Are you saying what I think you're saying - that you want me to…'

She nodded. 'I want you to make love to me.'

This time it was Joe whose eyes teared up, as he took his wife back into his arms and held her as though his life depended on it.

23

Jessie and Daniel had yet to come down that morning, so only Sarah, Peter and Anna were breakfasting when Emma swept into the room and headed towards the breakfast trays.

'Goodness me, Emma!' Sarah gasped. 'Whatever do you look like, coming in here looking wild and unkempt? Your hair! What has happened, is Juliet unwell?'

'No, Mama, I was up and about before Juliet came, so I managed on my own.'

'Well, you must send for her immediately, you look like an unmade bed,' Sarah scolded.

'Oh! Do I? I'll call her after breakfast then,' Emma answered dejectedly.

'You will send for her *before* you sit down to eat! David, please remove Lady Emma's plate.'

Emma watched as the footman took away her boiled egg.

'Go on.' Sarah ushered her to the door. 'I really don't know what you're thinking, darling. One must never sit down to eat in a state of undress – it isn't ladylike. You are a lady, and have a duty to always look like one.'

Emma glanced at her Papa who just raised his eyebrows.

'Sorry, Mama. It won't happen again.'

*

Juliet was duly summoned to Emma's room, unfortunately before she had time to compose herself. As Juliet re-dressed her and began to dress her hair, Emma tipped her head, noting Juliet's red swollen eyes.

'Are you alright, Juliet?'

'Yes, my lady,' she answered tremulously.

Emma turned to face her. 'But you look distressed.'

'I'm fine, honestly, my lady.'

Emma folded her arms. 'I'm sorry, Juliet, but something is plainly bothering you.'

Juliet's hands dropped to her side. 'Have I displeased you, my lady.'

'Displeased? No, why ever would you think that?'

'You don't seem to want my help anymore.'

Emma felt a pang of guilt. 'Oh, Juliet, please forgive me. I've been terribly insensitive to your feelings, haven't I? You have not displeased me at all. I was just conducting an experiment to see if I could manage on my own – like normal people do. But as you see, I failed miserably.'

'But why ever would you want to do that, my lady?'

'I have my reasons, Juliet, but rest assured, as long as I'm in this household, you will always be invaluable to me.'

Juliet halted her busy fingers as they arranged Emma's curls. 'Are you planning on leaving, my lady?'

'Well,' Emma put her hand to her chest, as she thought of Ben, 'I may marry one day, and of course you would not want to be parted from Joe - *if* I were to move away, would you?'

'No, my lady.'

'So, I might have to do without a maid.'

'But you're a lady, you wouldn't be able to do without one!'

'Mrs Chandler, our guest at the moment, manages without one.'

'Ah, well, I think she does most of the time, but I did dress Mrs Chandler's hair when the Montagues were here at the weekend.'

Emma turned around and took Juliet's hands in hers. 'I shall endeavour not to exclude you in future, but perhaps you can show me a simple way of putting my hair up myself – should I ever need to.' She added with a smile.

*

As soon as everyone had left for their respective days out, Emma unhooked the key to the Dower Lodge and told Joe that was where she was heading. Once outside, she headed for the barley field, running along the wild flower hedge, towards Ben's workshop, unaware that Sydney Pearson was watching her go with a heavy heart.

*

Ben was cutting a piece of leather when she arrived at his door and he felt a tingle at her presence. Jimmy Trevorrow was helping Ben, holding the leather still as he carved the shape of the pommel from the huge hide. As soon as the piece was cut, Jimmy made himself scarce, bowing to Emma as he left.

'Jimmy is a very perceptive young boy,' Emma smiled, 'he seems to know when to make himself scarce.

'For all his youth, he ribs me mercilessly about you.'

'Does he, really?'

'He thinks I should marry you.'

Emma stepped forward until they were close enough to feel the heat from each other's bodies. 'I think you should marry me too.'

Ben's lips curled into a wide smile.

'May I have a drink of water, the day is very hot,' she asked.

Breaking their gaze, he drew her a glass of water and watched her drink.

With her thirst quenched, she said, 'I see you watch me drink, and yesterday, at the picnic you watched me eat.'

'I'm just trying to memorise everything you do, for when I cannot be with you.'

'Do you think about me when I'm not here then?'

He laughed softly. 'Constantly.'

'When you're in bed?' she teased.

He quirked an eyebrow. 'That's a very leading question for a lady to ask.'

'Do you though?'

'Of course, I do, and now you have stirred something within me with your naughty question, I demand that you kiss me,' he whispered.

Her eyes glittered with happiness at the request.

Slowly wrapping his arms around her tiny waist, he kissed her full on the lips. The touch of her mouth roused within him a passion so fierce, he had to step away from her.

'What's the matter, Ben?'

'You know not what you do to me. Your kiss makes me want more – and more I cannot have. Now, it's gone very warm in here, don't you think. Do you have time to go for a walk?'

'I do.'

He grabbed a rug, locked his door and they walked as far as the stream to find a cool, green shady place to sit. Ben lay the rug on the ground and without embarrassment, Emma knelt down beside him and kissed him again. They lay back under the dappled shade of an ash tree. Ben wrapped his arm around her shoulder, so that she was laid close beside him.

She rested her hand on his chest, and with his shirt open to three buttons, he felt her fingers touch the soft hairs there.

'You're going to drive me wild with desire if you keep touching my skin as you do,' he said kissing the top of her hair.

'I'm sorry.' She moved her fingers away, but he grabbed her hand and placed it back where it was.

'I long to touch your skin, Em, but it would be wildly inappropriate before we wed,' he whispered.

'Then we must bring about our wedding day as soon as we have spoken to my parents.'

Ben sighed. 'I fear they will not take kindly to our union. Your papa will not want me for a son-in-law.'

'Papa loves me, I'm sure when he sees how much in love we are, he will only want the best for me.'

'And the best will not be me! I'm not your equal in class.'

'People cross the class divide all the time now, Ben – times are changing. We have the Chandlers staying with us at the moment, and Mrs Chandler was once a maid at the manor and now she is married to a gentleman – so it does happen. We must be positive about it. If my parents did not think you were a suitable friend for me, they would not have arranged for you to hire that suit for my ball. They like you - they always have, and when they see you all dressed up next week, well, you will look as good as any gentleman there. It will be fresh in their minds when we speak to them on my return from Italy. Oh goodness, I hate to think that I must leave you.'

'Don't remind me, I don't want you to go either.' He tightened his embrace.

'I'm sure all will be well, Ben.'

'And if it's not, are you still prepared to leave everything and come away with me?'

'Yes, and we'll live happily ever after.'

'Spoken like a true author. But you know, you may find the reality of living the way I live less romantic when you do,' he said seriously.

'You doubt my commitment to you?'

'No, Em, I don't, it's just... Well, my pa is worried about his position on the estate. You know, the house, his job. He's worried that if your father does not take kindly to our union, his position on the estate will become untenable.'

Emma sat up. 'Oh! Does your father know about us then?'

Ben sat up too. 'Emma, both my parents know how I feel about you. God knows, I've worn my heart on my sleeve for you for the past two years.'

'Only two years?' she teased.

'You know I've always liked you, but I've been hopelessly in love with you for two years and clearly unable to hide it!'

'Darling, Ben,' she kissed him, 'I'm sure your pa has nothing to worry about. If Papa is displeased with us, he certainly would not take his anger out on your father – he respects him too much.'

'I hope you're right.'

*

They spent a lazy hour lounging by the stream before they reluctantly made for home. Emma knew her mama would return from Boynton Manor around three that afternoon and would be bound to question Joe Treen as to Emma's whereabouts.

As they emerged from the clearing, Amara flew down from where she had perched high in the trees, to escort the couple on the journey.

'Ben, can we ride out to Dollar Cove tomorrow. I was listening to Jessie and Daniel Chandler speaking about how they first met each other on the dunes, because they shared a passion for swimming. It sounded so romantic - I should like to spend some time alone by the sea with you.'

'It's risky, Emma. We might be seen!' Ben protested.

'Dollar Cove is one of the quieter beaches in the summer. People prefer to spend their leisure days at Poldhu where refreshments are served.'

The thought of swimming and spending a few hours alone with Emma swayed him. 'Alright,' he smiled, 'I shall saddle my trusty steed Cara and meet you there at noon. It's not often I ride out on her for leisure purposes.'

'That's settled then. Don't walk back to the stile with me, in case your pa is about,' Emma suggested, 'there is no point in rocking the boat before we have the oars in place.'

They stopped at the end of the saddlery yard, glanced around to make sure no one was watching, before sharing a passionate kiss goodbye.

*

High on the roof of Polhormon farmhouse, Guy was repairing a hole in the thatch caused by some rooks. It was the flash of the white dove in flight which first caught his eye, and a moment later he saw something that he wished he hadn't seen - Emma and Ben's embrace.

*

That evening everyone gathered for pre-dinner drinks, and when Emma entered, her mama inspected her closely to make sure she hadn't tried to dress herself again. As they sat on the large comfortable sofas, enjoying an aperitif, there was much talk about the upcoming ball.

'Peter and I have been thinking,' Sarah said brightly, 'this is the first ball we've held in this house – except for the New Year's Eve parties of course, but they're on a different scale. The manor is not large so it doesn't really work as a venue for a ball, however a ball we shall have, for the first of our beloved debutante daughters.' She smiled at Emma, and then turned to Jessie and Daniel. 'As we have your children here, the Trevellicks are bringing their three children, Guy and Ellie will fetch their youngest, and as Lowenna and Theo have two small children, we thought we could do something special for them. They're all too young to attend the ball - and may well get under the feet of the grownups, so, I've had a word with Cook and she's happy to do a little party buffet for the younger children, which will be served in the conservatory adjoining the French drawing room. They will be able to hear the music from there, so they can have a little dance amongst themselves and be able to have a sneak-peek at the grownups in their ballgowns from the window.'

'What a lovely idea.' Jessie enthused.

Emma agreed. 'Thank you, Mama that *is* a lovely thing to do. Loveday in particular will be overjoyed,' she added.

'I shall tell Lowenna later,' Sarah said.

*

Later that night when everyone had made their way to their beds, Joe Treen set off around the manor to check that all the doors and windows were locked and secure. He'd watched Jessie and Daniel walk hand in hand up the stairs to their bedroom with a longing heart. Jessie would be gone from his life again in a week's time and he probably wouldn't see her again for a long time. It was probably for the best – her presence here had unsettled him, and there was no doubt that it had unsettled Juliet too by the way the conversation had gone earlier. He was pondering on that very conversation, as he climbed the stairs to bed, but he dared not get his hopes up just yet – perhaps it was just a spur of the moment thing Juliet had said to him earlier.

Juliet was normally asleep when he retired, but tonight she was propped up with her pillows reading.

It struck him that he normally got undressed in semi darkness so as not to wake her, but tonight the lamp was on and he felt strangely self-conscious.

'Shall I turn the lamp off?' he asked hopefully.

'Not yet.' She put down her book and smiled softly.

He took off his jacket, undid his collar and tie and pulled his shirt over his head. He glanced at Juliet – she was still watching him. He washed quickly and pulled on his nightshirt, before undoing his trousers whilst he sat on the side of the bed.

'Shall I turn the lamp off now?' he asked and she nodded.

He snuggled down into the bedcovers and turned to face Juliet. From the sifted light of the moon shining through the gap in the curtains, he could see her face illuminated.

'Are you tired?' she asked.

'Bone tired – why, do you want to talk a while?'

'Not talk, no.' She shifted closer, and wound her arm over him, making his body feel a sudden frisson of desire.

'Do you…. want me?' he asked.

'Yes.'

'Are you sure?'

'Yes,' she breathed.

Very tentatively, his hand touched her face and he began to kiss her gently on the neck. She pulled open the ribbon to her nightshift for him, and his lips moved slowly down to her breasts. He felt her shiver. 'You must tell me if you want me to stop,' he whispered.

'I won't ask you to stop,' she murmured, 'I want you to make love to me.'

'Oh, Juliet, my love, my love,' he whispered, and the years of waiting peeled away.

24

At breakfast the next morning, Jessie and Daniel were discussing their plans for the rest of the week. They were going to Poldhu beach that day and were taking with them Theo and Lowenna's children.

'Nanny can have a rest again today, because tomorrow she's promised to look after our children while we visit some very special parts of the coastline,' Jessie said, exchanging a loving smile with Daniel.

'It's very kind of you to take the Trevail children,' Sarah said. 'It's good for them to get out and about, though I think you must have had a busy day yesterday. I was speaking to Lowenna this morning, she said Loveday was exhausted when she returned yesterday teatime.'

'Yes, bless her,' Jessie smiled, 'she slept all the way home!'

'It's the fresh sea air,' Peter answered. 'It tires everyone out.'

*

The Chandlers weren't the only ones enjoying the sea air that day. Leaving their horses to graze in the field near Winwaloe Church at Gunwalloe, Emma and Ben shared a magical day on the beach. They ran out of the sea laughing and flopped down on their towels to dry in the sun.

'I'll have to move into the shade when I'm dry, otherwise Mama will go mad if she finds I've exposed my face to the sun.'

'And we don't want anything to spoil your beautiful face.' Ben kissed her.

Emma laughed. 'I do hope you've brought me one of your famous doorstep sandwiches.'

'I wouldn't dare not,' he grinned, producing a rather scrumptious cheese and pickle sandwich from his bag.

'You certainly know the way to a lady's heart. Maybe we could have these for our wedding breakfast.'

'I'm sure your parents expected you to have delicate cucumber sandwiches and a society wedding. But if you marry me…..'

'If I marry you, I shall be the happiest of brides.'

'I just feel sorry that I'll deprive you of a fabulous wedding day,' Ben said honestly.

'You'll be depriving me of nothing. A small country wedding will be perfect for us.'

He shook his head. 'I have no idea how we'll live, Emma. As I said before, I earn only enough to keep myself warm and fed.'

'Please do not worry, Ben. I have some savings, and I'm entitled to a sum of money from the estate, either on my wedding day or when I turn twenty-one - whichever comes first. It will keep us very well provided for.'

'So, I'm to be a kept man, am I?'

'I think the words "With all my worldly goods I thee endow" are spoken in the marriage ceremony,' she said, kissing him on the lips.

They lay back under the clear blue Cornish sky, then Ben asked presently, 'I take it Henry will be coming to the ball?'

'I'm afraid so,' she sighed. 'As this is my special ball, and he's shown an interest in me, he's expected to be there.'

'It's that interest I'm worried about. There is something about him that I don't trust.'

'I told you, Henry and I made a pact, to pretend to be interested in each other, until the last ball of the season – which will be the Queen Mary's ball just after I return from Italy. After that, we will break from each other. Now let's settle down and enjoy some time together, for I fear this will be the last time this week. I'll be quite busy with Mama finalising the ball, but of course, I'll be in your arms on Friday when I dance with you.'

*

Lyndon and Jenna FitzSimmons normally resided at the Trevarno Estate near Helston, but they had decided to stay over at Loe House – their weekend retreat - just for a couple of days following the garden party. Loe House sat in a prime position, perched on a cliff at Halzephron, just a short walk over from Dollar Cove.

Jenna had driven over to Winwaloe Church that day, to place some flowers on her late husband's grave, when a couple of people in the next field caught her eye as they readied their horses for mounting. She paused from arranging the flowers in the vase when she realised the couple were none other than Lady Emma Dunstan and the young man Jenna had mistakenly thought was her beau the other day. When she saw their passionate embrace, she knew then that she had not been mistaken – these two young people did love each other.

*

On Thursday evening, Lowenna was fastening the buttons on Sarah's gown of peach and cream silk. The dress Sarah would wear the next evening at the ball was a dark blue satin gown and was hanging from the picture rail along with Emma's dress, which was pale blue georgette - a colour that would match her eyes.

'How have your children enjoyed having some playmates this week, Lowenna?'

'They've loved it, my lady, though I've never seen Loveday so tired. I'm beginning to think I keep her too restricted. We should take her out more, let her walk and run free on the beach, perhaps her life here is too sedentary. She loves Stella though, it's nice for her to have another girl of similar age to play with. They giggle continually.'

'It's a shame Jessie and Daniel's son is only three, Lowenna. Poor Denny, doesn't have anyone to play with.'

'Well, you say that, and he was shy at first of Marina, but she soon brought him round and they're as thick as thieves now.' She smiled, finishing Sarah's hair with a flourish.

'Are they looking forward to their little private ball?'

'Oh, yes, they've spoken of nothing else since you announced it. I've been busy making a dress out of one of my old Sunday dresses for Loveday. The Chandler girls have such nice dresses, I want Loveday to have something nice too.'

'Goodness, Lowenna, we can do better than that. I shall speak to Nanny later – we have a trunk full of dresses in the attic that my girls have long grown out of.'

Lowenna put her hand to her heart. 'Oh, my lady - Loveday will be over the moon.'

*

On Friday the 11th of August, Ben stood in Thomas' Tailors and Outfitters in Coinage Street, Helston, dressed in a full evening suit, bow tie and black patent shoes. As a finishing touch, the outfitter folded a silk handkerchief and tucked it into his top pocket. 'And voila,' he said.

The outfitter stood back and Ben turned to look in the mirror, aghast at his refection. The saying "The suit maketh the man" sprang to mind. He certainly cut a fine figure.

'I suspect Sir will be visiting the barber later?' It was a suggestion from the outfitter, rather than a question.

Ben glanced at his unruly hair in the mirror. In truth he hadn't given his hair a thought, but now looking at his reflection, he knew exactly where he was heading next. 'Of course.'

An hour later, he'd been shaved and had his hair trimmed and with the suit in a calico bag over his arm, he boarded the wagon to Cury Cross Lanes.

The weather was changing for the worse. A cool front had moved in overnight and the barometer had indicated a storm before Ben had left home for Helston. He hoped for the sake of the farmers that it would only be a short summer storm and that their crops would not suffer.

It was five o clock, the ball started at seven, so Ben decided there was no point in going all the way home to Polhormon - he would bathe and change at his parent's house on the estate – that way he only had a short walk to the manor and would avoid soiling his suit.

As he walked down the long workmen's entrance drive, he noted there were already several cars parked along the front of the manor. No doubt belonging to the ones staying overnight after the ball. Although he was to be part of the grand party that night, Ben still thought fit to take the right-hand road which skirted the back of the manor to his parent's house. He did not like to flaunt his good fortune at being invited to this prestigious event.

*

Ben wasn't the only person on the estate getting ready to dress in clothes they didn't normally wear. When Loveday was presented with a pink net and chiffon party dress, she started to cry.

'Don't you like it?' Lowenna asked, thinking of all the hours she and Nanny had spent on adjusting the dress to fit her daughter.

'Yes,' she said rubbing her eyes with her knuckles. 'It's lovely,' she cried, 'It's a real ballgown.'

'Yes it is. It belonged to Lady Emma, and she wanted you to have it.'

Gathering the dress to her heart, she sobbed happy tears.

'Now come on, put it on and I'll pleat your hair.'

Once she was ready, Theo and Lowenna stepped back and clasped hands, marvelling at the delight on their pretty daughter's face.

'You've ruined her now, my love,' Theo teased. 'She'll expect to be dressed like this forever.'

'If we had the money she would be,' Lowenna sighed.

*

After bathing, Ben dressed in the smart suit, and had to ask his father to fix his bow tie. Once he'd smoothed down his hair, he was ready to join the ball. As he came downstairs, his ma gasped and shot her hand to her mouth.

'Well, my boy, you certainly scrub up well,' his pa said proudly.

'Mind your p's and q's now,' his ma said, brushing an imaginary piece of lint from one of Ben's sleeves.

'I will, Ma. I'll not let you down, I promise.' He kissed Ma warmly on the cheek, shook Pa's hand, then set off. What he didn't see was, his parents clutching each other's hands, worried sick as to where this was all leading to.

Walking along the kitchen courtyard to enter via the kitchen door, was stopped in his tracks when several excited children spilled out of Theo and Lowenna's cottage, making their way across the courtyard to the back entrance of the conservatory.

'Ben!' Loveday squealed and ran up to him.

'Loveday!' Lowenna shouted, 'mind Ben's nice suit now.' But she had already jumped into his arms. 'Sorry,' Lowenna mouthed.

Ben just smiled and hitched the child up on his hip. 'Hello, Princess. My, but you're going to be the belle of the ball, aren't you?'

'Yes,' she said confidently, patting her dress. 'I'm wearing Lady Emma's party dress.'

'So you are,' he said putting her back down. 'Off you pop then and have a good time.'

'You look nice too. Will you be dancing with me?' she asked.

'I think I have to dance with all the grownups this evening.'

She sighed. 'I can't wait to grow up, so I can dance with you.'

'And dance with you I will, one day,' he said happily.

'Come on, Loveday.' Lowenna gestured and then turned and smiled at Ben, 'You really do look very stylish, Ben. Have a lovely evening.'

As Ben moved through the manor, card games were being played in the library, and those who did not wish to dance had congregated in the Jacobean drawing room. When Ben approached the French drawing room, which was acting as a ballroom, there was nobody dancing yet, but music was playing from a small bandstand in the corner.

Emma spotted Ben as soon as he came through the door to the ballroom, and her face lit with love for him as she rushed up and pressed a dance card into his hand. She looked wonderful, dressed in a flowing pale blue gown with tall ostrich feathers in her hair.

'Ben, you look magnificent.' She cast an admiring look at him.

'It's flipping uncomfortable, but for you, I will endure the discomfort. I must say, you look gorgeous too.'

She giggled girlishly. 'Now, I have marked my dance card for the second dance - it's a waltz, is that alright?'

'Perfect, who gets the first dance with you?'

Emma pulled a face. 'Henry I'm afraid. It's protocol, as he has declared himself to me.'

Ben felt a curl of unease at this statement.

'Are there any more dances you're good at, we have five waltzes, six polkas, five quadrilles, one schottische, and one mazurka.'

'Goodness, are you planning on dancing them all?'

'Of course, it's my ball!'

'Well, I only know the waltz, so put me down for another one of those with you, and I shall watch you dance the others.'

Her beautiful face lit as she smiled at him. 'I'll put you down for three waltzes. I want you in my arms as many times as possible.' She quickly marked her dance card, just as the band announced that the ball would commence.

Henry was at their side in an instant. 'Lady Emma, this is our dance,' he said sternly, and moved her swiftly away from Ben.

*

As the polka began, Henry's face was set hard, but Emma was determined not to ask what was wrong. He seemed to be constantly irritated with everything.

About half a minute into the dance, he bared his teeth. 'What the hell is the estate steward's son doing here?' he demanded.

'You know why. Ben is our friend. I've told you often enough, he has a right to be here - he is practically family.'

'Well, I hope your dance card is full, so you don't have to put up with the undignified way he'll dance. I don't suppose he's ever danced more than a country reel.'

'Ben is more than capable of dancing, actually, and for your information, we have three dances marked at the moment.'

'You're making a fool of yourself you know, and a fool of me.'

'Don't be so ridiculous, Henry.'

'Dressing him up is fooling no one you know. A monkey in silk is a monkey no less.'

'Stop being so hateful, Henry. You are becoming quite a bore you know.' He pinched the skin on her back and she yelped. 'That hurt.'

'I'm just warning you, behave like a lady. We have a front to keep up and my parents are watching your every move – as am I.'

'This is my ball! I shall do whatever I like, and dance with whomsoever I please.'

*

Ben couldn't be sure, but he suspected Henry was displeased with him being at this ball – they did not look at all happy dancing together. In fact, they looked as though they were arguing! When they finished dancing, Henry led Emma over to his parents, instead of leading her back to Ben.

Agnes came to stand beside Ben. 'Shall we dance?' she asked. 'I feel a bit out of my depth with all these dandies,' she laughed. 'I need someone sturdy and grounded to lead me round this dance floor.'

'It will be my pleasure, I'm engaged for the next one with Emma, but I would love to after that.' They marked the fifth dance on their cards which was another waltz.

The band made ready for the next dance - time for Ben to collect Emma. He strode over to where she was standing with Henry, bowed to the Montagues who looked down their noses at him, and took Emma's hand to lead her away.

As they positioned themselves in each other's arms, they smiled at each other and began to dance as though they were the only people in the room.

*

The Bickfords and the FitzSimmons watched with interest as Emma danced with Ben.

'You know, I think Peter and Sarah are mistaken about who Emma would prefer to marry,' Jenna said to Hillary.

'I think you're right, Jenna. I do not like the Montagues at all — they look far too pleased with themselves. Having said that, Lady Montague looks fit to burst with indignation at the moment. Methinks she does not agree with the classes mixing. Oh hush, they're coming over to stand here,' Hillary whispered.

*

The Montagues moved around the periphery of the dancefloor, watching as Ben and Emma danced around the room. Emma was laughing brightly at something he'd said to her.

'What the devil is going on there, Henry?' his father asked.

'I'm not sure,' Henry answered through gritted teeth.

'Well, I think It's time you spoke to Dunstan about what we agreed, don't you?'

Henry narrowed his eyes as he watched Emma laughing with that commoner. 'I think you're right, father.'

Lady Montague fanned herself and glanced around to see if anyone else was appalled at the spectacle of Emma and Ben laughing and dancing, and noticed Hillary Bickford nearby smiling at them.

Moving closer to Hillary she said haughtily to her, 'Would you just look at Lady Emma. I fear her unchecked actions are outrageously wild - and not at all ladylike!'

Hillary shot her a cool look. 'Neither is your moustache,' she answered, before walking away, leaving Lady Montague, speechless, deeply affronted and fanning herself furiously.

25

When Emma and Ben's dance ended, Ben led her over to where Zack was standing, who was looking equally uncomfortable in his evening suit.

Fancy having to wear one of these suits every evening,' Zack said easing his collar.

'I admit, I do feel as though I have a washboard down my shirt,' Ben agreed. 'Are you not dancing, Zack?'

'I'm not much of a dancer – but I like the music. You two look very cosy together.'

Both Emma and Ben smiled a secret smile.

'Well, you make a fine couple.'

'We are working on becoming a couple,' Emma said happily.

'Yes, Ben mentioned that you're planning a life together. Good luck to you both, you deserve each other.'

Any more mention of their upcoming plans were halted when Agnes came up behind them.

'Zack. Daniel wants a word with you in the Jacobean drawing room.'

'We'll come with you and get a drink,' Emma said, 'I have a bye on my dance card and I'm parched.'

*

The children's party in the conservatory was in full swing, sandwiches and jelly were eaten and lemonade spilt down dresses and shirts, but the squeals of glee made for a jolly affair. Periodically the children gathered at the French dining room glass doors and surreptitiously pulled the lace curtains aside to peep on the grownups as they danced around the room.

Lowenna glanced at her daughter who had curled up on one of the conservatory chairs. The excitement of the evening seemed all too much for one little six-year-old.

*

There were several people in the Jacobean drawing room. Ellie was speaking to Jessie and Daniel, when Zack and the others joined them, Guy, however, was keeping company with Kit and Sophie in the other corner of the room.

Guy watched as Zack joined Jessie and Daniel, and saw his son shake his head when Daniel asked him something. Guy narrowed his eyes on seeing Daniel place a hand on Zack's shoulder, it looked as though he was urging Zack to do something of which he was shy.

'Damn the man for being here,' Guy muttered under his breath.

Kit turned and followed the direction Guy was looking. 'Guy, let it be.'

'I can't,' he hissed.

'You can, and you must.' Kit too could see the interaction between Zack and Daniel and knew exactly what he was urging him to do.

*

Zack felt a nervous flutter in his stomach at what Daniel was asking him to do and looked to his ma for guidance.

Ellie nodded to him. 'Daniel told me last week that you can play the piano, Zack, so I would like to hear you.'

'Zack doesn't just play, he has an extraordinary talent,' Daniel interjected.

Ellie smiled. 'Gosh! That is a compliment coming from you. You've certainly kept that quiet, Zack.' Zack just lowered his eyes.

'Play something,' Daniel encouraged, 'this is your chance to show your pa what you can do.'

'He won't like it,' Zack answered fearfully.

'How could he not. He will be so proud of you, I'm sure,' Daniel answered.

'Go on, Zack,' Ellie encouraged.

Zack looked nervously around the room – at least most of the people were in the ballroom, dancing. He glanced at the grand piano and sat in front of it. He could never resist the urge to play once his eyes had locked on the keys. He looked up at his pa who was watching him with a frown.

'What shall I play, Daniel?'

'Play the one you were playing when we first heard you. Debussy Clair de lune. It is a tune very close to our hearts, isn't it Jessie?'

'Yes, I remember you played it to me on your guitar in the dunes at Poldhu.'

Zack took a deep breath. 'Clair de lune it is then.' Zack stretched out his arms, flexed his fingers and started to play. The room fell quiet and everyone turned to listen, but Zack, lost in the music, had closed his eyes, to let his fingers dance upon the piano keys.

Debussy filled Zack's heart with joy as he played – he was lost to the world around him momentarily, until the slap of the palm of a hand on the top of the piano made Zack open his eyes.

Guy was standing beside him. Zack smiled but quickly realised the smile was not returned.

'Enough now, Zack,' Guy hissed, 'you're making a spectacle of yourself. No one is fooled that this is probably one of those pianos that play itself. So, enough!'

Zack ceased playing abruptly - a prickle of embarrassment washing over him.

'Guy!' Ellie scolded, and came to stand protectively beside her son.

Daniel too stepped forward in Zack's defence. 'I can assure you, Guy, Zack *is* playing this piano.'

Guy narrowed his eyes at Daniel. 'I didn't ask for your interjection, Chandler, thank you very much. The daft lad has clearly fooled you too.'

Sarah, noting the altercation, quickly moved over to the piano, and gently put her hand on Guy's sleeve. 'Zack really *was* playing this instrument. We do not have a pianola – this is my original piano,' she assured him.

Guy looked around at the faces looking back at him. 'Then what trickery are you playing on me here then?' he demanded.

'There is no trickery, Guy,' Kit said, as he too joined the group around the piano. 'Zack is a very talented pianist.'

Guy flared his nostrils. 'I don't understand – how can this be. We do not own a piano.'

'But we do!' Kit said.

Guy spun around to face Kit, anger clearly getting the better of him. 'I thought he was staying with you to do his apprenticeship, not wasting his time taking piano lessons.'

'Zack has had no piano lessons; I can assure you. He's just picked it up listening to Selene's piano teacher,' Kit answered calmly.

'He would have bettered his time buckling down to what he was there for. It's no wonder he's a useless cabinetmaker.'

Wounded by these words, Zack bit down on his lip to stem the emotion building in his throat.

'Zack is not useless, Guy,' Kit defended him, 'he's a very good carpenter. But Guy, listen, Daniel believes that Zack has a real gift for music. He'd like to help him on his path to becoming a great pianist.'

'Does he now!' Guy narrowed his eyes at Daniel. 'And who the hell do you think you are, coming here, filling my son's head with fantastical ideas?' he snarled.

Daniel stood his ground, determined to fight Zack's cause in this. 'They are not fantastical ideas. Zack has a rare talent, and an ear for music that cannot be taught. I'm an alumni of the Royal College of Music - one of the world's great conservatoires - who train gifted musicians from all over the world for international careers as performers, conductors, and composers. Zack is on par with someone who is near to graduation from such a college. He could come to London, stay with us, and I could introduce him to some very influential people…..'

'No!' Guy cut Daniel off.

'Please, Guy, give him this chance,' Daniel asked.

'Don't please Guy me,' he said through gritted teeth. 'I said no! Now keep out of my family's business - you've done enough damage already. Come away, Ellie.' He grabbed her arm and beckoned her away from the group.

*

The room had fallen silent, and quickly apologising to Daniel, Ellie followed Guy to the far end of the room.

'Guy that was incredibly rude of you,' Ellie hissed when they were out of earshot of everyone.

Guy drained his glass and said nothing.

'Guy, won't you even think about it?' she pleaded, glancing back at her only son, being comforted with a pat on the back by Daniel.

'I said no.' He looked around the room. 'Chandler has obviously turned your head too with this nonsense. I think we should go home.'

'No, Guy, we're not going. Stop being so churlish.'

The argument ceased when Peter chinked a glass to gain everyone's attention.

'Ladies and Gentlemen. If you could all return to the ballroom. There is to be an announcement.'

'What announcement, darling? Sarah asked moving to Peter's side.

'You'll see in a moment, Sarah. Emma, come with me,' Peter beckoned his daughter.

Guy, disgruntled that he could not leave now, reluctantly filed out of the drawing room, through the now empty library and into the ballroom, but he was seriously vexed.

*

Peter made his way to the bandstand where the musicians were playing, Sarah too stood by his side, looking slightly bewildered.

'Well, this is the penultimate ball of my eldest daughter's very successful season. Goodness, but it makes me feel old to know I have children old enough now to marry.' Peter smiled gently at Emma and she frowned back at him. 'And it seems, my darling daughter has found herself a suitor – well, rather more than a suitor. Henry, the stage is yours.'

As he beckoned Henry forward, Emma saw Henry's face beam as he left his parents side, suddenly she felt sick, and her eyes darted towards Ben. She saw him flash a look of panic back to her – both knowing what was about to occur.

Peter put his arm around Henry. 'This splendid chap here, came to me to ask for my daughter's hand in marriage, and as our ancient families are well known to each other, I couldn't be happier.'

Sarah, must have noted the shock and confusion on Emma's face, because Emma heard her whisper, '*Peter,* is Emma aware of this?'

'Hush, darling, all will be well, you'll see. Henry…' He gestured for him to speak.

'My dear, Emma, come, don't be shy.' Henry beckoned her forward.

Some women clasped their hands in glee, as the men raised their glasses, but Emma felt herself flush up to the roots of her hair with anger. Shooting another desperate glance towards Ben, try as she might, her legs would not move from the spot, until her papa came down to bring her forward.

'You make me very proud, my darling girl. You have chosen well. Clever girl,' Peter whispered as he kissed his daughter's cheek.

Realising it would be inordinately rude of her to flee the room at this very moment - which had been her first reaction, she looked at her papa who was beaming with delight, and then glanced at her mama for help.

Sarah stepped forward and whispered, 'Peter, I think this is not the time.' But Peter held his hand up to halt her protest.

Henry got down on one knee, holding up an enormous sapphire and diamond engagement ring in a velvet box, he said, 'Lady Emma Dunstan, will you do me the honour of becoming my wife.'

Before Henry had finished the words, Ben had left the room.

*

Ben could hear the cheers from the ballroom, as he ran blindly through the manor, exiting via the kitchen door. Ignoring the wind and rain as it buffeted him ferociously, he burst into his parent's cottage, pulled off his jacket, bow tie and shirt, then kicked off his patent leather shoes and pushed the trousers down his legs. Changing into his normal clothes, he ran heedlessly across the muddy fields towards the saddlery. When he got there, he could not stop, so set off down the valley to the cove, as far away from Bochym Manor as he could get.

At Poldhu, the sea was wild and angry, stormy grey rollers crashed onto the beach in a frenzy of white foam.

'No!' he roared into the wind, as the rain and sea spray soaked him through to the skin. 'No!' he cried again, and his empty eyes looked out to a future of loneliness, without his beloved Emma.

*

Back in the ballroom and after an endless round of congratulations, Emma was seething. She had not, in fact, said yes to Henry's proposal. Henry had pulled her hand to his, rammed the ring on her finger and shouted, "She said yes!" and the room erupted.

Emma's papa kissed her warmly. 'You have made me very happy, Emma. This union will be such a good one, not only for the family, but for you, my darling girl. Henry is a fine young gentleman, and he has assured me of his love for you, and that you will want for nothing. Well done, darling.'

Emma's heart imploded, not only at this farce unfolding, but at the fact Ben had witnessed it, and now she could not find him. As soon as she was able, she pulled Henry to one side, and whilst managing to keep a smile on her face, she hissed, 'What are you doing? We agreed that it wouldn't come to this.'

'Sorry, Emma, but father could see I was wavering every time your name was mentioned. You also didn't help yourself by so blatantly flirting with your commoner in front of my parents. So, father gave me an ultimatum. Either I marry you to check your wayward ways and settle down, or I lose my inheritance.' He gave a rather supercilious smile. 'And I have no intention of living on fresh air - as *you* seemed to have been planning on doing,' he raised an eyebrow. 'So, I spoke to your father last week, when you were with your low born friends, and now my dear, you're stuck with me. Cheer up and don't worry, I won't bother you much, and you will live a life of luxury in Devon. So, it won't all be bad.'

Emma was furious. 'I shall break the engagement in the morning. I shall tell my parents that I didn't actually say yes and that it was you who said it!'

'But you didn't say no either.'

'I could hardly shame you in front of everyone, could I? You left me with an untenable dilemma.'

'Well, it's too late to break it, Emma. It's signed and sealed now. I can tell you - and you must not tell anyone that I've told you - but our fathers have done a highly secretive and lucrative deal on the strength of this union. Your father has already invested a great deal of money, probably because he could see you and I were in agreement at a forthcoming marriage. If you break this engagement, your father will be financially ruined!'

Emma was momentarily speechless. 'Papa! Financially ruined! Oh, God! But I don't want to be married,' she said through gritted teeth.

'Correction, you don't want to be married to me, you mean. Come, come, Emma, you didn't think a saddler could give you any sort of life, did you?' As I said, methinks you were under a serious threat of your own ruin by throwing yourself at that commoner. No, my dear, you have saved me. I in turn have saved you from yourself. Together we'll save your father from ruin. Come, let's dance.' He tugged her back onto the dancefloor.

*

Zack had lain awake for most of the night. He'd left the ball shortly after Ben, but had not found him at home, so made his morose way to his parent's house. Ben was no doubt licking his own wounds somewhere. It hadn't been a great night for either of them!

Although he got soaked to the skin, he hadn't wanted to face the ride home with Pa, for he did not know if he could keep his promise to Ma not to press the issue of him going to London.

'I'll speak to him presently, Zack,' his ma had promised, though she didn't sound confident that she could sway Pa.

Zack had heard the others come in some two hours later, noting a prickly atmosphere in the house that was never normally there. He was sorry he had caused a rift between his parents, and that, coupled with his own misery, laid heavy on his heart.

26

When everyone had finally gone from the ball, which, after Henry's proposal and Ben's exit, held no joy for Emma, she took herself to her room, peeled off her beautiful dress, and left it in a pile on the floor.

Juliet came in, picked up the dress, turned down Emma's bed, but said nothing – there were no words which would help her mistress's distress. She helped Emma into her nightdress, gently laid a hand on Emma's shoulder in solidarity, before leaving her to her despair.

The clock in her bedroom, ticked away the hours, but Emma did not go to bed. Instead, she endured hours of discomfort, sat on the cold window seat of her bedroom, while the yawning empty future spread out before her. Her stomach churned - sick and desolate. The storm howled outside, as she rested her forehead on the cold window frame, looking out into the darkness. In her mind's eye she thought of the estate grounds where she had played with Ben throughout her childhood. The gardens where they had picked the first daffodils to present to their respective mothers. Beyond the garden, the stream which fed the boating lake down by the arboretum, bubbled over stones in the dappled sunlight while they fished for minnows and caught frogs. She virtually climbed the stile to the fields where all the children had helped with the harvest. Later at the harvest supper, Ben and Emma had first danced together. Her thoughts took her to the saddlery beyond the estate – the place which smelt of leather, where her beloved Ben worked, and where his white dove watched over them, as they first declared their love for each other.

'Ben,' she whispered into the darkness - the palm of her warm hand marking the window. The shock of the engagement still rendered her unable to shed a tear – the pain of losing Ben forever, cut so deep she could hardly breathe. How could Papa have taken financial risks at the expense of her happiness?

Truly believing she would never smile again, she vowed to endure this sense of loss and loneliness forever as a tribute to Ben – the real love of her life.

*

After sitting for an age on the wind-swept beach at Poldhu, Ben's limbs felt stiff and cold as he made his lonely way back home to his empty house. Peeling his wet clothes from his body, he lay on his bed and fell into a deep dreamless sleep. He woke at dawn as desolate as when he had gone to sleep. The storm outside had passed – the storm within him would take a great deal longer to abate – he knew that. He got up and lit the oil lamps, rousing Amara from her slumber. He put the kettle on the range to make tea that he had no desire to drink, fed his horse Cara, then without breaking his own fast, sat at his table and dropped his head into his hands desolately.

A noise outside made him raise his head - footsteps made his heart skip a beat. 'Emma?'

'It's Zack I'm afraid, old friend,' he said, popping his head around the door.

Ben slumped back down in his seat.

'I know it's early, but I couldn't sleep, so I came to see how you are.'

Ben turned his devastated face to meet his friends gaze. 'As you see.'

'Ben, I must tell you, Emma was distraught after you left - she had no idea that was going to happen last night. I left soon after you, but I couldn't find you. I spoke to Agnes when she came home last night. She'd managed to speak to Emma after the announcement. Apparently, Emma never said yes to his proposal – Henry just shouted that she had.'

Ben's heart accelerated. 'So, is there hope for us?'

'Well,' Zack sighed, 'here's the thing. Emma was so angry, she told Henry she would break the engagement today, but he told her she couldn't. Apparently their fathers have sealed some sort of financial deal on their union, which will lead to His Lordship's ruin if the pact is broken.'

Ben reached out his hands across the table and flexed his fingers as though grasping at some invisible help. 'So, Emma must go along with it.'

'We both know, Emma would not let her papa lose the estate - she loves him too much.'

He sighed, and murmured, 'Yesterday she loved me – we were making plans.'

'I'm sorry, Ben. If it's any consolation, she has no love for Henry. It's a crying shame that she's not allowed to follow her heart and marry for love.'

Ben's eyes flickered. 'I must let her go; I know that now.'

'I'm sorry, my friend.'

Ben nodded resignedly. 'What about you, Zack. I heard you play last night – you were magnificent.'

Zack flopped down in the chair opposite. 'Pa didn't think so - he won't speak of it. It seems neither of us can have what we truly want.'

'Perhaps you can,' Ben suggested.

'How?'

'If Daniel Chandler is offering to help you, you should let him – go with him.'

'I can't, he and Aunt Jessie are leaving today for London.'

'Then go independently. You're almost eighteen now. You said yourself it's a shame Emma has to do what her papa wishes, and we both know it will make her unhappy. Don't let your pa be the cause for *your* enduring unhappiness. Emma would say the same thing to you too,' he added sadly.

*

When Zack had taken his leave, Ben knew that Emma must be in turmoil. He must do the only decent thing – he must release them both from this sorrow – and let her go. He began to write his last letter to her.

*

Word of Lady Emma's engagement spread far and wide around Mullion and the surrounding area. A society wedding was on the cards, such has had not been seen for many a year.

At Polhormon Farm, the dairymaids were indoors milking, as the storm, although it had passed, had left the weather inclement. Merial Barnstock listened to the news of the engagement with interest. Undoubtedly, Ben would be upset today, perhaps he would welcome a shoulder to cry on, perhaps he wouldn't turn her away today, this was her chance to show him she could be a balm for his wounded soul.

*

With his letter written, Ben set off to the stile by the barley field. There he placed his letter for Emma to collect. He knew Henry and his parents had been staying that night at the manor, so he wasn't sure when she would pick it up, so he put a stone on top of the stile – their way of indicating a letter was waiting. Hopefully, she would find it soon, and it would settle Emma's mind that he understood, but he also wanted her to know how much she was loved. Perhaps she could endure a marriage to Henry, knowing there would always be someone in the world who loved her unequivocally.

*

Emma had no appetite for breakfast that morning – feeling nothing but a great void of emptiness inside. Standing at the window in the Jacobean drawing room, she could hear her parents in the breakfast room making plans with the Montagues - plans she had no desire to be part of, or undertake. The raindrops from a recent shower trickled down the windowpane as she looked unseeing at the vista beyond. Her heart was sore, and when she thought of her empty future, a great sadness built in her chest swelling into her throat.

It was a flash of a red neckerchief which caught her eye, and at first she thought her mind was playing tricks – but no, she could clearly see Ben walking away from the stile. That meant only one thing - a letter in the hidey hole! Though knowing there could never be a reconciliation with Ben now, and whether his letter contained his disappointment in her, the longing to read the words his beautiful hands had written to her for one last time, overpowered all other feelings. Slipping out of the drawing room, she took the exit by the kitchen side door and ran across the kitchen courtyard before anyone could stop her.

*

The servants were going about their business in the kitchen when they heard the side door bang shut. They all craned their heads to see who had exited.

Knowing how devastated she was by this engagement, Juliet whispered to Joe. 'Do you think she's running away?'

'I think not.'

'She was like a wound spring this morning when I helped her dress.'

'It looks like she has just uncoiled,' Joe said seriously.

'Poor Lady Emma,' Juliet breathed, and the others in the kitchen gave a collective agreement. 'This match with Henry Montague is not based on love.'

'I'm afraid that's how these old families work. Love may blossom between them,' Mrs Blair said to lighten the mood of her kitchen.

'There is a lot to be said for being working class. At least we can make our own choices in life,' Dorothy said, smiling at her husband David.

'I'll second that,' Juliet said smiling sweetly at Joe.

*

Ben had gone by the time Emma reached the stile, so she climbed over, scuffing her indoor shoes, and moved the heavy stone. Once she'd retrieved the letter from the wall she held it to her heart, as though it was Ben she was holding.

222

'What have you there then? A love letter perhaps?' Henry said appearing over the stile.

Emma pushed the letter down the front of her dress and walked past Henry without speaking to him.

He grabbed her arm. 'I saw him too, you know - lover boy. I wondered what he was doing, and now I know. There will be none of this when we're married – I won't tolerate it, do you hear?' He tightened his grip on her arm. 'And we *will* be married – there is nothing more certain, unless you want your father to lose all this. Our parents are gleefully arranging everything as we speak.'

Emma held her tongue, because what she wanted to say, should never pass a lady's lips. She wrenched her arm from him and ran back to the manor the way she had come - knowing that he would not follow her through the servants door.

Back in her bedroom, she pulled the letter from where it lay next to her heart, and ripped it open.

My dearest, darling Emma.

The hand that wrote this letter trembles with sadness, for this is the day I have dreaded.

Emma's eyes teared up - but she read on.

Zack explained what happened after I left, and why you must marry Henry now. I respect your father, I always have done, and I can only assume he was in financial dire straits, to make such a business deal at the expense of your happiness. So, for his sake and yours, it is my greatest wish, my darling, that you try to settle with Henry. He will undoubtedly give you a better life – one you deserve. Though it breaks my heart to let you go, let you go I must. So, I release you, my darling girl, from any attachment we had. Our dream of building a future together, is now, and perhaps always was, a pipe dream. But know this, Emma, I love you with all my heart - a heart that will surely break the day you marry Henry. There has never been anybody other than you for me, and I know there never, ever will be. The few stolen moments we have spent together this summer, have made precious memories that I shall keep until my dying day, though it is those memories which makes this parting more painful.

It grieves me now that the hand that writes this letter will never touch your beautiful face again. It will never open the door to find you standing smiling at the other side, or that my fingers will never gently push a soft curl of your golden hair back from where it has fallen. Instead, these hands must channel everything back into my work, but without doubt they will wipe the tears which I shall inevitably shed for the loss of you.

You know you have my heart forever, so, my darling girl, go gently in life, think of me sometimes, and keep my heart safe.

Ever yours, Ben.

'Ben, my Ben,' she sobbed, clutching the letter to her heart, as she wept into her pillow.

27

When Ben returned from delivering the letter, Jimmy was waiting for him, and from the look on his face, was deeply concerned about something.

'You have a visitor,' Jimmy whispered.

'Who?'

'It's Merial. I followed her up here after milking. She's been in there for half an hour.'

Ben clenched his teeth - she was the very last person he wanted to see today. 'Thanks, Jimmy.'

'Ben, I'm sorry about Lady Emma.'

'You and me both, Jimmy - you and me both. Right, I'll go and deal with my unwanted visitor, but Jimmy....'

'Yes, Ben?'

'Can you stay close and keep an ear out, she's unpredictable, and I simply don't trust her.'

'I'll watch from the high window in the stable.'

'Good man.'

Ben entered the workshop and it took a few moments for his eyes to adjust to the gloom of the room. Jimmy must have been mistaken because there was no sign of Merial. He began to relax, threw his coat over the chair, and walked to the kitchen to put the kettle on the stove. He turned to go and tell Jimmy to stand down, and it was then he saw the discarded clothes on the floor.

He wrenched back the curtain to his bedroom, almost pulling it from the rails, to find Merial in his bed, naked. Fury bubbled within him, and through the narrow aperture of his lips, he hissed at her, 'Get out of my bed, and out of my house this instant.'

'Oh, but Ben,' she whined, 'I've come to ease your sorrow. I know you've been disappointed. We've all heard about.....the engagement. Let me help you to forget her, I won't disappoint you, Ben,' she pouted, 'I won't disappoint you at all.'

Enraged, he dragged her from his bed. 'I said get out of my house – the sight of you makes me physically sick. You're a common hussy and the very last person on earth I would want in my bed. Now get away from me, and *keep* away from me.'

Merial stood by the bed, tears of humiliation and anger streaming down her face. 'You're no better than me, Ben Pearson, so don't think you are, and neither is your Lady Emma. She's the common hussy. I know you've been here with her alone, I know you've been with her in the long grass – there's probably a babe on the way. But you're not good enough to marry her, are you, Ben?' she spat, 'Is that why she's found herself a rich husband - to hide her disgrace? Well, if it is, it serves you right!'

Incensed, he grabbed her roughly by the arm, to drag her from where she was standing, but she shrugged him off, gathered her discarded clothes, and ran towards the front door, knocking her knee on the table leg as she went. She cried out in pain, and limped out of the door, as Ben slammed it behind her and locked it.

*

Merial stood in the front yard of the workshop, dressing as quickly as she could before anyone saw her. Her face scarlet with humiliation and her knee hot and swollen where she'd knocked it. Inspecting her arm, she found red wheals and no doubt bruises would follow by being so roughly manhandled. She limped down the path towards home. Ben would be sorry he did that.

*

Jimmy had watched the whole scenario unfold from his vantage point. He scrambled down the ladder and opened the barn door, catching sight, to his delight, Merial's bare bottom as she pulled on her clothes. He stifled a laugh and stepped back into the shadows.

Once she was out of sight, Jimmy knocked on the workshop door.

'It's only me, Ben. She's gone now.'

Ben unlocked the door.

'Blimey,' Jimmy said wide-eyed, 'I aint never seen a woman without clothes before!'

Ben laughed, despite his anger. 'I'm sorry your tender eyes witnessed that. But that is one woman I *never* want to see naked again.'

'Shall I tell Pa she's been here. He'll dismiss her in a heartbeat.'

'No, It'll just cause more trouble. I think I made myself pretty clear that she is not wanted here.' He nudged Jimmy. 'Hey, thanks for staying close by.'

'It was my pleasure,' he grinned. 'I'll have to scoot now, I've chores to do before I have a midday shift at The Old Inn.'

'Off you go then.'

Jimmy plunged his hands deep into his pockets and said, 'Are you alright though, Ben.'

Ben knew exactly what he meant and shrugged. 'I suppose I'll have to be.'

*

Henry had gone to play on the billiard table, though the game failed to cool his anger that Ben dared to continue his attachment to Emma, even now they were engaged. After an hour of knocking the balls about furiously, he rang for Joe.

'Tell my valet to bring my hat and coat, and have father's car brought round to the front for me,' he barked the order.

'Are you going far, my lord,' Joe asked.

'The Old Inn, Mullion. I'd be obliged if you can direct me to it.'

With directions lodged firmly in his head, and a fifty-pound note in his pocket. Henry drove to Mullion, with one thing only on his mind - to part that bloody saddler from Emma, once and for all.'

*

When Jimmy walked into The Old Inn, he received a clip behind the ear from the landlord.

'You're late.'

Jimmy rubbed his boxed ear and glanced at the clock he was one minute late!

'Get to work. The boats are in today – we'll be busy.'

As Jimmy collected the empty glasses, he noticed a toff sitting at the bar – not really the type who drank in this establishment, and certainly not on a day the fishing boats came in. Jimmy shrugged, put the glasses on the bar and went back to collect more. He smelt the Barnstock brothers before he saw them. They were fisherman just back from three days out at sea and stank as such. Jimmy watched with interest as the toff nodded to the brothers, then a moment later, the toff joined them at a table in the corner of the room. Curious, Jimmy busied himself near them.

'I want this done properly - you hear me?' Jimmy heard the toff say.

Bernard Barnstock grinned. 'We always do a proper job!'

'Make sure you do. That bastard broke my nose once. Here…'

Jimmy's jaw dropped when he saw the toff hand over a fifty-pound note.

'I shall expect that back in full if you don't fulfil the task – and rest assured I have ways of getting it back.'

Bernard grinned, but Barry Barnstock shifted uneasily on his seat as the toff stood up, put his hat on and left.

Suddenly Jimmy felt the landlord grab him by the ear and yank him towards the bar.

'Stop bloody nebbing and get on with your work, you lazy sod.'

*

The Chandlers took their leave shortly before luncheon, in order to avoid another meal spent in the company of the Montagues. Jessie had taken a great dislike to all of them, as they had to her, once they found out she'd been once a maid here.

'Thank you for having us, Sarah - it's been wonderful. Daniel is just gathering the children together.'

'Jessie, it has been a pleasure having you all here. You must all come back and stay with us again. And of course, you must come for the wedding, for Emma will be married from Bochym.'

'Sarah,' Jessie hesitated for a moment – she knew she would be speaking out of turn but speak she must, 'forgive me, as for Emma's marriage…..'

Sarah tipped her head questioningly.

'Perhaps you need to give Emma some time before you set a date. Call it intuition, but I don't think she is ready yet. I know she's your daughter, and you know her better than anyone else, but….'

Sarah placed her hand on Jessie sleeve. 'I agree with you, my intuition feels a delay is necessary too. The Montagues wanted a date before Christmas, but I've put my foot down and asked them to wait. I can assure you, Jessie, the wedding will not take place until we are absolutely certain she is happy.'

Jessie sighed with relief.

*

When they were all ready to go, Theo, Lowenna and their children, along with Juliet came to wave them goodbye, Sarah glanced at Joe Treen as he waved his old sweetheart off, instead of him looking sad at her departure, as she thought he would have done, he seemed to be beaming with happiness. Also, for the first time ever, Sarah witnessed a real tenderness between him and his wife Juliet. Perhaps Juliet had been a little in awe of the elusive Jessie, and they had got to know each other better now. Whatever the reason, the Treens looked happier now than they had ever done.

*

With Peter back in his office, the senior Montagues resting upstairs before luncheon, and Henry having returned from his drive, had now gone out for a walk, Sarah found she had a few minutes respite from everyone.

Sitting at her grand piano in the Jacobean drawing room, she thought of Zack sitting here last evening, and the revelation that he could play so professionally. She failed to understand Guy's refusal of Daniel's offer to take him to London to study music. Daniel had asked Peter to intervene with Guy before they left that morning, which Peter agreed to do. Everyone else could see that Zack was destined for bigger and better things than being a carpenter - everyone that was, except Guy!

While Sarah played a piece she knew off by heart, she glanced out of the window, to see her beautiful daughter walking forlornly down into the garden. After the excitement of her ball, Emma's mood seemed decidedly flat today. Perhaps it was down to an anti-climax, which often happened after a large event. She stopped playing, remembering what Jessie had said about Emma, she too was not completely convinced that Emma was entirely happy with this engagement, despite giving a show to her papa that she was.

*

Emma simply could not face another meal with the Montagues either, so took herself to bed before luncheon, sending word via Juliet to her parents that she didn't feel well.

Two minutes later, her parents came into her bedroom, not entirely convinced of her malaise.

'You must come down, Emma,' Peter protested. 'The Montagues have extended their stay another night so you can spend some time with Henry.'

'Wait a moment, Peter, to be honest, Emma has been out of sorts all morning – she hasn't eaten a thing,' Sarah said in her defence, as she sat on Emma's bed, placing her cool hand to Emma's forehead.

'I have a terrible headache. My tummy is upset and I feel dreadfully tired. Please excuse me to everyone,' Emma said pitifully.

'You probably drank too much champagne last night - I know I did!' Peter held his hand to his forehead.

'I genuinely think Emma is unwell, darling. The Montagues will understand,' Sarah answered firmly. 'Do we need to send for the doctor, Emma?'

Emma shook her head. *Not unless he can mend a broken heart.* 'I'm sure I will feel better tomorrow.'

*

Ben found he could not settle that day. What with losing Emma, and finding Merial in his bed, he was heartily sick of life. After stripping the bed of the sheets which bore traces of Merial's cheap scent, he paced the room in utter despair. In the end he could stand it no longer – he needed some fresh air.

Standing at the gate, he looked towards the sea, and then to the woods, undecided as to which path to take. Eventually, he took himself down to the woods to relive the heady happy days of not so very long ago, where they all, as children, had played until that unfortunate incident next to the oak tree.

He thought about that tree, and was sad and happy in equal measure that it had been uprooted by the April storm. He'd hated walking past it – for what had happened there could never be erased from his mind. Now though, with its roots exposed to the elements, and vast chunks of the trunk having been cut off for drying, to either burn or make furniture with, that dreadful location from four years ago had altered beyond recognition.

Still, like William, he didn't like to go near anymore, and skirted the area to collect dry twigs and branches for the fire. It was only by chance that a figure caught his eye, and when he saw who it was, he dropped the armful of wood. Keeping well out of sight, Ben watched as Henry Montague walked up to the oak tree, and when he heard him laugh heartily, a chill ran down Ben's spine, a chill he believed would never thaw. There, at that moment, he knew why his intuition had told him that he had met Henry before. Without picking up the wood he'd collected, he rushed back home, grabbed a sheet of writing paper, and penned one of the most important letters he'd ever written to William.

Dear Will,

I know we said we would never speak of this again, but I feel I must, as I think something very bad is about to happen.............

28

With a fifty-pound note to their name, Bernard and Barry Barnstock were in high spirits as they sat waiting for their supper to be served.

'How are we going to go about teaching Ben Pearson a lesson he'll never forget, Bernard?' Barry whispered.

'I don't know yet. I'm thinking on it.' Bernard was happy to act as hit man for the toff – he'd done it before and got away with it, for no rewards.

Merial limped in to serve dinner with her mother. As she put the plates down before them, her bruises were clearly visible on her wrist.

Bernard grabbed her arm and pushed her sleeve higher. 'What's all this then?'

'Ben Pearson hurt me,' she said sulkily.

'What?'

'Ben Pearson did it, when he manhandled me out of the workshop, and then pushed me out onto the path, making me fall to my knees.'

Bernard's face flushed with anger. 'When was this?'

'This afternoon.' She sniffed tearfully. 'I called on him, after I heard the news about Lady Emma's engagement. I thought a kind word from me might give me a chance of winning back his heart now that *she* was out of the way.'

'And?' he glowered.

'Well, he invited me in,' she lowered her eyes demurely,' but he took my offer of kindness and friendship the wrong way. He tried to make me lay with him,' she blinked a couple of times, glancing between her brothers. 'Of course, I wouldn't let him do that afore we're wed, so he was really rough with me when I refused.' She rubbed her bruised arm. 'And then... then he shouted at me, and called me a common hussy, then threw me out, that's when I hurt my leg,' she sniffed back a pathetic sob. 'It really hurts.'

Bernard gritted his teeth. 'Did anyone else see this happen?'

'No one was about......I felt quite alone and frightened.'

He grabbed her again by the wrist. 'Tell no one else what happened, you hear me? You just fell, alright?'

She squealed as he nipped at her skin, but nodded.

'We'll deal with Pearson. So, keep your trap shut!'

She nodded again, and as she limped away, awarded herself a smile – a beating from her brothers would teach Ben Pearson a lesson.

*

The Old Inn at Mullion was busy that night when Bernard and Barry Barnstock fought their way into the bar. They looked around for a table, found one with someone sitting at it, and told him to clear off.

After a couple of pints, Barry asked, 'So, do you have a plan, Bernard?'

'Aye, I do. We'll do the toff's bidding, and administer some justice for our Merial in one go.' Bernard's nostrils flared. 'I'll be damned if I'm going to let him get away with trying to force his way onto Merial only to toss her out like a used rag. Well, he'll not be messing about with any other young women again, high class or working class - you mark my words.'

Jimmy Trevorrow, who was working the evening shift in the bar, was clearing a table near the Barnstock brothers, stilled on hearing Merial's name - she'd obviously told a big fat lie to her brothers. He pushed himself into the dark alcove by the fire to listen some more.

Barry's lip curled cruelly. 'So, what do you propose?'

'Didn't our Merial say that he was cut up over Lady Emma's engagement?'

Barry nodded.

'Well, perhaps, he might go mad with jealousy tonight, perhaps he'll smash his workshop up, before throwing himself off a cliff.'

'Do you think he'll do that?' Barry asked in astonishment.

'No, you daft dork! That's what *we'll* do to him. We'll make it look like he's gone berserk before committing suicide.'

'Brilliant!' Barry grinned, bearing his rotting teeth.

'We'll have to be careful this time, do a proper job, like we promised - there are still rumblings about what we supposedly did to Harry Pine – though Pine never dare squeal on us.'

'What do you say, Barry, are you ready to teach Pearson a lesson he'll never recover from?'

'I say yes.' Barry cracked his knuckles.

'Come on, drink up, we'll need to fetch the horses.'

Jimmy felt his mouth dry - they were clearly going to kill Ben! He'd have to go and warn him, and be swift about it.

'Jimmy! Either collect those glasses or bugger off without pay,' the landlord barked at him. So, Jimmy put the tray on the bar and ran like the wind towards Polhormon Saddlery.

*

Ben had slept very little the night before and was bone tired. He was just contemplating his bed when he heard frantic hammering on his door. He glanced at the clock, ten to ten – who the devil was knocking at this time?

'Ben,' Jimmy gasped breathlessly, 'let me in, quick.'

Ben opened the door and Jimmy spilled in. 'What's wrong, what is it?'

'The Barnstock brothers are coming. I overheard them in the inn – they mean to kill you.'

'What? What for?'

'I think they have been paid to do it, but they're angry about what happened this afternoon. I think Merial's told a tall tale. Ben, they're planning to throw you off a cliff!'

Before Ben could think or do anything, the thunder of hooves could be heard outside, and every nerve in his body prickled a warning. Ben was strong and fit, but to take on both the brothers was going to be a task.

'Jimmy, go out the back door, get your father to come and help.'

Jimmy nodded and fled into the kitchen just as the Barnstock brothers kicked the front door open. He ran to the back door, but it was locked! He frantically looked around for the key but could not find it. He could hear things being smashed and furniture upturned as he searched the drawers and cupboards for the key, but all to no avail.

Ben circled the table as the brothers smashed their way through the room.

'Been free with our Merial have you?'

'No!'

'That's not what she says. Bruised and battered she is.'

Ben swallowed hard.

'Not denying that, are you?'

'I've done nothing wrong, except extract her from my workshop when she came flaunting herself at me.'

'Ah, yes! She's not good enough for the likes of you now, is she? You like the taste of a rich girl so we've heard.'

'Just get out.' Ben felt the panic rising. *Where the hell was Jimmy with help?*

Bernard upended the table, sending it crashing into Ben's legs, flooring him momentarily. Out of the corner of his eye, Ben saw Amara lift from her perch and flutter in panic. 'No!' he shouted when Bernard swiped at her with a chair and she fell to the ground in a scatter of feathers. Bernard laughed as he watched the bird roll under the bookcase, and then launched himself at Ben, punching him full in the face. When Ben tried to fight back, Barry hit him over the head with a chair. Stunned, Ben could see nothing but stars, as Bernard started to kick him in the ribs that had so recently healed.

Vomit rose, choking him as it lodged in his throat. A kick in the back dislodged it and he vomited over his rug. A kick in the groin made him throw up again and his body screamed in pain as Barnstock's boot rained down on him.

'Is he done for yet?' Ben heard Barry ask.

'He will be in a second.'

A moment later, a sickening blow to his head rendered him unconscious.

Jimmy was frantic and knew he must make a run for it to get help, but when he pulled the curtain aside, Barry was heading towards the kitchen, smashing things in his wake. He knew he couldn't help Ben now, but he also knew where they were going to take him, and decided that as soon as the brothers had gone, he'd go and fetch help. In his panic, Jimmy looked for somewhere to hide, and eyed the dresser cupboard. Cowering inside the cramped cupboard, Jimmy knew that as sure as eggs is eggs, if they found him, and knew he'd been a witness, they would do for him too. Peeping through the lattice woodwork of the cupboard door, Jimmy froze when Barry pulled the curtain to the kitchen down, revealing the devastation of the workshop. He bit his lip to stop himself from crying as he witnessed Bernard kicking and punching Ben who lay lifeless on the floor. He watched in horror, as Barry cleared the contents of the kitchen shelves to the floor, pulled the books from the bookcase and then suddenly upended the dresser, trapping Jimmy in his tiny tomb.

Everything fell silent for a moment, and Jimmy held his ragged breath long enough to hear Ben being dragged outside.

'Grab his legs and sling him over the back of my horse. A fall down a cliff will finish him off,' Bernard instructed. 'As I say, Barry, folks will just think he's gone mad with jealousy, over Lady Emma marrying someone else, and wrecked this place before killing himself. No one will pin this on us and we'll get away scot-free.'

Jimmy waited with bated breath in the stifling cupboard until the sound of hooves cantered away before he tried to kick his way out of the cramped cupboard. He tried and tried but he could not dislodge any of the sides of the cupboard.

'Pa!' he yelled, again and again until his voice turned hoarse. But nobody heard, and nobody came, and Jimmy cried with despair.

*

Ben regained consciousness when he landed on the soft mossy mound of grass. The fall had winded him, but the smell of fresh air, and the roaring sound of the sea brought him to his senses. His body cried out in pain whenever he took a breath, so he tried not to move. At first he thought he was alone, until someone grabbed his feet to drag him across the ground. Frantically he dug his fingernails into the earth to try and get some purchase, but could find none.

'Pick him up your end – I can't do this alone,' he heard a voice say.

Thank God! Ben thought, *someone had found him, help had arrived!* Whoever it was though, they were having a struggle to shift him. If only he could help. He realised he must have bitten his tongue, because he couldn't form any words, so he groaned and tried to wriggle free to help himself.

'He's coming to,' the voice said, as Ben felt the grip under his arms tighten and so too around his feet.

The noise of the sea began to roar in his ears as the wind buffeted his body - they were too close to the edge. *Oh, Christ!* he thought, *we're too close to the edge!* Then he felt it - the pendulum motion of being swung back and forth. He struggled furiously, as laughter rang out over the cliffs, a moment later he was falling in mid-air. His stomach heaved, as though it jumped into his throat, and then his body hit the first jutting rock and then another, each impact broke another bone in his body as he twisted and turned as he tumbled down the cliff. Almost in slow motion, sandstone rubble pelted him, the sound of the wind whistling in his ears grew ever louder, more bones cracked and flesh tore from his body, until the nauseating thud of impact stopped him dead and then Ben heard no more.

*

Merial was awoken by the sound of horses. Minutes later, her brothers came indoors in high spirits. Merial frowned, it was gone eleven. The Old Inn closed at ten thirty, and it was only a short walk, so she wondered where they'd been on horseback.

She heard them climb the stairs, laughing. "That'll teach him to slight our Merial," Bernard said, as they parted ways, slamming bedroom doors in their wake.

Merial smiled and snuggled down back into the covers.

29

Ben woke with a gasp, and through a slit in his right eye, could see it was still dark. The sea was splashing at his hot broken face, no doubt deciding whether to swallow him up and take him to a watery death. He was cold, so very cold. Numb at first to the pain of his broken body, until he tried to move and a tremendous pain wracked through him, as bone by broken bone introduced itself to his senses. For some reason he felt the need to wiggle his fingers and toes and when he did, the rock he was laying on gave way and he fell again, just far enough to land him on his back this time. Precariously close to the sea now as he tasted salty water, it was then he realised he could not close his mouth. His teeth appeared to no longer meet, and all he could smell and taste was blood. His body was grotesquely twisted at forty-five degrees, but there was no urge to move again. *You're a dead man*, a voice in his head whispered, as he drifted back into the void he hoped with bring death.

*

As dawn broke, Merial was awake, though enjoying a brief lie in that morning. It was her day off from milking, and she was glad of the rest, her knee still hurt from where she fell yesterday. She jumped when Bernard rattled on her bedroom door.

'Get your lazy backside out of bed. I need you to scrub our boots, they're caked with mud.'

'Clean your own boots, you lazy sod,' she uttered under her breath, and then pushed the covers away. It didn't do to annoy Bernard.

*

Ben had woken again as daybreak split the sky. He had no idea how long he'd lain broken on the rocks, except that it must have been several hours, as the last time he'd seen a clock, it had been ten to ten. He'd closed his eyes to his fate seemingly hours ago, how the hell was he still alive all these hours after being thrown off this cliff? Jimmy! Where was Jimmy and the help he was meant to bring? Where was Emma when he needed her smile and soft hands to comfort him? All gone. Everyone had deserted him.

In the cold light of day, through the narrow slit of his eyes, he saw again that his legs were pointing up the cliff at alarming angles. His clothes were shredded, and he had bones coming out of his thigh, ankle, and elbow. The horrendous pain from his hip, suggested that too was broken. Blood-stained saliva ran in a constant stream from his gaping mouth – he couldn't have felt more wretched. No one could come back from such injuries, nobody could withstand this, and mend again, besides, no one would find him, and if they did, he would undoubtedly be dead.

*

Emma stood with her parents that morning to see Henry and his parents off as they took early leave from Bochym Manor to set off on their journey to Devon.

'We'll see you very soon, Henry,' Peter said brightly as he waved the Montagues off.

Emma sincerely hoped they would not, she had never been so glad to see the back of their visitors, and was heartily sick of pretending that all was well with this forthcoming marriage.

As the family turned to walk indoors, Sarah smiled at Joe Treen. 'Thank you, and the staff for everything. I'll be in the garden if anyone wants me.'

'Yes, my lady.'

'Emma,' her Papa addressed her. 'I think that now you're engaged to be married, you must act as such. If you leave the grounds for any reason, you must either take a groom with you if you're riding, or Juliet if you're visiting anyone. Treen, I'll leave it to you to inform the groom, and ask Mrs Johnson to release Juliet as and when necessary.'

Emma's fingernails cut into her palms. She looked to her mama for help, but Sarah just smiled gently. 'You're papa is right, Emma.'

A great sense of indignation rose within her, but she was sensible to stay silent on the matter.

*

Emma ran upstairs to her room and stood behind the door, waiting for her anger to abate. This was Henry's doing - this constriction of her movements. Well, she was having none of it! While she had laid abed yesterday, she'd made the decision that she would refuse to set a date for the wedding until she was at least twenty years old. She would state that at eighteen she felt too immature to settle down. Her mama would agree to that, she was sure – she had said herself that there was no rush for a wedding. Emma had no business head, but thought that the delay in a marriage would mean that *if* her father had invested money with Lord Montague on the strength of the union, he would hopefully see a return for his investment by the time it became apparent that no wedding was ever going to happen – thus averting his financial ruin. Oh, goodness! She clasped her hands to her face, she had no idea the estate was in such financially dire straits, she just hoped that her plan would eventually work and they wouldn't lose this lovely house on the strength of it.

She needed to speak to Ben about what she planned to do. Yes, his lovely letter had released her from any attachment they had made, but she was not about to throw away hope that they would one day be together – it just wouldn't be anytime soon.

Without the help of Juliet, she dressed in her riding habit, carried her boots down the stairs so as not to make a noise, and slipped out through the laundry exit, putting her fingers to her lips when Izzy the laundry maid saw her. This way, Joe Treen wouldn't see her, and alert a groom to help her saddle her horse and consequently ride out with her. Skirting around to the stables, she quietly harnessed Saffron, threw on the saddle and fastened the girth, all the while softly whispering to her to keep her calm. She mounted Saffron inside and grimaced at every clip clop as they set off to the stable gates. It was then she saw the flustered groom run out from the stable lads hut.

'Give me a moment, my lady, I'll saddle Jet,' he said, trying to finish the toast he was eating.

'It's fine, I'm not going far, just a canter around the estate,' she said and set off like the wind before he could say another word.

*

It was the sound of a dog barking which roused Ben back into his agonising world. He opened one eye and groaned pitifully as the dog stood over him, barking and salivating. Perhaps, just perhaps this dog had an owner, Ben thought, and he would be found, and he would not die on this precipice.

'Flynn, Flynn, get down here,' a voice commanded. 'Don't make me come up there for you,' the voice warned.

Oh, God, please come up for him, Ben prayed, but the dog left his side and hope once again faded.

*

On Poldhu beach, Flynn returned to its owner and his lead was attached, but the dog was determined not to budge and began to bark again in the direction of Ben.

'For goodness' sake, Flynn. What is it?'

'Hello, Alan, what's amiss with Flynn?' Tobias Williams asked, as he and his wife Meg joined him on the beach.

Alan shook his head. 'He's seen something up there.'

'Here, hold on to these, Meg.' He handed over the scruffy little terriers to his wife. 'I'll go and look.'

'Be careful, Tobias, those rocks are slippery,' Alan said.

Taking little heed of the warning, Tobias scrambled over the rocks until he saw what looked like a pile of wet rags, 'Oh Christ,' he muttered to himself, 'a body.' He'd been a policeman in his day and fished many a bloated person from the sea.

'What is it?' Alan shouted.

'A body, I think.' Tobias moved nearer, expecting the usual stench of decay to hit his nostrils, and then he heard a guttural moan, harsh, raspy, and almost inaudible.

Tobias's eyes widened and quickly rushed to Ben's side, almost slipping on the slimy rocks underfoot. 'Jesus, are you alive, mate?'

When Ben emitted another groan, Tobias scrambled back down the rocks.

'We need the police, and an ambulance, and some strong men. It looks like someone has fallen off the cliff – he's badly hurt.'

'Who is it – is he local?' Meg asked.

'I don't recognise him. He's had a terrible battering.'

'I'll take the wagon up to Mullion and get the constable, he'll phone for an ambulance,' Meg offered, 'I'll alert Guy and Ryan on the way to come and help.'

Tobias nodded. 'We need to fetch the board from behind the tearoom, the one we use for rescuing holidaymakers from the sea. Then I'll go back up to him - the poor bugger looks like he's been there a while.'

Soon, Guy, Zack and Ryan had joined them on the beach, so too had Ellie and Betsy. Tobias scrambled back up the rocks to Ben, while the others carried the board over the slippery rocks after him.

It's alright mate,' Tobias said when he got to Ben, 'help is coming.'

*

Emma dismounted outside the saddlery to find Farmer David Trevorrow approaching. Her heart fell a little – her plan to see Ben alone scuppered.

'Good morning to you, my lady,' David Trevorrow doffed his hat.' May I offer congratulations from me and my good lady wife on your engagement.'

'Thank you, Mr Trevorrow,' Emma said jadedly. 'Are you here to see Ben?'

'Well, I'm looking for our Jimmy actually, have you seen him? He's been out all night. The Mrs is frantic with worry, we've only just realised he didn't come home to bed last night. I thought perhaps he might be here with Ben - he spends most of his time here now - though he never spends the night out normally!'

'Let's see then, shall we?' Emma knocked on the door and they both waited. When no one came, Emma said, 'It's quite early, Ben may not be up yet, perhaps if you tried the door, just in case he is in a state of undress.'

David turned the knob, and the door opened, but as he stepped through, he gasped audibly. 'Oh, good God, whatever has happened in here?'

Emma was behind him in an instant, both standing open mouthed at the devastation of Ben's furniture, upturned, and broken. It was then they heard a frantic knocking sound.

'Ben, Ben, is that you? Where are you?' Emma shouted.

They followed the knocking until they found the dresser, which was laid face down, plates smashed all around it. Together they took one end of the dresser and righted it, and the knocking became fiercer. Emma bent down and opened the cupboard door and Jimmy spilled out onto the floor along with a strong smell of urine.

'Jimmy, what the devil were you doing in there?' his father asked as he lifted his son to his feet, but Jimmy's legs gave way after being cramped in the cupboard.

Jimmy's face was distraught and tried to speak, but his voice was hoarse from shouting all night, and his neck had a crick in it, which made him wince as he tried to straighten it.

Emma drew a glass of water from the tap and gave it to him to ease his throat.

'Oh, Pa. I was hiding,' he rasped, 'I heard the Barnstock brothers plotting to come and beat Ben up last night, so I ran here to warn him, but they were hot on my heels. Ben told me to come fetch you, but I couldn't get out - the back door was locked, I thought if they found me they would beat me too, so I climbed into the cupboard to hide from them.' He took another long drink of water and sobbed. 'I could hear them beating Ben, I heard him groaning in agony and then Barry Barnstock upturned the dresser and I was trapped inside. Oh, Pa,' great fat tears began to stream down Jimmy's face, 'it went quiet and I heard them drag Ben outside.'

David shook his head. 'Good God, why ever would they do this?'

Jimmy quickly proceeded to tell them all he had heard in The Old Inn, including the toff and the fifty-pound note. 'The toff said, "I want this done properly - do you hear me? And make sure you do - that bastard broke my nose once." Jimmy looked up at his pa. 'I don't know if that is important or not, or if they were talking about Ben - otherwise I would have come and told Ben yesterday afternoon!'

David patted his son to calm him. 'Tell me exactly what you heard the Barnstocks plotting.'

'Well, I think this is all something to do with Merial,' he sobbed, 'I think she told her brothers a great fat lie about what happened yesterday.'

'Why, what did happen yesterday, Son?'

Jimmy told them about Merial's visit to Ben and how Ben had asked him to keep watch while he dealt with her. He told them exactly what he'd seen - that Ben had found Merial naked in his bed, and that he threw her out. 'I think he might have bruised her arm, when he shoved her out of the workshop.'

'Oh!' David shot a worried glance at Emma.

'Who is Merial?' Emma asked.

'She's a milkmaid at my dairy – someone not to be trusted, she's been the bane of Ben's life, forever fawning at him, though the feelings were never reciprocated.'

'I think they've killed him, Pa!' Jimmy sobbed.

David patted his son to calm him. 'Why do you say that?'

'I heard Bernard say, "Grab his legs and sling him over the back of my horse. A fall down a cliff will finish him off. Folks will just think he's gone mad with jealousy, over Lady Emma marrying someone else, and wrecked this place before killing himself. No one will pin this on us and we'll get away scot-free." Jimmy looked up at Emma sheepishly.

Emma felt her face flush. 'Oh, good God!' Emma breathed, 'we must do something, quick! I'll ride to the police station, Mr Trevorrow,' she said tremulously. 'We need to get them to search the cliffs immediately.'

They followed her out to her horse, and David warned his son, 'Now Jimmy, for your own safety, do not breathe a word of what you've just told us until you've spoken to the police. Tell them everything mind. Even the bit about the fifty-pound note - it might be relevant.'

Emma mounted Saffron. 'I've known Ben all my life, Mr Trevorrow,' she said, 'and I've never known him to break anyone's nose!'

'Still, son, tell the police everything, just in case. Goodness but let's just hope we're not too late. Godspeed, my lady.'

30

Ben was delirious, drifting in and out of consciousness, he had lain on this rock for so long, he wasn't sure he could still feel pain – his body felt completely numb.

'We shouldn't really move him, Pa in case his back is broken,' Zack said.

'We can't leave him here until the ambulance gets here. He'll be a goner.'

As they carefully circled his broken body, trying to avert their eyes from the jutting splintered bones, they managed to wedge the board under his shoulders and drag him slowly from the rock. Ben was shivering with shock, and as they carefully picked up the board he screamed in agony with every movement.

When they neared the bottom of the rocks, the constable was waiting for them on the beach.

'Is he still alive?' the constable asked.

'Aye, just,' Tobias said.

'An ambulance is on its way.'

As they manoeuvred the board up the beach, Zack was nearest to Ben's head, and when the pain became unbearable, Ben's eyes snapped opened, and then they rolled back as though he was going to faint. Zack looked down, his step faltering, almost dropping his end of the board, he recognised those eyes immediately.

'Ben! Is that you, my friend?' Zack cried.

'Ben?' The policeman looked questioningly at Zack.

'It's Ben Pearson – the saddler.'

'Oh, good God, so it is,' Guy said.

*

Emma rode like the wind down to Mullion, only to find the police station unmanned. When a neighbour heard her knocking, she came out wiping her hands on her apron.

'The constable has gone out I'm afraid – some incident at Poldhu Head.'

Emma felt every nerve in her body stand alert. 'Thank you,' she shouted as she pulled her horse to the mounting steps and set off to Poldhu as fast as Saffron would carry her. As she turned up towards Poldhu Head, she looked down, and noticed people on the beach – lots of people. Pulling her horse to a halt she took in the scene and her spine chilled when she saw they were carrying a body on a stretcher.

'Ben!' she screamed, but the wind caught her words. She galloped back down the hill, turning swiftly onto the dunes, just as the ambulance pulled up.

'No, no, no, no!' Emma slid from her horse, leaving it untethered, as she ran to the stretcher the four men were carrying. 'Ben,' she cried, clamping her hand to her head in anguish. 'Is he alive?' She looked frantically at the men carrying him.

'He's in a very bad way, Emma,' Ellie said, grasping her by the arms to pull her away. 'Let them take him to the ambulance.

'Oh, my goodness, Ellie,' Emma sobbed.

The constable approached Emma and said, 'We think he slipped down the cliff - his body is completely broken.'

Emma grabbed the constables sleeve. 'May I have a word please,' she said, pulling him out of earshot of everyone. 'Ben didn't slip!'

'Now, now, what's all this then?' The constable asked.

'I've just come from Ben's workshop and the place has been turned upside down – it's in a terrible mess. David Trevorrow and I found young Jimmy Trevorrow trapped in a cupboard. He said the Barnstock brothers came and attacked Ben last night.'

'I see,' the constable straightened his shoulders, 'and do the Barnstocks know they were being watched?'

'Jimmy says not, but he couldn't get out of the cupboard to alert anyone.'

'Right,' the constable narrowed his eyes, 'I'll go and speak to Ben's parents to tell them what has happened, and then I'll go and see the lad. Can you keep this information to yourself, my lady. I don't want the perpetrators to get wind that we know anything just yet.'

*

Ben was being transferred to a proper stretcher by the ambulance men, he'd been given a sizable injection of laudanum to keep him asleep and pain free in readiness for the journey. Emma watched as they placed him carefully in the ambulance, and had to be stopped from hitching her skirts up to get in with him.

'Emma,' Ellie pulled on her arm, 'let them take him.'

'But I need to go with him, he needs someone with him,' she turned her distraught face to Ellie, 'he might die!'

'He's in good hands, Emma. You must let them take him so they can treat him. Come with me. I'll make you a cup of tea.'

'I don't want tea,' Emma cried, as the ambulance set off up Poldhu Hill. 'I want to go with Ben!' Emma crumpled to the sand and sobbed broken-heartedly into her hands.

Guy came to help Ellie lift Emma back onto her feet.

'Come on, Emma, let Ellie look after you,' Guy said gently. 'Zack, can you get Emma's horse and tether it in the stable, please.'

*

Ellie sat Emma down at one of the tables and set about making her a cup of sweet tea, all the while glancing sympathetically at the distraught, dirty, dishevelled girl - her face streaming with tears. Everyone knew how close Emma was to Ben, so Ellie could understand her distress.

Pouring the tea, Ellie said, 'Here, drink this.'

'He's going to die, Ellie, he's going to die and I'm not with him!'

'Emma, you must think positively. He has survived all night on those rocks. Yes, his body is broken, but broken things can be mended, so you must not lose hope. I know you care deeply for Ben, but Emma, be strong for him and pray that he comes back from this. Now wipe your tears and sip your tea. Forgive me but I must get on,' Ellie said glancing at the clock, 'we open in an hour.'

'Of course, I'm sorry,' Emma's lip trembled again and more tears fell.

'You don't have to go yet. Stay there and gather yourself while I get the counter ready.'

*

Every time Emma tried to control her tears, more rolled down her cheeks. There was only one place she needed to be, and being sat here drinking sweet tea was not it. Picking up her cup she took it to the counter.

'Thank you, Ellie, but I must go.'

'Are you well enough to ride – you've had quite a shock. I can get Guy to take you home.'

'Ryan can ride your horse home,' Betsy added, 'he's good with horses.'

'No, thank you both for your kindness, I'll be fine.

'Take care then, and Emma…' Emma turned, 'Ben *will* get through this,' Ellie said gently.

Emma smiled, unconvinced.

Zack was with Saffron in the stables, and he took Emma into his arms. 'We have to be strong for him, Emma,' he said firmly.

'I'm trying,' she said, 'I'm trying.'

Once she had mounted, she rode like the wind back to Bochym Manor, slipped off the saddle with ease before the groom could help her, picked up her skirts and took the quicker route into the house through the kitchen side door.

'Treen, where is Papa?'

'Lady Emma, thank goodness you're here – your parents have been worried sick about you.'

They both turned as Sarah appeared from the drawing room, clearly shocked at Emma's dishevelled appearance.

'Mama,' she cried, where is Papa?'

'Emma, go to your room and tidy yourself, and then come and see me in the drawing room,' Sarah said sternly.

'But Mama, I need to see Papa. Ben Pearson has been found seriously injured at the bottom of a cliff and I need someone to take me to the hospital.'

'We are aware of what has happened to Ben,' Sarah said firmly. 'The police have been here and the Pearsons have gone to hospital.'

'But, Mama, I need to go too,' Emma pleaded.

'Emma!' Sarah scolded. 'Go and change. Treen, please send Juliet up to Lady Emma to assist her.'

'Yes, my lady.'

As Emma passed the school room, Anna came out to meet her. 'Ooh, Emma!'

Emma spun around. 'What?'

'You are in so much trouble for going out alone,' she whispered.

'That is the least of my worries at the moment,' Emma snapped.

'Anna! Come back and finish your French lesson this instant,' the governess shouted her back.

Anna rolled her eyes.

Emma had shed her riding habit before Juliet got to her and was pulling a travelling dress out of the wardrobe.'

'Let me help, my lady,' Juliet said.

'Juliet, we must hurry. I must find Papa. Ben has been badly hurt! I must….' Her face crumpled and she started to cry.

'Yes, my lady we've heard. We understand he was found at the bottom of a cliff.'

Emma nodded as her tears fell freely. 'I think he will die, Juliet.'

'Let's hope not, my lady,' she said sympathetically.

'Oh, Juliet,' she wiped the tears with the back of her hand, 'I must go to Papa and get him to take me to hospital - Ben will need me.'

'Let's get you dressed then,' Juliet said softly.

*

Both her parents were waiting for Emma in the drawing room, her Papa in particular looked very angry indeed. Nevertheless, Emma ran up to him.

'Papa, I'm sorry I went out alone, but can we address that another time. I need someone to drive me to hospital,' she pleaded. 'Ben was in a terrible state, every bone in his body was protruding through his flesh. His mouth, oh Mama, Papa, his mouth gaped open at such a strange angle, the ambulance men said his jaw was broken. I don't think he is going to survive, I really don't. I need to be with him.'

Peter held her by the arms and shook her gently. 'Emma, calm yourself,' he said sternly. 'You cannot go to the hospital. Ben's parents are with him, and as Pearson is a valued member of my staff here, I have offered to pay for whatever treatment he needs. Ben will get the best care. We have done all we can, for the moment.'

'But I want to be with him!'

'Enough, Emma. You're engaged to be married to Henry. You must leave this childhood friendship where it belongs, in the past. These declarations about needing to be with him, must stop. Whatever must the servants think of your unguarded comments.'

'I don't care what anyone thinks!'

'That, my dear, is blatantly obvious by your disregard for our authority. You may be eighteen, Emma, but until you are married you will obey your parent's wishes. So, If we say you must always take out a groom when riding, we mean it. I had a mind to dismiss Tomkins, the groom allocated to escort you, until Treen told me he followed you on bareback, but could not find where you had gone. I shall dock him a week's wage instead!'

'No, Papa, please don't do that. I sneaked out – it wasn't his fault, really it wasn't. I promise I will not do that again.' *If Ben died she would never need to do it again,* and with that thought she broke down in tears.

Sarah sat Emma down and put her arm around her. 'Darling, we were just worried about you, that's all,' she said.

'Well, I'm worried about Ben!'

'We know darling, we all are.'

'Then let me go to him,' she pleaded as she glanced between her parents.

'No, I say. You will be in the way. This is a time for his family only,' Peter said, 'and that is my *last* word on the matter. Now, I suggest you go and apologise to Tomkins – you have made a lot of trouble for him.'

'Please don't dock his wages, Papa. He's saving to get a cottage so he can marry his sweetheart.'

Both Sarah and Emma tipped their head beseechingly to Peter.

'Oh, very well, but if it happens again…'

'It won't, Papa, I promise.' She got up and flung her arms around his neck and kissed him.

'Now, darling, your Papa and I are going down to the tearoom at Poldhu. Papa wants to speak to Guy on a matter. I suggest you do as Papa says, and apologise to Tomkins and then go and lay down for a while – you've had a terrible shock, seeing what you've seen. As soon as we get word from the Pearsons we will let you know.'

*

Jimmy had given his statement to the police, and after milking, he and his father had returned to Ben's workshop. The police were there, trying to find evidence of what had happened. The place was in turmoil, every scrap of furniture had been damaged. It would take a lot of time to get it back spick and span, but David and Jimmy had vowed to do it for Ben – they just hoped he would survive to come back to the place. There was a letter on the table picked up off the floor by one of the officers - it was addressed to Lady Emma's brother, William, in Oxford, so Jimmy put it in his pocket. He'd put a stamp on it and send it for Ben – it was the least he could do.

'There is something under here,' an officer said reaching under the sideboard.' Ugh!' he retracted his hand. 'It's a dead bird!'

'Oh, no, Amara!' Jimmy scrambled to his knees, reached under the sideboard, and brought the dove out. She was filthy and dishevelled, but her little heart was still beating. 'She's still alive, Pa, but she's injured, what shall we do?'

David Trevorrow inspected the bird. 'Take him to Ryan Penrose - Betsy's husband from the tearoom. He's good with horses and most animals, he might know what is best for her.'

'It looks like it needs clubbing over the head to put it out of its misery,' one officer said grimly, but Jimmy cradled Amara close to his chest, and set off to Poldhu in search of Ryan.

31

By the time the Pearsons got to the hospital in Truro, Ben had been taken down to surgery. All they could do was pace the waiting room for news. They were both white with grief by the time the police arrived at the hospital two hours later.

'We believe there has been foul play.'

Rose gave a strangled cry.

'We have a witness, a young lad, who says he knows who did this and why. Now, as it's attempted murder, we're keeping our witness under wraps for now for his own safety.

'What on earth was the motive for such an attack?' Sydney asked aghast.

'It seems it was a crime of passion.'

'Pardon?'

The officer took a deep breath and began. 'Apparently Ben threw over a young woman from the village, when she believed there was a promise of marriage on the horizon.'

'What nonsense is this?' Sydney demanded.

'The young woman visited Ben often at his workshop - they had danced openly at the harvest dance and she told people they were walking out together.'

'Who is she? We know of no woman from the village - Ben never mentioned this!'

'I can't tell you at the moment, but the witness we have says her relationship is all fabricated. Undoubtedly she did visit Ben while he was working, but there was never any suggestion that they were sweethearts.'

'And...?' Sydney asked cautiously.

'Apparently a friend of Ben's - a lady friend whom Ben cared for very much, recently came back from abroad. The other woman, claiming to be Ben's sweetheart, felt put out that Ben was no longer interested in her.'

Sydney pursed his lips. 'You're painting a picture of Ben's life that we have no knowledge of. Go on.'

'We understand that the woman Ben cared for has recently got engaged to someone else.'

Sydney suddenly felt a curl of unease in his stomach. The newly engaged woman could only be one person – Lady Emma, but still he asked, 'And the name of this newly engaged woman is…..?'

'It is not for me to disclose such things – it was probably only a friendship. However, my witness says that everyone in the village knew Ben was upset by the news, so the young woman who had her nose pushed out, went to Ben to offer comfort, and by all accounts, her body, but Ben threw her out, and was quite rough as he did it.'

'This is preposterous - this sounds nothing like our Ben!'

'The young lad witnessed the whole thing. I understand Ben was quite forceful in removing the young woman from his workshop. The lad said he could see she had bruises on her arm where Ben had manhandled her. We believe she was upset and humiliated and must have told her family about what Ben had done to her - and as was her way, fabricated a story.'

'So, a member of her family did this and is still free to walk around after doing what he did to Ben?'

'There were two of them involved.'

'Then why have you not arrested them?'

'The thing is, Mr Pearson - we only have the young lad's account. He'd overheard two men in the inn, speaking about Ben trying to force himself onto their sister and then roughly manhandling her when she refused him, they said that Ben needed to be taught a lesson. The lad ran to warn Ben, but they were hot on his heels.' The constable then proceeded to tell them what had happened after that. 'The witness heard one of the assailants say…' he opened his notebook, 'and I quote, "A fall down a cliff will finish him off. Folks will just think he's gone mad with jealousy, over his lady friend marrying someone else, and wrecked this place before killing himself. No one will pin this on us and we'll get away scot-free." The police officer had omitted Lady Emma's name from the quote.

Sydney shuddered. 'And that's what they're doing – getting away scot-free! Damn it, man, why can you not arrest them?'

'We're going to interview them – as part of our ongoing investigation, but the thing is, Mr Pearson, the courts may not hear the young lad's story. He's a minor. We need to hear it from your son.'

'My son is in a critical condition; he's being operated on now.'

The policeman nodded. 'When he comes out of surgery, if you could call us, we'll come back and speak to him.'

'And if he doesn't survive?'

'Oh, Sydney don't,' Rose slumped down, dropped her head into her hands and sobbed.

'Well?' Sydney stared at the police officer.

'We would have to find more evidence.'

'Then find it, God damn it! If my son dies........' he paused suddenly tearing up, 'if he dies and those bastards get away with it, I will personally hunt them down and serve justice!' He wiped the tears with a swipe of his hands, but his body was trembling with rage.

When the police left, Sydney took his wife into his arms to comfort her, the action also helping to stem his own tremors.

'The young lad must be Jimmy Trevorrow,' Sydney breathed, 'he's always at the saddlery. If the police do not do their duty. I will get it out of Jimmy who has done this, I swear I will.'

'And damn Lady Emma for teasing our boy like that,' Rose snarled. 'We warned him' Sydney, didn't we? We warned him that no good would come of their burgeoning friendship. *This is all her fault.*'

'Now, now Rose, you can't blame Lady Emma for this.'

'I can and I do.' Rose folded her arms defiantly. 'Lady Emma bewitched him! Why else would this other woman, whoever she is, have felt put out by Lady Emma's attachment to our Ben. It's not right to promise a girl and then drop her when someone better comes along.'

'I do not believe that Ben promised this other girl anything – he would have told us,' Sydney said firmly.

'Well, *she* obviously did! To have her family do this to our boy! This is definitely all Lady Emma's fault. The flighty madam came home from Switzerland, turned Ben's world upside down again, then promptly got herself engaged to some rich man, leaving my poor boy broken hearted. I'm telling you, Sydney, she'd better not come anywhere near our Ben again or I'll not be responsible for what I say to her.'

'Now, Rose, remember, we work for the family. You must not say a word.'

*

It was midday when two police officers arrived at the Barnstock's door. Bernard parted the lace curtains and snorted angrily.

'You two, get upstairs and keep quiet,' he hissed to Merial and his mother.

'What have you done?' his mother cried.

'Nothing, get upstairs and shut up. Merial, if anyone asks we came home from the inn at quarter to ten. Alright?' He held his fist up to her in a warning and she nodded, and then he wrenched the front door open. 'What do you two want at my door?'

'Mr Barnstock,' one of the officers spoke, 'we need to speak to you about an incident which occurred last night.'

Bernard shrugged. 'Oh yeah, what's it got to do with us?' Bernard leant against the door jamb, arms folded, determined not to let the officers in.

'We need to know where you were last night.'

'The inn, ask anyone.'

'What time did you leave?'

Bernard shrugged again and looked at Barry who had come to stand beside him. 'About quarter to ten.'

'Where did you go when you left the inn?'

'To our beds.'

'Can anyone verify that?'

'Aye, our Merial probably heard us come in.'

'Is she in?'

'She might be. Merial,' he yelled, 'are you up there?'

Merial came to the top of the stairs wide-eyed.

'Get down here a moment,' Bernard barked, giving her a warning look.

Merial limped downstairs and looked nervously at the officers.

'Can you verify when your brothers came home last night?' the officer asked.

'Aye, I can, ten to ten - they were making a right old racket.'

'And did they go out again afterwards.'

'Well by the sound of the snoring coming from their rooms, no.'

'What is this all about anyway?' Bernard asked angrily.

'Ben Pearson was found at the bottom of Poldhu Head this morning.'

Bernard laughed. 'Probably threw himself off. The whole village knows he was pining because Lady Emma was to marry another.'

The officer cleared his throat. 'We found footprints in the mud at Poldhu Head.'

'Well, you don't think he flew up there, do you?' he answered sarcastically.

'There were two sets and neither belong to Ben! The officer looked down at the brothers boots, both were clean and shiny.

Bernard lifted his boot to show them off to the officer.

'A lot of people walk about at the top of the head – the odd few are stupid enough to go too close to the edge.'

Bernard glowered at the police officers. 'Now, if that is all, we have work to go to.'

The officers glanced at each other. 'Why are you limping, Miss, and can you explain the bruises on your arm?'

Bernard roared with laughter. 'You're not suggesting our Merial chucked Pearson off that cliff, are you?'

Ignoring the question, the officer looked at Merial for an answer.

'I fell yesterday and hurt myself.'

'Where did you fall?'

'In the back yard,' she lied.

'Right, we'll be in touch.'

'What the hell for?' Bernard demanded.

'Good day to you.' The officer said and ushered his colleague away from the door.

'So…is Pearson dead?' Bernard asked nonchalantly.

'Sorry, we can't disclose that information.'

Bernard slammed the door shut and turned to Merial. 'Good girl.'

Merial folded her arms. 'What have you done?'

'Nothing anyone can pin on us,' Bernard grinned. 'But rest assured, Pearson won't be slighting you anymore. We made damn sure of it.'

*

News of what had happened to Ben must have travelled like wild fire, for Poldhu Cove was extremely busy that day, so too was the tearoom. Everyone wanted to know what had happened. What was Ben doing on Poldhu Head in the dead of night? Had he tried to kill himself? Was he murdered?

Tobias Williams, as the one who first found him, fielded many of these questions, but kept his counsel about what the officer had told him about the Barnstock brothers. With only Jimmy Trevorrow as a witness, Tobias was concerned that the brothers would get away with this again, like they did on the attack of Harry Pike. Tobias had been sworn to secrecy in order to let the police do their job. He just hoped that Ben would survive long enough to put those two away for a very long time.

*

Ellie greeted Peter and Sarah warmly at the tearoom, seating them at one of the outside tables she'd reserved for them where Guy was already sitting, reading yesterday's newspaper. It was unusual for Peter to join them for tea – he was a busy man, but when the reservation for a table was sent down to her that morning from Bochym, Ellie knew the reason for the visit. Before Jessie and Daniel had set off home, they had called in to say goodbye and Daniel told her that he'd asked Peter to intervene, and speak on behalf of Zack. Ellie silently wished Peter luck, because although she loved the bones of her husband – Guy could be as stubborn as a mule sometimes.

'How is Emma?' Ellie asked, 'she was dreadfully distressed when they brought Ben down from the rocks, but then, he was in a terrible state. I can't believe he will survive those injuries.'

'She was rather hysterical, when she got back from her ride - *without* taking the groom,' Peter said glancing at Sarah.

'Darling,' Sarah placed her hand on his, 'you know Emma, she will go her own way, she's young.'

'Well, look where it got her. A groom would have kept her as far away as possible from seeing Ben in such a state.'

'Do we know how it happened?' Peter asked.

'Not yet. We must hope Ben pulls through to find out the reason,' Guy said gravely.

'Poor Ben,' Ellie said, placing the tea tray on the table. 'Zack has taken the accident hard. They've been friends a long time.' She nodded to the dunes where Zack was sitting staring out to sea, and everyone followed the direction of her gaze.

'About Zack, Guy,' Peter said, clearing his throat.

'What about him?' Guy said cautiously.

'It's one of the reasons for my visit today.'

'Oh!'

Peter took a deep breath – he didn't like to interfere in other people's families, but he felt this was an exceptional case. 'Daniel is offering Zack a rare opportunity.'

'*Don't* speak to me about that man!' Guy gritted his teeth. 'God damn it, he was instrumental in my brother Silas's demise,' he shook his head humourlessly at the pun, 'and now he wants to take my only son from me.'

'He doesn't want to take him away. He wants to help him to grow and shine. I'm sure that's what you want for Zack too.'

Guy glanced out to sea and remained silent.

'You heard Zack play the piano at the ball. Did you not know he could do that?'

'No! I sent him to Kit's to get an apprenticeship in carpentry, not to play the damn piano! Forgive my language again, ladies,' he said to Sarah and Ellie.

Peter felt his shoulder muscles tense – knowing he was on thin ice here, but continued, 'And Zack has honoured your wish to get a skill and is nearing the end of his apprenticeship, but really, have you spoken to Kit lately about Zack?'

'What is there to say – a working man needs a skill.'

'Yes, but apparently Zack has no passion for cabinet making – Kit says he's good, but his passion lies elsewhere.'

'Why has Kit told you this and not me?'

'Kit has only just found out that Zack can play the piano – apparently he was teaching himself in secret.'

'I do not care how well he can play the piano - he needs to buckle down, finish his apprenticeship and start earning, otherwise he'll never have enough money to settle down.'

Peter shook his head. 'Settling down is the last thing on Zack's mind – he needs to find his wings and fly a little first.'

Guy was trying very hard to keep his temper. 'With respect, Peter. You might want to look at what is happening to your own offspring before you try to tell me what to do with mine.'

Peter felt a frisson of displeasure. 'To whom are you referring?'

'Emma.'

'Emma!' Peter frowned. 'What about Emma?'

'Guy.' Ellie gave him a cautionary look. 'Perhaps now is not the time.'

Peter cut a glance between Guy and Ellie. 'What about Emma?' he asked more seriously.

'Emma is not in love with Henry.'

Peter laughed. 'Of course, she is – you were there the other night when they announced their engagement!'

'That's as may be, but…'

Peter felt the small muscles in his jaw contract. 'But what, man?' he asked, fast losing his patience.

'I believe she is only going through with it because it pleases you.'

'It does please me! Henry's father and I are old friends – the union would be financially beneficial for both he, myself, and Emma.'

Guy remained silent.

Peter narrowed his eyes and pushed his cake away – his appetite fast waning. 'Would you like to explain yourself more?' he asked, folding his arms.

Guy twisted his mouth, glanced at Ellie, who gave him no other indication as to whether to pursue this, so he continued, 'We believe, Emma cares for another.'

'Damn you man,' Peter hissed, 'are you saying she is taking young Henry for a fool?'

Guy held his hand up to stop Peter protesting. 'I'm sure she's not, and seeing her resignation the other night at the engagement, I have no doubt she will honour Henry with her hand in marriage, but it's not where Emma's heart truly lies.'

'Good God, Guy – I never put you down as a romantic.'

'Well, I've had my moments,' he smiled at Ellie. 'Many of our mutual friends witnessed your Emma's consternation at the engagement. Tell me, Peter, did Emma know Henry was going to ask her that night?'

'Well, no, but of course an announcement was imminent – Henry had declared to her in May.'

'And was she happy with that declaration?'

Peter glanced again at Sarah. 'Emma seemed pleased that the declaration allowed her to come home. She was weary of all the balls, I understand, isn't that right, Sarah?'

Sarah nodded in agreement. 'She couldn't wait to come back home.'

Guy raised his eyebrows.

'Are you saying she wanted to come home to someone else, Guy?'

Guy stayed silent.

'So, come on, man, who is this mystery man my daughter really cares for?'

Guy breathed out a sigh. 'Perhaps you need to ask her. Perhaps take note of her distress at the moment, and for whom.'

'Guy!' Ellie warned, her eyes indicating caution.

'You mean Ben Pearson? Don't be absurd. Emma's distress was immense, I admit, but come on, they've been friends from childhood – all our children have grown up together - it's natural that she finds what has happened distressing.'

'If you say so. But if it isn't Ben she cares for, it certainly *isn't* Henry.'

Peter turned and looked away into the far distance, then turned back to Guy when he'd collected himself. 'How come you know more about my daughter's heart than I?'

'Perhaps because I'm emotionally detached from her.'

Peter folded his arms.

'Peter, I don't want us to quarrel over this – I just felt you needed to be aware. Emma is such a lovely young woman, I'm sure you wouldn't want her to marry someone she did not fully respect.'

'Well then, can we both agree to do what is right for our children,' he countered.

'No, my mind is made up. It's time Zack earned a living,' Guy said adamantly.

32

Zack sat with his arms encircled around his legs, very much afraid of many things that day. The very worst was that his good friend Ben might be about to lose his life. His poor friend, battered, and broken – not only physically, but emotionally. After Ben had so excitedly shared his plans of making a life with Emma – no matter what the consequences were, he had watched his friend's face shatter when Henry had announced his intention to marry Emma. Life was so unfair. He picked up a stone and threw it down the beach. His dream of becoming a pianist was just a pipe dream now, but this paled into insignificance after what he'd witnessed this morning. He remembered Ben's words though, "If Daniel Chandler is offering to help you, you should go independently to London." Zack shook his head - but how could he go now?

*

Peter and Sarah drove back in silence to Bochym, it was only when they pulled up and David opened the car door for them, did Peter lead Sarah over to the love seats in the front garden.

'What do you make of Guy's theory about Emma and Ben?' he asked tentatively.

Sarah folded her hands on her lap. 'I think perhaps Guy and Ellie have seen how close a relationship the two have developed over the years, that's all.'

Peter leant back and raked his hands through his pomaded hair, making it stand on end. 'They are close though, aren't they?'

'Yes, they are. I noticed it myself over a year ago. I didn't want to alert you to something that might not have been there, but I thought her year in Switzerland at finishing school would break the bond between them.'

'Have they been much in each other's company since she came home from her season, do you know?'

'Not that I am aware of. Emma did insist that Ben attend her ball though, she was quite angry that he had been omitted from her birthday dinner at Easter. She said if Ben wasn't invited, she did not want a ball.'

'Was that just loyalty to him as her friend, do you think?'

'Perhaps. Emma has always known that she would be expected to choose a husband from a good family, so I'm sure she would never have let her feelings for Ben turn to more than friendship.'

Peter nodded. 'So, you think Guy and Ellie are just surmising she is in love with him, having seen her so distressed at Ben's injuries this morning.'

'Perhaps. But Peter, I think you need to speak to Emma about Henry - she does seem a little hesitant around him.'

'Well, I hope all is well, as you know Henry has asked if he can join our holiday in Italy – you haven't said anything to Emma yet, have you?'

'No, you asked me to keep it as a surprise. I just hope it is a nice surprise for her.'

'I'll go and speak to her now.' Peter pushed his hands to his thighs to get up.

*

After apologising to Tomkins, the groom, for her misdemeanours, and assuring him he would not have his wages docked, Emma had spent a couple of hours trying, without success, to read a book – her mind was in such turmoil for Ben.

She was surprised when her papa had sought her out. He seemed in a strange mood, as he leant against the piano with his arms folded, just looking at her for a good few seconds, as though he too was fighting some inner turmoil.

'Are you happy with Henry, Emma?' he asked eventually.

The question had stunned her momentarily, but seeing the concern in her papa's eyes, and remembering Henry's statement, that if she broke this engagement, Papa would face ruin, what could she say? If she had not made such a big thing about initially accepting Henry as her beau, Papa might not have settled on this financial deal with the Montagues? This was all her own fault, so she gathered herself to answer, 'Of course, I am, Papa,' she said, trying to sound convincing, 'though I would like to wait a while before we marry - I'm still very young,' she added, thinking she may as well put her plan into action now.

He nodded. 'We would have to speak to the Montagues about that.' Then he tipped his head and looked at her strangely. 'I love you, Emma, you know I would not wish you to be unhappy.'

Emma's lip trembled. 'I know, Papa.' The voice in her head was screaming, *tell him, tell him the truth about who you do love,* but she could not say the words, she could not do that to her beloved Papa. It was only when Papa vacated the room, did she let her guard down and cry broken heartedly.

The emotion of the day finally overwhelmed her, fatigued and exhausted she must have fallen asleep, because it was late in the afternoon when she was woken when Joe Treen knocked on the drawing room door.

'Begging your pardon, Lady Emma, I'm sorry to disturb you,' Joe said.

Emma blinked sleepily. 'That's alright, Treen,' then asked suddenly, 'is there something the matter?' Very much afraid that there was.

Joe cleared his throat. 'Forgive my impertinence, but Mr Pearson has rung from the hospital and spoken to His Lordship. I thought perhaps you would like to know.'

Emma stood up in an instant, brushed the creases from her dress and fled from the room. Halting for a moment at Papa's study door, she gathered herself for bad news and then knocked.

'Papa, may I come in,' she said peeping around the study door.

'Ah, I see the jungle drums are working?'

Emma smiled weakly. 'What news of Ben?'

Peter sighed heavily. 'Nothing good to tell you, except that he has been operated on to mend several broken bones. It's just a case of wait and see, now. You must not worry, my darling.'

Emma nodded. 'Thank you, Papa.'

As Emma was leaving the study, her mama was just coming in and heard her papa say gravely, 'Ah, Sarah, close the door, would you.'

Emma felt her spine chill, and though she knew she shouldn't, she pressed her ear to the door, knowing instinctively that her father had not told her the truth.

'I understand there has been a phone call from Mr Pearson. How is Ben?' she heard Mama ask.

'It's not good, Sarah. Pearson broke down when he told me that the doctors are not certain he will make it through the night. His injuries are catastrophic. Pearson and his wife are staying by his bedside.'

'Good gracious. I take it you didn't tell Emma.'

'No. I'll tell her if the worst happens, but she's been so upset today about it, I'd like her to have a little respite from her distress. Pearson has said he will keep us informed.'

Emma felt her heart implode as tears once again streamed down her face, she was very much afraid that she would never see her beloved Ben alive again.

*

Ben woke at five the next morning. He did not know, but his parents had sat in vigil all night, praying that their son would make it through these critical hours. Within seconds, the enormity of pain in Ben's body made him gasp audibly and fight for breath.

Chairs scraped back and hands touched him.

'Oh God, Sydney, he's in terrible distress,' Ben heard his ma cry.

'Stay calm, Son, stay calm,' his father's voice soothed. 'Rose, go and fetch somebody.'

'Argh!' Ben cried as he tried to open his eyes but couldn't. 'Argh!' He tried to move his arms, but was held down. He could not make his mouth form any words other than indications of pain, and his face felt as though it was in a vice. 'Argh!'

'Ben, Ben it's your pa here. Ben, stay still, help is coming.'

Oh God, am I still on that cliff? Movement around him panicked him. *Don't touch me, please don't pick me up - the pain, oh God the pain is unbearable.*

'Ben, you must listen to me,' a strange voice came through the turmoil in his head. 'You've had an operation to fix your broken bones. You're going to be in considerable pain in the top half of your body for quite some time. We are going to try to keep your pain under control, so I'm going to give you an injection to keep you calm and sleepy, so you don't undo the surgeons work.'

Someone wiped his face free of tears, as another put in needle into his arm. Suddenly a calmness ensued, the pain left him and his heart reduced to a slow, thump, thump, thump......

*

Sydney Pearson held his wife in his arms as they watched their son drift back into unconsciousness. They sat down to continue their vigil, and when eventually Rose succumbed to sleep, Sydney went in search of the doctor.

'He had quite a lot of fight in him, when he woke,' Sydney said to the doctor, 'is that a good sign?'

'It's adrenalin he's running on, I'm afraid. I saw it several times during the war – I suspect you did too,' he answered darkly.

Sydney made a guttural noise in his throat. 'I saw a man decapitated once by a wire fence; he ran headless for ten yards before he collapsed.'

The doctor nodded – indicating he'd probably seen much the same.

'So, our son may still die?'

'I'm sorry, Mr Pearson, I can't give you any really positive prognoses at the moment. Ben has lost a great deal of blood, and the infections from his compound fractures - and there were five in all - may overwhelm his system. His body may not be able to cope with what has happened to him.'

Sydney Pearson sat down heavily and the tears he had withheld since hearing the news, burst forth like a waterfall. 'I'm sorry,' he said covering his face with his hands.

The doctor patted him on the shoulder. 'We'll do our best for him.'

It was several minutes before Sydney recovered enough to ask, 'When you spoke to Ben when he woke, you told him his upper body would be in a great deal of pain.'

'I did.'

'And the lower part of his body….?'

'It's a little too soon to know for sure, but at the moment he has no reflexes in his legs.'

'Is he paralysed?'

'As I say, it's too early to tell.'

*

Later that morning at Polhormon dairy, the dairymaids gathered together to discuss the terrible tragedy that had befallen Ben. Although David and Jimmy Trevorrow had been sworn to secrecy about what they knew for sure, it was common knowledge that the police had been to the Barnstock's door yesterday in regard to Ben's accident.

When Merial walked into the milking parlour, the other three dairymaids turned, folded their arms, and glared at her.

'What?' she asked, feigning innocence.

David Trevorrow joined them and matched their stance. 'You have a bloody nerve showing your face here,' he said.

'W...Why?'

'You know why, now get out of my milking parlour, and off my land this instant.'

'But, but....' Merial was stunned for a moment *How on earth could they know? Bernard said nothing could be proved.*

Jimmy bent down, scooped up a handful of cow muck and hurled it at Merial. 'Pa said go.'

Shocked, her mouth dropped as she looked down at the mess on her dress and then another handful hit her right on the mouth.

'Bullseye,' Jimmy shouted, 'perfect for a mouth that spews shit about people.'

Merial staggered back, spitting and retching, trying to rid herself of the taste. 'My brothers will hear of this,' she cried.

'And I'll have the police down on them again like a ton of bricks,' David Trevorrow snarled, and then ushered everyone into the milking parlour, slamming the door on her.

*

After a disturbed night, Emma rose the next morning, puffy eyed from crying herself to sleep, feeling a sense of dread she had never experienced before. When Juliet came to help her dress, she found Emma had long since bathed and got ready.

'You'll do me out of a job, Lady Emma,' Juliet said to lighten the mood.

'I'm sorry, Juliet, I couldn't sleep, so I thought I would get up.'

'You should have rung me.'

'I have a lot on my mind. Has there been any word from the hospital?'

'None that I know of. Maybe go out and get some fresh air after breakfast. You look terribly peaky.'

'I can't leave the manor until I know that Ben has made it through the night.'

'I know what you and Ben mean to each other. Go out for some air and I'll come looking for you just as soon as a phone call comes through.'

Once again tears began to stream down her face. 'Thank you, Juliet.'

*

Theo and Lowenna Trevail had also experienced a sleepless night. Since the children's party on the night of the ball, Loveday had been terribly lethargic, not even wanting to get out of bed. It was most unlike her. Only a few weeks ago she had been as lively as any six-year-old girl could be. Concerned at what ailed Loveday, Lowenna had sent word with Theo that she wished to stay with her daughter, and wondered if someone could stand in for her to see to Her Ladyship. If Loveday were sickening for something - it could not have come at a worse time. Theo and Lowenna were due to accompany the Dunstan's to Italy the day after tomorrow. It wasn't an unusual thing for them to leave the children in the care of Nanny when they accompanied the Earl and Countess anywhere – this was all part of the job. But if Loveday got any worse, Lowenna could not think about going and leaving her.

33

Zack had the princely sum of eight pounds in his pocket and a bag of clothes. After Ma told him that Peter Dunstan had tried to argue the case with Pa for Zack to go to London, all to no avail, he'd made the monumental decision to leave Cornwall.

When Zack kissed his ma goodbye that morning, supposedly to go back to Kit's, he'd held her slightly longer than normal —unsure when, or if, he would see her again.

He would, for all intents and purposes, take the Helston wagon, but would not alight at the St Keverne road junction as normal, so as to walk down to Gweek. He had a train to catch. London was calling him.

Several times he felt the pang of guilt, doing what he was doing, knowing his friend Ben was fighting for his life in hospital. He'd call the hospital from London to check on him, and he was sure that Ben would have urged him to take this momentous step, if he'd been able.

As the train passed Truro and the mighty cathedral came into view, he felt a slight tremble - he'd never been beyond Truro before. Taking Daniel Chandler's card from his pocket, worn now from having been looked at many times, he read and re read the address where he would be staying tonight. He should have rung Daniel before he set off, he knew that, but he had no time, and he was confident that Daniel and Jessie would accommodate him. He may be on a wild goose chase, and the music conservatoire might laugh at his strange way of imitating the great composers. If so, he would try to forge a new path for himself in the capital, for whatever he did in the future, it would be better than making coffins.

*

In Gweek, Kit walked into the kitchen as Sophie was finishing washing the breakfast plates. He circled his arms around her waist and kissed the back of her neck.

'Has Zack turned up yet? It's not like him to be late.'

'Perhaps he missed the Mullion wagon, or it didn't turn up.'

'He'll be on the next one no doubt. I'll be working on the boat. Tell him to come find me when he arrives.'

By midday, and still no sign of Zack, and confident that he was not ill as Zack never ailed anything, Kit allowed a seed of doubt to manifest that Zack was not coming. He was very much afraid that Zack would not be here today, or for that fact, ever again. It was after luncheon when he shared his concerns with Sophie.

Sophie stopped collecting the plates. 'What do you think he's done?'

'Well, Zack was upset at the altercation between Daniel and Guy on Friday night. I think he's taken Daniel up on his offer.'

'And gone to London!'

Kit nodded.

'Do you think it was all arranged?'

'I don't know. I don't think so. I never saw Zack speak to Daniel again that night, and of course he and Jessie set off back on Saturday. If Daniel were going to take him with him, Zack would have gone then.'

Sophie picked nervously at the linen tablecloth. 'Zack isn't world wise - he could get into all sorts of trouble alone in London.'

'I know.' He pushed back his chair and stood up. 'I'm going to phone Daniel. Perhaps he'll go and meet the Cornwall train. At least we'll know then if that is what Zack has done.'

Sophie reached over to touch his sleeve. 'I'm sorry, Kit.'

'What for?'

'All those years of training him.'

Kit shook his head. 'In all honesty, his heart was not in it, and you know you have to love your craft to do it well. If he's gone to pursue his real passion, well, good for him!'

'Well, I don't envy you telling Guy.'

'Mmm,' he agreed as he picked up the phone.

It was Jessie who Kit spoke to. Daniel was at a rehearsal and she was shocked, but not surprised if Zack was making his way to the capital.

'Guy can be so pig headed sometimes,' Jessie said, 'he will not see reason. We had hoped to build bridges with him last week, but he simply won't forgive us. Anyway, if Zack is on his way, he's taken the only action left for him. I'll go to the station. I can meet him if he comes off the train.'

'Thank you, Jessie. Will you report back to me if he does turn up. I feel it my duty to inform Guy and Ellie.'

'I will.'

*

Merial was scrubbing the cow manure out of her dress when Bernard and Barry arrived back from Mullion harbour after getting the fishing boat ready to sail on the evening tide.

'What's all this then?' Bernard scowled.

'I've been dismissed and abused, that's what!'

'Why, what have you done?'

'It's what you've bloody done. They know, Bernard. When I asked why I was being dismissed, David Trevorrow said that I knew why.'

Bernard snorted, and then caught her by the chin and hissed, 'They can't bloody know. They're only surmising. I told you - we did a proper job on Pearson. No one saw us, and he's most probably dead, so cannot link us to it. So, *you*,' he squeezed her face with his calloused hands, 'had better keep your trap shut.'

*

In hospital, Ben became agitated again just after midday, and the doctor was brought to administer more pain killers. The more they could keep Ben still, the better the outcome for his recovery. The Pearsons watched on, white faced and anxious, as Ben moaned and whimpered in his sleep. At regular intervals, all his wounds were checked for seepage and sniffed to see if anything was turning putrid.

'No infection yet,' the doctor assured them, 'I think the fact that he was soaked in sea water is probably a factor in this – salt is good for wounds. So, in that he was lucky.'

Sydney looked mournfully down at Ben's broken body. *Lucky! His only son was paralysed, and the doctor says that he's lucky.* He glanced at his wife, sitting anxiously by Ben's bedside, hoping for the best, he hadn't the heart to tell her what the doctor had told him last night.

*

There was a great sense of unease in the Bochym household by mid-afternoon Monday – the doctor had been called to see Loveday Trevail, because Lowenna was concerned that her condition had worsened throughout the day. There had been two cases of children dying from a sore throat on the Lizard in the last month, but though she was showing no signs of any fever - something was clearly wrong.

Despite the obvious worry about the child, and empathy for Theo and Lowenna, there needed to be urgent discussions as to what would happen when the family set off for Italy, and who would accompany them, if Theo and Lowenna were needed here to nurse their sick child.

Molly, the housekeeper, sat with Joe in his office to discuss the scenario.

Cupping her hand around a mug of tea, Molly said, 'I saw to Her Ladyship this morning, Joe, and I was happy to stand in for Lowenna, but I simply cannot countenance going with them to a hot country. I can't even cope with the heat in the height of summer here.' She fanned herself at the very thought.

'It might not come to that, Loveday might just be getting a summer cold, children come down with things all the time. The doctor has taken some blood and driven up to the hospital with it. Perhaps when he returns with the results he'll administer something to help the poor girl, and she'll be as right as a clock tomorrow.'

They exchanged a glance that said that was highly unlikely.

'Would you go?' Molly asked.

'Well, I've stood in on occasions for Theo, so I might have to.'

'As Juliet has assisted Lady Emma since she came home from finishing school, you might both be going off on a second honeymoon to Italy.' Molly grinned.

'We never had a first one!' Joe said, drumming his fingers on the table. The thought of a honeymoon with Juliet gave him a warm feeling. After the other night, his kind words and gentle nature, had won Juliet's trust enough for her to be able to relax enough for him to really make love to her. From then on, each night together had been blissful. A couple of weeks in Italy might be rather lovely.

'Joe? Joe?' Molly's voice brought him back from his reverie. 'Gosh, you were already in Italy then, weren't you.' She grinned.

'Sorry, Molly, I did rather drift off there. Yes, I suppose I would like us to go, but certainly not at the expense of little Loveday's health.'

*

It was six o clock when the train pulled into the station in London that evening, and Zack pulled on his coat and checked his pocket for his wallet and Daniel's card. A sudden frisson of alarm hit him - the card had gone! Frantically, he searched the other pockets to no avail. It had definitely been there when he bought a sandwich for his dinner – it must have fallen out as he pulled his wallet out. In his panic, he could not remember the address, even though he'd read the card many times! His eyes darted to his fellow passengers, maybe someone would know Daniel, especially as he was famous. When he tried to ask them, some just laughed, but most ignored him - too busy to bother with him while they were getting ready to leave the train. He felt his lip quiver slightly, but swallowed and held his head high. *For Christ's sakes don't blub!* He got off the train, unsure of what to do or where to go, so sat on a bench. There were hundreds of people about – this wasn't like Poldhu, where everyone knew everyone else. Panic brought more tears to his eyes, and people were staring at him. *God damn it, man, get a hold of yourself – you're almost eighteen now!* he scolded, and lifted his head. There was only one thing to do, he'd have to phone Kit for the address, and he in turn would tell Pa, who would come and drag him back home and his dream would end before it began! He dropped his head in his hands as tears began to fall. It was then he heard someone calling his name. He lifted his head and thought his eyes were deceiving him. Aunt Jessie was there, behind the barrier, smiling and waving. He sniffed back his tears, beamed a thankful smile, and ran to the barrier to give in his ticket.

'Aunt Jessie! Oh, God, I'm so glad to see you.' He practically fell into her arms. 'But how….'

'Kit phoned. When you failed to turn up in Gweek, he suspected you were on your way to us. Zack, you should have called us to tell us you were coming.'

'I'm sorry, it was a spur of the moment thing. I just needed to get away. But I've been foolish, Jessie. I lost the card Daniel gave me with your address on. I didn't know what to do, I thought I'd have to go back home.' He wiped a stray tear.

Jessie smiled sympathetically. 'Hush now, don't get upset. You're here now, and I'll take you home – to our house.'

*

In the Chandlers beautiful parlour, Jessie handed him a cup of tea and a slice of cake.

'You must think me a real cry-baby,' he said quietly.

'I do not. I think you've been very brave undertaking this journey. I don't suppose this is just a visit?' she asked with a smile.

'No, It's not just a visit. You said Kit rang you - has he told Pa?'

'No, he's waiting for me to confirm that you're here safe and well.'

'Pa will be so angry. Please don't send me back.'

'We won't, Zack. You're very welcome to stay with us here, but you must write to your parents immediately, to tell them you're safe here and put their mind at ease.'

'Yes, Aunt Jessie.'

Jessie sat beside her nephew and cupped her hand over his and squeezed. 'Welcome to the start of your new life.'

*

When Kit came off the phone to Jessie, he ran his hands through his hair anxiously.

'Is he there then?'

Kit nodded.

Sophie bit her lip. 'It's a bit late to go over to Guy's.'

'I think I must though,' he sighed, 'he's going to be so angry with me.'

'It's not your fault, Kit.'

'Oh, I think it is – it was I who introduced Zack to Daniel.'

*

Kit was welcomed into Guy and Ellie's kitchen with curious looks.

'What on earth brings you all this way at this time of night?' Guy asked. 'Is everyone well at home?'

'Yes, yes, everyone is fine. Guy.....I think you need to sit down.' He proceeded to tell him what had happened, all the while watching Guy's face fill with rage. 'I'm sorry, to bring this news to you. But I thought you needed to know sooner rather than later. At least you know he's safe. When I realised what might have happened, I phoned Jessie, and she met him from the train.'

'Damn Jessie, and damn Chandler for his interference.' Guy thumped the table. 'I could bloody kill him for this. He's not content with ruining my brother's life, now he's taken my only son from me!'

'He hasn't taken him from you, Guy. Zack is only in London – he hasn't gone forever.'

'He bloody well *has* gone forever! He'll not set foot in this house again for defying me.' Guy began to pace the room like a caged lion.

'Guy, you're upset. Don't say rash things like that,' Ellie said quietly.

'I told him he couldn't go. I told him, and he still went!' Guy turned to Kit. 'Did you know? Did you know he was planning this?'

'Of course not. But to tell you the truth, I'm not surprised. It's what he wanted to do.'

'It's only what he wanted to do after Chandler put those bloody stupid ideas into his head.'

'No, Guy. Zack has been hankering to do something other than carpentry for some time now.'

'Well, he's certainly wasted your time, damn him! All those years, doing his apprenticeship, only to swan off to London, just like that. I mean, how the hell has he got the money to go there?'

'Well, I do pay him for the work he completes.'

'You should have kept him busier and away from that bloody piano.'

'In truth, I didn't know he could play like that until just recently. He'd been listening into Selene's lessons during his tea break and he just picked it up. We only found out he could play by accident.'

'I will never forgive Zack for this, never!'

'Guy,' Ellie stood up to put her hand on his arm, 'calm yourself, please. There's nothing we can do. Zack has made his decision.'

Guy narrowed his eyes at Ellie. 'You seem not to be shocked by this news. Did you know he was going to do it?'

'No, but I'm not surprised he's gone either.'

'Damn you, Ellie if you knew something like this was going to happen..... If you'd have had any inkling he was going to do this, you should have told me. I would have stopped him – I would have nipped it in the bud.'

'You can't stop him forever – he would have gone eventually. He's not a child anymore. Your vocation in life was to be a Thatcher. Zack believes his is in music,' she argued.

'He will never earn a living playing the piano. He'll be destitute in no time and living off the Chandlers, and it serves them alright!'

'Not necessarily, Guy. You heard him play. You heard how fabulous he was. You can't deny it. Everybody says he has a real talent. Daniel thinks….'

'I don't care what that man thinks,' he yelled, 'the sound of his name makes my blood boil. So enough, enough I tell you. I don't want to talk about it anymore.'

Kit glanced at Ellie. 'I think I should take my leave. I'm sorry.'

Guy grunted a goodnight.

'Thank you for coming to tell us, Kit. I'll see you out.' Once outside, Ellie patted Kit on the arm. 'He's angry. He'll come round, eventually. I just hope Zack has done the right thing.'

'Time will tell.' Kit kissed Ellie on the cheek. 'We'll see you soon.'

34

When Kit left, Guy took his rage outside and walked up to the Marconi buildings. He'd batted Ellie away when she tried to stop him from going out, and told her to go back when she tried to follow him.

He sat alone now on the damp grass, hatless and coatless, ignoring the chill wind biting at him. He felt bitterly betrayed by Zack. All this time, providing a safe warm home for him as he grew up. Realising, albeit reluctantly, that he was not cut out for thatching, he'd arranged for a good apprenticeship in a craft that was much needed. He'd almost secured him a business, where he'd be set up for life! And what had he done? He'd thrown it all back in his face, that's what! Bloody Daniel Chandler – he could wring his neck for him. Twice now he had split his family up, and there was nothing he could do about it. He thumped his palms against his head in desperation. He fancied that he should go to London and drag him home, that's what he should do, but Zack would be eighteen on Wednesday - not a child anymore. The unhappy alternative was to cut him off for his betrayal, though he knew he would have a battle on his hands with Ellie. She was like a lioness when it came to her children – she would fight to the end to protect Zack from being banished forever, and would not allow him to cut him off completely. Well, so be it, on this matter he would stick to his guns, and Ellie would have to have the same relationship with her son as she did with Jessie, from a distance, and by letter, because he would not back down on this one. Zack would never be welcome in his house again.

*

After waiting in all day for a phone call from Mr Pearson, Emma finally went out to the stable that evening to groom Saffron. She hadn't been there more than five minutes when Juliet came rushing in.

'There was a phone call just now, my lady.'

Emma handed the curry comb to the groom and rushed out of the stable with Juliet. 'Was it Mr Pearson?'

'I don't know, my lady. His Lordship picked the call up before Joe got to it. I thought you might like to know.'

'Thank you, Juliet.'

Emma stood for what felt like an age outside her papa's study until Joe checked the line and found it to be available again, and Emma knocked on the door.

'Ah, I take it you heard the phone ring.'

'Yes, Papa, was that from Mr Pearson at the hospital?'

'No, darling, it was from Kit.'

'Oh!' Emma's shoulders drooped. 'I thought it might have been about Ben.'

'I'm sorry, darling, but no. It seems that Zack has taken himself off to London to live with the Chandlers.'

'Oh! Well, good for him,' she said meaningfully.

Peter's mouth curled into a smile. 'So, you agree with defying one's father then, do you?' he teased.

'In this case, yes. Guy is a lovely man, but he doesn't see his son's potential. Zack was really upset after my ball.'

'I'm sure Guy's heart is in the right place and just wants what's right for Zack.'

'To be a carpenter, when he could have a fabulous career in music?' she stated.

'Well, that remains to be seen. Now, I must get on.'

'You will let me know when you get news from the hospital, won't you, Papa?'

'I will, my darling, and remember, no news is good news. The fact that they haven't rung, must mean that Ben made it through the night.'

When Emma came out of her papa's study, Juliet was waiting. 'Well?'

'Not from the hospital, I'm afraid.'

'Oh, I'm that sorry for getting your hopes up.'

'No matter. Thank you for coming for me though.'

They both turned when they saw Joe escorting the doctor through to the Trevails cottage.

'I hope Loveday is alright, my lady, that's the second time the doctor has been today,' Juliet whispered.

'Yes, so do I.' It struck Emma that she was not the only one worried about a loved one.

'Come, my lady, we may as well get you ready for dinner.'

Juliet was just dressing Emma's hair when a knock came to her bedroom door and both women stilled.

Emma reached for Juliet's hand and squeezed it. 'Please let this be the news I'm waiting for – please let it be good news.'

When her bedroom door opened, it was Emma's mother who came in. Emma took one look at the distress on her mama's face and suddenly felt the world spiral out of control!

*

In London, Daniel arrived home, took one look at Zack, smiled brilliantly, and shook his hand warmly.

'Well, this is a lovely, if not rather unexpected surprise.'

'I'm sorry to drop on you like this, it's just that….'

'Don't apologise, we're happy to have you here, as I'm sure my lovely Jessie has told you. Does your father know?'

Zack nodded his head.

'How old are you now?'

'I'll be eighteen on Wednesday.'

'Ah, good. I don't think your father will come looking for you.'

'No, I don't think he will. Kit went to see him and apparently he's washed his hands of me.'

Daniel gave a pained frown. 'He's probably upset, perhaps he'll come round.'

'I very much doubt it, he still hasn't forgiven Aunt Jessie for falling in love with you!'

'Well, I'm sorry if he doesn't, but rest assured, we will look after you until you find your feet here. I think it's time to make plans for your future. And a birthday party is on the cards too by the look of it.'

*

Emma came round to the pungent aroma of ammonia and ethanol and quickly batted the smelling salts away from her nose. With mournful eyes she looked up at her mama and Juliet as they fussed around her. Seeing that her mama's eyes were filled with tears, Emma felt them building in her own.

'Ben?' she cried.

'No, darling.' Sarah brushed the hair back from her face. 'I'm sorry I gave you a shock, Juliet explained that you were waiting for news of Ben, but I do have some other dreadful news.'

'What is it?' she asked fearfully.

'It's little Loveday – the doctor says she is very ill. He's taking her to hospital in his car, and Theo and Lowenna have gone with her.'

*

After breakfast, the next morning a telephone call came, not from the Pearsons, much to Emma's dismay, but from Theo Travail. He rang to say Loveday was having more blood tests, but the doctors seemed to be very worried about her condition.

With the trip to Italy imminent, it was clear that the Travails were needed at their daughters bedside, so after a long discussion with Joe Treen, it was decided that Joe and Juliet would travel with the party as valet and lady's maid to Italy. A prospect that had a double-edged sword for Joe and Juliet. It was a very unexpected adventure they were embarking on, marred only by the dreadful reasons they were going.

*

Italy was the very last place Emma wanted to journey to at this moment in time, so went in search of her mama. She

287

found her in the garden, discussing the autumn borders with Mr Hubbard the gardener.

'In light of what is happening to poor Loveday, are you sure you still want us all to go to Italy, Mama?' Emma asked.

Sarah knelt back. 'Yes, there is little we can do to help the Travails. Loveday is in the best possible place. We've asked the Treens to make themselves ready to accompany us. That should put Lowenna and Theo at ease, so that they do not have to bother about us at the moment, and can focus on Loveday getting better.'

Emma's shoulders sagged. 'I was hoping we would not go at all.'

Sarah gave her daughter a sympathetic look. 'All the tickets are bought. Justin and Ruby are expecting us, and we promised William that we'd spend a little time with him there before he goes back to university.'

'But Mama, please could you ask Papa if I could stay behind and not go to Italy.'

'No, Emma, you cannot stay here alone,' Sarah said getting up from where she knelt. 'It's out of the question. Justin, Ruby, and William will be very upset if you didn't come.'

'But Mama, I'm eighteen now. I'll be fine here, and I simply can't face leaving when Ben is so ill – he might die!'

'Darling, there is nothing you can do for Ben. Like Loveday, he is in the best place possible with the best treatment available to him.'

'But we've heard nothing from the Pearsons yet!'

'That can only be perceived as a good thing, Emma. His parents are with him, and they will be all he needs at the moment. By the time we return from Italy in three weeks, Ben may be up to seeing people.'

'That's if he doesn't die!' she sobbed.

Gathering her daughter into her arms. 'Emma, darling. We must all be strong and pray for Ben's recovery. You know Ben, he is a strong-willed young man – he was alive when they found him, and to fall from such a height and sustain so many injuries and still be conscious, well, it just shows how strong his will is to survive. Your papa has given David, who will be acting Butler while we're away, instructions to send a telegram to your uncle Justin just as soon as he knows what's happening with both Loveday and Ben. Now, my darling, dry your eyes. Juliet has never been abroad before - she may need your help with what to pack.'

*

In London, after a day of sightseeing with Jessie, Zack watched as Daniel breezed into the house, first kissing his wife lovingly, then all his children, finally shaking Zack's hand.

'Have you all had a good day?' Daniel asked.

'We have, darling. We visited Crystal Palace and stood at the gates of Buckingham Palace.'

'Excellent. So, Zack, do you feel ready to show off your talents to my fellow orchestral musicians.

Zack nodded. 'It's what I came for.'

'Well, we're extraordinarily lucky at the moment. The London Symphony Orchestra often have guest conductors, and at the moment we have Sergei Rachmaninoff with us. You could not have arrived at a better time.'

'Sergei Rachmaninoff!' Zack gasped.

'Yes, and he'll see you tomorrow.' He winked. 'He owed me a favour, he stayed with us for a couple of days when he came over to England, until he could find his own accommodation.'

Zack sat open mouthed then asked, 'What will I play?'

'Do you know anything by Sergei Rachmaninoff?'

'I know everything he wrote.'

'Excellent, of course you do,' Daniel laughed and slapped him on the back.' What will you play then?'

'Perhaps, Ten Preludes?'

'Perfect. I suggest you go and practice until supper.'

*

While the Dunstans and their entourage, boarded the train to London to embark on the first of the five train journeys it would take to get to Italy, Zack was sat in the auditorium where Daniel and his fellow orchestral musicians rehearsed. He had never felt more at home in an environment as he did here.

The sound of an orchestra in full rehearsal mode was something to behold. His whole being wanted to sit at the grand piano, as his fingers itched to touch the keys. The gentleman playing the piano was lost in the waves of music whilst still being able to take his lead from the conductor. Starting and stopping, the pieces were worked on, and played again, until at last they played the whole concerto through. Zack had to literally stop himself from clapping at the end and felt himself colouring up at the passion it had roused in him.

Zack felt the adrenaline start to run as instruments were put away, and everyone said their goodbyes to each other, but Daniel stayed seated until they had all vacated the room. Now it was Zack's turn to shine.

'Maestro, may I introduce Zackary Blackthorn – the pianist I was telling you about.' Daniel beckoned Zack down from where he was seated.

Sergei shook his hand. 'Now then, young man. Mr Chandler here speaks very highly of you.'

Zack smiled, unable to find his voice for a moment, and Sergei, returning his smile, gestured him to sit at the piano.

Sending a nervous glance in Daniel's direction, who nodded back at him, Zack sat for a moment, adjusted his seating position a couple of times, and flexed his fingers. Just as he was about to start, Sergei asked, 'What are you going to play for us – you appear not to have any music with you.'

'I'm going to play Ten Preludes – I err, I don't need music.'

Sergei's lip curled with amusement. 'When you're ready then.'

While Zack played, some of the other members of the orchestra came in to listen. Daniel watched Sergei with interest. He had folded his arms and lent back against the podium with a look of astonishment on his face, until suddenly he shouted, 'Stop!'

Zack lifted his hands from the piano in shock, clearly waiting to be berated for fudging a note, though he was sure he hadn't. He glanced between Sergei and Daniel but nothing was said.

'Play Debussy, nocturne,' Sergei requested.

Zack licked his lips, swallowed hard and began to play note for perfect note.'

'Stop!' Sergei walked up to him. 'The piece we were rehearsing, do you know it?'

'I'm not familiar with it, but I listened intently to it.'

Sergei raised his eyebrows with interest. 'Well then, let's see if you can pick things up quickly. Play.'

Zack had to clear his head of Debussy and homed back into the music he had listened to all afternoon. They had only run through the whole passage once, so he doubted he could do it justice. *Come on, Zack, try,* the voice in his head urged. He flexed his fingers and very tentatively began to play. Daniel picked up his cello and began to play along with him, and then one by one, several members of the orchestra came and sat down until a cacophony of instruments accompanied his playing.

When he finished, Zack placed his hands on his lap for a few seconds, all was quiet in the auditorium - everyone waiting to hear what Sergei would say.

Sergei walked up to the piano and asked, 'How do you think you did, Zackary?'

Zack looked quite dejected. 'It would be better if I could do it again. I think I fudged a key.'

'You did my boy – you *fudged* one key in that whole piece of music. I'm astounded.' Everyone in the auditorium stood up and clapped, and Zack looked at them all in awe.

'We need to polish things up a little. You will need to learn how to take direction from your conductor, and how to read music and start sitting your exams, because you're ready to do so. Welcome to the world of music, Zackary.'

If Zack could have smiled a broader smile, it would have met from ear to ear!

35

After spending the night in the Dunstan's London residence, the party took the train to catch the boat to Calais.

On the boat, Joe and Juliet sat appropriately apart from the family, though after they made their journey via the Blue Train from Calais to Paris, they were to board the night train from Paris to Milan from where their personal space would be very different. Emma and Anna would have their own cabin, while Juliet would share a cabin with Her Ladyship and Joe would share His Lordships, that way in their capacity of valet and lady's maid they could help their master and mistress dress without awkwardness.

As the boat engines began to rumble, Joe could feel Juliet trembling at the thought of the crossing. She had never been on the sea before.

'How on earth can something as big and heavy as this float?' she asked tremulously.

'I can assure you it will, my love.' Joe put a comforting arm around her shoulders.

'Poor Lady Emma,' Juliet sighed. 'It was such a shame there was no news of Ben when you rang David this morning at Bochym.'

'I know, she's going to be beside herself by the time we get to Italy. There was no news of Loveday either, so we'll all have to wait now for both outcomes.' Joe sighed. He glanced over at His Lordship, who seemed to be looking around for someone. 'I may have to leave you for a moment, Juliet. I think His Lordship is looking for me.'

As he pulled his arm from around Juliet's shoulders, Juliet saw who His Lordship was searching for, and gave an audible gasp. 'Oh, no! Look who the cat's dragged in, Joe,' as Henry and his valet strode over to the Dunstan party, 'Lady Emma will not be happy about this!'

*

Emma was quietly disenchanted with everything that morning – having no news of Ben's condition or Loveday for that matter. That meant with two days travelling before they got to Italy, it would be at least Friday before word might get through via telegram. She looked up from her despair when her papa suddenly stood up and smiled. She followed the line of his gaze and her heart plummeted. *What on earth was he doing here?*

'Ah, here you are, you made it then,' Peter said, shaking Henry's hand. 'Emma look who's here!'

Without getting up, she shot him a sharp look, and said, brusquely, 'What are *you* doing here?'

'Emma,' Sarah frowned, 'mind your manners.'

'Yes, that's not the sort of welcome I expect from my fiancée,' Henry teased.

Emma's face flushed. 'Nevertheless, what are you doing here?' she reiterated in exasperation, then felt a curl of dread - realising exactly why he was here.'

Henry smirked. 'I'm on my way to Italy!'

Emma's eyes cut from her papa, who was smiling broadly, back to Henry, who wore a malicious glint in his eyes.

'Yes, my dear, I'm staying in a villa in Tuscany – isn't that right, my lord?'

'Certainly is, my son.' Peter patted him on his shoulder. 'I thought it would be a nice surprise for you, Emma. A chance to get to know each other in more informal surroundings.'

'But where will he stay, Papa? There is only room for our party,' she stated bitterly.

'I've spoken to Justin and he says his neighbour Barclay Graham is away at the moment, so Henry and his valet can take his villa and share it with William. So, the boys will be quite separate from us at night.'

Not separate enough, Emma thought, as her papa gestured Henry to sit down with them.

*

The first part of their journey to Paris was taken on the famous Blue Train - and meant to be the highlight of the journey. It was an opulent train, used by the rich and famous where they could be fine dined and waited on in absolute splendour for a few hours. Now, having Henry tagging onto a holiday that Emma absolutely did not want to be on, was almost too much to bear. Fortunately, the journey to Paris passed without them having to exchange a single word, as they were seated on different dining tables for luncheon. It was later when they boarded the sleeper to Milan, that Emma found she could not avoid Henry any longer.

Her papa must have seen Emma's reticence towards Henry over dinner when she'd been seated next to him, because he leaned forward and said to Henry, 'Emma is quite upset at the moment, you'll have to excuse her melancholia. Her good friend Ben befell a terrible accident before we left for this holiday, and she is quite desperate for news on him. Aren't you, my dear?'

Emma felt her eyes water and Henry shot her an icy look.

'Did he now! Well,' he turned to smile at Peter, 'It's a good job I'm not a jealous man, for a jealous man would wonder why my fiancée is crying over another man.'

Peter laughed softly. 'No need for jealousy - you know they grew up together. It's just genuine concern for a friend.' He glanced at Emma and smiled. 'Dry your eyes, my darling girl – all will be well, I am sure.'

'So, how bad are his injuries,' Henry asked nonchalantly as he took a sip of wine.

'Catastrophic his father tells us,' Emma's breath hitched as she spoke.

'And pray tell, how did he come about these *catastrophic* injuries?'

Emma felt sure there was a mocking tone to his question. 'They found him at the bottom of a cliff.'

'Oh dear - that *was* clumsy of him,' Henry whispered, unfolding his napkin.

Emma felt her bile rise. She threw down her napkin, her appetite having left her, and excused herself from the dining table.

'What's happened?' Peter asked.

As Emma made her way out of the dining carriage, she heard Henry answer, 'I really don't know, my lord.'

*

At Emma's cabin, Juliet knocked and gained entry.

'Oh, my lady, I'm so sorry you have to endure this unexpected guest on our journey,' she soothed.

'I can't bear it, Juliet, I just can't bear the man. There, I've said it out loud.' She looked tearfully at her.

Juliet nodded. 'Perhaps you need to speak to your papa then.'

Emma dropped her head and shook it. 'My fate is sealed, Juliet. I'll have to marry him – I can't tell you why, I just have to.' She began to cry, and Juliet gathered her into her arms to comfort her.

*

Henry and his valet retired early after dinner, and after taking Anna to her cabin and checking on Emma, Sarah returned to the dining carriage to have a nightcap with Peter.

'I'm beginning to wish we hadn't invited Henry to join us,' Sarah whispered.

Peter hummed in his throat. 'I don't think there is anything to worry about, Sarah. Once Emma gets word that Ben is alright, she will not be so emotional and will settle down to a nice holiday with Henry.'

'Well let's just hope that Ben *is* alright, because if he isn't, I don't think our daughter will ever get over it.'

*

In Tuscany, Ruby was putting the finishing touches to the villas in readiness for their guests, one of which was due any moment now. Justin had gone down to Florence station to meet his nephew, William, from the Roma train.

They arrived with a toot of the horn and Ruby ran to welcome William to their home.'

'Gosh, Ruby, don't get too close. I've been travelling for weeks and only bathed in the sea. I don't think I smell too fragrant at the moment.'

Ruby laughed and kissed him. 'Then go and shower and we'll eat as soon as you're ready. Come, I'll show you to your room for tonight.'

'For tonight! Why only for tonight, are you going to throw me out tomorrow?' he grinned.

'We're *moving* you out. Your mama, papa, Emma, and Anna will arrive tomorrow, along with Henry and his valet. We thought you, Henry, and the valet can stay at Barclay's villa as he is away in England at the moment.

William put his bag down. 'Oh, right, so, who is this Henry chap?'

Because William had been travelling for weeks, and didn't know about Emma's engagement, Ruby and Justin had decided not to spoil the surprise of letting Emma tell him about it, so Ruby said,' You're father asked him along – he said you knew him – I believe he came to Bochym once - Henry Montague.'

William blanched, and sat down on the bed heavily.

'William! Are you alright? You look awfully pale all of a sudden.'

'Yes, yes,' he said raking his fingers through his dirty hair. 'Weary from travelling, I think.'

'Well, I'll leave you to get cleaned up. We'll eat early so you can get some sleep. I suspect some good food, wine, and a comfortable bed will revive you by the time everyone arrives tomorrow.'

*

William's mind was in turmoil as he stood in the shower letting the cool needles of water pummel his body. He had to think, and think fast, because he couldn't stay here - not with Henry Montague coming.

*

In the hospital, Ben had drifted in and out of consciousness briefly over the last few days, but his sheer agitation and obvious pain, meant he had to be suppressed by sleeping drafts. The Pearsons were still no nearer knowing if their son's body would succumb to his terrible injuries, but when Ben woke again on Friday morning - the sixth day after being brought to hospital, the doctors decided not to sedate him again.

Very slowly the pain crept into Ben's psyche, building with each second, until an involuntary moan escaped his throat, and his skin slicked with perspiration.

'I'm going to check your body for any sensation,' a doctor hovering over him explained.

Ben tried to speak, but found he could not. He tried to turn his head, but there seemed to be a large frame clamped to his face.

'Your jaw is broken, Ben. You may not be able to form proper words, but just blink twice for yes to my questions.'

Ben moved his tongue around his mouth – he was so dry.

'Nurse, bring something to moisten his mouth please.'

A stick with some wet lint was put to his lips and his painful tongue sucked on it thirstily.

'Now, Ben, I'm going to check your body for pain.'

Ben tried to speak, but the doctor halted him. 'Just blink twice for yes, alright?'

Ben blinked twice.

'Any pain in your right arm?'

Two blinks.

'Left arm?'

Two hesitant blinks

'Neck?'

Another hesitant two blinks

'Your hips?'

Ben stared at the doctor.

'Legs?'

No blinks.

The doctor nodded solemnly. 'You've sustained catastrophic injuries in your fall, I'm afraid. The breaks in your arms, legs, hands, ankles, and jaw should take about six weeks to heal, but unfortunately your pelvis was also broken, so that will take longer to heal. You will be with us for quite some time I'm afraid, but you're on the road to recovery. You've been very lucky, Ben.'

Ben closed his eyes – he certainly didn't feel lucky.

'We will begin to give you some thin broth now you're awake. Eating solids will be out of the question for quite some time. I can see from the perspiration on your face that you're struggling with the pain at the moment, but we needed to see how bad things were. The nurse will bring some pain relief for you now, but it won't be as strong, we would rather you stayed more lucid, so that we can monitor you better.'

'Doctor?' Ben heard his mother's voice. 'Why can he not feel his legs?'

Ben closed his eyes in despair – *because I'm bloody paralysed, aren't I!*

'He has a small injury to his spine – hence the body splint. That helps for us to move him regularly without doing more damage – an essential action so as not to get bed sores. Also, his pelvis is fractured. Many of the important leg muscles and abdominal muscles are attached to the pelvis, and allow for body motion and function. Until the pelvis and the spine begins to heal, we do not know if he has any function in his legs.' The doctor looked down at Ben. 'So, do not give up hope.'

'When will he be able to speak again,' this time it was Pa who spoke. 'The police want to ask him some questions. We believe there has been foul play afoot.'

'I see.' The doctor nodded. 'Not for at least five weeks I'm afraid. He'll be able to form some words that you can understand, but his jaw is clamped so he has very little mouth movement.'

Foul play! Ben felt himself suddenly being drawn back into the nightmare of that night. The violence in the saddlery and then the moment he had been thrown over the edge of the cliff. The moment his life - as he knew it - ended. The thought of the Barnstocks caused him great agitation - he must have them convicted of this. If he couldn't speak, then he must write and tell the police what had happened. He tried to flex his fingers, and yelped, the pain in his arms and hands almost made him sick.

The doctor looked down in alarm. 'Ben, all your fingers are broken too, so although I'm sure you need to give your side of the story to the police, I'm afraid you will not be able to do so by handwriting either.'

Ben groaned in despair. Laying here, broken, and desperate, it angered him that the Barnstock brothers were getting away with this.

Once the doctor had gone, his ma and pa loomed over him.

'Now you're awake, Ben, your ma and I are just nipping home. It's Friday today, we've been by your side since you came in. But we'll be back. Do you understand?'

Ben blinked twice.

'You mustn't worry about anything,' his pa added, 'His Lordship has paid for all your treatment, and this room, he's been very concerned about you – they all have. We'll let them know you're on the road to recovery now.'

Road to recovery! Recovery to what? A life spent in a wheelchair – a life without Emma – a life that was finished?

His ma put her hand on his shoulder. 'We'll send them a telegram. The whole family are on their way to Italy at the moment, staying with Her Ladyship's brother in their villa. They're meeting William there, aren't they, Sydney? And they have taken Henry, Lady Emma's fiancé – so that will be nice for them all to be together, won't it?'

Ben's eyes widened as he gave an audible groan. *Oh, God, no! They're taking Henry with them, and meeting William there!* That day, that awful day by the oak tree flooded back into his memory. And the letter! The letter that he wrote to warn William when he'd seen Henry laughing by the tree that day – it hadn't been sent, but then with William travelling, he probably wouldn't have received it anyway! *Oh, William, I'm so sorry, I can't help you now!*

'Ben, Ben, calm yourself,' his pa said, seeing how agitated he'd become. Sydney pulled Rose away and hissed, 'Now look what you've done, Rose. You shouldn't have mentioned Lady Emma – we need to keep him settled, not upset him.'

'Well, he has to know that she is getting on with her life with someone else now. It's no good getting his hopes up,' his ma said loud enough for him to hear.

'We'll leave you now, son,' his pa said apologetically, as he led his wife swifty out of the room. 'We'll see you later.'

When they'd left him, Ben took several deep breaths to calm himself down. There was nothing he could do, and well, if William were to meet Henry out there in Italy, at least he would find out about the engagement then – and would surely stop a marriage from happening.

Suddenly his heart constricted, and he allowed his guard to drop and the tears streamed down his face. *Oh, Emma, Emma, why are you so far away from me when I need you the most – and with him, that monster!* For sure Henry was a monster - he had no doubt about that, after seeing him laughing by the oak tree. Ben knew what he was capable of. In all honesty, Ben could not believe that Emma had gone to Italy and left him, knowing what had happened to him! After all, had he not a vague memory of hearing her scream his name when he drifted in and out of consciousness on the beach. If so, why had she abandoned him? *Why Emma, why?* Unable to wipe the tears away which were trickling into his ears, he decided crying wasn't the best idea he'd had all day. Fortunately, a nurse came, smiled, and dabbed his tears away.

'That's it. It's good to have a cry,' she said gently, feeding him a spoonful of laudanum for the pain. She returned a few minutes later, raised his head slightly, and placed a bib to his chin, then spoon fed him a thin soup for which his stomach thanked her for, by emitting a cavernous groan.

'Can you swallow comfortably?'

He blinked twice and she smiled again. 'That's a good sign,' she whispered, and he cried again.

After wiping his tears again, and giving him a sip of water, the nurse left him to settle back down.

Very slowly he ran his tongue across the back of his teeth, which felt dirty to the point of being furred. One by one he probed with his tongue to check to see if any were missing – remarkably they all seemed intact – though his jaw ached terribly. The dreadful metallic taste must have come from the blood in his nose, which he was told had been broken, but set straight again. What with the taste of blood, combined with the soup, his mouth felt wretched. As he tried to speak and form some words to himself, his breath smelled revolting. What he would give for a sip of mint tea to freshen his mouth. If only he could write to make himself understood. He flexed his fingers again and moaned in agony as a sharp pain shot up his arms and caused a prickle of perspiration to form on his forehead and upper lip.

Although the Barnstock brothers had done this to him, Merial had invariably instigated it - of that he was sure. It angered him that he was laid here, probably paralysed for life, while they went scot-free for their misdemeanour – just like they had done when Harry Pine had been attacked. The sooner he could tell the police his story the better. They needed to hang for what they had done. Eventually the painkillers began to work and his senses were dulled to the pain. Only the deep pain of loss in his heart remained.

36

The weary travellers were greeted at Florence train station by Ruby and Justin.

'Welcome one an all,' Ruby said in true Cornish fashion.

After kissing everyone she knew, she shook both Henry's, and his valet's hand.

'You must be Henry, Emma's fiancé.'

'Correct,' Henry answered coolly, 'and this is my valet, Clive Gibb.'

Ruby always prided herself on her instincts, and the first impressions of this man were not at all favourable. Pushing her feelings aside, she hugged Joe and Juliet tightly.

'Oh, my dear friends, you are going to love it here,' she enthused. 'I'm so glad you could come, though poor Theo and Lowenna, what a dreadfully worrying time this must be. Come, I've put you both in the summer house, so you can be near enough to help Sarah and Peter, but still have your own space.'

'Is William here?' Peter asked.

'Yes, he arrived yesterday,' Justin answered. 'We had dinner together last night, but he was awfully tired so retired early. We've seen neither hide nor hair of him today. We think perhaps he's ensconced himself in Barclay's villa ready for your arrival. He seems to have had a wonderful time touring Italy.'

'Did you tell him I was coming?' Henry asked.

'We did, and he was quite taken aback!' Ruby answered, noting that Henry appeared to be smirking.

'Come,' Justin beckoned them, 'we've brought two cars.'

*

Outside the train station, as Peter and Sarah headed to Justin's car, Henry tapped Peter on the shoulder. 'I say, my lord. Could we ride with you?' he lowered his voice and added, 'I don't trust a woman at the wheel.'

Peter frowned. 'Of course, but that's a rather old-fashioned attitude to take.'

Henry shrugged. 'Call me old-fashioned if you will, but a woman's place is not behind the wheel of a car. They're far too emotional to be good drivers.'

Taken aback by Henry's chauvinistic attitude, Peter said stiffly, 'You'll have to change your tune soon, Henry, Emma intends to learn to drive!'

'Does she now!' Henry answered stiffly.

As they climbed into the car, the conversation abated, but Peter felt a curl of unease about Henry. He very much hoped this young man wasn't going to try and clip his beautiful daughter's wings.

*

Justin took Henry and his valet to settle in Barclay's villa, and called out to William, but received no response.

Justin frowned. 'I wonder where he is. Never mind, Ruby has prepared three rooms for you all, I'll just check which bedroom William has taken, and then you can choose yours.' After inspecting all the rooms, Justin came back scratching his head. 'Well, William seems not to have settled in yet, so gentlemen, take your pick. Luncheon will be served at one, at our villa, we all share the same table, so Mr Gibb you will also join us for meals, as will Joe and Juliet – we don't stand on ceremony here. I shall leave you to settle in.'

When Justin left, they chose a bedroom and smiled at each other, looking forward to the fun they would have in here.

'If I'm not mistaken, it looks as though William has run away with his tail between his legs. Methinks he didn't want to stay and say hello. I wonder why?' he smirked. 'Lock the front door, Clive, we've a delicious hour to kill, before we take luncheon,' he curled his lip disdainfully, '…. with the *staff!*'

*

After Juliet and Joe had seen to the needs of Sarah and Peter, they settled themselves into the summer house at the back of the villa.

It was a beautiful clapboard building, whitewashed inside and out. They had their own bathroom, small kitchen, lounge and airy bedroom with a ceiling fan and a view out to the Tuscan hills behind the villa. They looked at the bed, dressed in cool white sheets and smiled at each other.

Joe pulled her into an embrace. 'Happy honeymoon, Juliet.'

'And the same to you, my darling husband,' she kissed him.

'Shall we…' he nodded to the bed.

'What? In the middle of the day! Oh no, Joe. It's not proper – it's not decent in daylight hours! Is it?' Her cheeks flushed alarmingly at the question.

Joe's eyes twinkled. 'There is only one way to find out.'

*

With everyone settled, Ruby began to prepare the simple lunch of tomatoes, mozzarella cheese, thin slices of local ham, and crusty bread. It was then she noticed the letter on the mantelpiece addressed to *Mama and Papa*. Without knowing the contents, Ruby sensed that William had gone, and she suspected it had something to do with Henry coming.

*

Taking the letter from Ruby, Peter read it, trying unsuccessfully to keep his temper. He handed it to Sarah, not trusting himself to speak for a moment.

Dear Mama, Papa, Emma, and Anna.

I am so terribly sorry that I couldn't stay to see you all. Please forgive me, but I have had to start my journey back to Oxford. It seems that I lost all track of time, travelling, and have some important work to do before the start of university. I do hope my departure does not mar your holiday.

Your loving son, William.

'I can't believe William would do this, Peter. Granted, if he had to leave sooner than expected, you would have thought he would have waited to say hello at least!'

'Has William gone somewhere, Mama?' Emma asked walking out onto the hot terrace to join them.

'Yes, back to Oxford it seems,' Peter answered curtly.

Sarah looked up at Ruby and asked, 'And he said nothing about this to you yesterday.'

'Not a word.'

'Well, I think it's damned rude of him.' Peter folded his arms. 'Sorry, ladies for swearing, but I shall have some strong words to say to him when next I see him.'

'Darling,' Sarah put a calming hand on his arm, 'this is so unlike William, I'm sure he must have had a very good reason to go back so soon.'

'He had better!'

*

Henry and Clive lay in the tumble of white bedsheets, both spent and covered in a sheen of perspiration. Clive turned onto his front and lit two cigarettes, handing one to Henry - they both took a satisfied drag.

'I say old chap, you might want to rein in your bigoted views on women - you quite ruffled His Lordship's feathers earlier, you know!'

'I can say what I want – I *will* be Emma's master.'

Clive gave him a sideways glance. 'Stop it, you'll make me jealous. All I'm saying is take care. Dunstan could have this marriage stopped if he thinks you won't treat his daughter well. That will mean you will lose your inheritance, and I don't know about you, but I don't want to live in some squalid accommodation, I rather enjoy the lifestyle we live now.'

'Stop worrying. I have everything under control. Come on,' he slapped Clive hard on his bare backside, 'I've worked up an appetite now.'

*

Joe and Juliet stood at each side of the bed to tidy the sheets, hiding all evidence of how they had spent the last half hour, except, that was, for Juliet's cheeks, which were still pinked with excitement.

They'd both been told to dress more comfortably for the heat – their normal black clothes relegated to the back of the wardrobe for the duration of the stay. Here, in these informal surroundings, they still had tasks as valet and lady's maid to undertake, but they also felt very much part of the family.

'Fancy us sitting down with the Earl and Countess, Joe,' Juliet said, as she pulled on one of the three summer dresses Lady Emma had insisted she bring with her. She twisted back and forth to admire herself, in a cool white linen dress printed with sprigs of lily of the valley.

'It will be rather unusual,' Joe said, looking quite out of character dressed only in a white shirt and beige trousers. 'Oh dear, I feel so underdressed like this.'

'I know what you mean,' Juliet said nervously as she came to stand beside him at the full-length mirror.

Joe reached out and curled his fingers around Juliet's.

'Now, we must, of course, always refer to His Lord and Her Ladyship as we would at home. No matter how informal things get at meal times.'

'Don't worry, I could no more call them Sarah and Peter than fly in the air.'

*

With ten around the table for lunch, Emma was seated next to Henry, but thankfully with Anna to her other side.

'No William?' Henry asked nonchalantly.

Peter cleared his throat. 'No, sorry, Henry. It seems William had some pressing work he needed to get on with in Oxford. He left a note, and sends his apologies, hoping it will not detract from our holiday.'

'That's a shame,' Henry smirked. 'I was rather looking forward to making his acquaintance again.'

Ruby paused from putting the food down on the table. Instinct told her William's disappearance was definitely something to do with Henry.

They were just about to start lunch when the bell of a bicycle was rung and immediately Juliet gave a stifled cry, to which Joe placed a comforting hand over hers to calm her.

While Justin got up from the table to deal with the postboy, Juliet apologised for her outburst. 'I'm so sorry,' she said holding her hand to her heart, 'it's just that the sound of a bicycle bell still fills me with dread, even now, four years after the war.'

Henry snorted derisively and everyone looked at him. Ruby in particular narrowed her eyes at him. 'The sound of a bicycle bell, invariably meant bad news from the front, during the war, Henry.'

This prompted Emma to give a small cry.

'Sorry, Emma, I know you're waiting for news from home,' Ruby said, 'but Henry needs to know that it's nothing to mock about.' She looked sternly at him. 'Thankfully you were too young to understand how dreadful the war was, not only for the men fighting in it, but for the loved ones waiting at home.'

Everyone nodded in agreement, but Ruby noted Henry's teeth clench at being so publicly reprimanded.

Justin handed the telegram to Peter, who put his spectacles on to read the missive. He nodded before handing it to Emma.

Emma took a deep breath - her hands visibly shaking as she read:

BEN AWAKE. RECOVERING.

'Oh, Ben, thank God, thank God,' she cried into her hands.

Ruby watched with interest as Henry rolled his eyes.

'I take it that was good news?' Justin asked.

'Yes, my steward's son, Ben – you'll remember him. Well, he met with a terrible accident last weekend, it was touch and go as to whether he would survive,' Peter answered and then turned to Emma. 'Now, my darling, hopefully this will put your mind at rest. I know how upset you've been.'

'It will, Papa, but I'm not so sure it was an accident!' Emma said seriously.

Everyone looked at her.

'What makes you say that?' her papa asked.

'I cannot say at the moment, but I'm sure - it was *not* an accident!'

Peter frowned. 'Then we must hope the perpetrators are hanged.'

'Amen to that,' Emma uttered.

Again, instinct made Ruby glance at Henry, just in time to see his Adam's apple move at Emma's statement.

'So,' Peter raised his glass, 'let's all toast Ben's recovery.'

Everyone raised their glasses, though Ruby noted Henry did so very reluctantly.

Peter too must have seen Henry's hesitancy, and said, 'Now then, Emma, now you know Ben is on the road to recovery, it's time to give Henry your full attention. The poor man has come all this way with us so you two can get to know each other better. We all know your mind has been on another, but I think Henry has shown great patience, which shows his good character.'

Henry bowed his head gratefully. 'Thank you, my lord.'

Emma, however, squirmed uncomfortably on her seat.

*

Later that night, Ruby lay in Justin's arms, not able to settle.

Justin kissed her. 'You're agitated, my love. What's bothering you?'

'Henry is bothering me. There is something about him that I do not like, and if I'm not mistaken, Emma doesn't like him either.'

'Are you sure?'

'I'm rarely wrong with my gut instinct as you know. I'm going to ask Joe and Juliet tomorrow if they can shed any light on why Emma has coupled up with Henry.'

37

The opportunity for Ruby to speak to Juliet came as they visited Florence that next morning. Henry and Clive had gone off sightseeing on their own, not caring to join the others in the Uffizi gallery. Though Peter had urged Emma to go with them, she politely refused.

'I would rather see art than the Arno, Papa,' she pleaded, so he reluctantly allowed her to join them in the gallery.

'Emma seems not herself for some reason – or are my instincts incorrect,' Ruby said when she got Juliet alone.

Juliet looked around cautiously. 'She's been very upset about Ben.'

'I noted her passionate emotion for Ben's predicament.'

'Lady Emma is very fond of Ben,' Juliet said tentatively.

'Fond?'

Juliet looked around to see if Joe was listening, but he was studying a painting. 'I believe she's in love with him.'

'Oh! So where does Henry come into this equation then?'

'Henry declared himself to Lady Emma in May. I think she agreed to the match so she could come home from her London season. Unfortunately, Henry dropped the bombshell of the engagement onto Lady Emma at her ball. In truth, she's not happy at the prospect, but there is something that is binding her to the engagement, but she won't say. Joe thinks it's because her Papa is keen for this alliance to go ahead for some reason.'

'I see, and do Sarah and Peter know of Emma's reluctance to this match?'

Juliet shook her head. 'You know Lady Emma – she will do anything to please her papa.'

'And so, she is to be condemned to a marriage without love, to the self-righteous Henry.'

'Yes, and I'm that sorry for her,' Juliet said sadly.

Ruby nodded, wondering what she could do to intervene.

*

In the hospital, Theo and Lowenna Trevail held onto each other as the doctor delivered his diagnoses as to why their little girl was so ill.

'I'm so dreadfully sorry to tell you both this, but Loveday has leukaemia.'

Lowenna emitted a strangled cry, and grasped at her husband's arm.

Theo swallowed back the lump which had formed in his throat. 'Is she going to ….' he asked tremulously - unable to finish the sentence.

'Die. I'm afraid so.' The doctor nodded sadly.

'But, but…. can nothing be done?' Theo was aware that his voice was high pitched and desperate.

'Very little, I'm afraid. They did try to give blood transfusions from siblings, to see if they could change the patient's blood, but it didn't work. And of course, although radium has also been found to be effective in leukaemia, it is widely acknowledged that patients might even succumb to the poisons released into their system.'

'Doctor, are you sure of this prognosis? I seem to remember Her Ladyship's brother Justin Devereux thought he was dying of a blood disorder, but our local doctor found that that was not the case, and he lived!'

'Yes, Dr Martin mentioned the Devereux case during our deliberations. I understand that Mr Devereux had mistakenly been diagnosed with pernicious anaemia, but it was in fact a bleeding ulcer.'

'That's correct, so, could this be a misdiagnosis?' Theo asked, grasping at straws.

'No, I'm afraid not. I ran the tests twice to make sure, and as you see, your daughter is covered in the bruises associated with the type of leukaemia she has contracted.'

Suddenly their world imploded, as Theo looked down at Lowenna who was sobbing inconsolably into her hands.

'What can we do?' Theo asked, his own tears now falling freely.

'You can take her home tomorrow - there is nothing more we can do here for her. Just let her enjoy what she can. She'll become increasingly tired, but carry her out into the fresh air and let her feel the sun on her face. I'm so sorry we can't do more.'

'Is she in pain?'

'No, she is just incredibly tired. I'm so sorry.'

'How long have we got with her?' Theo asked, his voice hollow. 'We've only just noticed her malaise!'

'Hard to tell. Everyone is different. Sometimes it's months, but by your daughter's poor condition.....'

With the silence at the unfinished sentence, Lowenna began to keen like a wounded animal.

*

The telegram from Bochym arrived at Casomi Villa at five that afternoon, just as everyone had sat down for aperitifs.

On hearing the bell, Emma stood up – a look of deep apprehension etched on her face.

'Oh no, please don't let this be news that Ben has relapsed,' she cried.

Henry grabbed her arm and pulled her back in her seat. 'For heaven's sake, Emma, calm your hysterics will you – you're wearing thin on my nerves,' he hissed.

Once again, Justin passed the telegram to Peter to open.

'Oh, good God!' Peter gasped.

'Papa, what is it?' Emma stood up again, shrugging off Henry's attempts to pull her back down.

'Oh, no, darling, it isn't Ben, it's....' Peter's breath caught in his throat and everyone tensed. 'It's Loveday - she has leukaemia - she's dying.'

The devastation was such, that no one wanted to eat that evening. Tears were shed, stories of how the little girl had touched everyone's heart were shared, and the mood of the party plummeted to depths of despair that were unfathomable.

*

Failing to share their misery, and weary of the maudlin mood towards yet another servant, Henry excused himself, and took off with Clive to their villa, taking a loaf of bread and a side of ham, along with three bottles of fine claret from Justin's cellar.

Deciding to take their picnic to bed, Henry bemoaned the fact that no one had been in the villa to make their beds, and decided to use the only remaining bed left that was still freshly made. As they lay in bed, tipsy and sated, Henry felt increasingly annoyed that there was no housekeeping in this villa, that they had to eat with members of the staff, and now, for goodness' sake, he had to put up with the family grieving over some common brat. He was also keenly aware that Ruby had got the measure of him.

He shared his thoughts with Clive, who shifted into a more comfortable position before nodding.

'Good God, but the Dunstans really need to get their priorities right,' Henry said picking a piece of ham from his teeth. 'Did you ever see such a ridiculous display of exaggerated emotions for a member of staff – well not even a member of staff – their silly little brat! I mean, leave the lower classes to lick their own wounds for goodness' sake - don't let it mar the holiday! They're all soft in the head if you ask me! I'm sick of Emma mooning over that damned saddler, and even William did me out of.... well.... you know what!'

'Were you not even a little bit concerned about William, after what happened last time you saw him?' Clive asked draining his glass.

Henry took a satisfyingly long drag on his cigarette. 'Not even a fraction. He wouldn't have dared raise any objections to me being here – because I warned him, good and proper – he knows what would have happened.'

'You're very sure of yourself, aren't you?'

'I leave very little to chance you see!' he said with a flourish of hand. 'So, I think it's time to go, and leave this family to their shallow lives, weeping over their damn servants. I'm bored sick of them all, especially Emma. Besides, I have a feeling that there will be no more clean beds in this place after tonight, and I'm damned if I'm making my own! I think we'll have a little adventure of our own, as we wind our way back to old Blighty.'

*

In hospital, Ben was dreaming – he was laid beside the stream in the woods. The sun was shining down on him, and Emma was by his side. They were making plans for a future together, all was well in the world, until he was awoken from his dream by hearing Pa speaking to Ma. Try as he might, he could not lull himself back into his beautiful dream, and then his attention was suddenly brought back to the real world.

'Oh, goodness gracious no, Sydney.' He heard his mother cry, 'tell me this isn't so.'

Convinced their distress was something to do with news of his injuries, Ben, unable to speak, emitted a mournful groan, that quickly brought his pa to his bedside.

Wide-eyed, Ben looked searchingly into Pa's eyes, waiting for him to deliver the bad news.

'I'm so sorry, my son, did we wake you. It's just…., well, I've just spoken to Theo Trevail in the corridor here,' he paused for a moment, 'Loveday was brought in to hospital a couple of days ago….' For a good few seconds, Sydney Pearson could not speak, he just bit down on his lip making Ben frown.

'The little girl is dying of leukaemia, Ben. How dreadful is that? The Trevails are devastated.'

Oh no! Ben closed his eyes, his breath became ragged, and more uncontrollable tears fell.

*

When Henry and Clive came up to the villa for breakfast, they found only the Earl and Ruby at the table.

As Ruby placed coffee, warm bread, and cheese in front of them, they received it without thanking her, so she took herself back inside, not wanting to sit with them.

'The others are still naturally distraught at last evenings news,' Peter explained.

'Naturally,' Henry answered, hardly able to keep the sarcasm from his voice.

'I'm going down to Florence to put a call through to Bochym this morning, but I don't think collectively we will be doing anything much today - but don't let that stop you two.'

'Actually, my lord, what with William not being here, and well, you have to admit that Emma, and in fact all of you, are preoccupied with one predicament or another, so my valet and I have decided to leave the family to deal with your sadness. You do understand don't you?'

'Of course, Henry, I'm just so sorry this trip has turned out to be marred with problems. And I'm sorry, Lady Emma was so preoccupied with Ben – she's been friends with him for a long time. If you get yourselves ready, I'll take you with me to Florence. I'm sure you can adjust your train tickets there.'

'May I see Emma before we leave?'

'Of course, you can. I'll go and ask Ruby to see if Juliet has helped the ladies to dress yet.'

*

Emma was dressed, but on hearing Henry's voice she had gathered a plate of food to take back to her bedroom, instead of going outside for breakfast.

When Ruby came to tell her about Henry, despite her sorrow for little Loveday, Emma felt a surge of elation to hear that he and his creepy valet were leaving.

'He wants to say goodbye,' Ruby said.

Emma nodded, brushed the crumbs from her dress, and with a lightness in her step that Ruby hadn't seen before, went out to see Henry.

*

When Henry saw Emma emerge from the villa, he walked over to greet her.

'Walk with me, Emma,' he said grabbing her by the arm and pulling her around the side of the house towards the laundry. When he found no one about, he shook her violently. 'You'll be pleased to know that I'm going,' he hissed.

'You're right, I am pleased,' she replied tersely.

'Next time I see you, I don't want to hear another word about Pearson, do I make myself clear? You will humiliate me no longer with your ridiculous mooning over another man.'

Emma struggled under his grip. 'You're hurting my arm, Henry, let go.'

'I will hurt you if you defy me in this! Not that lover boy will be a nuisance for a while,' he smirked, 'but I still don't want you anywhere near him – now he seems to be recovering.'

Every fibre in Emma's body prickled. 'You're glad he's injured, aren't you?'

'Oh, for Christ's sake, I'm not wasting another thought on that wastrel. Now, heed my warning, or else!'

*

Having seen Henry grab Emma roughly by the arm to lead her away from everyone, Ruby moved stealthily through the villa until she came to the laundry, and stood by the open window to listen to them outside. Not liking what she heard, Ruby opened the laundry door and folded her arms.

'Is everything alright, Emma?' She could see the relief on Emma's face was palpable.

'We're having a private conversation, if you don't mind,' Henry sneered.

'The conversation is over,' Emma said, and walked to Ruby's side.

Henry shot Ruby a derisory look and stalked off back to the front of the house.

'Emma, *is* everything alright?' Ruby asked anxiously.

'Yes, Ruby, nothing to worry about,' Emma said. 'Thank you.'

*

After dropping Henry and Clive off at the train station, Peter had rung through to Bochym and relayed a message to David for the Trevails. They were to be excused duties as and when necessary, and whatever Loveday wanted, she was to be granted. At the villa, while the rest of the family sat about in the sunshine, Juliet offered to go down with Ruby to clean Barclay's villa and were both shocked and disgusted at the state of the place! There were food and wine stains, and well, goodness knows what else on the sheets! Every bed had been used, the bathroom was awash with water, and wet towels were strewn everywhere.

'Good grief! What on earth have they been doing in here to get it in such a state? They were only here for less than two days!' Ruby grumbled, as she helped Juliet tie the sheets and towels in a bundle, holding them at arm's length as they walked them up to the laundry. 'I'm going to have to boil these to get them clean!'

In Cornwall, later that day, Ben opened his eyes to find a nurse standing over him, smiling gently.

'Ben, you have a visitor.'

His brow creased - he didn't really want to see anyone.

'It's Theo Trevail. He says you know him, and he would like to ask you a favour. Blink twice if you want to see him.'

He thought of poor Theo, Lowenna and Loveday and blinked twice. If he could do anything for them - even in the state he was in - he would.

Theo came to his bedside – his eyes red and bloodshot from weeping, and Ben tried to convey with his eyes how desperately sorry he was for them all.

'I'm really sorry to disturb you, Ben,' Theo said, his voice raw with grief, 'you look like you too have more than enough on your plate.'

Ben blinked slowly.

'It's just that ...well, Loveday heard you were in the hospital too. She won't let us take her home until she's seen you,' his voice wavered. 'We don't want to deny her anything she asks for, and she was always so fond of you. Are you up to seeing her before we take her home?'

Ben blinked twice. *Hoping she wouldn't be frightened by the look of him like this.*

The nurse who was by his side, said, 'Ben says yes.'

Ben's heart went out to Loveday, when Theo carried her in a few minutes later and sat her down by Ben's bedside. Her bright rosy complexion was yellowed, and dark circles dimmed her normally sparkly eyes.

'Oh!' Her lips pouted. 'It doesn't look like you, Ben! Why are you wearing that funny wooden hat? And why have you got a dirty face?'

Ben has had an accident, Loveday, that hat, you call it, is keeping his head still,' the nurse explained.

'Are you poorly too, Ben?'

''es,' he said through the narrow aperture of his lips.

'What did he say, Papa?'

'He said yes. Ben can't speak very well at the moment, darling,' Theo explained, 'he has a sore mouth.'

'You have lots of bruises, like mine, look!' She pulled her sleeves up to show off her bruised arms.

It took all Ben's resolve not to cry at the sight of her little arms.

'But I'm better now, I can go home. When will *you* come home?'

'Ben has to stay here for a while until his broken bones mend,' Theo answered, 'I think we should leave him now – he's very tired.'

'I'm tired too, Papa.' She reached up for him to pick her up.

With his daughter safely in his arms, Theo said, 'Say goodbye to Ben.'

'Bye, Ben, I'll see you soon.'

''es,' was all Ben could say, conscious that he may never see this lovely little girl again.

*

Although everyone's mood was subdued by the terrible news about Loveday, the atmosphere at the villa lightened considerably once Henry and Clive left.

'Goodness where have you two been all afternoon? We were about to send out a search party.' Justin kissed Ruby on the lips.

'Washing and cleaning for two very messy guests,' Ruby murmured.

'Well, as there is a general consensus that we can do nothing for poor Loveday, we may as well try to enjoy the holiday. We thought we'd all take a walk down to Giovanni and Rachel DiRienzo's vineyard, to sample their fine wine and cuisine. I think it will be nice to while away a few hours there, while we plan what else to do on this holiday.'

Ruby kissed Justin on the lips. 'That sounds like just the ticket.'

*

Again, that night, Ruby could not sleep, and it had nothing to do with the amount of wine they had consumed, or the heat.

Justin leaned over to her. 'Go to sleep,' he said, gently stroking his fingers down her face. 'We have an early start in the morning, if we're to drive to the coast.'

'I can't sleep.'

'Why, what's bothering you?' he said sleepily.

'Henry,' she answered quietly.

'Henry's gone now - you can relax.'

'He is not all he seems to be, Justin, and I'm dreadfully worried about Emma.'

Turning on his back, he put his arms behind his head - very much awake now. If Ruby had an inkling all was not well, it was not to be ignored.

'Well, I think we've all found him to be a very proud, self-satisfied individual, but he's young, and youth sometimes brings arrogance. He'll mellow with marriage.'

'It's more than that,' she breathed, unsure of what to say next.

'Tell me.'

'Every bed had been used in the villa.'

'Yes, so you said, maybe Henry couldn't find one to his liking – it strikes me that not a lot is to his liking.'

'No, I believe Henry and Clive shared the beds!'

'Pardon?'

'There were used wine glasses and plates of leftover food, on each side of the bedside tables, in every room!'

'They probably just relaxed on the beds to chat - they were left on their own for the most part.'

Ruby fell silent.

'What are you thinking?'

'I scrubbed and boiled those sheets today to get them clean,' she curled her lip disdainfully, 'they had most definitely not just been laying on the beds.'

'Oh. Oh, I see!'

'I've nothing against them doing anything, but I do not feel comfortable knowing Henry is not true to Emma.'

'Do you want me to speak to Peter?'

'I think you should speak to Sarah first. Don't say anything about my suspicions – it's not for me to judge him, but tell her to look more closely into Emma's feelings for Henry. I think Emma is hiding her dislike for Henry from her parents for some reason.'

*

After trips to the beach and sightseeing trips to Rome, Luca, Siena and Assis, the trip to Italy came to an end, and once Henry and his valet had left, everyone had relaxed into the holiday. It had been a shorter trip this year - ten days - they normally stayed a fortnight, but the tickets had been booked so they could return home with William in time for the start of his new term at university. Peter was still annoyed with William, that he hadn't bothered to stay around to holiday with them, and vowed to write for an explanation as soon as he got back to England.

*

William had slowly made his way back to England, and arrived back in his rooms at Oxford, around the time his family were boarding the train to return to England.

He threw his case on the bed. He was bereft at missing the holiday with his family, but what else could he do? If he lived to be a hundred, he would never want to see Henry Montague again. He sifted through the letters awaiting him, and found one which was rather dusty and crumpled, but had the word Urgent on the front. Slitting open the envelope, he read Ben's letter, and his legs almost gave from under him.

Dear Will,

I know we said we would never speak of this again, but I feel I must, as I think something very bad is about to happen. I never got a clear vision of the person who attacked you that day in the woods, I was so angry I just kept punching his face until he was unrecognisable. Nor did you reveal his name, but I think, in fact, I am certain, that I know who it is now. Henry Montague, I'm not wrong, am I?

I'm not sure if you know this nugget of information, as Emma tells me that you have been travelling this summer. She may in fact have already told you if you met up with her in Italy as she hoped you would. If so, I hope you have done something about it already. However, if for some reason you don't know - Montague has been to Bochym Manor, courting Emma! I met him on a couple of occasions, and neither encounter was pleasant. Call it intuition, but I felt that there was something vaguely familiar about him, but could not put my finger on what it was. To my dismay - as you can imagine - Emma became engaged to Montague on the night of her ball, though I'm told she had been coerced into a union with him, because of your father's business plans with Lord Montague. As I said, I didn't like him from the moment I laid eyes on him – though I knew not why, and it seems the dislike was mutual. It was the day after the engagement, that my intuition about him gained some veracity. You see, I surreptitiously saw him in the woods - visiting the oak tree. As they say, criminals return to the scene of a crime, though this criminal didn't look like he was there to 'make things right, or to try to 'undo the past.' I have to tell you - he was laughing heartily.

So, my friend, what are we to do? I know neither of us can sit back and let this marriage happen, but how do we go about it, without revealing what happened. Whatever we decide, we both know, Emma cannot marry that man - that monster.

I await your return letter.

Ben.

'Oh, good God, no!' William buried his head in the pillow and wept like a baby.

*

The Dunstan's party arrived back in England on Thursday the 31st of August and Emma in particular had a much more pleasant journey back, without Henry, than when they went. Emma was keen to go back to Cornwall, but as it was only five days until the Queen Charlotte's Ball, she reluctantly had to defer going, as her Papa decided they should stay in London until afterwards. After having looked forward to The Queen Charlottes Ball all summer, knowing now that Henry would be there - demanding she dance with him - had quite taken the shine off the whole event.

*

David, the footman, had been informed of the families delay in their return to Bochym, so there were letters waiting for them which had been redirected to their London residence. Within them was a letter to Emma from Zack.

Dearest Emma,

You will no doubt have heard of my escape to the big city and I'm so glad I took the plunge. London is proving good for me. I have been seen and heard by the greatest of men – Sergei Rachmaninov. He has set me on a path which I never thought possible. I am a student in the London conservatoire and have already sat two of my exams. I need to continue to study music. As you know, I could not read a note, but that has all changed now, with Daniel's help. I am told that I'm a genius, imagine that - me a genius! Daniel thinks it will not be long before I'm allowed to play in an orchestra. All my dreams have come true. Of course, my happiness is marred by what happened to Ben. What a dreadful accident. Have they found out what happened? Daniel allowed me to phone the hospital, but of course, as I'm not a relative, all they could tell me was that he had pulled through the operation. I hope perhaps you have more news. I suspect you've been to see him. When you go again, tell him I'm sorry to have left him at such a terrible time, but as he always encouraged me to follow my dream, I don't think he'll hold it against me.

I have no idea when I will return to Cornwall. Pa has refused to have me in the house again. Ma, of course is happy for me, as is Agnes, so I do have some allies. I'm sure I can count on you to be one too. If you're ever in London, please come and call on me. I'm staying with the Chandlers indefinitely, at the address above. I must say, Daniel and Jessie have been inordinately kind to me. Their children are exhausting me, but I love them very much – I feel like one of the family here.

Regards. Zack

*

Juliet was just putting the finishing touches to Sarah's hair when Emma knocked on the door to her bedroom.

'Mama, I've had a lovely letter from Zack, I wonder, can we visit him - he's staying with the Chandlers.'

Sarah smiled. 'Better still, we'll ask them all over for dinner on Saturday evening. Your father wants to speak with Zack anyway.'

'I hope he's not going to try and persuade Zack to go back to Cornwall. He's doing very well for himself here in London.'

'No, my darling. I think your papa would like to act as a go between to settle this estrangement. Now, I think we're finished here; Juliet, my hair looks lovely, you have a nice touch. You can go with Lady Emma now to help her dress.'

'Thank you, my lady.' Juliet turned to Emma with a twinkle in her eye. 'I'll be with you shortly, my lady.'

Emma knew from the look Juliet had given her that she had news, and paced the floor of her bedroom while she waited for her to come.

'Well?'

Juliet smiled. 'Joe has rung through to Bochym, I thought you might like to know. I don't know what has been said, because once Joe had dressed His Lordship he went to the kitchen to make sure dinner was on schedule.'

So, as soon as Juliet had dressed her, Emma went to Joe Treen's office.

Joe stood up and bowed slightly as Emma entered his room. 'Lady Emma. How can I help?'

'What news of Ben Pearson? Juliet told me you had rung through to the manor, I'm desperate to know more.'

'Of course, my lady. David spoke to Mr Pearson this morning. He said Ben is still very poorly. Both legs and arms sustained terrible fractures which they have splinted. His pelvis is broken and at the moment they're unsure if he will walk again I'm afraid.'

This news made Emma's breath catch. 'Oh, this is terrible news for him! I must go and see him as soon as we get back, poor Ben.'

'Mr Pearson told David that no visitors are allowed at the moment. Ben cannot speak, due to a head brace he has to wear. I believe it is keeping his jaw stable as that too was broken.'

'Can he write?'

'No, all his fingers are broken – it will be five more weeks before he can communicate.'

'Oh, my goodness!' She dropped her head in her hands. *Five more weeks before he's able to tell the police what happened, all the while the Barnstocks walk free.*

39

At dinner, Ben had been the focus of discussion throughout the meal, as the prognosis was not looking good for him. Emma could hardly eat a bite, she was so upset, and felt tears welling up at the thought of him being paralysed.

'Darling don't get upset.' Sarah placed a comforting hand over Emma's. 'Ben is having the best care. Your father has paid for everything he needs.'

'Thank you, Papa. I just wish we could go home.'

'We will, my darling, after the Queen Charlotte's Ball,' Sarah said gently.

'In truth, I don't want to go to the ball, Mama.'

'But it's one of the balls you were looking forward to, darling.'

That's before I knew I had to spend it with Henry. 'Yes but with this news tonight, my heart just isn't in it.'

'Who is Queen Charlotte?' Anna asked confused. 'Isn't Queen Mary George V's wife?'

'Yes, my dear,' Sarah explained. 'The Queen Charlotte's Ball is a prestigious event held every year. It was created by King George III in 1780 as a birthday celebration in honour of his wife. It's where all the debutantes file past an enormous 5ft cake, made to commemorate the anniversary of Queen Charlotte's birthday. They then curtsy to whichever dignitary or minor royal is presiding over the occasion. They cut the cake and the debutantes take a small slice to eat before the music starts and the dancing commences. I thoroughly enjoyed the ball when I attended.'

'I'll go, if Emma doesn't want to go,' Anna asked hopefully.

'Your time will come, Anna,' her papa said gently, 'I need to keep my little girl for another year or so, before I have to marry you off too.'

Anna gave an exasperated sigh.

Sarah squeezed Emma's hand. 'As his fiancée, Henry will expect you to be there.'

'I suspect he doesn't want to go either – he has no liking for balls.'

'Well, in truth, my time would be better put to use at home on the estate,' Peter said, and Emma's heart lifted. 'We could arrange to go home tomorrow.'

'It will have to be the day after, darling,' Sarah said, 'I've just sent an invitation to the Chandlers to dine with us tomorrow.'

'Saturday return it is then. Treen, can you notify the Bochym household. I'll inform the Montagues that we won't be attending the ball,' Peter said.

Emma could hardly contain her relief that she wouldn't have to spend any more time with Henry for a while. And she could hardly wait to be excused from the table, she needed to write to Ben. She needed to let him know that she was going to be there for him, no matter what. And even if he could not lift his limbs to read or write, one of his parents would read the letter to him – she was sure of that. With that in mind, she had to choose her words carefully.

My dearest friend, Ben.

The hand that writes this letter trembles for you. She smiled, hoping that the start of this letter would make him smile too. *Be it your ma, pa or a kind nurse who is reading this to you, as I understand you're not able to use your hands at the moment, I want you to know, you are very much in my thoughts. My heart goes out to you that you have suffered this terrible setback. I cannot even begin to understand what you are going through, but Ben, do not lose hope, you will get through this. Everyone will help you, and you have a strong will and mind and I know you will pull through. Bones heal. Scars fade, but there is still life to live. I will help as much as I am able, so that we can get you back to your workshop.*

In response to the last paragraph of your last letter, I want you to know that everything you said, I truly reciprocate. Just as soon as I am allowed, I shall come to visit you, but I am afraid Zack won't be coming any time soon. He has taken himself off to London, as I think we both knew he would. He asked me to tell you that he will write to you soon. He is carving out a new life for himself, and that, my dear friend is what you will have to do too. Stay strong, Ben, you will come through this.

Forever your friend, Emma.

After writing her letter, Emma flopped down on her bed, with Joe Treen's words going around her head. "They're not sure if he will walk again."

'Oh, Ben, how I wish I could hold and comfort you,' she cried into her pillow.

*

When both Emma and Anna had retired to their rooms, Peter and Sarah enjoyed a nightcap.

'I'm secretly glad we're not going to the ball, Peter. I think a little distance is needed between Emma and Henry.'

Peter frowned. 'Why do you say that?'

'It's something Justin said before we left. I've been mulling it over trying to make out if it has any verification.'

Peter tipped his head.

'Justin raised some concerns about Emma and Henry, and to be truthful I have some myself.'

Peter flashed a look of concern, which Sarah couldn't decide was for their daughter's welfare or the business Peter had with the Montagues. 'What sort of concerns?' he asked steadily.

'He said that Ruby had picked up on quite a few things that disturbed her with their relationship.'

'So, they're not Justin's concerns?'

'No, but Ruby was the housekeeper in this house for a long time and she's very perceptive to things that are not as they should be. Ruby would not have said anything to Justin if she wasn't sure.'

Peter put his brandy down. 'But Henry was only at the villa a couple of days - they hardly spent a moment together, and, of course, Emma was preoccupied with Ben's predicament at the beginning of the holiday. Perhaps Ruby picked up on the fact that Henry's patience was being sorely tested.' He raised his eyebrows. 'You have to admit it must have been difficult for him to watch his fiancée so distressed over another man!'

'It's more than that. Ruby believes that Henry is untrue to her – she didn't elaborate - it was just a suspicion she had.'

'Another woman, you mean, did he flirt with any women while he was in Italy?'

'I don't know, perhaps.'

Peter relaxed. 'Darling, many men sow their wild oats before marriage.' Sarah's eyebrows raised. 'Now, I'm not condoning it if he is doing so, I'm just saying.'

'Even so, Peter, I do think we should ask Emma again if she is truly happy with Henry.'

'We've asked her before, Sarah, and she always says yes.'

'Yes, but I'm sure you noticed she seemed to enjoy the holiday once Henry had gone, and you have to admit they're not the happiest of young engaged couples.'

'Again, I reiterate, Emma has been too preoccupied with Ben!'

'I think she cares for Ben more than Henry.'

'I know,' Peter said seriously, 'I think Henry knows that too, so you can understand his frustration with her.'

'Let's just give Emma some time, Peter, she is still very young. After all, she did request a delay in setting a wedding date.'

'You were eighteen when I married you,' he smiled warmly at her.

'Well, I had no concerns about marrying you, darling.'

*

On Friday evening, Daniel, Jessie and Zack arrived in a flurry of handshakes and kisses.

'I'm not going back,' Zack whispered to Emma as he kissed her on the cheek.

Emma hugged him tightly. 'Hush, I don't think that is the point of tonight's invitation.'

'I sincerely hope not.'

'So, Zack,' Peter said as they enjoyed a predinner drink, 'you've made your entrance into the big wide world then?'

'Yes, my lord,' Zack answered cautiously.

'And what an entrance it has been,' Daniel interjected. 'Zack has impressed many people with his playing, in fact he's been given the opportunity to play in his first concert in December.'

'What splendid news,' Peter slapped him on the back.

Zack smiled ruefully. 'I'm going to send tickets to my family, but I don't think Pa will come.'

Peter smiled. 'Don't give up hope, the concert is a while away – things may have changed by then.'

Zack didn't feel hopeful. 'I'd like you all to come too,' he said tentatively.

'Of course, we'll come. We wouldn't miss it for the world.'

Peter's enthusiasm made Zack's father's rejection even worse.

Around the dinner table, the conversation turned to Ben and what they knew of his injuries.

'Have they found out what happened yet?' Zack asked.

'Well for some reason, Emma doesn't think it was an accident – but she won't enlighten us as to why,' Peter said curiously.

Zack glanced at Emma questioningly, but she shook her head and stayed tight lipped.

'Well, darling, if it wasn't an accident, and there are people who would do such a thing walking free, then you must promise your papa and I that you will not ride out alone when we get back home. Do you promise us this time?'

'Yes, Mama.' *I have nowhere I need to go now anyway.* She mused sadly.

Zack moved closer to whisper to Emma. 'Do you think Ben knows it wasn't an accident?'

'I do, but until he can communicate, it's best for me to keep tight-lipped.'

Zack smiled. 'Understood.'

During coffee and brandy, they listened to Zack playing the piano and when they all started to move and say their goodbyes that evening, Peter pulled Zack to one side.

'As soon as you send the invitations out for your concert, I'll speak to your father, Zack. I'll act as a go between for you, and try to make him see sense. But can I suggest you send your father a letter now. Tell him that you respect the fact that he only wanted the best for you. But tell him how your life has changed and that you feel fulfilled in the path you have taken – just as he does as a thatcher. Tell him you just want to make him proud. I think it might help in the long run.' He patted him on the shoulder.

'Thank you, my lord, I will,' Zack said warmly.

*

The family arrived back at Bochym Manor late Saturday afternoon, to the overpowering aroma of beeswax, and a house and contents which shone like a new pin – Mrs Johnson and her staff had clearly been busy.

Although weary from travelling, Sarah and Peter went straight to Theo and Lowenna's cottage, to reiterate their offer to do whatever they could for them. They found them both strained and moist-eyed. Lowenna in particular was in a controlled state of turmoil as they tried to make life as normal as possible for a little girl who did not know her coming fate.

To Loveday's delight, Sarah had purchased a doll for her, dressed in traditional Italian costume. She'd also brought back a couple of boxes of the famous Gianduiotto chocolates, for both Loveday and Denny, who, Sarah suspected, would have been feeling very much pushed to the side-line.

'Is Loveday able to get about?' Sarah asked quietly.

'She is, to a point, my lady,' Theo said, 'though many times we have to carry her, as she is so tired. I take her to see the horses in the stables every day. When you rang from Italy, and gave us permission to use the gardens to sit in, Loveday was thrilled.'

'Bless the poor little girl,' Sarah breathed. 'Now, Lowenna I shall speak to Mrs Johnson, so that she and Juliet can take care of your duties.'

'Thank you, my lady,' Lowenna said tearfully.

'And Treen will take on yours, Trevail,' Peter added, 'you will, both of course, be on full pay.'

'Thank you so much, my lord, my lady,' Theo answered, 'but if you don't mind, I think I need to resume my duties to you, my lord while you're at home. I need something to occupy my mind.'

'Of course, Trevail, I understand, but if I travel I shall take Treen.' Peter put his hand on Theo's arm. 'We're so dreadfully sorry this is happening to you all.'

*

Later that evening, after the family ate an early supper and retired to the comfort of their own beds, a soft knock came on Joe's office door – it was Molly Johnson.

'Ah, I see you have not gone up yet.'

'I'm just partaking in a small glass of claret we had left over from the dinner. Care for one?'

Molly smiled. 'I don't mind if I do.'

Joe poured two glasses and they raised them.

'Did you have a wonderful time then - you and Juliet look as though you have caught a little colour. In fact, I don't think I have ever seen Juliet look so happy.'

'It was truly marvellous, Molly. Marred only by the dreadful news of Loveday. How are Theo and Lowenna coping?'

'Theo is holding himself together, and they're trying to make everything as normal as possible, but poor Lowenna...I keep finding her hiding in corners away from Loveday, weeping broken heartedly. I simply can't think of anything worse than losing a child, can you, Joe?'

Joe smiled tightly. *Never having one perhaps.*

40

Emma was up bright and early the next morning, hoping to catch the Pearsons before they set off to the hospital. Juliet had told her that Ben's parents took the Bochym car to hospital every day, but that Mr Pearson drove it back home after a couple of hours, so he could get on with his work, leaving Mrs Pearson to sit with Ben. Mrs Pearson then returned by train later in the afternoon, to be picked up from the station.

Emma watched from her bedroom window, as her papa spoke with Mr Pearson by the gates to the front garden. Even from this distance, the estate steward looked pale and drawn when her papa patted him sympathetically on the shoulder. *Oh, Ben, I hope you're alright.*

'I'm just going to see Mr and Mrs Pearson, before breakfast, Juliet - it looks like they are making ready to go to the hospital.'

'Yes, my lady. Let me help you on with your coat. There's a rare chill in the wind this morning – it's not like Italy.'

Emma smiled, as the coat gave her a little bit of snug comfort. 'I agree, the Cornish weather is a little bit of a shock, isn't it?'

With her letter for Ben in hand, Emma knocked on the Pearson's door. As Rose opened the door, she was putting her own coat on.

'Oh! My lady,' she said, almost blanching at the sight of Emma.

'Forgive me for calling so early, Mrs Pearson. I've been desperate for news of Ben. Mr Treen tells me he is out of danger now.'

Mrs Pearson pursed her lips. 'But certainly not out of the woods.'

Emma was taken aback by her abrupt manner. 'No, but we all wish him well and hope for a speedy recovery.'

Mrs Pearson lowered her gaze and nodded.

'Could you give this letter to Ben, please?'

'He can't use his hands, so he won't be able to read it.'

'No, I understand that, perhaps you could read it to him – just so he knows I'm thinking about him?'

Emma noted there was a slight hesitation - almost reluctance, to take the letter from her hand, but then Rose gave a curt nod as she pushed the letter into the handbag she was carrying.

'I must go, Lady Emma, Sydney is waiting,' she said stiffly, pulling the door closed behind her.

'Of course. Give Ben our good wishes too. We're all praying for him, and a happy outcome to all this,' she said, as Rose walked smartly past her and up the path to the waiting car.

*

While the family gathered for breakfast, a return letter arrived for Peter from William, but to Emma's dismay, he took it to his study to read.

Dear Papa,

I am deeply sorry that I spoiled the trip to Italy for you all. Your letter demanded to know the real reason I left. Well, the truth is, I hate Henry. I cannot tell you the reason, I am sorry, but there it is. He fell out of my favour some years ago, and I have no intention of ever renewing my acquaintance with him. Since my return to Oxford, I have learned, from Ben Pearson, that Henry is to become part of our family. This news has shocked me to the core. If this is true, I beseech you, Papa, to break this engagement, for the sake of Emma, my beloved sister. I cannot believe Henry has wormed his way into our family. He has clearly hidden his true character from you all.

William.

Peter sat back and dropped the letter on his desk. He felt quite shaken at the strength of William's hatred towards Henry. What was it that others could see in Henry, that he could not?

He cast his mind back to the only time William had met with Henry. They had gone out to play, and granted, within the hour Henry had come back in a terrible state – some tale about being attacked by a ruffian in the woods and that William had run off, leaving him to the beating. Lord Montague had been furious, and had driven Henry to hospital to have his broken nose fixed. Peter too remembered his own fury, as he waited for William to come home. He had called William a coward for leaving a defenceless boy to a beating, and then sent him to bed without supper. He'd also made William write to Henry to apologise for leaving him.

Peter drummed his fingers on his desk. Could there have been more to that incident than he knew. For sure, Henry didn't hold a grudge about that day – after all, hadn't he been looking forward to seeing William again? So, why did William hate him so?

Peter put the letter away for safe keeping – he wouldn't show Sarah yet. Perhaps it was just some schoolboy disagreement that had rumbled into adulthood. He would confront Henry about it when next he saw him. Perhaps he could shed some light on why William disliked him so much, and then they could smooth out this problem – for it would be a problem.

*

Having asked her Papa what was in William's letter, he'd replied that William had, in fact, had some pressing work to complete in Oxford and had apologised for spoiling their holiday. So, Emma sat down to write her own letter to him.

Dear William.

I understand a letter came to Papa from you, though he only shared a little of its contents with us. He was very angry about your swift departure from Italy, I suspect he said as much in the letter he sent on our return to England. I too was very disappointed, but I understand you are busy with university work, so don't feel too bad about it. Justin and Ruby told us all about your adventures, and I long to see you so you can tell me about them.

I have two pieces of news for you, first and more importantly, Ben was attacked and thrown from Poldhu Head on the 12th of August - the day after my ball. He sustained, what the doctors say are catastrophic injuries, and could be paralysed. William, I am distraught. He is allowed no visitors, nor can he communicate in any way. Until he does, the police cannot move on with their investigations. We must pray for his speedy recovery.

My other news is, on the night of my ball I found myself to be unintentionally engaged to Henry Montague! I do not love him; I do not even like him. Thankfully, Mama and Papa have noticed my reticence, and I am hopeful, of breaking the attachment soon. You and I both know there is only one man I want to marry, unfortunately he is in hospital at the moment.

I long to see you, William. Christmas is such a long way away.

Write soon if you have time.

Your loving sister Emma

*

Sitting in his halls of residence, William read Emma's letter, feeling shocked and relief in equal measure. Whereas one catastrophe had been averted, another had befallen his friend Ben. If Ben could not communicate at the moment, there was no point in writing to him. He would wait for more news from Emma on his condition.

*

At the hospital, Ben was asleep. His pelvis had been giving him pain these last few hours and the doctor had prescribed a stronger painkiller which made him very sleepy. Rose took the letter Lady Emma had given her from her handbag and ripped it open, watching continually in case Ben woke.

She read the letter, shaking her head at the first line, thinking the words - *the hand that wrote this letter* - was a silly way to start a letter. Once read, she put it back in her bag. There was no way she was going to read that letter to Ben. What did she mean - *In response to the last paragraph of your last letter, I want you to know that everything you said, I truly reciprocate.* Lady Emma would do well to leave Ben alone now she'd made her choice with the Montague gentleman. What right had she, to write such a letter, telling him that his friend Zack was carving a new life out for himself, when Ben's life was over! And to offer him help to get back into his workshop! Well, that was just a ridiculous thing to say. Ben would never work again - she was just giving him false hope. She must do everything in her power to keep Lady Emma and her son apart from now on. She would intercept his letters, so that he could forget her. Ben would be crippled now, and she, his ma, would be the one to look after him!

*

There had been complete silence surrounding the fate of Ben Pearson in the Mullion area. With the ongoing police investigation, his recovery progress had been contained within the circle of the staff at Bochym Manor and the Trevorrows at the dairy. So, to all intents and purposes, everyone else believed that Ben was still unconscious – this allowed the Barnstock household to relax, that was until Bernard walked into The Old Inn and the landlord threw him a letter addressed to him.

'I'm not a bloody post office, you know!' the landlord snarled. 'If you're doing anything underhand, use your own bloody address, not mine.'

Bernard ripped the envelope open.

You promised me a proper job, and you have not yet delivered. I hope you haven't spent the fifty pounds.

They had spent it, well, a considerable amount of it anyway. Bernard showed the letter to Barry, who began to quake in his boots.

'Stop worrying. It's been three weeks now. If Pearson hasn't woken up by now, he's not going to. He's a goner, for sure,' he assured Barry. 'Besides, the toff won't come near if there is a sniff of foul play.'

*

Taking His Lordship's suggestion, Zack had written a letter to his Pa. He thought long and hard about what to say, and screwed up several pieces of writing paper, until in the end, he wrote what Peter had told him to write.

Dear Pa.

Please would you forgive me, for going my own way, I had to follow my heart you see. You followed your heart onto all the roofs you thatch, and I am proud of the skill you put into your work. I want you to be proud of me – and you never would have been if I had taken up your offer of making coffins forever more. I would have dulled in your estimation over time - more than I already do. As you had a passion to thatch, I have a passion to make music. I want to do something that fills your heart with pride for me, where you look at people around you and say, "that is my son there." I believe I am now on the road to making you proud – I just need you to follow my journey so that I can show you the man I want to become.

Your forever loving son, Zack

*

The letter duly arrived at the Blackthorn's residence at Poldhu Cove with all the other post. Ellie glanced at the letter addressed to Guy – she'd know that handwriting anywhere, so popped it on the mantelpiece for Guy to read when he came back from work.

While Ellie dished out the supper to her family that evening, she said, 'There's a letter here for you, Guy, it looks like it's from Zack. It's on the mantelpiece.'

Guy paused a moment then carried on eating.

'Has Zack sent a letter to me too?' Agnes asked.

'And me,' Sophie joined in.

'No, just one for your pa today,' Ellie answered, watching Guy's blank reaction.

When the supper was over, Guy stood up and everyone watched to see if he would pick the letter up, but he walked past it, sat beside the fire, and picked up his newspaper to read.

Ellie glanced at her daughters and pulled a tight smile. 'He'll read it later,' she whispered, but he didn't, and the letter stayed where it had been placed, unread.

*

Emma decided that she would write a letter for Mrs Pearson to read to Ben every week. That way he would feel like he was outside living the life he should be. Ben's letters had helped her when she was stuck in London – hopefully, her letters would help Ben.

My dear Ben,

The hand that writes this letter, picked the posy of flowers I have sent to you – they are from Mama's garden and we hope they cheer you. The borders are still in full bloom from the summer, I wish I could bottle the fragrance and send it to you with this letter, hopefully the bouquet will transport you to the garden.

I've been to see Jimmy Trevorrow this week at the dairy, and have good news for you. He found Amara in your workshop the day you were taken to hospital. The poor bird was injured, like her master, but Jimmy took her to Ryan Penrose, who has cared for her. I took it on myself to visit Ryan, and I can tell you that Amara is on the mend now. She is shedding enough white feathers to fill a pillow case though, which I believe is a sign that she is stressed without you. Hopefully, you will be reunited with her very soon.

Everyone at the Poldhu Tea Room sends their best wishes. The visitors to the cove have diminished now, and I took a dip in the sea last Sunday with Agnes and Jake – the water is really warm at the moment!

Little Loveday says she wants you to come home, as do we all. Theo brings her to the stables each day, so I sit her on the front of my saddle with me and take her for a trot around the estate. Poor little mite, she smiles all the time, unaware of what is going to happen. We all pray to God that she lives long enough for you to come back home – it's all she asks for, I think you were her favourite person in all the world.

All for now, Ben. I will write again next week. Enjoy the flowers.

Ever your friend. Emma.

*

The flowers, Rose could not deny her son, but told him that the Countess had sent them for him. The letter she had read and stored in her handbag, along with the others, which included one from Zack Blackthorn, apparently lording it up in London. What on earth was everyone thinking – writing about places and things that were so out of Ben's reach now. It was a good job she had taken it on herself to hide these letters from him. It would just upset him.

*

Ben glanced at the flowers from Her Ladyship – at least *she'd* thought of him. He forced himself to stem his disgruntled thoughts - His Lordship was doing everything possible to help as well – this room, his treatment - all paid for by him. It was just…..well, where were his real friends, Emma, William and Zack when he needed them most? Why had they abandoned him? Emma perhaps, he could understand why, he had no doubt Henry would have prohibited her coming to him. But William, why had he not written to him? After all that had happened between them! Ben had been there for William in his hour of need, why had he not returned the help? He'd recovered enough to receive visitors, but none came, no one it seemed cared, and he was starting to feel very much alone in the world.

41

On the 25th of September, the brace supporting Ben's jaw was taken off. Very slowly, with the help of a nurse, he moved his jaw slightly, which sent shooting pains to his ears.

'It will be a few days before you can use your mouth to speak and eat again, so you will be on thin soup for a while longer,' the doctor said. 'Just very carefully start to open and close your mouth a fraction.'

Next came the removal of the splints from his limbs.

'We'll start to exercise your limbs in the morning when you've got used to being without the constraints of the splints. I'm afraid we will have to keep you prostrate for a while longer just to let your pelvis properly heal, and then we will get you into a chair.'

'The Earl de Bochym has purchased the best wheelchair he could for Ben,' his ma said proudly to the doctor.

The mention of the chair brought on a fog of depression, and Ben closed his eyes to the inevitability of the life he would live now he was chair bound.

Later that evening, when his ma had left the hospital, Ben started to recite the alphabet through the narrow aperture of his teeth. The sooner he could speak, the sooner he could put the Barnstock brothers behind bars for what they had done to him.

He mouthed, A, shuddering when a sharp pain shot through his jaw, then he tried to mouth, B. He waited a moment for the pain to subside before continuing, C, D, E, another shooting pain came with 'F' which made his attempts cease for a while. An hour later, the pain lessoned as he tried to mouth B and F again. He practised for most of the night, until he could almost speak legibly before finally dropping asleep in the early hours. When the nurse came the next morning to see if she could bring him anything. He replied, 'Yes, the police!'

*

Bernard and Barry Barnstock were hauling in the catch of the day. They fished from Mullion harbour on Captain Sawle's boat The Quest.

Clem Sawle had no liking for the vulgar, ill-bred Barnstock brothers - they could be bullish and argumentative at times with other members of the crew, but they were strong and worked hard, and that's all that mattered on a fishing boat. They were sailing back into harbour that evening when Clem caught Bernard boxing the ear of Johnnie Bray - the youngest member of the crew.

'Hey,' Clem growled a warning at him. 'See to your own work, Bernard and leave the lad alone, or look for another job.' Clem beckoned the fearful lad to work at his side.

Bernard bared his teeth at Johnnie, who trembled at the thought of the retribution to come.

Pulling up alongside the harbour wall, the crew made ready the baskets to be hauled up from the boat. Once the catch was unloaded and the deck swilled, Clem went back into his cab to make sure all was shipshape while the crew began to climb the iron ladder to the harbour. Johnnie, carrying the harpoon for Clem, made to put his foot on the first rung, but Bernard dragged him off. 'Get me into trouble would you?' he snarled. 'Well, I'll have you, you little bugger when Clem isn't watching.' Bernard gestured for Barry to climb the ladder first then Bernard followed him, breaking wind into Johnnie's face with every step he took.

Suddenly a scuffle began at the top of the ladder, and when Johnnie looked up, he saw four policemen, two of which had apprehended Barry Barnstock. Bernard, seeing what was happening, started to make his descent back down the rungs to make his getaway.

A policeman blew his whistle, and shouted, 'Don't let him get away.'

With Bernard's backside looming closer, Johnnie jabbed the harpoon into it so hard Bernard howled in agony, halting his descent long enough for the other two policemen to grab him by the scruff of the neck and haul him onto the harbour.

The crew looked on agog as one of the policeman said, 'Bernard and Barry Barnstock, I am arresting you both on the charge of the attempted murder of Ben Pearson. You do not have to say anything, but it may harm your defence if you do not mention when questioned something that you later rely on in court. Anything you do say may be given in evidence.'

As they marched them off to the waiting Black Maria, young Johnnie punched the air in delight.

*

News of the arrest spread like wildfire around Mullion. Merial and her mother, knowing full well Bernard and Barry were guilty of this heinous crime, and therefore would never return, quickly packed up all the belongings they could carry. But by the time they set foot outside their cottage, the neighbourhood was waiting for them. By the time they'd reached the wagon terminus, they were covered from head to foot in egg, rotting vegetables and the contents of several chamber pots.

*

Ben, hearing of the brother's arrest, was a hollow victory for him, now that he faced the prospect of life in a wheelchair. Since the splints had come off his limbs he had started to move his hands, arms, and fingers. The one person he knew could save him from the black fog descending on him, was Emma, so with hope in his heart he painstakingly picked up a pen and wrote.

Dear Em, Sorry, the broken hand that wrote this letter is shaky.

I know I have no right to ask, but please come and see me. Ben

'Ma. Could you make sure Lady Emma gets this, please, and don't look at me like that. I need to see her.'

Rose took the envelope, gave a sharp nod, and stowed it away in her handbag.

*

Zack had been studying at the London conservatoire for nearly two months and had made a few friends there. Slowly he ventured out into the London scene with some of them, visiting Jazz clubs and dance halls – it was all a far cry from life in a sleepy village at the far end of Cornwall. He did, of course, have the occasional pang of homesickness. He missed the sea, the coast, and the countryside. He missed his family too. Agnes and Sophie wrote to him, so did his ma often – they all understood his need to break out and find himself, but it seemed Pa wanted nothing more to do with his wayward son. According to Ma, his letter remained unopened.

During these outings in London, Zack was introduced to many young women, often finding himself thrown together to dance, but he had no desire to link up with any of them. They were nice enough, and fun for the best part, but they were too wild, too painted, sometimes almost boyish in their looks. He had never been any good with girls - with the exception of Selene Trevellick - who he'd got on with like a house on fire. He wrote to Selene, so too Kit and Sophie, and once he realised they were not angry with him for taking off as he had, they corresponded quite regularly. He'd been told that he would always be welcome at their house, and for that he was deeply grateful. It gave him the option to return to Cornwall, if only to see his friend Ben when he finally came out of hospital, which by all accounts would be months away. He'd written to Ben, apologising for leaving him at a time when Ben could probably have done with his friends about him, but he hoped he would forgive him for following his dream. He had not expected a reply, Emma had told him that at the time Ben could not speak or hold a pen, so he hoped that some kind person had read the letter to him.

So, for now, this was his life. He was earning nothing at the moment, but Daniel and Jessie had told him that he could stay forever if he wished – their children loved him.

By the end of September, a fellow student, Simon Dance, urged him to come out with him to a secret club. The club was in Soho – an eye opener in itself.

'Where the hell are you taking me?' Zack said, trying to avert his eyes from the many women touting their wares.

'It's a club, similar to an American speakeasy – do you know what I mean?'

'No,' he said in all honesty.

'You'll love it. Come on, it's down here.' They nodded to the man on the door and walked down a narrow staircase where the music became louder and louder the deeper they went into the bowels of the building.

The room was hot and lit only by candlelight on the tables, except for the stage which was dimly lit with amber lights. Tobacco smoke hung in ribbons from the low ceiling, making Zack wrinkle his nose at the smell.

'We're a bohemian lot down here. What happens here, stays here,' Simon said as he handed Zack a cocktail which looked and tasted like nothing he had experienced before.

Zack scanned the room. There were ladies of the night, albeit high class ones by the look of them. A band was playing, people were dancing, people were…no, they couldn't be, people were practically making love on the sofas at the edge of the room.

'Come with me,' Simon said, beckoning Zack through a curtain into another room.

Zack stopped dead in his tracks as his eyes scanned the room, and then he saw something that made him baulk. Henry Montague was on one of the sofas in a rather compromising position - with another man! He glanced around the room, to find men dancing together, men kissing each other!

'Christ, Simon, where the hell have you brought me?'

'Oh, I thought you'd like it here.'

'Why?' he said backing back out of the curtain.

Simon frowned and followed him back into the bar. 'So, you're not....'

'Not what?'

'You know.' Simon flicked his head back to the room they had just vacated.

'No, I'm not!' Zack could have punched Simon in the mouth for suggesting such a thing. 'Why? Are you?'

Simon looked unsure of himself for a moment, then he bit his lip and nodded.

'Oh, I see! Look Simon, I can't stay here, I'm sorry, I must go.'

'I'll come with you then,' Simon said following him.

Once outside, Zack stood in the rain trying to clear his head of what he had just seen.

'Do you hate me?' Simon asked.

'No, of course not. But Simon, you must be careful about these things. The law is against you. What if you were caught in a place like that? You would be thrown in prison.'

'I'm afraid its only places like that that we can be ourselves.'

Zack ran his hands through his hair. 'Well, I'm sorry for you. Truly I am. I'm not very worldly, but I do understand the predicament you face. But whatever gave you the impression that I was that way inclined?'

'You don't seem to like any of the girls the others have introduced you to. I thought...well, you know what I thought.'

'I'm eighteen years old, Simon, I come from a sandy cove at the far end of England. I haven't come across many girls except the ones from school and my sisters. I've come here to London, and have been given a great opportunity to follow my dream. I'm not interested in girls at the moment!'

'I'm so sorry, my friend.' Simon patted him on his shoulders. 'Can I still call you my friend?'

'Of course, you can. Just….. don't take me to places like that again, promise.'

'Cross my heart.'

42

Peter had become aware that his steward was growing increasingly morose during their morning walks around the estate.

'How is Ben's recovery coming along?'

For a moment Sydney couldn't answer, struggling to keep his emotions in check.

'Has there been some set back?' Peter pressed.

'I think Ben has lost the will to live. He's plummeted into such a state of depression, no one seems to be able to lift him out of it.'

'Oh dear, I'm so sorry. You would think the conviction of those two rogues would have made him rally.'

'I think he just wanted to live long enough to see justice – now his mind can only focus on his disabilities. He says he doesn't want to live life as a cripple.'

'You know, Pearson, Guy Blackthorn - the thatcher - suffered from an injury to his back some twenty years ago. Why don't you go and see him – ask him to visit Ben. If Ben could see Guy, fit and able to scramble over rooftops to thatch, after what happened to him, it might, just might give Ben hope for the future.'

*

Ben's depression was such, he could barely be bothered to do the exercises given to him to get his broken limbs working again. He picked at his food, was unresponsive to his ma's constant chattering, and wallowed in self-pity at the lack of visitors and letters from people he thought cared for him. Even his letter to Emma to come visit him, had fallen on deaf ears. Therefore, Ben was surprised to see Guy Blackthorn walk into his room in early October.

'Well, well, I thought I'd been abandoned. Even your Zack hasn't been to see me,' Ben said coldly.

'You've not been well enough to accept visitors,' his ma said in her panic.

Ben's eyes cut from his ma to Guy.

'Zack hasn't been because he ran off to London, the day after your accident,' Guy said bitterly.

'Oh! Did he?' He frowned, 'I would have thought he'd have written to me then. Is he alright?'

'I'd rather not speak about Zack - it's rather a sore point.' Guy twisted his mouth. 'I'm here to speak to you about your predicament. I understand your mood is low.'

Ben snorted. 'That's an understatement. It's so low I might as well be underground.'

'*Ben* don't say things like that,' his ma scolded.

Guy turned and smiled at Rose. 'Mrs Pearson, may I have a few minutes with Ben alone.'

Rose seemed reluctant to leave the room.

'Please, Mrs Pearson,' Guy asked.

Once she'd left the room, Guy pulled up a chair, glanced around the stark hospital room and sighed. 'I too have known this despair, Ben. Twenty years ago, I found myself in much the same predicament. I had cracked my back after someone tried to kill me. I was in the depths of despair. I thought I'd lost Ellie, because of reasons I won't go into now. I truly thought I'd never walk again - let alone work. As far as I was concerned my life was over, and I wanted nothing more to do with it. Thankfully, I had nurses who would not let me wallow in my own self-pity. My back mended, and with their help, and through sheer hard work and determination, the nurses got me back on my feet. I'm here to tell you not to give up, but to throw yourself into your recovery. It worked for me.'

'But I might be in a wheelchair forever!'

'So, you'll be in a wheelchair. You'll have to learn to live a different life, but you do still have a life to live. Believe me.'

*

It was the following weekend that Guy and Ellie dined at Bochym – something they did at least once a month.

'I went to see Ben on Tuesday,' Guy announced.

Emma stopped eating and looked at him in surprise. 'You went to see Ben! In hospital? I thought no visitors were allowed.'

'Well, Sydney Pearson asked me to go. He thought as I broke my back twenty years ago, and seeing how that worked out, it might give Ben something to live for.'

Emma felt a chill run down her spine. 'Why? Is his state of mind in jeopardy?'

'Understandably, yes, I too went down that road. I thought I would never walk again either.'

'Have the doctors confirmed that Ben will never walk again?' She looked stricken between Guy and Papa. 'Has Mr Pearson said as much, Papa?'

'It's still early days,' Peter said to calm her concern.

Emma looked back at Guy. 'Can he not move any of his limbs?'

'His arms and hands yes,' Guy smiled.

Emma felt a pang of unease. *If he could use his hands, why had he not answered her letters?* 'Is the movement in his hands and arms a new development, Guy?'

'I believe not. He's been able to use them since shortly after they came out of splints a couple of weeks ago.'

Emma's eyes began to water, and Guy noting her distress, said gently, 'Emma, I regained the use of all my limbs as you can see. That's what I told Ben, I told him not to give up hope.'

'Do you think he'll take heed?' she asked tremulously.

'It takes a strong will and determination, and Ben has those qualities. There is always hope.'

'How long were you in hospital, Guy?' she asked.

'Six long months, but things have moved on in the last twenty years. They plan to get Ben sitting up in the next couple of weeks, he will probably be home for Christmas.'

'I wish I could go and see him.' Emma placed her utensils on her plate – her appetite having diminished. 'I write to him every week but I get no letter back.'

'Give him time,' her papa said.

'So, what news of your wedding plans, Emma?' Ellie asked tentatively.

Sarah answered for Emma. 'We're not in any rush to set a date.'

'We might not be, but that was Lord Montague on the phone before dinner, Emma. He rang to say Henry and Lady Montague are coming down tomorrow. They're keen to set the date.'

Emma's heart dropped as she glanced between her parents.

'Henry wants Easter Sunday,' Peter added, 'but of course that is such a busy date in the ecclesiastical calendar.'

'Easter Sunday! What date would that be?' Ellie asked.

'1st April, I believe,' Emma said dryly.

'Well, I think that's probably a joke on Henry's part,' Peter added.

I'm not laughing, Emma grimaced.

Sarah must have seen Emma's consternation and said firmly, 'Keen or not, Peter, *we* will set the date when Emma is ready and not before.' Emma could have kissed her.

Later that evening in her bedroom, Emma felt a little more settled that her Mama was going to fight her corner and defer this wedding. She was dreadfully worried about Ben and his state of mind though. If only he would write to her. She'd sent four letters now - each one she'd written on the front – please could you read this to Ben. This time she would write one from the heart, and mark it private, so he would know how much she still cared for him.

*

On Sunday morning, Peter received a phone call from the Montagues informing him that the train to Cornwall could not run that day, due to a large tree across the line, so they would attempt to come down another day. Emma couldn't have been more thrilled at the news.

'I'm just heading off to the Pearson's cottage for a meeting,' Peter announced, 'I need to tell him that the trains are not running this morning.'

'I'll come with you, Papa. I have a letter for Ben,' Emma said hoping that what she'd written would help ease his melancholia.

*

Now that Ben was out of danger, physically, though not mentally, Sydney Pearson had returned to work full time, while Rose took the train to Truro every day to sit with Ben. The Bochym car took her to the station every morning and though His Lordship had suggested in the past that if he didn't need the car, the chauffeur could take her to the hospital, Rose always refused. She was grateful for the offer, and it would have been a lot easier, but she knew if the car were going all the way to Truro, Lady Emma would try to take advantage of the ride, so that she could see Ben – and that would never do.

Rose had successfully intercepted every letter Lady Emma had written, but was worried that Emma might send a letter to Ben by post. She'd explained to the nurses that Ben had been terribly hurt when someone he thought loved him, had got engaged to another. She'd said that the woman in question kept sending letters which upset him, and that was the last thing she wanted for her son, with all he had to contend with. She'd requested that any letters coming by post to Ben were to be given to her instead. Rose truly believed she was doing this for his own good. In her opinion, the longer the estrangement between Ben and Lady Emma, the sooner he could put her to the back of his mind and concentrate on getting better.

Rose could not wait for Lady Emma's marriage to happen, the sooner it did, the sooner she would have her son all to herself again.

*

When Peter and Emma approached the Pearsons, they found them waiting for the car to take Rose to the station, but before Papa could explain about the train, Emma smiled and handed her the letter for Ben.

'I understand Ben can use his hands now, so he will be able to read this *himself*,' she said.

Rose forced a smile and put the letter in her handbag, but when Peter told her there were no trains to Truro, Rose clamped her hands to her face. 'Oh goodness gracious, whatever shall I do?'

'I'm sure Ben will manage without you today,' Sydney said to calm her.

'Ben cannot manage at all!' she cried almost hysterically.

'Mrs Pearson, please be calm,' Lennox will take you to the hospital and bring you back after your visit,' Peter suggested.

'Oh!' Emma said brightly, 'if that's the case, may I come too and say hello to Ben?' she asked hopefully.

'No!' Mrs Pearson said sharply.

Emma was taken aback by her vehemence.

'I beg your pardon, my lady,' Rose quickly apologised for her outburst. 'It's just that Ben doesn't want to see anyone at the moment.'

Peter put his arm around his daughter. 'Don't worry, Mrs Pearson, Emma understands, don't you darling?'

As Rose climbed into the car with the chauffeur to drive away, Sydney also apologised. 'You must excuse my wife. She…. we… are desperately worried about our boy.'

'Think nothing of it, Pearson. We do understand,' Peter said, tightening his arm around Emma's shoulder. 'Now, shall we conduct our morning walk?'

As everyone left her, Emma felt a curl of unease that something was very wrong here. After all these years of friendship, she did not believe that Ben wouldn't want to see her.

*

In the back of the car, Rose picked out the envelope marked private and slit it open, pursing her lips at the ridiculous way she always started her letters.

My Darling Ben.

The hand that wrote this letter would give anything to stroke your lovely handsome face and help you to feel better. Now this letter is private, I can open my heart to you. I love you - you know I love you. I hope knowing this will give you something to live for. I am attempting to stall this wedding indefinitely - hoping that Henry will eventually give up on me, so I beseech you, please don't give up on us, my love. It's time to make your body strong again, so that you can come back to your home at the saddlery and I can help to heal your troubled soul and we can be together again. Please, write back to me, Ben, so that I know you still want me.

Forever your love, Emma.

Rose practically screwed the letter up in her hand. Had that woman no shame? Why couldn't she leave her son in peace? Pretending that the wedding wasn't going to go ahead – what nonsense was she talking. It was all just false hope again. That young woman would be the death of her son!

43

The Montagues arrived by train late Monday morning, much to Emma's dismay, and try as Sarah might, they would not be dissuaded from going to see the vicar at Cury Church. Before they set off though, Peter beckoned Henry into his study.

Henry blanched momentarily when Peter told him of William's letter.

'Did he say why he dislikes me?' Henry asked anxiously.

'No. Can you shed any light on this matter? Was it a schoolboy tiff you had that day in the woods, that William will not tell me about?' Peter asked.

'I'm sure I do not know to what he is referring, my lord. I was rather enjoying our little game in the woods, until that ruffian came upon me and attacked me,' he said without any hint of irony. 'I'm sure he'll come around when we become brothers-in-law.'

'Very well,' Peter said, dismissing Henry to join the ladies.

*

At Cury Church, and though the vicar put up a good argument for not holding a wedding on Easter Sunday, Henry had offered him a princely sum of money that swayed him otherwise. So that was it! The wedding date was set for all fool's day, and Emma could not help feeling that Henry had made a complete fool of her. As she looked at his smirking face, all she felt was anger for having been so incredibly gullible to have ever been taken in by him.

As they emerged from the church that day, it was purely by chance that Jimmy Trevorrow was walking past and spotted Henry Montague with Lady Emma. It was then he realised that this was the toff who had handed Bernard Barnstock the fifty-pound note.

*

Emma waited for a whole week, but still no letter came from Ben. In the end she wrote to Zack. Something in the back of her mind was telling her that all was not well. She received a letter back from Zack by return post.

My dear Emma,

Your letter regarding correspondence from Ben, aligns with my own concerns on that matter. I have written to him twice now and if, as you say, that Ben is able to write letters, I cannot understand why neither of us have heard from him.

I, like yourself do not believe that our friend would not want us to keep in touch with him. I am seriously wondering if our letters are going astray somehow.

I am also dismayed for you that your wedding date has been set. Henry is most definitely not for you! Stay true to Ben – I think all will be well in the end.

Fondest wishes, Zack.

Emma was puzzled – what did Zack mean by 'all will be well in the end.'

*

Zack had spent the whole week in turmoil after seeing what he'd seen at that dreadful club. Emma's happiness was at stake here, but he needed more information before he could act on what he'd seen. Simon, his friend, had unfortunately been away at his parent's house all week, but as soon as he returned, Zack questioned him if he knew Henry Montague and if he frequented the club often.

'Oh, yes,' Simon said with a flourish, 'everyone knows Montague. He comes to the club around nine every Thursday, Friday and Saturday, without fail. Why do you ask?'

'Oh, I knew him from a while back, that's all,' Zack answered nonchalantly. 'I had no idea he was a homosexual.'

'Well, we try not to broadcast it – for obvious reasons.' Simon grinned.

'Quite!' Zack nodded.

'I trust you will keep that under your hat too?' Simon said more seriously.

'Of course,' Zack said with his fingers crossed.

Later that night, knowing that Emma was desperately unhappy with the prospect of marrying Henry, and after a long deliberation, Zack took it on himself to write to Peter Dunston.

My Lord,

Forgive me. I could so easily have sent this letter anonymously, but I felt it my duty to lay before you the evidence that Emma's intended is not a man of honour. My life in London has seen me attend many parties, where the Bohemian life is taken to another level. I must therefore tell you that I came across Henry at a club the other night in a very compromising position – with another man! I dare not confront him of course, the Montagues are a powerful family, and it is no business of mine what he gets up to. However, I do believe the happiness of a beloved friend is my business, and for Emma to enter into a marriage with a man who will not respect her, is, to me, unacceptable.

In case you do not take my word for what I have just written, I do have it on good authority that Henry frequents The Kitty Club in Soho every Thursday, Friday and Saturday nights, around nine o clock, should you wish to see for yourself.

I beg you, my lord to take action. Henry will destroy your beautiful daughter with his unconventional ways, and as you know, if he is ever found out, and believe me, he is alarmingly promiscuous with fellow homosexuals, this will happen. If this is ever made public; Emma will suffer greatly, as will his family, and indeed your own, by association.

I must also tell you that Emma has no love for Henry, she is marrying him because you endorse the union, and she would never do anything to hurt you. I have known Emma for a long time and I know that she is deeply unhappy with the upcoming nuptials.

I do not wish to expose Henry to Emma, so I write to you, hoping that you allow her to be released from this engagement - without further question.

May I be so bold as to remind you that you fought my father by putting my case forward to allow me to have the life I wanted. I now put to you that you let Emma be allowed to live the way she really wants, and it is not being married to Henry.

If I can help in any way, please ask.

I beg to remain, Sir, your most humble and obedient servant.

Zack Blackthorn.

*

The letter arrived on a platter for Peter Dunstan at the breakfast table. He put down his newspaper and slit the letter with his opener, and clenched his teeth so hard his jaw ached. He got up from the table, leaving his coffee untouched, threw his napkin down and left the breakfast room.

In the privacy of his study, he read the first paragraph of the letter again. This could not be true, surely not! But why would Zack say such a thing if it wasn't? He rubbed his chin. He had to find out for himself – but if this place was some den of iniquity as Zack told him, he would have to tread very carefully. He lifted the phone receiver and put a call through to his lawyer.

At dinner that night, Peter kept glancing at Emma, wondering if she knew this about Henry but was afraid to tell him. She was certainly unhappy, especially since the date of the wedding had been announced.

'Are you alright, Papa?' Emma asked when she caught him looking at her.

'Of course, my darling, just glancing around at my beautiful family.'

Sarah smiled and reached over to put her hand on his.

'I'm going up to London tomorrow, I have some urgent business there. Treen, I shall need you to accompany me.'

'Yes, my lord.'

'Shall I come with you?' Sarah asked.

'No, darling, I shall be preoccupied for a couple of days. I would rather go alone.'

'Whatever you wish,' Sarah said slightly puzzled.

*

On Friday evening, on leaving the bright lights of Soho, Peter, his trusted lawyer Mr Sheldon, and Mr Elliot - a private detective Peter had engaged, followed Zack down a dark dank back street towards The Kitty Club. They waited in the shadows for almost an hour before Henry Montague strode up to the door of the club with his arm around his valet.

'Right, Mr Elliot, that is Montague!' Peter said.

'Very well, my lord. I shall report back later tonight.'

As Elliot walked to the door of the club, Peter turned to the others. 'This will go no further,' he hissed. 'Once I have the evidence, I shall deal with this matter my way. Emma must never know. You understand!'

'Of course, my lord. You have our upmost discretion,' Mr Sheldon and Zack agreed.

After dropping the lawyer off, and then Zack at Daniel's house in Mayfair, Peter shut himself in his study at his Belgravia home to wait.

*

Elliot had been greeted at the door, but refrained from giving over his coat and hat. He'd taken a seat at the bar and ordered a drink he'd no intention of drinking. He waited, biding his time. Presently he pulled the curtain to the back room and slowly walked through the throng of people, shrugging off the many hands of high-class prostitutes pawing at his sleeve. His eyes adjusted to the low light, his nostrils picking up the strange aromas of sweet tobacco. Glasses were raised to him, eyes beckoned him to sit. Men and women were entwined with each other, lipstick smeared and clothes array. He walked past a sofa where three women were enjoying each other's company, and then a ménage à trois involving two men and a woman. As he moved amongst the discarded sequin wraps and dinner jackets strewn across the backs of chairs, his eyes latched on to what he'd come to see. Henry was laid on a sofa, muttering soft expletives to a person he was engaging in some explicit act with. Elliot surreptitiously, took the first photo via the camera hidden in his coat. The light could have been better, but he was a good photographer to know the photo would come out. Henry's face contorted in whatever kind of ecstasy he had reached and two more photos were taken. Henry must have noted someone standing over him because he opened his eyes.

'Mr Montague?' Elliot asked.

'Yes, yes,' he held his hand up and slurred with drink, 'but you'll have to wait your turn though, I've not finished with my friend here yet.'

'Mr Montague,' Elliot repeated, and Henry narrowed his eyes crossly at him.

'What?'

'The Earl will see you in his study at Belgravia at nine prompt in the morning.' He then turned on his heel and marched out.

*

It took a couple of seconds for the sentence to sink in before Henry pushed his companion off him and straightened his clothes. He left the club almost immediately, with Clive swiftly on his heels, but once outside, the man was nowhere to be seen.

'Oh, for Christ's sake!' Henry raked his hands through his hair and tried to shake off the excessive drink he had consumed. 'The Earl must have sent him.'

'The Earl's not going to tell anyone, Henry, calm down.'

Henry spun around and grabbed Clive by the lapels. 'Shut up, Clive, I need to think.'

'Think? Think about what?'

'How the hell I'm going to get out of this mess! What if he tells my father?'

'Deny it. It's that man's word against yours. You just plead to your father that Dunstan has obviously decided his daughter wants to break with you, and to save his daughter's face he's making up outrageous lies about you.'

Henry stopped and leant heavily against the wall of a building, digesting this suggestion. 'Yes, yes. That's what I'll say. Come on, let's go home. I have an important meeting in the Earl's study in the morning - and I'm going to rather enjoy it.'

*

It was almost a quarter past midnight when Elliot knocked on the door in Belgravia and handed an envelope of photographs to Joe Treen.

Peter dismissed Joe for the night and then spread the photos out on his desk. He drank two glasses of brandy in succession and then sipped the third one more slowly as the evidence played in his mind. What he'd seen could not be unseen, no matter how much alcohol he threw down his throat. He had no feelings for or against anyone's sexual orientations, but what he did abhor was Henry's deceit to his beloved daughter. This man, who clearly preferred the company of men, was about to enter into a marriage which would be false and untrue. A marriage that would be intolerable for his darling Emma to countenance should she ever find out about his sexual exploits after the wedding. Peter was not about to allow that to happen, but this had to be managed delicately.

If there was one thing Peter was sure of, Henry would try to wriggle his way out of this situation. It was fortunate that so many people had tried to warn him against Henry. He knew his character now and Peter was ready for him.

*

It was nine thirty before Henry saw fit to call at Belgravia and breezed brightly into Peter's office – as though he had already won this war.

'Sit.' Peter barked at him.

Henry smirked and relaxed into the chair.

'Sit up in my presence!'

Henry's head nudged a little at the order, but manners told him to straighten his back in the presence of the Earl.

'So, what have you to say for yourself?'

Henry frowned. 'About what, my lord?'

'About duping my daughter into an engagement – when you so clearly have *other* preferences.'

Henry folded his arms. 'I think you'll find she said yes to me.'

Peter fought against the curl of anger rising. 'But she did not know what you were then!'

'I'm sorry, my lord, I don't think I comprehend what you're saying.'

'Don't come clever with me, Henry, you know exactly what I mean. Your despicable behaviour sickens me, therefore your engagement to my daughter is over. Now, for my daughter's reputation to remain unsullied by this broken engagement, it will be widely known within our social circle that it was Emma who broke from you. She will not have to give a reason; it is in her rights not to. For the moment, I shall not make Emma party to this decision, but I shall expect you to write to her as soon as possible, expressing your regret about her decision, but that you fully understand that you are not the right man for her, and agree to her ending the engagement.'

'I don't think so, my lord.' Henry crossed his legs and brushed his sleeve with his hand as though the request soiled him. 'If I allow Emma to break off this engagement, it will sully *my* reputation and lessen my chances of finding a wife. I must marry, you see, my father has threatened to disinherit me if I don't, and I'm not about to allow that to happen and let my brother Charles take all the riches.'

'I couldn't care less about you, Henry. Just as you so clearly do not care one iota for my daughter's happiness, or any other poor woman's, it seems. If you do not agree to my terms, I will very happily tell your father what I know.'

Henry snorted. 'It's your word against mine, my lord. I shall tell father that you are making up outrageous lies about me to save your daughters reputation. I shall tell him that it is I who wish to call this wedding off, because your daughter has sullied herself with another man. You cannot deny it, my lord, she clearly favours another. Ben Pearson! Need I say more? So, my lord, we will do this on *my* terms, or *I* could go to the papers, I could give them such a story about Lady Emma, it will be she who will be scandalised, not I.'

Peter stared at Henry with loathing, allowing him his short triumph before calling through to the adjoining room.

'Did you hear that blackmail threat, Mr Sheldon?'

Henry turned quickly to the door ajar into the next room to see a gentleman emerge.

'Henry, meet my lawyer, Mr Sheldon.'

Henry's face paled significantly.

'I sent a private detective to that *dreadful place of iniquity* you frequent, after I was tipped off by a third party about your indiscretion. I have the measure of you now, Henry, you see. It took a little time, but I started to take heed of all the people who warned me not to trust you – even my own son hates you - and he only met you once! So, understanding your true character, I knew that I must leave nothing to chance.'

Peter leant back and steepled his fingers in satisfaction.

Henry's face whitened. 'It's still my word against yours,' Henry said in an attempt to pull back some authority.

'I think not.' Peter pushed the newly developed photos towards Henry. 'Though the light was poor, his skill is so that he managed to take these shots of you in your *compromising position.'*

Henry baulked at the photo – although it was grainy, and he could perhaps argue that it was not him, he could see quite clearly his opulent signet ring - embossed with the Montague crest - on his hand, as it had been clamped over his companion's head. He slumped back in his chair defeated.

'The knowledge I have of you and the photographs shall remain a secret. I have no desire to see you thrown into jail – your sexual orientation is your own business. So, I shall expect my daughter to have a letter from you, acknowledging her decision to end this engagement, by next Tuesday at the latest. If not, I *shall* speak to your father, and show him the evidence. It will be up to him whether you languish in jail or not. Now, get out of my sight.'

Henry left the room as quickly as he could and as he slammed the front door, Peter looked up at Mr Sheldon with gratitude and poured two whiskies. 'I know its early, but....'

Mr Sheldon took his glass and raised it. 'Never too early for a good result.'

When Peter showed Mr Sheldon out, Joe was swilling a bucket of water down the front steps.

'I beg your pardon, my lord,' Treen said, 'but I think Mr Montague must have been feeling ill – he was violently sick when the fresh air hit him.'

Peter and Mr Sheldon exchanged a knowing glance.

44

William was in the university library on Saturday afternoon when a freshman came looking for him.

'Your father is waiting for you in your rooms, Lord Dunstan.'

William felt a pang of unease. This would be the first time he'd seen his father since he'd absconded from Italy. 'Thank you,' he said, and straightened his mortarboard.

'Papa, this is a surprise,' William said, placing his books on his table. 'You should have told me you were coming.'

'I've been in London, so I thought I'd take the train and drop in.'

William smiled in confusion. 'I've been at Oxford for over two years – you have never just dropped in before.'

'Well then, I won't beat about the bush. Your disappearance from Italy, and your letter pleading with me to stop Emma marrying Henry, perhaps you would like to enlighten me as to why?'

William, crestfallen, said, 'I can't, Papa.'

'As far as I know, you've only met Henry once.'

'Yes.' William felt his eyes begin to fill with tears.

'William. Did Henry do something to you when he was at Bochym four years ago?'

The lump which had formed in his throat rendered it impossible to answer.

'Please tell me, William. I can see that something is upsetting you deeply. I've been thinking about that day and remember that your mama and I saw a change in you afterwards. Your reluctance to venture further than the estate grounds. Your reticence with your friends afterwards, I know now it was not down to some adolescent emotion we thought you were going through at the time. I think it's time you told me. I think you're carrying a burden that you need to offload, and I think I know what it is.'

'I think not, Papa!' William said swiping a tear away.

'Henry Montague's true nature is known to me now. Rest assured - the wedding is well and truly off. Now, my boy, what happened to you that day?'

William crumpled into a chair. 'You will think of me differently if I tell you.'

'I love you, my son. Nothing can change that.'

William took a deep breath, but great sobs wracked his body before he could speak.

Peter reached over and placed his hand over William's. 'Have a good cry, son, and then wipe your eyes and tell me what you should have told me years ago.'

It took a good couple of minutes for William to compose himself – the horror of that day racing through his head, he shook his head, but his father squeezed his hand again.

'In your own time, William.'

Wiping his eyes, he began. 'That day, that dreadful day, it comes back to me often, and hits me like a steamroller. When Henry Montague came to visit, you made me go out and play with him, while Lord Montague did business with you. I was reluctant at first – because Henry kept looking at me in a strange way. He was giving me the heebie-jeebies, but I knew not why, but you and Lord Montague practically pushed us out of the door to go and play.'

Peter shifted uncomfortably in his seat.

'Henry fetched a coil of rope from his father's car. "Let's make a rope swing," he said and I reluctantly agreed. We walked into the woods where the stream trickles through the undergrowth, and looped the rope over a sturdy branch of a great oak tree. I believe it was recently uprooted in a storm - thank the lord for small mercies,' he added. 'Henry told me to hold the rope as far up as I could reach so he could tie the rope around my wrists so I wouldn't slip off it. Like a bloody fool I allowed him to do so. He held onto my waist and told me to walk backwards, so I could get a good arc when I swung, and guided me towards the tree trunk.'

William dropped his head, visibly shuddering at the thought of what happened next, so Peter squeezed his hand again for him to continue.

'Henry said, "You have some fine muscles on you," and squeezed my waist, and then…..' William gritted his teeth, '….and then he ran his hands over my body, touching things he should not touch, and said, "You're a handsome lad as well, aren't you?" Every fibre of my being stood on end, Papa, and I shouted, "Hey, what the hell are you doing? Untie me now." Henry told me to shut up whining, and pulled a handkerchief tight around my mouth, and then he whispered in my ear, "Let's see you in the flesh." I struggled frantically, kicking my feet back at him, I kicked so hard my shoes came flying off and then he pulled my breeches down to my ankles and pushed me hard against the tree trunk. He hissed in my ear, "This will be our dirty little secret, William. Say one word to anyone, and I'll say you made me do it – you forced me to do it to you, and you'll go to prison."

William dropped his head in his hands and sobbed. 'Oh, Papa, what happened next, was truly painful and terrifying, if it hadn't been for Ben coming to rescue me after hearing my muffled screams, I……'

'Ben! Was it he who beat Henry up that day?'

'Yes. When he saw Henry behind me, and what he was doing to me, he went berserk. He dragged Henry away from me and started punching him in the face and kicking him until he howled in pain, and then Henry managed to scramble away. Ben was staggering from the exertion, his eyes wild with rage when he came to help me down. My legs had given way and the knot had tightened, so he had to cut me loose with his pocket knife. I fell to the floor and eased the rope from my wrists. I remember pushing Ben to one side, while I vomited violently, and then I crawled to the stream, discarded my breeches, and sat in the freezing water to try and take away the shame and pain. Ben picked up my shoes and clothes and brought them to the side of the stream ready for me to put back on. He put his hand on my shoulder to comfort me, but I flicked his hand away - I couldn't bear anyone to touch me.'

'William, are you saying Ben knew that it was Henry Montague who attacked you? Because if he knew, and he never said a word about his character when he found out he was Emma's beau, I will personally strangle him!' Peter said angrily.

'No, Papa, Ben didn't know who it was – I wouldn't tell him, I just said he was the son of my father's friend. To be honest, Ben had been so intent on punching him, he never got a clear view of Henry's face. Ben wanted me to tell you what he'd done to me, but I grabbed Ben by the shirt, almost pulling him down the muddy bank into the stream, and told him to promise me, that he would never breathe a word of this, this, disgusting thing that had happened to me. Poor Ben, he was struggling to keep his balance as his hands sank deeper into the mud, but I wouldn't let go until he'd promised me. When he did, I remember I dropped my head into my hands to cry, knowing I couldn't go home until Henry had left. When Ben said that he'd made a bloody mess of him – broken his nose for sure - we were fearful that someone might come looking to see what had happened. I got dressed, and Ben, bless him, gave me his jacket because I was shivering with shock. He took me to the woodshed in the woods and then went off to watch for Henry leaving the manor. I remember crying again, sobbing like a baby, thinking what a fool I had been to have let him tie my hands like that.' William paused and looked up at his papa. 'Ben kept his promise, you know, he fielded questions from the others as to why I would not venture near that bloody tree again – he is truly the best of men, I'll never forget his kindness to me that day.'

'My poor boy, and to think I berated you and made you send a letter of apology to Henry. Can you ever forgive me?'

William nodded and then swallowed hard. 'Are you disgusted at me now?'

'No, my boy. I'm not, and nor should you be for what happened. It was completely out of your control. Thank God for Ben.'

'Amen to that,' William agreed. 'Poor Ben. Emma wrote and told me about Ben's attack,' he shook his head, 'what happened to me, now pales into insignificance. Have the perpetrators been caught?'

'They have. It was the Barnstock brothers, and they will undoubtedly hang for sure. Thankfully, there was a witness, who verified Ben's account of the attack.'

'It was actually Ben who told me about Henry's engagement to Emma. He sent me this letter - he must have sent it before he was attacked. William handed the letter over to Peter. 'It posed such a dilemma. I couldn't let him marry Emma, but I didn't know how to warn you about Henry's character without telling you about what happened to me.'

'Oh, bless you my boy.'

'I feel damaged though, Papa. How can I ever have a normal relationship with a woman, knowing this happened to me. I feel that Henry has ruined my life.'

'He can only ruin your life if you let him. You must not let things like that define you, if you do, you will always be a victim. We Dunstans are made of stronger stuff than that, William. It happened, it was horrible, and I won't trivialise it, but you must refuse to be a victim, and in the end that will make you the victor.'

'So, Papa, how *did* you find out about Henry's real character?'

'That, my son, will be my secret. I don't ever want Emma to know what sort of person he is. Next week, we will put it out to everyone we know, that Emma has broken the engagement, for reasons she does not wish to reveal - that should be the end of it.'

*

Peter returned to Cornwall the next day in a speculative mood. After learning of Henry's despicable attack on William, he felt now that Henry had got off too lightly. Peter was not a vindictive man, but my God, he wanted to teach that damned upstart a lesson. He was unable to act on anything though, for he could never expose what had happened to William. He had to pull on all his reserves when he got home to hide his disquiet from Sarah.

*

On Monday, the 16th of October, three households - the Trevellicks - the Blackthorns and the Dunstans received their invitation to Zack's London debut concert which was to be held on the 20th of December. At Bochym there was also a letter waiting for Emma in the post.

'Oh, my goodness!' Emma gasped, causing Peter and Anna to look up from their breakfast. She placed her hand to her heart and burst into tears of elation. 'I can't believe it!'

'Emma, what is it?' Peter said tentatively, hoping that Henry had done his bidding.

Emma could hardly breathe. 'It's from Henry. Our engagement is off!' Her eyes glittered with happy tears.

Peter watched his beautiful daughter emerge from her doldrums like a butterfly from its chrysalis, and was deeply regretful that she'd felt the need to bottle up her despair.

Emma must have noted his expression, because she quickly added, 'I'm so sorry about my unchecked reaction, Papa. This is no way for me to act, I know.'

'I'm ashamed, Emma,' Peter said grimly.

Crestfallen, Emma answered, 'I'm sorry I've shamed you, Papa.'

'No, my darling girl, I'm ashamed of myself, not of your reaction. I had no idea that the thought of marrying Henry was so disdainful to you. You should have said – I asked you often enough.'

'I know Papa,' her voice trembling, 'but I dare not say.'

'Why on earth did you agree in the first place?'

'I didn't! It was Henry who said I'd said yes, and I could not let Henry look a fool for asking me in front of all those people. I was so angry with him though for dropping it on me like that. When I told him later that I would revoke the engagement when everyone had gone home from the ball, Henry said I couldn't. He told me that his father would disinherit him if he did not marry me. He also said you would face financial ruin if the wedding did not go ahead.'

'Did he now!' Peter gritted his teeth. 'What does his letter say?'

She handed him the short missive.

Lady Emma,

After much deliberation, I think that an end to our engagement would mutually suit both of us. Please return the ring.

Henry.

Peter felt the muscles in his jaw tighten – this was not the letter Henry had been told to send, damn him.

'Oh, Papa, I'm sorry. I cannot think why he has said this. What is to be done now? Will you be ruined like Henry said you would? Will we lose Bochym?'

Listening intently, Anna dropped the knife she was holding and looked fearfully at her papa. 'Will we, Papa?'

'Lose Bochym! No, of course not, my darling daughters. Emma, I think Henry has told you a tall tale there. I *have* done business with Lord Montague, but it is he who has invested in a financial deal with me - not the other way round. The deal certainly had nothing to do with a favourable outcome of your wedding with Henry - I would never gamble on your happiness, my darling girl.'

Emma broke down and wept again - this time in relief, and Peter got up and gathered her into his arms. 'If only you had told me what Henry had threatened - we could have stopped this engagement in a heartbeat. I can see from your elation that this news makes you very happy.'

'It does, Papa, I can't tell you what a relief it is.'

'However, I will not allow Henry this claim. Treen. I need you to convey to the rest of the servants that it is Lady Emma who has broken the engagement with Henry, and it is not, as Henry states, a mutual decision. I will not insult you by asking that you conceal what you have really heard this morning.'

'Indeed, my lord.'

'Oh, and if Lord Montague phones – I'm away from home. I don't think I want to speak to any of the Montagues at the moment.'

'Yes, my lord.'

*

In the Blackthorns cosy kitchen at Poldhu, Ellie smiled when she saw Zack's handwriting on the envelope and opened it with relish. She loved to hear what he was doing in London.

'Oh, how wonderful!' Ellie placed her hand to her heart.

'What is it?' Guy said shrugging on his coat.

'It's from Zack. He's playing in his debut concert on the 20th of December. He's sent us four tickets. He says he's invited the Dunstans and the Trevellicks as well.' She held the tickets aloft, her face beaming with delight.

Guy stilled for a moment, but said nothing.

'Guy?' Ellie tipped her head.

'I'll see you tonight,' he said, picking up his tool bag and left without saying goodbye.

Dropping the letter and tickets, she followed him out into the yard. '*Guy!*'

'I don't want to talk about it, Ellie, alright.' He got into the wagon and barked at the others to get in.

Agnes frowned and looked at her ma and mouthed, 'What's happened?'

'I'll tell you later,' Ellie answered, too angry to speak more.

45

Emma could hardly contain her happiness at the news that she was free of Henry at last. At her writing desk, she pulled out a piece of paper to write the good news to Ben. It might just be the tonic he needs to pull him out of the doldrums.

My Darling Ben.

The hand that wrote this letter has been clasped with my other hand in happiness. You see, my love, I am free. Free of Henry. Papa has allowed me to call off our engagement and I, as I am sure you are, will be thrilled with this news. Henry lied to me you see. He lied that Papa would face financial ruin and this was not the case. My love, please let me come and see you? I long to hold your hand so that you will know how much I love you. Whether you are wheelchair bound, or not, you are still my Ben.

Until I see you again, I'll send my love and good wishes in this letter, I hope my news helps to make you strong again, so you can return to me and we can be together as we planned.

Forever, my love. Your Emma x

Emma had just sealed the envelope when her mama knocked on the door.

'Well, Emma. Your papa has told me what has happened. I will endeavour to write to convey to everyone that it was you who broke the engagement – we do not need to give a reason. But darling, you should have told us what Henry had threatened. Did you really think your papa would gamble on our home and your happiness? Don't you know that your happiness is our top priority.'

'I do now, Mama. I'm so thankful it is all over. But I have no idea how this has really come about.'

'Whatever has happened, we are both glad that you're happy with the prospect. Now darling, you do know what this means. You must go through a second season and hopefully we can find someone more suitable for you.'

'No, Mama! I don't want to go through another season.'

'But Emma you must! Otherwise, it will greatly reduce your chances of finding a good match.' Sarah reached out and took Emma's hands. 'I promise you, that we will endeavour to make sure you are much better placed this time – with someone you can trust and respect.'

'I would rather fate find me a husband, Mama. I want to marry for love, not particularly a position in life.'

Sarah got up. 'Well, we shall see when the time comes, but your papa will have the last say about next season. As your parents we must do what is best for you.'

When her mama had gone, Emma's elation dipped slightly. She had won this battle, but there was still a war to fight.

*

Rose Pearson smiled through gritted teeth as she took the letter from Lady Emma's hand, noting Private on the envelope again. Knowing that the letter could contain personal words of love and encouragement as the first private letter did, it went against her sensibility to open any more private marked letters. So, this one would remain unopened with the others, but stowed away for safe keeping away from her poor son's eyes.

*

When Peter set off on his rounds with his steward he was still mulling over what to do about Henry. He had clearly not followed his instructions about the letter, which had put a partial blame on Emma for the dissolvement of the engagement. And of course, now that he had learned of the despicable attack on William – he felt that Henry had got off too lightly. When they reached the perimeter of the grounds, Peter glanced at his steward, noting that he too was mulling over something, he asked, 'Is something troubling you Pearson?'

'Yes, my lord.'

'About Ben?'

Pearson cleared his throat. 'Indirectly, yes.' Pearson stopped and looked around him.

'Well, spit it out man.'

'You see, my lord. There has been some new evidence come to light, about Ben's attackers.'

'Good! The more the better if it will mean those two rogues are hanged for their part in this.'

'Indeed.' Pearson pulled his lips tight a couple of times, unsure how to proceed. 'The thing is this, my lord - Lady Emma's fiancé, Mr Montague, was seen in The Old Inn at Mullion with the Barnstock brothers, the day of the attack.'

'Go on,' Peter breathed.

'Well, Jimmy Trevorrow was collecting glasses at the Inn at the time and he overheard a gentleman say to Bernard Barnstock, "I want this done properly - you hear me - the bastard broke my nose once." Then the gentleman handed over a fifty-pound note to Bernard.'

The bastard broke my nose once. Peter shuddered - *that could only be Montague.* 'So, why has this only just come to light. Why wasn't it in Jimmy's original statement?'

'It was, but as no one knew who the gentleman was, the police couldn't link it to the attack. It was only by chance that Jimmy saw Mr Montague coming out of Cury Church with Her Ladyship and Lady Emma the other day, and realised he was the gentleman he'd seen with the Barnstocks.'

'I see. Can Jimmy's statement be verified?'

'Yes, the police have asked at the inn, and the barmaid said Bernard tried to buy drinks with a fifty-pound note that night, she refused it, and told them to take it to the bank in Helston to change. Further investigation show that on the Monday after Ben's attack, the bank ledger at Helston showed a fifty pound note had been changed. I'm sorry, my lord but when this evidence is made public, it will impact on your good family's name – and of course Lady Emma's future.'

'Rest assured, Pearson. Montague is no longer attached to our family in any way. Lady Emma has called the engagement off.'

'Oh, I see.'

'So, let the police do their worst.'

'Yes, my lord.

*

After finishing the rounds with Pearson later that morning, Peter walked through the side entrance door to be greeted by Joe.

'Lord Montague has been on the phone, my lord. I explained that you were away from home.'

'Did he say anything else?'

'Only that he was in France on holiday with Lady Montague at the moment and would speak to you on his return to bring about fixing this broken engagement. He sounded rather angry, my lord.'

Peter grimaced at the audacity. 'Thank you, Treen. I'll be in my study.'

Peter sat down on the highly polished leather seat and thought of Ben. Could it be that poor Ben suffered these dreadful injuries because he'd helped William in his hour of need? If so, Henry Montague really was a monster. Well, Henry, the buck stops here. He lifted the telephone receiver. 'Operator, could you put me through to Helston police, please.' When he was connected, he said, 'Lord Dunstan – The Earl de Bochym here. I understand you have received some new evidence about the attack on Ben Pearson. Evidence linked to Mr Henry Montague.'

'Yes, my lord. We were about to come and see you about it before we spoke to Mr Montague – we understand that he is engaged to Lady Emma.'

'Not any longer – Lady Emma broke it off. I'm phoning you because I believe the evidence against him to be true. It has been brought to my attention that Mr Montague had a grudge against Mr Pearson that we knew nothing about. Now, I understand the senior Montagues are from home, but I have it on good authority that you can find Henry Montague in the back room at The Kitty Club in Soho every Thursday, Friday and Saturday night from nine p.m. I expect to hear about his arrest from you shortly.'

'Yes, my lord. Thank you for the information.'

When he finished the call, a knock came and Sarah entered.

'Is everything alright, Peter, you look flushed?'

'It will be, my darling - It very soon will be.'

*

Emma received an unexpected letter the following Saturday, from Jenna FitzSimmons.

My dear Lady Emma.

Your mama spoke very favourably to me a few weeks ago about your writing, and also told me that my dear late husband James encouraged you. I am still very much involved with James's publisher and have spoken to him about you. He asks if you could send him a sample of your work to see if he can help in any way. I have enclosed his address for you. Remember to enclose a cover letter saying that I endorse your writing.

We shall look forward to a happy outcome.

Yours sincerely

Jenna FitzSimmons.

Emma's mouth formed an O – life seemed to be getting better by the minute.

'Good news, Emma?' her papa asked.

'Yes, look!' She handed him the letter.

'Do you have anything to send?'

'Yes, though I haven't written much over the summer, what with one thing or another, but I do have a novel half finished, and a few short stories he could look at.'

'Well, I wish you luck, my darling,' Peter said, as David the footman came to the breakfast room door to tell him there was a telephone call waiting for him.

*

Peter sat in his study, steepling his fingers. He was sitting on the satisfying news that Henry Montague had been arrested on the charge of the attempted murder of Ben, and a charge of gross indecency, having been caught in a compromising position with another male. It would be in the papers on Monday. He must speak at once with Sarah, as they would, of course, as a family have to deal with the fall out, but for now, Peter congratulated himself that he had avenged, not only Ben, but William and Emma too.

*

On Monday, the newspapers ran the story of Henry's arrest and with him being the son of Lord and Lady Montague, the story made the front page.

There was no hiding the story from Emma, Peter and Sarah knew that everyone would have read it by the end of the day. So, the paper was kept out of the way until Anna had finished her breakfast and gone up to the school room.

'I think I'll take Saffron out this morning, Papa, will someone inform Mama?' Emma glanced at Treen, who bowed his head.

'Before you go, darling, you need to see this.' Peter handed her the newspaper.

'What is it?' she smiled.

'Read the front page.'

Emma glanced at the paper and then stood up, almost upsetting her cup and saucer. She threw the paper down as though it had burnt her.

'Oh, good Lord,' she said in utter disbelief, feeling the blood drain from her face. She grasped the table for stability and both Peter and Joe stepped forward to assist. Putting her hand up to stop them advancing on her, she sat down heavily. Glancing at the headline again, she stole herself to read the story. 'Arrested on the charge of the attempted murder of Ben Pearson!' she said almost inaudibly. 'Oh Papa, to think that monster has been a guest in this house, and on our holiday!'

'I'm so sorry, Emma,' Peter cupped his hand over hers. 'He certainly hid his true character from us.'

'From you and Mama perhaps,' Emma said spikily.

Peter nodded in agreement.

Calmer now the initial shock had passed, she said, 'And a charge of gross indecency! She looked straight into her papa's eyes, 'I take it that means….'

Peter cleared his throat. 'I believe it does.'

'Oh, goodness, I feel ill,' she said clutching her throat.

'Shall I get you a glass of water, my lady,' Joe asked.

The offer fell on deaf ears. 'But why? Why would Henry want to kill Ben? What did Ben ever do to him?'

Peter remained tight lipped.

Silence ensued for a moment, and all that could be heard was the ticking of the clock, and then Emma clamped her hands to her face. 'He tried to kill Ben because of me, didn't he, because of my friendship with Ben?'

'It's not because of you, my darling girl - don't ever think that. Henry was a very controlling individual – it seems he would do anything to get what he wanted. He tried to kill Ben because he and those dreadful Barnstock brothers are vile and evil.'

'Yes, yes they are,' she breathed. 'I hope they hang – all of them. Thank goodness the engagement had been broken, Papa. Perhaps Henry knew this story was about to break and he did that to lessen our family's association with him?' Emma said trying to find some positive in the situation.

'No, darling, I won't allow him any credit for doing so - he deserves none. I know for a fact that Henry Montague does not possess an ounce of decency.'

Emma looked blankly at her papa, and suddenly realised, that Papa had been instrumental in the broken engagement.

'Now, my darling. We must manage this situation the best we can.'

'Will I be notorious, Papa - having been linked to him? Will it affect our standing in society?'

'Fortunately, we as a family distanced ourselves from him. Your mama wrote to everyone she could, to tell them you had broken with Henry. I believe we will avert a scandal. There may be rumblings of course, it's only natural, but our good family name will rise above everything. The Montagues will take the brunt of the whole sordid affair, of that I'm sure.'

*

In the Pearsons household, Sydney and Rose read the report in the newspaper, though they had been forewarned about it by the police. The police had left it to Sydney to tell Ben, but they hadn't in fact told him yet, and were undecided whether to or not at the moment. Ben was in such a fragile state of mind, they feared it would be too much for him to deal with, if he found out the Barnstocks had been paid to kill him. He would have to know of course, certainly before the trial, which had been due in November, but would not now take place until after Christmas, in light of the arrest of Henry Montague. Ben would have to be told of the change in trial date, but not the reason, at the moment.

'To think my poor boy is going to be crippled for life, just because he was *friendly* with Lady Emma!'

'You don't know that was the motive, Rose.'

'What else could it be? I'm telling you, Sydney, if when Ben comes home, Lady Emma comes within a foot of my door, I'll, I'll....'

'You'll do nothing, Rose. You must remember our position here. Besides, I don't think she will come. To be truthful, I think the friendship, or whatever it was between them, is well and truly over. As far as I know Lady Emma hasn't even written to our boy in all the time he has been in hospital.'

Rose had to turn away from her husband to hide the fact that her cheeks had coloured up. Lady Emma had handed her another letter for Ben only yesterday.

'Talk of the devil, the postman is here,' Sydney said, 'I'll be off on my rounds with His Lordship. I'll leave you to get ready for the car coming to collect you.' He kissed his wife and headed off to work.

Rose took the letter from the postman, noting the envelope had the embossed de Bochym crest on it. From Lord William, perhaps. Rose was in a quandary now. Should she give the letter to Ben – what if he mentioned that Henry Montague had tried to kill him – for sure they, and His Lordship, knew a few days ago before it broke in the newspaper – His Lordship was bound to have told his son. Rose glanced at the time – the car would be here in a couple of minutes, 'Oh lord forgive me,' she said as she steamed the letter open.

My dear Ben.

My apologies for not having written before. I was late hearing about what happened to you, and I am so deeply sorry that you have found yourself in this predicament.

As you may know I was travelling through Italy during the summer. I would have learned sooner, if I had as planned, made a stop off at Uncle Justin's villa, but I got wind of the fact Montague of all people was going to be in the family party. As you can imagine, it floored me. I had no idea why he was coming, there had been no mention of the engagement between him and Emma. I understand since, that my family were going to surprise me with the news – and what a dreadful surprise that would have been! I took myself off before they arrived, therefore did not learn of the attachment Henry had made with Emma until I got home to Oxford and your letter was waiting for me. As you can imagine, I was astounded, shocked and dismayed by the news of the engagement. I replied to you immediately, unaware of the dreadful situation that had befallen you. I also wrote to Papa informing him of Henry's unsuitable character and that he must have Emma break the engagement forthwith. I couldn't tell him, of course, why I thought him to be unsuitable, and at first I think Papa thought I was just over reacting. Thankfully, other people had raised concerns about him and when Papa delved deeper into Montague's character – his true colours came to light. I have to tell you, Papa knows the secret you and I kept, and he says he will be eternally grateful for what you did and your discretion. And now my friend, we have this dreadful news that Montague paid to have you killed. His evilness, it seems, holds no bars. It must be a relief to us both that my beloved sister is free of that monster. I wish you God's speed in your recovery, Ben. I shall be home at Christmas to see you.

Your friend, Will.

Rose folded the letter back into its envelope and knew not how to process the contents. She couldn't show it to Ben - it contained too many things that she would rather keep secret from him. But she was very much afraid, that her actions in reading this letter had made her party to something so secret, so dreadful, that only a few people knew of it and those who knew could not speak of it. This in itself, would eat into her curiosity until her dying day.

The letter was duly put with the others. On the day it would inevitably come to light that William had sent Ben a letter, Rose would claim it must have been lost in the post.

46

By the end of October - a month after Guy's visit - Ben had rallied, if only to get out of this place. Pushing his self-pity aside, he'd done everything asked of him to get his limbs moving, but there were still weeks of therapy ahead of him. He could now move himself from the bed to the damn wheelchair – a contraption he hated, but at least he could manoeuvre himself about, allowing him to manage the toilet by himself which gave him some dignity back.

He spent his days by the window - though his view was of other hospital buildings, but occasionally he would see the birds in the trees beyond. He thought of Amara - poor Amara – he'd seen that brute Bernard swipe her with a chair and she'd fallen to the ground, she could not have survived, he was sure of that. His mind turned to everyone he'd lost, all his friends seemed to have forsaken him. He'd been in this hospital three months now, and not a single letter from any of his friends. Yes, they were all busy with their lives, but one of them could have written at least! All he'd received was the occasional message via his pa from His Lordship wishing him well. Well, he needed more than the occasional well wish. Ben was a person who needed his friends around him - didn't they know this - had they learnt nothing about him during the years they had grown up together? He cast his mind back to the letters he'd sent to Emma while she was stuck in London. The way he'd described nature in all her changes to her so that she wouldn't feel homesick, she could have done the same for him! But what had Emma done for him when he needed it most, nothing, absolutely nothing. According to his ma she was busy arranging her wedding. He shook his head at the thought of her marrying that monster. He honestly couldn't understand why that wedding was still going ahead – surely William had found out about it now! He could only surmise that he'd been wrong about Henry being William's attacker. Had his sheer hatred for him, twisted his memory of who he'd seen that day? But he would have thought William would have written to him to put the record straight if that was the case. Ben had never felt more alone. The only constant in his life were his parents – namely his ma, who visited every day without fail. He loved her dearly, but wished she wouldn't because he was heartily bored with her company.

*

Since that dreadful newspaper report, Emma had kept to the grounds of Bochym Manor. Most mornings she rode Saffron, almost always taking little Loveday for a quick trot first. The child seemed to rally a little when she was with Emma - pretending she was a princess trotting around her great estate.

'I miss Ben, Lady Emma, do you?' Loveday said one such morning.

'I do,' Emma answered sadly.

'Are you going to marry Ben when he comes home?'

Emma's heart constricted – Ben wouldn't even answer her many letters. 'I think Ben will be too poorly to get married, Loveday.'

Her little body almost deflated as she sat at the front of Emma's saddle. 'When he's not too poorly, will you marry him? Because you said I can be your bridesmaid, didn't you? And if you don't do it soon, I shall be so tired I will sleep through the whole day!'

Emma gave the child a little squeeze, but felt too choked to speak.

In the afternoons, Emma took herself down to the Dower Lodge to write, finding that heartache and disappointment fuelled her writing like nothing else could. As they always say – write about what you know.

Emma was eternally grateful for Jenna FitzSimmons's help. James Blackwell's publisher had been kind and informative when he'd seen her work, and wrote to her saying that there was potential in the short stories, but they were naïve, and she needed to grow more as a writer to learn how to craft a story properly. He had sent her a report on how to fix many of the great errors that new writers often stumble on. Emma had devoured the report, and through the early part of the winter, she had completely re-written the novel on which she'd been working. She desperately needed something to distract her from her unhappiness.

*

At the beginning of December, Ben started to experience, what he believed to be phantom pains in his legs. He remembered speaking to the Polhormon farm hand, John Ellis, who had lost his arm in the Great War. He'd told Ben that he could still feel the pain of where the shrapnel entered his arm, even though his arm was no longer there. Ben couldn't flex his feet or feel his toes, so he knew it must be something similar he was experiencing, but still, it was quite strange to feel something again after all these months.

On the 15th of December, his doctor told him that there was little more the hospital could do for him now. The exercises he had been given were to be done for the next few months in order for him to gain the greatest movement in his upper limbs. His parents had been told to make a room ready in their cottage, because Ben would be home by Christmas. But as the festive season approached, the winter winds blew bitter and cold in Cornwall, so too did Ben's heart when he thought of Emma. Because she had forsaken him, the very last place he wanted to be was to be near her in the steward's cottage at Bochym Manor!

*

On Sunday 17th December, Sarah returned home from taking tea at Poldhu and went in search of Peter.

'I've just come from Ellie, Peter, and she is in such a quandary about this trip to London to see Zack. Guy has practically forbidden her to go, though she says she will, but she would rather have his blessing. She wondered if you could talk some sense into him.'

Peter raised an eyebrow. 'I interfered before if you remember, all to no avail.'

'But now, Zack has proved you were right to fight his corner and Guy knows it. Please, Peter.'

'Very well, but I'm busy for the rest of the day. Where is he working?'

'Ellie said, he's thatching West Wind Cottage in Cury.'

'I'll go and see him tomorrow then.'

*

There was a crisp cold nip in the air when Peter had his horse saddled the next morning. He had left Pearson to do the rounds of the estate by himself and had given him the rest of the day off. Ben was due to come home on Wednesday, and because of being in a wheelchair, a bed had to be set up for him in one of the ground floor rooms.

Peter rode up to West Wind Cottage and called up to Guy, 'Can you give me a moment?'

Guy sighed heavily, pushed a spur into the reed and made his way down the ladder. 'I know why you're here, Peter, and you're wasting your time,' Guy said, brushing the reed dust from his sleeves.

'Your pride will drive an irrevocable wedge through your relationship with your only son. It has already hurt Ellie.'

'Ellie?'

'Yes, your pride has kept Ellie from seeing her best friend Jessie these last ten years. Don't make her become estranged to her son as well. Your prejudice against Daniel Chandler has gone on too long and is totally unfounded. Yes, he had an affair with your brother's wife, but even you cannot deny she was estranged from Silas at the time, and he was not a good husband to her. Now don't give me that angry look,' he said seeing Guy's eyes narrow, 'you know in your heart that Silas did not do right by Jessie, nor were Jessie and Daniel to blame for Silas's death.'

Guy folded his arms. Peter could see the truth clearly biting hard at him.

389

'Guy, we have been friends for many years, and I do not say this lightly, but I shall think you a lesser man if you drive your only son away on a ridiculous notion that Daniel Chandler is on a mission to deprive you of your kin. By all accounts, Zack is doing really well in London. He has found his niche in life, as you did in yours as a thatcher. Daniel has been instrumental – if you'll excuse the pun, in guiding Zack down the right path. Please be happy for Zack – he is the best of men and a credit to you. Put your prejudice and pride away, and pack your bags for London. If you don't, you will regret it for the rest of your life.'

When Peter returned home, Sarah looked at him hopefully. 'Well?'

'I've done all I can. It's down to him now.'

'Thank you for intervening, darling.'

*

On the morning of December 19th, the Dunstan's car drew up at Poldhu Cove to collect the Blackthorns. Ellie ushered the two girls out to the car with their cases, while Guy stood, arms folded and stony-faced.

'I distinctly remember that I forbade you to go to London!'

'I believe you did,' Ellie said picking up her bags.

'So, you would defy your husband then?'

'As you see.'

'I'm warning you, Ellie…'

'What?' she turned on him - her eyes ablaze. 'I have never had cause to defy you before, and I never thought I would have to, but in this instance, I will! I'm proud of our son, and I want to share in his success. This grieves me to say this, Guy, but if you cannot put your silly prejudice to one side, I think we will have to discuss our future life together when I return.'

Guy opened his mouth, but closed it again, and watched as they climbed into the waiting car.

Half an hour later, Guy, with a face like thunder, met with Jake and Ryan to go to work. Betsy was handing out the packed lunches that day because Ellie was away.

'Where's Agnes?' Jake asked.

'Defying me, like her mother is!'

Jake shot a glance at Ryan and Betsy who both grimaced. They all knew about the concert in London, but they also knew Guy had forbidden his family to attend.

'So, you'd better take heed, Jake, of her lack of disregard for authority,' Guy grizzled. 'This is how the women in my family treat their men - if you ever manage to tie Agnes down.'

Jake gritted his teeth. 'If Agnes marries me, the last thing I would want to do is to tie her down and clip her wings if she felt she needed to do something!'

Guy snorted.

'The only reason Agnes will not marry me, is because of you! Do you know that?' Jake continued. 'She knows that as soon as we marry and falls pregnant, you will stop her from doing the thing she loves – thatching.'

'And you would risk a pregnant wife on a roof would you?' Guy countered angrily.

'As long as she could climb a ladder, yes!'

'And what about afterwards? Will you risk the mother of your children on a roof?'

'Ellie and Betsy risk the fathers of theirs on a roof.'

'That's different.'

'No, it isn't! Times are changing, Guy. People want different things – like your Zack.'

'Don't mention his name,' he snapped.

Jake shook his head. 'I'll tell you what, Guy. If I'm lucky enough to have children. I shall hope that I'm a decent enough father to listen to what my children need, so that they are happy in their lives.'

Guy threw his tools in the wagon.

'And another thing. 'I am going to ask Agnes to marry me again, and I shall tell her, that if you refuse to employ her afterwards, I will set up my own thatching business with *her* as an equal partner and therefore leave her free to shinny up and down that bloody ladder whenever she wants to!' With that, Jake too threw his tools in the back of the wagon.

Ryan glanced nervously at his wife Betsy, who mouthed 'good luck' back to him, and as he climbed into the cab with the others, he could have cut the atmosphere with a knife.

*

When Guy returned home from work that evening, the smell of cooking met him and he could hear someone in the kitchen. Feeling a hint of triumph that Ellie had seen sense and decided not to go, he put his tools down on the table by the door and walked into the kitchen with a victorious smile on his face, only to be met by Betsy.

'Ah, there you are,' Betsy said, 'Ellie asked me to put a beef and vegetable pot to cook in the oven for you. I shall leave you to it – my brood are waiting for their supper.'

Guy sat at the table, moving his fork around the plate of food he'd ladled out. Though the range was still warm, the kitchen felt cold and soulless without his family around the table. Afterwards he built the fire up in the sitting room, and despite the shovels of coal, the flames remained sad and unwelcoming.

Glancing at the clock when it chimed six, he knew his family's train would be arriving in London now. He swallowed a lump that had formed in his throat. He'd been at loggerheads with Jake all day, and frankly Jake did not deserve his wrath. It was dawning on him that he'd been a fool - a pig-headed fool. He'd managed to alienate everyone he cared about. He thought of Peter's words to him the other day, "Put your prejudice and pride away, and pack your bags for London. If you don't, you'll regret it for the rest of your life."

He glanced up at his invitation, along with the letter on the mantelpiece – it had been sat there unopened and dusted around for the last few weeks. He picked the letter up, turned it over in his fingers and for a moment, aimed it at the fire, but then ripped it open.

He read and re read the letter, the last part in particular.

........*As you had a passion to thatch, I have a passion to make music. I want to do something that fills your heart with pride for me, where you look at people around you and say, "that is my son there." I believe I am now on the road to making you proud – I just need you to follow my journey, so that I can show you the man I want to become.*

Your forever loving son, Zack.

Placing the envelope back on the mantelpiece, Guy put on his coat and headed out into the cold night.

47

Kit, Sophie and family were staying with Daniel and Jessie. Meanwhile Ellie and her two daughters were housed at the Dunstan's house in Belgravia, where all were to convene for dinner that night.

Joe and Juliet had accompanied them once again to London, and it was while Juliet was helping Sarah to dress for dinner, that Sarah noted Juliet looking decidedly queasy. Suddenly Juliet clamped her hand to her mouth and fled from the room to the family bathroom.

Sarah listened at the door in dismay as Juliet retched.

'Juliet,' Sarah knocked on the door, 'can I get you anything?'

Juliet wore a sickly pallor, pale and slicked with perspiration when she emerged, covering her mouth in shame, she apologised, 'I'm so dreadfully sorry, my lady.'

'Nonsense.' Sarah led her back into the bedchamber. 'Are you ill, my dear?' she asked handing Juliet a glass of water.

'No, my lady, not ill…. pregnant.'

'Juliet, that's wonderful news! Joe must be over the moon.'

Juliet lifted her watery eyes. 'I haven't told him yet.'

'Why ever not?'

'I didn't want anyone to know I was bringing a new babe into the world, especially as the Trevails are about to lose Loveday.'

'Oh, bless you.' Sarah took her hand. 'But you cannot keep this a secret forever. I think it's time you went and told Joe.'

'But I've Lady Emma and Lady Anna to see to.'

Sarah smiled. 'I think they can wait a few more minutes.'

*

Joe Treen could hardly contain his joy as he welcomed all the visitors into the house at Belgravia - and this time it wasn't because his old sweetheart Jessie was among the guests.

As he served drinks, he simply could not stop himself from smiling, and knew His Lordship was giving him strange looks. Try as he might, he could not adjust his face to a more fitting countenance for serving drinks in the drawing room.

'You look very pleased with yourself, Treen,' Peter said eventually, 'in fact you look almost fit to burst. Has something happened we should know about?'

That was it, Joe could not hold his elation back a moment longer. 'Yes, my lord, something rather wonderful has happened. I've just found out I'm to be a father!'

The room erupted with good wishes, handshakes were offered, a drink was thrust into his hand, and a toast was raised to Juliet and himself.

Jessie came and kissed him on the cheek. 'You will make a wonderful father, Joe. I'm so happy for you both. I must go and congratulate Juliet.'

'She's a little bit nauseous at the moment. She's having a lie down.'

'Oh, bless her. Tell her it will all be worth it in the end.'

*

As the excitement died down, and the dinner gong was rung, they all made their way through to the dining room.

'Have you heard from Ben,' Zack asked Emma.

'Not a peep, you?'

He shook his head. 'I've written three times.'

'I've written every week since it happened, but they just go unanswered, I don't know whether to stop now – it seems fruitless. William said he wrote to him too, but he didn't get a response either. I can't even go and see him - Mrs Pearson says he doesn't want any visitors.'

'I'm worried about him, Emma. It's not good to be so alone when something like this has happened. I cannot understand it – this is not like Ben.'

'Perhaps the old Ben is no longer there. But I'm telling you, just as soon as he comes home, I'm going round there and I'll make him see me!' she whispered.

'I would too, but I don't know when I'll be back in Cornwall. It certainly won't be this Christmas. I'm spending Christmas with Daniel and Jessie. They've become my second family now.' He smiled affectionately at them.

Kit saw him looking over, and asked, 'Are you nervous about tomorrow night, Zack?'

Zack laughed. 'No, I'm excited. I never thought I'd get this sort of chance so soon. I know it's not a professional orchestra, it's an amateur one for the students of the conservatoire. It's part of our exams, but I can assure you, no one is put forward for this unless they have excelled in their musical field. So, there should be no fudged notes to endure – I hope.'

*

Later that evening, when Ellie climbed into the beautiful feather bed, she looked around what Sarah and Peter called the Chinese room, and angry frustrated tears welled in her eyes. This was her first time in London and she was not sharing it with Guy!

'You stubborn, stubborn man. I'm not sure I can forgive you for this, Guy Blackthorn,' she wept.

*

The next morning at Poldhu, Jake and Ryan knocked on the Blackthorn's door, but nobody came. They began to get the wagon ready and by the time Betsy came over with their lunches, Guy was still nowhere to be found. Fishing the key out of her apron pocket, Betsy opened Guy and Ellie's door and after a sweep of the house, came back out and shrugged. 'He's nowhere to be seen.'

'God, but I hope he's alright,' Ryan said, 'he was in such a mood yesterday.'

'What shall we do?' Jake asked.

'I suggest you go to work. Perhaps he will turn up later,' Betsy said.

*

Ben Pearson arrived home in an ambulance that same afternoon. He was lowered down by hoist, and thankfully wheeled into the cottage before anyone saw him.

His pa wheeled him down the passage, into the far room on the ground floor and stopped him in the middle of the room.

'Your ma has made a good fire in the grate for you, and has been busy making everything homely.'

Ben glanced at the fire, but it could not lift his mood. His eyes fell on the bed on the far side of the room. Some of his books, brought from his workshop, were on a bookcase, low enough for him to reach. A commode stood in the corner and a clock ticking on the mantelpiece, told him this was his life now.

'Now what would you like - a nice cup of tea perhaps?' his ma asked.

No, I want my life back.

Rose tipped her head at his silence. 'I'll make you one anyway while you settle in.'

Settle into what exactly? A life lived in a room no bigger than twelve by twelve feet – is this it?

His pa patted him on the shoulders. 'She'll fuss like a mother hen now you're home, as for me, I'm off back to work. The family are in London for a concert. From what I understand, Zack Blackthorn is making his debut as a pianist there. Fancy that, eh? The Trevellicks have gone, and so too have all the Blackthorn family, except Guy I believe. I understand he's still sore that Zack went off to London without a by your leave. Still, I'll not say a bad word about Guy – he got you to rally didn't he? I must say, we feared you would never pull out of the doldrums enough to come home.'

Ben clenched his teeth together for it was taking all of his resolve not to cry. *Zack making his debut as a pianist, yet he could not be bothered to send him a letter telling him so.*

Ben was still where his pa had left his chair when his ma brought in the tray with two cups, a teapot, and a freshly baked cake. She poured and handed a cup to Ben.

'Now, this is nice, isn't it? Better than that dreadful hospital room. We can all be a family again now. Would you like some cake?'

Ben shook his head and put down his cup. 'Ma, do you mind if I rest awhile?'

'Of course not. I'll help you onto the bed and I'll sit with you. I can read to you if you want.'

'No!' he said more sharply than intended. 'I'll manage myself, and I can read my own books!' He took a deep breath, and added more softly, 'thank you.'

'Oh!' Rose's bottom lip quivered. 'Well, if you think you can manage. I'll pop back in a minute to see if you're alright.'

'No, Ma. I can manage. Now please, leave me be. I want to be alone. I'll be fine.'

He watched her eyes well with tears, but hardened himself to it. He needed her to understand that he wasn't a useless invalid, and after five months of no privacy, he just wanted to be left alone.

Rose closed the door after her with a bang to show her displeasure, and Ben wheeled his chair over to the window. He lifted the lace curtains, but he had no view – just the blank wall of the back of the manor staring back at him. He'd been told he could be wheeled into the garden to sit, but to do that, would expose him to Emma, and she was the last person he wanted to see now. He could not forgive her for abandoning him. He winced as his legs suffered the dreadful phantom shooting pains. He'd said nothing to the doctors in case they kept him in that damned hospital a moment longer. They kept him awake most nights though, fizzing, prickling, and stabbing him mercilessly, until he slapped them to cease!

*

In London that evening, the auditorium was filling up in the concert hall, and there was a buzz of excitement from other family members of the orchestra, they were all feeling the same sense of pride Ellie felt. They had wonderful seats, right in the middle of the auditorium. Ellie settled in her seat with the yawning gaping void of a vacant chair next to her - the others were seated to her right. Everyone looked up when there was movement behind the curtain and scraping of chairs and shuffling of feet.

A gentleman came out onto the stage to say, 'Five minutes to the performance ladies and gentlemen, if you could all take your seats.'

After a couple of minutes, the room dimmed slightly and Ellie looked across at the others in the row and smiled with anticipation. She didn't see the person making their way towards the vacant seat until she felt a presence next to her. She shifted uncomfortably, she had hoped that because Guy still had his ticket at home, that no one would have taken his place.

'Just in time,' the voice said next to her, as the lights went down and the curtain came up. Ellie tried to distance herself from the man who clearly felt himself free to speak to her – she would endeavour to ignore him. Suddenly the stage was flooded with light, and there he was, her boy Zack, her handsome son, in a tail coat and black tie at the seat of the grand piano.

'That's our boy,' the man's voice said, as he curled his hand over Ellie's. She turned in astonishment to find Guy sitting beside her.

'I'm sorry, Ellie,' he whispered.

*

The concert drew to a close, and with genuine tears in their eyes, and hands clasped tightly together, Ellie and

399

Guy could barely believe how fantastic their son had been. No one to the left of Ellie had seen Guy arrive, so oblivious, they all stood up to shuffle out of the row. Daniel had sent word from further down the row, for everyone to convene in the bar until Zack could join them, and then they could go on to dinner afterwards. Agnes turned to relay the message to her ma and stood open mouthed at the sight of her pa.

'How long have you been there?' Agnes gasped.

'For the duration of the concert.' Guy smiled.

'You'll stay to see Zack?' she pleaded.

'Well, I haven't come all this way not to see him.' He grinned.

When they joined the others in the bar, Guy came face to face with Daniel and Jessie, while the others held their breath.

Guy held his hand out to Daniel and shook it firmly. 'Thank you for doing what you've done to show my son's potential. You could see in him what I could not. I've been far too blinkered, for so long.'

Daniel nodded. 'It's been an honour to help him, Guy.'

Guy glanced at Jessie, and then back to Daniel. 'I also want to thank you for giving Jessie the love and the family she so craved, and which my brother Silas denied her. I'm ashamed of my treatment of you both. I thought to blame you for everything, but I have everything to thank you for.'

Guy smiled at Jessie. 'You have a beautiful family, and I can clearly see how happy you both are. I'm so dreadfully sorry for my behaviour.'

Jessie's lip trembled. 'Forgiven,' she said stepping forward to kiss Guy on the cheek.

'So, I'd like to extend an open invitation to you all, to come and see us at Poldhu anytime you wish.'

It was then that Daniel spotted Zack making his way through the crowd of people. 'Oh look, here is the maestro himself.'

Zack was beaming with delight, as people he didn't even know patted him on the back as he made his way to the others, and then he saw his pa and faltered.

'You came!' he said in astonishment.

'I did, and you were wonderful tonight, son.' He pulled him into a warm embrace, and then said out loud, 'Ladies and Gentlemen, this is my son, Zack, who played the piano for you tonight, and I am the proudest father in the world.'

There followed a resounding round of applause, and Guy whispered in Zack's ear, 'Can you ever forgive your stupid old Pa?'

'Of course, I can,' Zack said, his voice cracking with emotion.

'Well, I think this calls for a celebratory dinner,' Daniel announced. 'I have a table booked, if you would all like to follow me.'

*

In the opulence of one of London's finest restaurants, Guy leant over to his daughter Agnes.

'Next time, Jake proposes, say yes.'

Agnes twisted her mouth.

'I promise that I will never stop you working on the roof - no matter how heavy with child you get, or how many children you bring into the world. You can give birth on the roof if you want.'

This time Agnes grimaced. 'No thank you. I would rather do it in my own bed.'

'Well,' he smiled, 'I'm just saying.'

'Thank you, Pa,' she kissed him on the cheek, 'but I doubt Jake will ask me again – I've refused him several times.'

'Oh, he will, and you can be sure by the passionate way he spoke up for you when he handed me some home truths yesterday, that he would never restrict you in any way either!' He winked and added, 'He wouldn't dare.'

48

When the Cornish constituents returned home from London, Zack was with them to spend Christmas with his family.

With a flurry of hugs and kisses at Helston train station, the three families were about to part ways after setting a dinner date for Boxing Day.

Emma said to Zack, 'Ben is coming home for Christmas, so when you come on Boxing Day, I think you and William should go and see him – make him see you. I simply cannot believe he would cut us all out of his life like this!'

*

When Juliet dressed Emma for dinner later that evening, she confirmed that Ben had indeed come home.

It took all of Emma's resolve to not call on Ben until after noon the next day, so as to give him time to get up and about. When she did, she was met at the door by Rose Pearson, who stepped out onto the path and pulled the door closed behind her to speak to her.

Emma furrowed her brow. 'Hello, Mrs Pearson. I understand Ben is home. May I see him?'

'I'm afraid not, my lady. Ben doesn't want to see anyone,' she said firmly.

'Please, Mrs Pearson. Could you just tell him, it's me. I'm sure he'll want to see me.'

'No. I'm sorry, my lady, but no. Please don't come back.' She turned and went inside, closing the door on her.

'Was that someone at the door, Ma?' Ben asked. His pa said that William was coming home for Christmas, and wondered - no, hoped with all his heart, that he would come and see him.

'Just the post,' Rose replied.

*

On Christmas Eve, Theo Trevail approached Sydney Pearson with a special request.

'We understand that Ben is adjusting to being back at home, but, well, Loveday knows that Ben has come home, and she would very much like to see him.'

'We're not sure how Ben feels about people seeing him in a wheelchair.'

'Well, Loveday saw him in hospital, covered from head to foot in splints. I should think he looks a darn sight better now.'

Sydney nodded. 'I'll ask him.'

'Thank you, it would make my little girl very happy. She is so fond of Ben.'

When Sydney conveyed Theo's request, Ben agreed immediately.

When Sydney brought Theo and Loveday through the house to see Ben, Rose Pearson followed them stone-faced into Ben's room, secretly praying that Theo would not disclose all they had kept from Ben. If he should get wind of Lady Emma's broken engagement, well, goodness knows what would happen then.

Loveday squealed with delight and ran to Ben's arms.

'Hello, Princess,' Ben said, choked at how thin and tired she looked. 'Thank you, Ma, Pa. We'll manage on our own,' Ben said dismissing his parents. 'Now then, how is my favourite little girl.'

'I'm a bit poorly, aren't I, Papa? I can't go to school anymore because I keep falling asleep. I don't mind because I didn't like school.' She giggled. 'But Papa carries me to the stables every day and Lady Emma lets me sit on her lovely golden horse with her. I sit side-saddle,' she said proudly, 'just like a lady. We trot down to the arboretum and back. Lady Emma is lovely, she said I can still be her bridesmaid on her wedding day.'

Ben's heart constricted momentarily, but he rallied, and said, 'Well, you'll be the prettiest bridesmaid ever.'

'Why has your chair got those big wheels?'

'So that I can move about, look.' He wheeled it backwards and forwards.

'Why don't you use your legs?'

'Loveday,' Theo cautioned.

'My legs are tired.'

'Like mine?'

Ben nodded.

'Can I have a ride on your chair?' Before Ben could say another word, she'd climbed onto his knees.

'No, Loveday. Ben's legs aren't strong enough to hold you.' Theo made to pick her up, but Ben stopped him and began to wheel her around the room.

Loveday giggled, yawned, and then promptly fell asleep.

'Oh, bless her,' Theo said, 'let me take her.'

'She's fine, let her sleep a while. So, my friend, how are you bearing up?'

Theo shook his head. 'There is not a day I don't shed a tear. Poor Lowenna, she's relinquished all duties with Her Ladyship, she is so distraught at the prospect of what is to come.'

'How long?' Ben whispered.

'We don't know, she has good days and bad days.'

'I'm that sorry for you, my friend.'

'What about you, Ben. Are you planning on going back to the saddlery when you feel stronger? I know Jimmy Trevorrow keeps asking about you.'

'Does he?' He sighed. 'I don't know if I could manage.'

'Well, since the Great War, many people have gone back to work with similar afflictions. I myself thought my working life was over when I lost an eye in the war, but His Lordship believed in me when I didn't believe in myself. Don't lose hope my friend. Now, let me relieve you of at least one burden.' He reached over and picked Loveday up. 'May we come again one day.'

Ben smiled. 'Of course.'

'Have a lovely Christmas, and I hope the New Year brings a turnaround in your life.'

'Thank you, Theo. Give my good wishes to Lowenna.'

As Rose showed them out, she whispered, 'Theo, could you keep this visit to yourself. Ben made an exception for you and Loveday. He doesn't want to see anyone else yet.'

'Of course. We won't say a word.'

When Rose came in to tidy Ben's room, she did so with trepidation, but Ben said nothing about Lady Emma, and for that she was truly grateful to Theo.

*

Although the Manor was decked with fronds of spruce for Christmas, and they had the largest Christmas Tree ever, Emma could find no cheer in the season. She had hand delivered a Christmas Card containing a letter through the Pearsons letterbox.

My Darling Ben,

The hand that wrote this letter trembles. From your silence towards me, and your refusal to see me, I can only deduce that you no longer love me.

My heart is broken for us. It's broken for you having had to endure this dreadful predicament, and for the lost future we thought we had together. I shall leave you to your family for Christmas and the New Year, perhaps in January you will change your mind and admit me, so that you can tell me face to face that you no longer want anything to do with me. I hope, I tremble, that that is not the case.

Warmest season's greetings to you, my one and only love.

Your Emma x.

*

Rose Pearson had seen Lady Emma walking up to the door, but thankfully it was only to push an envelope through. *When would that woman give up?* she thought as she put it with the others in her handbag.

*

On Boxing Day, Rose opened the door to Zack and William, who proved to be a little more difficult to refuse entry.

'Just let us see him, Mrs Pearson. 'Just for a moment. We're worried about him.' Zack had practically stepped over the threshold.

'No!' she said forcefully, glancing between the men.

Zack retracted his foot and William looked at her pleadingly.

'I'm sorry, but please respect my son's privacy at this dreadful time. He does not want to see anyone!'

*

Zack and William reconvened with Emma in the library. She looked hopefully at them, but they shook their heads.

'Something is definitely amiss here. We've all known Ben for years. He would not refuse us entry, I'm sure. We need a plan to get past that woman.'

'I agree, but she guards him like his jailer,' Emma breathed.

'Has anyone got past her, Emma?' Zack asked.

'Not that I know of, and she doesn't go out! I'm beginning to fear for Ben's sanity. Mrs Pearson is a nice enough woman, but if she's the only company Ben has had these last months, he'll be in dire need of rescuing.'

'What if he doesn't want to be rescued. What if he's become a recluse,' William said seriously. 'Sometimes things happen, and the only way you can deal with it is to hide away. It may be that he just needs time to adjust – time alone.'

Zack and Emma looked at him unconvinced.

'Well, I'm just saying,' William added.

'I know what we should do,' Zack said, 'we need to give Mrs Pearson a false sense of security. Though it pains me to say this, but we won't call on Ben again this holiday. Mrs Pearson will think we've given up. Then in the New Year, she might go out and leave him alone. That will be your chance then, Emma.'

*

Unbeknown to Ben, his pa had declined their invitation to the New Year party from His Lordship, knowing someone undoubtedly would tell Ben about all they had kept from him. He would know soon enough about Henry Montague's part in Ben's attack, but they both wanted to give him a few more days respite before he had to relive the horrors of that night at the trial. So, January 1923 broke with fireworks. The sound of music coming from the manor, told Ben that everyone, including his so-called friends would be at the celebration. Heartsore that he hadn't even received an invitation – not that he would have gone - Ben had never felt more wretched or lonely.

The 1st of January saw a thick frost coating the windows every morning – at least it masked his normal view of a blank wall. His legs were paining him every single hour now, and since coming home, he'd found that he could straighten his left leg, which, he had been told, he probably would never be able to do. Whenever he could hear his mother upstairs, he tried to stand on this leg, but more often than not, it would give way. He remembered his nurses saying that the more you move a limb, the stronger it gets, so day after dreary day he did the same repetitive movement of standing and falling back. By the 2nd of January, he found he could straighten the right leg too. He tried very hard not to get his hopes up, but if he could get some movement in his legs, perhaps he would be able to manage on sticks. Perhaps he would be able to get away under his own steam, far away from Cornwall and Emma and everyone else who had neglected him.

*

On Wednesday the 3rd of January, Sydney beckoned Rose outside to speak about the upcoming trial.

'We have to tell Ben, about Henry Montague. We've waited as long as we could, but now is the time. His Lordship's lawyer wants to speak to Ben on Thursday to fill him in on the proceedings.'

Rose clenched her teeth at the prospect. 'As soon as he knows, he will learn about Lady Emma's broken engagement and then what? He'll be filled with false hope that she's going to take up with him again. Our boy has been through enough heartache, Sydney.'

'Nevertheless, he must be told – we'll do it tonight. As for Lady Emma, you know as well as I, she hasn't been near our Ben. It's over, Rose. Whatever it was between them is well and truly over. Now, why don't you catch the wagon to the market today and get something nice to make for our dinner. It may soften the blow when he finds out about Montague.'

'But I can't leave Ben on his own,' she said flustered.
'You will have to leave him one day, Rose. You need to go back to shopping in Helston every week. The gamekeepers wife can't keep doing it for you forever. So, you will be on that wagon today to go to the market. Alright? Ben will be fine. I'll check in on him.'

49

Emma was in the stable grooming Saffron when an excited Juliet came looking for her.

'Is everything alright, Juliet?'

Juliet nodded and gestured for her to follow her.

'What is it?'

'My lady, I've just seen Mrs Pearson walking up the drive with her shopping basket. It's Helston market today, she must be going there. I thought perhaps....'

'...I could go and see Ben! Thank you, Juliet.' Going back into the stables she told the groom not to saddle Saffron yet. Outside, she checked for signs of Mr Pearson, and saw him in the far distance with Papa. At the door of the steward's cottage, she gave another swift look around her, then turned the handle and stepped through.

*

Ben was sat quietly watching the flames of the fire for want of something better to do. At last, his ma had gone out and left him - he was heartily sick of her fussing.

His head lifted on hearing footsteps in the house, and sighed, thinking Pa must have been put in charge of watching over him. Then he heard Emma's voice call out.

'Ben, Ben, it's me, Emma.'

Oh, God no! Panic set in. After desperately wanting to see her for months, he suddenly didn't want her to see him in this wheelchair.

'Ben are you in there?' she knocked on his door.

'Emma, go away, please, I beg you.' But she opened the door and stepped into the room.

By instinct he tried to get up to flee to another room, and to his amazement, his foot withstood his weight for a second or two before he slumped down again.

'Ben, you stood up then!' she said in amazement.

'Oh, Emma, please go away. I don't want to see you.'

'Is it because you're in this chair?'

He averted his eyes for he could not look at what would be pity in her eyes.

'Ben,' she knelt beside him, 'Ben, look at me.'

He closed his eyes and shook his head.

'You're still my Ben. You may be in this chair, but you're still my Ben.'

He opened his eyes and looked tearfully at her. 'I'm not though am I! I'm not yours anymore. You're engaged to Henry Montague.' He saw a deep puzzled frown form on her face.

'No, I'm not! Have you not heard - have you not read any of my letters?'

'Letters, what letters? You sent me nothing.'

She sat back on her heels. 'Yes I have! Every week I wrote, sending you my love, offering to help you get back on your feet. Did you not get any of them?'

'I received no letters, Emma! Nobody has written to me, and no one came to see me!'

'But I gave them to your ma – she put them in her handbag.'

Ben felt his face pale.

Emma nodded knowingly. 'We did wonder if they were going astray somehow. Oh, Ben, nobody has been allowed to come and see you. I've been turned away by your ma, so too has Zack and William at Christmas. William has written to you, and Zack has sent at least three letters to you. We've all been worried sick as to why you didn't want to see us or write back to us.'

Ben looked around the room in confusion. 'I admit I was worried about seeing *you,* because I'm not the man I used to be.'

'Of course, you are, my darling, Ben.' She cupped his face in her hands.

'I never told Ma to turn anyone away though. I just can't believe she'd do such a thing. I've been so lonely, Emma.

'Oh Ben, my darling Ben.' This time she kissed him full on the mouth and his body fizzed with elation.

He grabbed her hands. 'Is the engagement really off.'

'Yes, oh goodness, surely you know now that Henry caused this to happen to you. He was the one who paid the Barnstock brothers to kill you.'

'Pardon?' He felt suddenly dizzy with shock.

'Did you not know – has no told you?'

He shook his head in disbelief.

'That man is well and truly out of our lives. He will surely hang for what he did to you.'

Ben shook his head, unable to take in what she was saying.

'Darling, Ben, don't you see, we can be together now.'

'Oh, Em, don't. That's just a pipe dream now.'

'No, it's not!'

'I'm crippled!' he yelled. 'I can't support myself, never mind you.'

'What nonsense is this. Your hands and arms work, don't they? Why have you not gone back to the saddlery? Jimmy would help you. He's desperate for you to come back, and Amara is fretting so much she's almost bald!'

'Amara! But Amara's dead - I saw her fall.'

'No, my darling, Ryan Penrose brought her back to health for you. You must come back to the saddlery.'

Ben's eyes blurred as they welled with tears.

'Come on, Ben, you need to rally yourself. You need to work again even if you have to do it sitting down. You need something to get up for in the mornings. Anyway, I saw you stand when I came in.'

'For a second, perhaps, but they're useless.' He slapped his thighs in frustration.

'Ben, if you can stand for a second, you can learn to stand for longer. Have you any feeling in your feet?'

He stared at her glassy eyed.

'Have you?' she demanded.

'Yes, a little. There's something there, yes. Pains — the occasional pinpricks.'

Her eyes glittered with happy tears. 'Then there is hope.'

'No, Em, even people with amputations can feel pain and things in their missing limbs!'

Ignoring his protest, she stood up and held her arms out. 'Grasp my arms and get up again.'

'I can't.'

'Yes, you can, do it now.'

Reluctantly he grasped her arms, as she did his.

'I'm going to pull you up onto your feet after three. One, two, three.'

With all the strength he could muster, he heaved himself up, only to flop down again.'

'See,' he said.

'See what?'

'I can't do it.'

'You can, and you did. Come on, this is mind over matter. Concentrate. Tell your brain that your feet and legs need to work. Ready, one, two, three.' Just as she pulled him onto his feet, Ben's ma's voice rang through the house.

'I've been waiting for over a quarter of an hour for the Helston wagon......' she said stopping in her tracks just as Ben flopped down again. Livid, she shot a steely look at Emma. 'Lady Emma, I specifically told you my son does not want to see you.'

'Ma, please, it's alright.'

'It's not alright. What the hell were you just doing?'

'We're trying to see if I can stand,' Ben explained.

'What is this nonsense. Of course, you cannot stand.'

'He *will* stand again, Mrs Pearson, he's done so today. He just needs to get his limbs working again.'

Rose Pearson, put down her handbag, and took a great measured intake of indignant breath. 'With respect, Lady Emma. I am his mother and I know his capabilities now.

You are giving my boy *false* hope, and I'll not stand by and see you destroy him again!'

'*Ma!*' Ben snapped, as Emma stood back from her onslaught - stunned at her accusations.

Ignoring her son's rebuke, Rose kept her gaze on Emma. 'Please leave us in peace,' she said, pointing Emma to the door.

Emma glanced awkwardly at Ben who looked furious, then she headed for the door, with Rose in hot pursuit.

'Lady Emma, I do not wish to be rude, but please do not come back to our door with regards to Ben.'

Emma ignored her and left without saying goodbye.

Rose walked back into Ben's room with her arms folded. 'The cheek of that woman, coming in here, making you stand on your poor legs.'

Ben held up his hand to stop his mother from speaking. 'You were incredibly rude to Emma, Ma.'

Affronted, she said, 'Well, I only have your best interests at heart.'

'I'm not sure you do, Ma. Now leave me alone. I do not want to speak to you at the moment.' He locked his eyes on her until she flounced out of the room, and then wheeled his chair to the door to turn the key in the lock.

Almost as soon as Rose vacated the room, she knocked, and in a light singsong voice called through, 'Ben I've left my handbag in there, can I have it please?'

Ben glanced down at the handbag. 'Go away, Ma,' he shouted back, picking up the bag, he tentatively opened it to find all the letters that had been withheld from him.

*

It had taken Ben almost an hour to read all the letters. After reading the last one, he dropped his head in his hands and wept with joy – he truly hadn't been forgotten. When he recovered and wiped away the tears, he unlocked the door and his Ma was in the room in an instant. She glanced first at her handbag and then the letters on Ben's lap.

'Have you anything to say to me about these?' he asked. 'The letters from my friends. Friends I believed had forsaken me!'

'It was for your own good, Ben,' she said fiercely. 'You were in that hospital crippled, while your friends were getting on with their lives. It would have killed you to read about such things.'

'And do you not think I should have been privy to the fact that Henry Montague was the one who paid to have me killed?'

'Damn Lady Emma!' Rose stamped her foot. 'We were going to tell you tonight, because Mr Sheldon, His Lordship's lawyer is coming to see you on Thursday to talk about the trial. We kept it secret from you till now in case it gave you false hope that Lady Emma was free again, or worse still, knock you back into your depressive state. We didn't want that for you.'

Ben shook his head incredulously. 'I'm not a child anymore, Ma. You can't make my decisions for me.'

'I can, and I will continue to do what is right for you – you are my son! Only a mother knows what's best for her children.'

'Enough, Ma. I'd like to see Pa when he comes in from work. Now please leave me alone,' he said before he shut his door.

*

Sydney Pearson scratched his head in disbelief at Ben's request to go home to his workshop.

'But how will you manage, son?'

'I'll manage,' he said calmly. 'Everything is on the level.'

'But shopping, you can't go out to buy things!'

'I'll manage. Jimmy will help.'

'You're ma is distraught. She says Lady Emma was here and has upset you.'

'Emma has not upset me, but Ma has! Emma has been truthful to me, and made me understand that I do have a life to live.'

'You're disabled, Ben. You're not the same man you were when you left the saddlery.'

'I *am* the same man! I can work again - my arms are fine. I need to be independent again, Pa. Please, can you arrange to take me home in the morning?'

50

Juliet breezed into Lady Emma's bedroom the next morning, with news that Mr Pearson had requested use of the de Bochym car.'

'Oh, really - where is he going?' Emma felt a curl of unease that her visit yesterday had somehow set Ben back and he needed to go back to hospital.

'Well, that's the thing, my lady. He needs the car to take Ben home to the saddlery!'

Emma pushed back the covers and jumped up. 'That means I'll be able to visit him whenever I want!'

Juliet nodded excitedly.

'I'll ride down to visit after breakfast,' she paused then said, 'no, I won't visit - I'll leave him to settle in on his own.'

'But will he manage, my lady?'

'Yes, he'll have to. It's the only way he'll get back on his feet – so to speak. I've no doubt Jimmy Trevorrow will find out he's home and offer his help, which I think Ben will accept willingly. Ben needs to find his independence again – I think his ma has tried to strip him of it.'

*

As the chauffeur driven car pulled up outside Polhormon Saddlery, for the first time in many months, Ben felt a rush of adrenaline at the prospect of life getting back to almost normal. Ben waited in the back of the car until his wheelchair was unloaded and refused help from either the chauffeur or his pa as he shuffled himself out and onto it. It was a bumpy, difficult ride to the doors of his workshop with it being rough grass, but Ben looked around at the view down to Poldhu, and his heart filled with gratitude that he'd lived to see this vista again.

From what he remembered of that dreadful night, when all he could hear was the crack of wood and the crash of crockery as he laid dazed on the ground, he expected the workshop to be in a terrible state. To his surprise, it looked pristine, albeit missing three chairs and most of the crockery from the shelves. He wheeled himself in and looked around – a lump forming in his throat, thinking this day to be an impossibility. Hearing a flutter of wings, Ben looked up, to see Amara flying down to him.

'What the...' The chauffeur batted the bird out of the way until Ben shouted for him to stop.

The dove settled on the bookcase, a dishevelled, almost bald version of her former self.

'Amara,' Ben called and she looked curiously down at him. Lifted her wings and circled wearily before settling on his shoulder. 'Oh, my poor girl - I thought you were dead, you *have* missed me, haven't you?' The dove closed her eyes and gently touched his cheek with her head. 'I'm back now,' he said stroking her neck.

'Well, I never...' the chauffeur gasped, 'I've never seen the like before.'

Sydney put a basket of food on the table which held a pot of stew Ben's ma had made and shed tears over.

'Shall I build a fire?' his pa asked.

'No, thank you, I'll manage.'

Sydney shook his head. 'How are you going to manage, really, Ben?' he said, deeply concerned at leaving him here alone.

'I'll manage, Pa.'

They all turned as they heard footsteps running towards the workshop and Jimmy burst in, breathless with the exertion of the sprint.

'Ben, you're back!' He threw his arms around his friend. 'Ben I'm so sorry I couldn't get out of the back door that night, it was locked,' he sobbed, 'I hid in the dresser and then they trapped me in, and.........'

'Hush now, Jimmy, you helped me get them arrested, didn't you?'

He nodded tearfully.

'All's well that ends well then.'

'And you're back with Amara. She's in a bit of a state though, she's moulted with stress. She looks a darn sight better than when I found her cowering under the bookcase. She was in a poor state, we thought she was a goner, but Ryan Penrose nursed her back to health. I brought her back here last week. I thought she'd feel better in her own home.'

'Thank you, Jimmy, and send my thanks to Ryan.'

'We've all been waiting for you to come home, Ben. We didn't know when you would come back, but we thought we'd get everything ready for when you did, so Pa and me, widened your privy so you could get in with your chair.'

Ben felt an overwhelming warmth of gratitude that the Trevorrow's never doubted his return. 'Thank you, that will really help.'

'Well then, my boy,' his pa said, 'do you need me to do anything else for you?'

'No, thank you, I *shall* manage from here.'

Sydney sighed heavily. 'Well, if you can't, you must send young Jimmy here to fetch me, and I'll bring you straight home again.'

'That won't be necessary, Pa. I'll be fine.'

'I'll tell Mr Sheldon where you are then. He wants to go through the trial proceedings.'

Sydney beckoned the chauffeur out of the workshop, and when they'd gone Ben looked at Jimmy, who beamed a smile so wide it reached ear to ear.

'So, you're back for good then?' Jimmy asked.

'Well, I'm going to give it a try.'

'To work?'

'Once I settle in, yes. But I'll need an assistant full time. I'll need someone to go and buy the hides from the tannery. Someone who knows the quality I need to do the work I do, and when it arrives I'll need someone to carry it for me – just until I get back on my feet.'

'Are you going to walk again then?'

'I'm going to give it a damn good try, Jimmy,' he grinned. 'So, are you up to the job?'

'What? You want me to be your assistant!'

'I can't think of anyone else to do it.'

'Blimey, yes, Ben, thank you.'

'Jimmy, I didn't say as much to my pa, but I might need you to do the odd job for me, if you would?'

'Name it. I'm just so glad to have you back.'

'I don't want you to fuss around me. If I need help I'll ask, alright?' The sound of hooves cantering up to the workshop halted the conversation.

'Now, who's that?'

Jimmy ran to the window. 'It's Lady Emma.'

'Oh, no!' Ben groaned. 'I'm not ready yet.'

They both waited for the door to open, but instead, an envelope was pushed under the door, and a few seconds later the horse galloped off.

Ben wheeled the chair to the door, and smiled when Jimmy didn't try to pick the envelope up for him.

'Don't you want to see Lady Emma again?' Jimmy asked seriously.

'I do, but not yet. Not until…. Well, not until I feel more like my old self.'

'You don't look any different to me – a bit thin perhaps. You're just sat on your arse that's all.'

Ben and Jimmy laughed.

'And then might you and Lady Emma……?'

Ben raised an eyebrow.

'Don't look at me like that, Ben. I know all about you two - I've covered for you often enough. It's just that, well, she's free of that nasty toff she was engaged to, now I got that bastard arrested.'

Ben straightened up. '*You* got him arrested?'

'Blimey, Ben, don't you know? Didn't your Ma or Pa tell you?'

Ben shook his head. 'They appeared to have kept a lot of things from me.'

'Well, I overheard Montague say to the Barnstocks, "I want this done properly - the bastard broke my nose once," and then paid him fifty-pound.'

Ben felt his spine chill. *Oh God. The court will want to know why I broke his nose!*

'And guess what, Ben? 'The constable told me that Montague was caught in a compromising position with another man when they arrested him! Fancy that, eh?' Jimmy grimaced. 'He was charged with a gross act of indecency, and sentenced to hard labour. Montague is to be brought to court again on Monday on conspiracy to murder - on *my* evidence!' he said proudly. 'What's up, you look like you've seen a ghost,' he added.

'It's…it's a lot to take in that's all,' Ben answered.

'Anyway, Ben, shall I do anything for you while you read Lady Emma's letter?'

Ben tried to calm his unease. 'Yes, Could you light the range for me?'

As Jimmy set about his task, Ben opened the letter.

My dear Ben.

The hand that wrote this letter longs to knock on your workshop door again - to find you there making your beautiful saddles. When you feel ready to admit me back, send a letter with Jimmy. Until then, I will let you do what you need to do to settle back in.

Sleep well in your own bed, my love, enjoy being with everything around you that belongs to you.

Forever yours, Emma.

He smiled. After waiting for him all these months, she knew him well enough to give him time to mend.

*

It would indeed have been a feat of endurance for Ben to attend the trial that Monday if not for the generosity of His Lordship, who had offered the Dunstan's car and chauffeur to take them all the way to Exeter.

The courtroom was stuffy, despite it being early January. A watery sun slatted through the thin windows of the room, sending shafts of light-filled dust motes onto the proceedings.

When Ben had been wheeled in to sit at the front with Mr Sheldon, there had been a murmur of sympathy for him, which Ben hated. With his returning to some sort of normality, he would not be a victim anymore. Hopefully, this trial would mark the beginning for him of carving a new life out for himself.

The presiding judge came in, and everyone rose, except Ben who bowed his head courteously. Now it was time to see the men who had put him in this wheelchair, charged.

*

At Bochym Manor, Peter stood in his study with his hands behind his back. Today, Ben would get justice for what those men did to him. The only downside was that in that justice, the Dunstan's name would be forever associated with the scandal. For now, Mr Sheldon had kept their name out of the papers. But all that would change today. The evidence and motive for Henry's part in the affair, first pointed to words he'd uttered in The Old Inn, "The Bastard broke my nose once," and then of course, his jealousy of Ben's friendship with Emma while Henry had been engaged to her was the other catalyst for the attack. These two factors were necessary, to verify Henry's motive for the attempted murder. Both William and Emma would not come out of this unscathed, if that was the case. After today, nothing would be the same.

*

Ben watched with loathing as the Barnstock brothers walked into the court, and once they were in the dock they glowered at him.

He then watched as Henry Montague shuffled into the court room. Gone was the tall, arrogant, self-satisfied man, in his place was a meek and broken man who had clearly suffered in prison - for what he was. Ben awarded himself a secret smile.

'Apparently Lord Montague has not, as we thought, sorted out the services of the best lawyer in town for Henry,' Ben's lawyer whispered. 'It appears Lord Montague has disowned him and left him to rot in prison.'

'Good!' Ben said justly.

The judge presiding over the case, listened as the evidence against the Barnstocks was read out. With Jimmy being a minor, he had not been called to court, but his evidence, and the fact Ben had been able to verify all but the conversation that Jimmy had overheard between the Barnstocks and Henry, was heard. There was no doubt about their part in the attack. This, along with a statement from Mr Henry Pike, who still had trouble walking, and had sustained a speech impediment since the beating at the hands of the Barnstocks three years before, gave credence that the Barnstocks were a law unto themselves. The judge said he would take this into account when he passed sentence.

Henry Montague was then made to stand and had to be held up by two court officials, as Jimmy's evidence against him was read out.

The judge then addressed Ben. 'Mr Pearson, Do you know any reason why the accused, Mr Henry Montague would pay to have you killed, and did you, as he says, break his nose once?'

Over the last few days, Ben had deliberated long and hard about Henry's part in his attack. If he gave any credence to Henry's claim that Ben had once broken his nose, and that was one of the reasons he wanted him dead, Ben would have to explain what had happened that dreadful day in the woods. And then of course there was the claim that Henry wanted Ben out of the way because of his friendship with Emma. In his heart he knew to give credence to either of these claims, would incriminate both William and Emma. He'd learned that the Dunstans had managed, so far, to keep Emma and Montague's fateful engagement out of the papers. And in so doing, they had stopped any whiff of scandal for the family's association with him. Emma's reputation would be ruined forever if this were made public. The Dunstans had been inordinately kind to Ben throughout his ordeal, so, Ben was faced with a dilemma - tell the truth, and have Henry hanged for attempted murder, or……..

'Mr Pearson?' The judge prompted.

'No, milord, I cannot think of a single reason, and I have never broken anyone's nose.'

A murmur reverberated around the court, and Ben glanced at Henry, who could scarcely raise his head to acknowledge this, so wretched was he, in his new circumstances.

*

Outside the court, Mr Sheldon shook Ben's hand – justice had been done. The Barnstock brothers had been sentenced to hang for their crime.

'I shall telephone His Lordship, Ben, and explain what has happened.'

'Yes, sir, thank you for everything.'

When they got into the car for the return journey to Cornwall, Sydney turned to his son questioningly.

'Why?'

'Why what?' Ben said knowing exactly what he was referring.

'Why did you let Montague off the hook.'

'I have my reasons. Anyway, I hardly think he's been let off the hook. You saw him. I don't think Henry will be troubling anybody for a long time. I don't even think he'll survive prison. He may not hang for his part in my attack, but he will suffer a lot more, and for a lot longer, than he would have done with a rope around his neck.'

51

It had been a long day, and Ben was terribly stiff from the journey. Every bone in his body seemed to be protesting as he poured himself a brandy as a nightcap. He had just recorked the bottle when he heard a car pull up. Any noise after dark, sent a chill down his spine.

When the knock came to the door, he shouted tremulously, 'Who is it?'

'Peter Dunstan.'

Ben manoeuvred to open the door. 'My lord! Please come in.'

Peter walked through and put his hat on the table and looked around the workshop.

'May I offer you a drink, my lord. I'm treating myself to a celebratory brandy.'

'I won't, thank you. I'm aware that it's late and you've had a trying day, but I had to come and see you. Mr Sheldon phoned when you came out of court – he told me the outcome.'

'Yes, my lord, I shall sleep more peacefully now the Barnstocks have been sentenced.'

Peter nodded. 'And Henry was acquitted.'

'From a murder charge, yes, my lord, but he's not escaping punishment – I assure you.'

'Ben, you must know that I owe you a great debt of gratitude for what you did today. Your loyalty to my family, and your selfless actions today, have saved the reputation of two of my children – Emma and William.'

Ben looked up sharply.

'Yes, you see, I know what you did to help William in the woods that day. He told me all about it.'

'I see,' he breathed. 'Well, my lord, I love them both dearly.'

Peter stepped forward and hugged Ben as a father would his son, then stepped back unashamed at the gesture. 'William said you are the best of men, I heartily agree with him. I'll bid you goodnight.'

*

The next morning, Emma was furious on hearing that Henry had not been charged with attempted murder.

'The evidence did not hold up, darling,' her papa told her, 'Henry's statement claimed that he'd lost a fifty-pound note while drinking at The Old Inn. He refuted that he'd ever spoken to the Barnstock brothers.'

'He was lying then!' Emma folded her arms. 'Jimmy Trevorrow is not one to tell tales.'

'Nevertheless, although we've distanced ourselves from Henry with the broken engagement, if he'd been charged with attempted murder, your name would have been bantered around court and sullied by association with him, we wouldn't want that now, would we?'

'No, Papa,' she said with a shudder.'

'Rest assured - Henry *is* being punished in more ways than one.'

*

It was the end of February before Ben felt able to see Emma again. Farmer David Trevorrow had commissioned the carpenter who'd taken on Old Mr Gray's carpentry shop, to make Ben a pair of crutches. Every day, Ben had stood on his numb feet, and very slowly had begun to take a few tentative steps. Whereas his feet were numb, his legs were painful to say the least, and they troubled him terribly through the night - but if they pained him, they were not useless!

Ben had received his first commission for a saddle, and they had taken delivery of several hides. It was difficult to work - Ben could not lie, not being able to kneel or crouch made life tricky, but Jimmy was his right-hand man, he simply could not manage without him.

Sydney Pearson had called in on his son every day during his first week back, but when he'd been sent away with the usual, 'I can manage,' he gave up and left him to his old life. His ma, well, his relationship with Ma remained strained, to say the least. He'd not seen her since he left their cottage – leaving her arguing that what she'd done was in his best interests. Ben struggled to forgive her though, for keeping the letters from him, the very letters which could have stopped him slipping into the deep depression he had suffered with.

It was on St David's day when Ben sent Jimmy on a special mission – a letter for Lady Emma. 'You know what to do at the stile?'

Jimmy nodded. 'I'll put it in the hidey hole and put a stone on the top to say it's there.'

'Good lad.'

'Will she notice it though?'

'Oh yes – she'll notice it,' Ben said confidently.

*

Emma had not wasted her time whilst waiting for Ben to send for her. Apart from almost completing her novel, she'd been taking driving lessons from Lennox, the chauffeur, believing it may come in handy should Ben not get his full mobility back. There wasn't a day that went by though that she did not glance at the stile, desperately waiting for news. And then, on that sunny, albeit chilly day in March, her dreams were answered.

My darling, Emma.

The hand that wrote this letter, is ready to open the door to you again. Thank you for waiting for me.

P.S. Please don't expect too much of me. I am still a long way from being who I used to be.

Your Ben.

As soon as she read the letter, all plans for her day were shelved, and she saddled Saffron.

*

From his study window, Peter was watching Emma cantering up the main drive, when Sarah knocked on his door and breezed in on a cloud of delicate perfume, to kiss him warmly.

'We have a wedding invitation!'

Peter raised an eyebrow.

'Agnes and Jake are to marry on March 25th.'

'Ah, at last! Tell me, Sarah, where do you think Emma is going in such a rush?'

'I don't know, perhaps she's had word from Ben – I know she's been waiting until he feels a little stronger before she visits him.'

'Visit him?' Peter raised his eyebrow. 'Sarah, she should not be seeing him alone. She should have taken a groom with her.'

'Darling, she's missed him terribly, let her have some time with her friend. You know how close they are!'

'That's what I'm worried about.' Peter folded his arms. 'She really should be getting ready to embark on her second season. It will be harder for her this year - not having secured a husband in her debut year.'

Sarah cleared her throat. 'Well, I need to speak to you about that. Emma does not want to go through another season.'

'What does she want then – to be an old maid?'

'I think we should leave her be. This business with Henry really upset her.'

'Yes,' he looked out into the far distance, 'how wrong could we have been about Henry. I should have listened to everyone who raised concerns about him!'

'Well let's listen to our daughter now. Let's give her time.'

*

Unable to settle since he sent Jimmy with the letter to Emma, and unsure of when she would come to see him, Ben tried unsuccessfully to concentrate on the saddle he was making. He'd managed to sweep the workshop clean one handed, while supporting himself with the walking stick he now used. He'd set out two cups and had a kettle boiling for the last half hour. She may not come of course - she may be out, or perhaps in London. Oh, he hoped not. Now he'd sent for her, he didn't want to wait another moment. He wanted to show her, how much his mobility had improved, though he was, as stated in the letter he'd sent her, a long way from being who he used to be. He'd sent for her because he needed to know - to look into her eyes and see if she still really wanted him – as broken as he was. Ben put down his work, feeling a tingle of excitement when he heard the clatter of hooves in the yard. He glanced at Jimmy, who grinned and knew to make himself scarce.

Supported by his stick, he moved to the door. *Now Ben, remember, keep everything polite and formal until you know how she feels.* He opened the door to find her standing there smiling.

'Hello, my love,' she said, her face open and hopeful.

All formality was forgotten, as he took her into his arms – his stick falling to the floor with a clatter.

'Oh, Em, my love, my one true love.' He inhaled the beautiful scent of her, felt her soft blond curls brush against his face, and the trimness of her tiny waist in his arms.

Emma held him close and murmured. 'I never thought I would hear you say that again. I thought for so long you didn't want to see me.'

Finally parting from their embrace, he shook his head. 'Oh, my darling, I've read all your letters now. I found them in Ma's handbag. All those words of love you wrote – they would surely have pulled me through the darkness faster.'

'But why, why did she do it? Why did she deprive you of them?'

'She misguidedly thought she was protecting me from anymore hurt. Mothers, eh? Come, sit with me. Could you…' He nodded to his stick and she bent to retrieve it.

'Well, this is an improvement on the last time I saw you.'

'I'm a long way from mending completely – if I do at all.'

'As I say, you're still my Ben.'

Amara flew down from the top of the bookcase and sat on Ben's shoulders as though to tell Emma that Ben belonged to her also.

'Amara looks a lot better than the last time I saw her – we feared she would not survive.' She reached over to hold Ben's hand. 'My biggest fear was that *you* would not survive. I don't think I would ever have got over your loss.'

'I have no idea how I did survive. Possibly because I have the constitution of a horse,' he smiled and tipped his head. 'Do your parents know you're here?'

'No, but I will tell them when I get home. I'm not going to hide anything from them anymore.'

He reached up to touch her cheek. 'Please tell me they're not making you go to London again for another season.'

'No, I refuse to go. I'm quite capable of finding my own husband,' she said, her eyes glittering with love. 'I just need to see if he still wants me as a wife.'

Ben smiled warmly. 'It's what I want more than anything in the world, Em, but can we wait until I'm a little fitter before you present me as a fait accompli to your parents. It was going to be difficult enough for them to agree to our union before I became a bag of broken bones.'

'Don't make me wait too long.' She kissed him gently on the lips.

'I won't,' he breathed.

52

Poldhu Cove was drenched in Spring sunshine when the wedding party made their way from Cury Church to the Poldhu Tea Room for the wedding breakfast.

Jake Treen had finally managed, after a courtship of nearly three years, to put a gold wedding band on Agnes Blackthorn's finger.

Agnes wore an ivory silk wedding dress, which was elegant, but without frills, as befitting Agnes's personality. No veil was worn, only a simple coronet of gypsophila, made from Bochym Manor's hot house blooms, adorned the thick tumble of dark curls which fell like a waterfall down her back.

*

After the reception, Peter watched as Agnes and Jake, accompanied by William, Emma, Zack and Ben walked slowly down the beach. Whether it was the uneven surface of the sand or deliberate, Peter did not know, but Ben and Emma continually bumped into each other as they walked. At the water's edge, they all draped their arms around each other's shoulders and looked out to sea.

When Guy came to stand beside Peter, he said, 'It's been a lovely wedding Guy.'

'Not as grand as we wanted for her, but you know Agnes, she calls the shots. God, Peter, but I feel old all of a sudden. One minute they're children round your feet, the next you're walking them down the aisle and handing them over to someone else to look after.'

Peter and Guy glanced down to look at their offspring. 'It's true, they're all growing up fast,' Peter said. 'Look at them, stood with their arms around each other. What a year it has been, and nothing has shaken their bond, has it?'

'I don't think it ever will. Everyone has friends during each stage of life, but only lucky ones have the same friends in all stages of life. Kit and I grew up together. We attended the same school – we belong in each other's life.'

'I can understand it between same sexes, but what of Ben and Emma's friendship, Guy? Her bond to him is going to mar her chances of securing a husband from her own sphere. I fear their relationship *is* more than friendship, as *you* once suggested.'

Guy, deciding to play the devil's advocate asked, 'Would it bother you if it was?'

'Would it have bothered you if Agnes attached herself to a man who, let's be honest, is far from able to provide for her.'

'Money isn't everything, Peter, but happiness is. Zack made me see that. I wanted him to work at something to earn money and be financially secure, but everyone around me, even you, could see Zack needed something else in his life – something that made him happy.'

'I hear you, Guy, but I don't want Emma to throw her life away. You can see for yourself Ben has not fully recovered from that attack - and may never do so. Would you want your daughter to be a nurse to an invalid for the rest of her life?'

'Love conquers all.'

Peter sighed. 'Is it love though? Is it proper love.'

'It's not for me to say, Peter. It's for you to find that out,' Guy answered.

Peter watched as the friends turned from the water's edge, everyone's arms falling back to their sides, except Emma and Ben – they lingered in their closeness.

*

Walking slowly back up the beach at a pace Ben could manage, Emma and Ben's fingers brushed against each other with a tantalising frisson.

'Well, that's one of our gang married!' Ben said. 'When is it to be your turn, William?'

'God, not yet a while. I need to finish university, and then throw myself into the running of Bochym before I cast my eyes around for the next Countess de Bochym.'

'What about you, Zack?'

'No, I have concerts to play, and the world to tour at the moment. So, that just leaves you two.' Zack grinned at Ben and Emma.

'I agree with Zack,' William said casually, 'you and Emma should marry. If nothing else it will stop my sister from attracting anymore unsuitable beaux like bloody Henry Montague.'

Emma slapped her elder brother for his cheek, all the while exchanging a secret smile with Ben.

'Come on, I've worked up an appetite for more of Ellie's delicious scones,' Emma said.

Ben laughed. 'I honestly don't know where you put everything, Em. You eat like a horse and you're still as slim as a rake!'

'I am a horse – a thoroughbred,' she smiled, 'and you can't fatten a thoroughbred.'

*

It was only by chance that Peter was glancing out of his study window the next day and saw a young boy running up the barley field. Reaching for his binoculars, he focused them on Jimmy Trevorrow - Ben's assistant. Peter waited a moment, but Jimmy didn't climb the stile. instead, he put a rock on top and ran back down the field.

A few minutes later, he saw Emma running up to the stile. She climbed over it in a very unladylike fashion, and then a moment later she scrambled back over with a letter in her hand and ran down to the gardens.

Now what on earth is going on there? Peter puzzled.

*

Emma sat amongst the spring borders to read Ben's letter, clasping it to her heart after her eyes skimmed the words.

My darling, Emma.

The Hand that Wrote this Letter.

The hand that wrote this letter, is almost ready to lift the veil of my beloved on our wedding day.

I love you, Em, I want to go to sleep with you in my arms every night and wake up with your lovely face next to me every morning. You have given me the strength to find the man I once was. I can't hide the fact that life here at the saddlery will be challenging for you – being so used to the luxuries of the manor. I have said this many times before, but you always push my concerns away. I hope and pray that life with me will not be a disappointment. All I can promise you is that you will never have a moment of unhappiness under my roof.

If you still wish to be my wife, as I think you do, we must start to make plans again. I long for the day we are together forever. Let's hope your papa doesn't skin me alive for my impertinence of thinking that I am good enough for you.

Come, see me soon. Your presence lights my life, like the sun lights the day, and the moon lights the night. I need you, my darling girl.

Ever yours. Ben x

Back in the house she called for Juliet to help her change into her riding habit. Juliet, who was by now seven months pregnant, was by her side as swiftly as she could.

Seeing her puffing and blowing from climbing the stairs, Emma took her hand and led her to the bed to sit down. 'Oh, Juliet, I'm sorry, I could have dressed myself – I didn't think.'

'It's alright, my lady, I'm fine – just not as swift as I was. But by the look on your face, you've received some good news today.'

'I have. And I think you know what it is.'

*

An hour later, with plans firmly made, Emma could hardly contain her joy as she rode back to the manor. Picking up her skirts she ran through the side door and up to her bedroom.

'My lady, thank goodness you're back,' Juliet said, running as fast as her pregnancy would let her.

'Goodness, Juliet, slow down. You shouldn't be running like that.'

'It's your papa, my lady,' Juliet said all a fluster, 'he's been in your room – he's taken your letters.'

With great trepidation, Emma lifted the lid of her leather box where she kept her letters – they had indeed all gone! At first Emma felt only anger at this gross disregard for her privacy, but then, she did live under her papa's roof – he was entitled to do as he pleased.

'Where is Papa now, Juliet?'

'He had his horse saddled about half an hour after taking your letters.'

'Oh Lord. He must be on his way to see Ben.'

'What will you do, my lady?' Juliet asked anxiously.

'Nothing - I can do nothing. If Papa has read those letters, he will know the full extent of our love. There will be a row - I have no doubt, but I'm determined on this. Ben loves me! In fact, I've just come from Ben's, and we've made plans to speak to my father next month. This has just hastened the process. Oh, poor Ben. We wanted to do this together.'

'Did you think your Papa would agree then?'

'We don't know, but we had decided that if he refuses to allow us to marry we were going to elope.'

Juliet looked stricken. 'Oh, my lady. I'm going to lose you, aren't I?'

'Juliet,' Emma took her hands in hers, 'don't fret so. You'll soon have a little baby to occupy your time.'

'I rather thought I might carry on with you, you know, after the baby, like Lowenna did with Her Ladyship.'

'And you will, though not with me. I'm afraid I won't be able to afford a maid. Now, there is nothing surer, Ben will have told Papa our plans, and if he refuses to let me marry Ben, I may have to steal away in the night. I might need you to smuggle some things out for me. Would you do that for me?'

'Of course, I will.'

Emma reached out for Juliet's hand. 'You've been such a good friend to me. I shall miss you when I've gone.'

*

Ben looked up and stopped what he was doing when he saw who his visitor was. He grabbed his stick and stood.

'No, don't get up,' Peter said, but Ben remained standing.

'My lord, what can I do for you,' he said glancing at the letters in his hand – his letters! He took a deep breath and straightened his shoulders.

Peter walked around the workshop in silence – a silence which grew louder with every second. When he came to the table he leant back against it and folded his arms, the letters now in clear view.

'I see you recognise these,' Peter said quietly.

'Yes, my lord.'

'Very eloquent letters, I might say.'

Ben remained silent.

'It is clear from these that you have forged a relationship with my daughter beyond a childhood friendship.'

'Yes, my lord. I love her.'

Peter glanced again around the workshop. 'Does my daughter reciprocate your love?'

'She does. We hope to marry.'

Peter laughed lightly. 'And when pray were you going to come and ask my permission or did you plan to elope?'

'Em and I planned to tell you next month.'

'Em?' Peter closed his eyes and inhaled deeply. 'Emma is a lady you know – you should address her as Lady Emma.'

'She's Em to me, my lord.'

Peter tipped his head. 'Why next month?'

'I should like my legs to be stronger - to be able to walk her down the aisle unaided, my lord.'

'And this will happen next month?'

435

'My right foot feels almost normal, but my left foot still feels strange and my balance isn't as it should be.'

'Yes, I noticed yesterday at the wedding that you needed to lean against my daughter to walk.'

'I'm getting better every day. Thanks to you, and what you did for me in hospital.'

Peter nodded slowly. 'And this is how you repay me.'

'Yes, my lord.'

Peter twisted his mouth. 'This love you proclaim – how deep has it progressed.'

'Enough to know that she will stay in my heart until I draw my last breath.'

'Is she…, he glanced away, 'have you…?'

'Goodness, no, my lord. Our love is pure.'

'I see, and are you able,' he cleared his throat, 'I mean, do you function as a man should?'

Ben knitted his eyebrows. 'I do, my lord, yes,' he answered without embarrassment. 'But I can assure you, nothing like that has happened between us.'

With a nod, Peter stood up straight. He glanced momentarily to inspect the saddle Ben had been working on,

'I know I'm not what you wanted for your daughter, but I love her and I want to marry her. I have work coming in again so I can provide for her, albeit not in the manner she has become accustomed to, but she seems willing to live the life I can offer her.'

'Well, that may be so, but I'm *not* willing to allow my daughter to live like this.'

Ben's eyes flickered with disappointment - all their hopes and dreams had been dashed again.

'So, Ben, this is what I propose.

53

When Peter returned to the manor, he dismounted at the front gate as his groom took the horse from him.

'Give him a good rub down, I've ridden him hard,' he said.

Joe Treen opened the front door for him, and as Peter strode up the path, he glanced up at Emma's bedroom window and saw her looking down at him.

'Treen, have Lennox take the car to Ben Pearson's saddlery – he's expecting it, and then please fetch Mr and Mrs Pearson. I'll see them in my study in ten minutes.'

'Yes, my lord.'

'And can you give these to Juliet for her to take to Lady Emma.' He handed over the letters. 'Tell Juliet to inform Lady Emma that she must stay in her room until I send for her.'

'Very good, my lord.

'Where is Her Ladyship, I need to see her first?'

'In the library, my lord.'

*

Rose Pearson quickly fussed over her hair after Sydney told her His Lordship had sent for them both.

'What do you think he wants with us, Sydney?'

Sydney plunged his hands deep into his jacket pockets. 'I didn't want to tell you, but…. It seems Ben has taken up with Lady Emma again,' he said gravely. 'I went to see Ben last week and Lady Emma's horse was outside. So, I think it's what we feared – his foolery has lost us our position here.'

With their heads low, they knocked on the side door near the kitchen and followed Joe Treen to the Earl's study in grave resignation.

*

Noting their deep apprehension, as they shuffled into the study, Peter sensed they knew why they'd been summoned.

'Thank you for coming. Take a seat please.' He took a deep breath. 'Now, you may or may not know that your son has declared that he wishes to marry my daughter.'

Sydney looked stricken as he answered, 'Oh, goodness, my lord, I'm so sorry, both Mrs Pearson and I have tried without success to keep them apart. We've told him, warned him, not to take this further. I can only offer my apologies at any offence his thoughtless declaration has caused you and your family. Ben is a good lad - he will not have done anything other than profess his love for Lady Emma, of that I can assure you.'

Peter let Sydney speak until he finally ran out of words and fell silent. He then leant forward and steepled his fingers. 'You understand, this alters our professional working relationship?'

Sydney lowered his eyes and nodded dejectedly. 'We do, my lord.'

'Then we have much to sort out.'

*

Emma sat down heavily on the bed when Juliet conveyed the message that she'd been confined to her room until sent for.

'Joe said the Pearsons have been summoned to your papa's study, my lady, and that the car has been sent round to Ben's workshop.'

'Oh lord! Papa must be having them all sent away. Goodness, Juliet, what has our love done? We never wanted this to happen. I can't believe Papa would take it out on the Pearsons.' She began to pace the room like a caged lion - fearful of what was to come. 'We must prepare, Juliet. If Ben has been sent away, he will inevitably send word to me where he is, and I *will* go to him.'

They quickly began packing a small enough overnight bag for Emma to take, should she need to steal away in the night. Emma opened her wardrobe door and selected certain items of clothing that she might need Juliet to smuggle out at a later date. They quickly closed the wardrobe door and stood to attention when a knock came to the door.

'Your parents request that you join them in the Jacobean drawing room, my lady,' Joe said.

Exchanging a fearful glance with Juliet, Emma followed Joe down the stairs. At the drawing room door, she tried to swallow the lump which had formed in her throat, as Joe opened the door to admit her in. Brushing down her already tidy dress, she held her head high as she walked into the room. Suddenly her breath caught in her throat, there, sat around the roaring fire, were her parents, along with Ben and *his* parents – the latter looking more than a little uncomfortable in their opulent surroundings.

'What's happening?' she asked tentatively.

'Ben has something to say to you,' her Papa said.

Emma swallowed hard, and expecting the worst, turned to Ben.

'Em, my Em, forgive me if I don't kneel – I'm not sure my legs are strong enough to get back up, but,' he smiled broadly, 'your parents have given their blessing for me to ask you formally if you would do me the honour of becoming my wife.'

A shiver of delight washed over her. 'They have!' she breathed, glancing at her parents. 'You have?'

They both nodded.

'Well?' Ben tipped his head.

Momentarily dazed, she looked back at Ben. 'Sorry?'

He laughed. 'I'm still waiting for your answer.'

Her eyes sparkled with happy tears. 'I think you know the answer, my darling. Yes, yes, yes.' They laughed and fell into each other's arms. She turned to her parents, 'Oh, Papa, Mama, thank you, thank you.' She kissed them both, hardly able to believe what was happening.

'Well, my darling girl, yet again we failed to see what was right in front of our eyes. We can see now how happy you are at this prospect,' Peter said. 'So, I had a long chat with Ben about where you will live.'

'We shall live at the saddlery,' Emma said reaching out to hold Ben's hand.

'You will not!' Peter said firmly. 'I simply cannot let you, as a lady, live in that workshop! So, you and Ben will take up residence in the Dower Lodge after the wedding and will be assigned staff to look after you.'

Emma glanced at Ben, who seemed delighted at the prospect. 'Thank you, Papa, but what about Aunt Carole and Grandmama?'

'They mostly reside in France now, and if they visit us, they will simply have to stay in the manor!'

'My lord, my lady,' Ben moved forward, 'you have been so kind to me and my family over the last few months, and now this is a dream come true. I promise you – I'll never give Emma a day of unhappiness.'

Peter nodded. 'I know you won't, son.' He patted him on the arm. 'I think I said to you, only a few weeks ago, that you are the best of men.' He gave Ben a knowing smile.

Sarah rang the bell for Joe. 'I believe this calls for a celebration. Treen, please could you locate Anna and William - they are both somewhere in the house, and then fetch champagne and send some to the kitchen. Ben and our darling daughter are engaged to be married.'

Joe, unable to keep the smile from his face, said, 'Yes, my lord,'

'Oh, and tell Cook there will be three extra for dinner tonight.' Peter glanced at the Pearsons who, though stunned at the turn of events, nodded. 'We'll have a celebratory dinner to welcome the Pearsons into the family fold.'

54
Saturday May 19th, 1923

Emma stood in front of her mirror, admiring her beautiful drop-waist wedding gown, made from ivory chiffon moire, embroidered extensively with pearls and golden thread.

Sophie Trevellick had made the gown for her, which was an almost exact replica of the gown Lady Elizabeth Bowes-Lyon had worn to marry Prince Albert, Duke of York on the 26th of April 1923 at Westminster Abbey. While Sophie fiddled with the last-minute adjustments of the dress, Juliet was putting the finishing touches to Emma's headdress. She was wearing a long lace Victorian veil, which her mama had worn on her wedding day, though Emma wore it draped over her head to fall like a waterfall at her sides, which was of the fashion. It was anchored with a coronet of myrtle, cream roses, and a froth of gypsophilla, which Juliet, with hair pins held in her mouth, was studiously securing to the veil.

Juliet stepped back to admire her handiwork. 'There, you look beautiful, my lady.' Suddenly she put her hand to her tummy with an involuntary, 'Ooh!'

Sarah, Sophie, and Emma turned in alarm.

'Are you alright, Juliet?' Emma asked.

Juliet blew a puff of breath out. 'I think so, my lady - a little twinge that's all.' She cradled her tummy again. 'The doctor says we'll not be meeting baby Treen for at least another week, so nothing to worry about.'

Sarah and Sophie exchanged knowing glances to the contrary – both had delivered a babe a good couple of weeks before their due date.

'Perhaps you'd better stay here, Juliet,' Sarah suggested.

'Oh no, my lady! Wild horses wouldn't keep me from seeing Lady Emma and Ben marry.'

A knock came at the door, and Anna and Loveday, resplendent in their bridesmaids dresses, were ushered in by Nanny. Loveday had been so excited when Ben and

Emma asked her to be one of their bridesmaids, it had seemed, Lowenna said, to give her little girl a new lease of life.

Loveday has had a nap, so she's ready to carry the basket of petals to pave your way up the aisle,' Nanny said.

Everyone looked down at the little girl – so changed with fatigue. Dark circles shadowed her hollow eye sockets, but the smile she wore through this adversity, because she had a bridesmaid dress on, told everyone that at least one of her dreams were coming true.

Another knock came at the door and Joe handed a letter to Juliet for Emma.

Recognising the handwriting, Juliet smiled. 'It looks like it's from Ben, my lady.'

'Oh, goodness gracious!' Sarah clutched her hand to her heart. 'Why is Ben writing to you? He's not calling it off, is he?'

'I shouldn't think so, Mama. It would sooner snow red ink than Ben call this wedding off.'

'Well, what does it say?'

My Darling, Em.

The hand that wrote this letter, will put a band of gold on your finger this day - a day I dreamed of, though thought would never happen. Now this hand will take yours, and we will never be parted again, as we walk hand in hand through life together.

Yours forever. Ben. X

Emma smiled and lay the open letter on her dressing table for all to see. 'As you see, I have chosen the very best of men as my future husband.'

*

Peter waited in the library for Emma to come down the stairs. There had been a last-minute flurry of activity in the French drawing room, where the finishing touches had been put to the wedding breakfast. Emma had insisted on a cold buffet reception, so that Cook and the domestic staff could attend the church ceremony. Peter smiled to himself – the class barriers were well and truly breaking down – except perhaps with his mother and sister. Their excuse for not coming over from France to celebrate the wedding of their granddaughter and niece respectively, was that his mother had a heavy cold. Peter laughed sardonically, believing it to be more to do with Ben being a *commoner*, as Carole had so eloquently put it, when she found out whom Emma was marrying. It probably didn't help that the Dower Lodge was no longer at their disposal!

Still, everyone who mattered was coming to the wedding. He watched the car make its way down to the Dower Lodge to collect Ben, his best man William, and Zack his usher. He was so grateful that Zack had had the courage to speak up for Emma about Henry. To think he might have subjected Emma to a life of purgatory with that dreadful man. Peter had watched Emma blossom with happiness these last few weeks, as she prepared to marry her real heart's desire.

*

In Cury Church, bedecked with the heady perfume of early summer flowers, Loveday Trevail put her little heart and soul into scattering rose petals to pave the way for Emma to take her place next to Ben. When she had completed her task, she curtsied to Emma before reaching for her pa's arms where she promptly fell asleep. Theo and Lowenna smiled thankfully, knowing that their little girl had had her day.

'*Dearly beloved,*' the vicar began, '*we are gathered here today in the sight of God, to join this man, and this woman in holy matrimony.*'

Juliet's brow furrowed when she felt another twinge in her tummy, and shifted slightly on the pew.

Joe turned with a questioning look. 'Are you alright?' he whispered.

Juliet nodded.

'.........*Not to be entered into lightly, holy matrimony should be entered into solemnly and with reverence and honour. Into this holy agreement these two persons come together to be joined.*'

Another twinge came, and this time Juliet emitted a low gasp and dug her nails into Joe's leg. 'I think you're going to meet your son or daughter,' she whispered.

'........ *If any person here can show cause why these two people should not be joined in holy matrimony, speak now or forever hold your peace.*'

A scuffle of shoes on the stone floor made everyone, including Emma and Ben, turn in alarm.

'Do you have something to say?' the minister asked.

'The baby is coming – I'm going to be a father!' Joe said, as he led Juliet out of the church as fast as he could.

Molly Johnson leapt up from her seat, made her apologies and followed them out of the church.

Ben and Emma looked at each other and laughed.

'I think we can continue now,' Ben said to the vicar.

*

When the wedding party arrived back at Bochym Manor, the doctor and Molly were with Juliet, and Joe was proudly holding the son he never thought he would have, in his arms.

Champagne was sent to their cottage as the speeches were made. A toast was given not only to the bride and groom, but to Joe and Juliet's new arrival. The bridesmaids too were toasted and Loveday was presented with a teddy bear wearing a replica bridesmaid dress which she hugged protectively.

At seven that evening, after Ben had danced around the floor with little Loveday - as he had always promised her he would, Theo and Lowenna said their goodbyes to the happy couple. Loveday was now fast asleep in Theo's arms - the day had exhausted her.

'My lady. Ben.' Lowenna bobbed a curtsy. 'Can I just say you have made our little girl very happy today. All she ever dreamed of was to be a bridesmaid – and not just anyone's bridesmaid - *your* bridesmaid. I never told anybody, but somehow she had got it into her head that one day you two would marry – and she was right! We're so happy for you both.'

'Thank you,' Emma said, 'Loveday made our wedding day complete.'

'We'll bid you good night then,' Theo said. 'Is it alright if Denny stays? He's enjoying himself dancing with Jessie and Daniel's eldest daughter.'

'Of course. We'll make sure he gets home safely later, don't worry.

*

In their tiny cottage, Theo placed Loveday on the bed, and her thin little arms flopped to the sides. Theo glanced at Lowenna with a shared look of deep unspoken concern.

Loveday opened her sleepy eyes. 'Please can I keep my bridesmaid dress on? I want to wear it forever,' she said, her voice almost inaudible.

'Of course, my love.' Lowenna's lip trembled, fighting hard to keep the tears at bay, as she covered her with the bedsheets, tucking her new teddy under the covers.

Loveday smiled and her eyelids drooped. 'I had the best day of my life today, but I'm very tired now. Will you both stay with me,' she said sleepily, reaching out to them.

Lowenna, her throat raw with grief, shot a pleading look to Theo to answer, knowing that if she had spoken, the floodgates would open, and that would ruin them all.

'Of course, we will,' Theo said, his voice wavering as he kissed his daughter's soft cheek. 'Sweet dreams, darling girl. We will be right by your side.'

'Night, night, then,' Loveday murmured.

*

In the next-door cottage, Joe sat on the bed with Juliet as she nursed their newborn son in her arms. The overpowering feeling of love that seared through Juliet's body when he was laid to her breast, surpassed anything

445

she had ever felt before, and she truly believed this feeling would never leave her.

'You have made me the happiest of men today, Juliet,' Joe said touching his son gently on his chubby cheek.

'I know, my love. I'm just so sorry I made you wait so long.'

'The best things come to those who wait.'

They smiled at each other as music and celebrations from the ongoing wedding reception filtered through the open window.

'We're missing all the celebrations,' Joe said softly.

'No, we're not, Joe.' Looking down at her son, sleeping peacefully in her arms, Juliet smiled, she might have been instrumental in helping Lady Emma be with Ben, but she would not change that celebration for this one.

*

Later, in the privacy of the Dower Lodge, Emma and Ben stood before each other as man and wife. Ben smiled with love into Emma's eyes, and the hands that wrote all those letters, softly and gently began at last to discover each other.

*

As the night gave way to the dawn, ribbons of Cornish mist lay across the beautiful gardens that Sarah so lovingly cared for. Nocturnal creatures ceased their rustling in the undergrowth ready to curl up and sleep, and three couples on the Bochym Manor Estate woke to a very different future.

BOCHYM MANOR

Please note, Bochym Manor is a private family home, and the house and gardens are not open to the public. They do however have holiday cottages available. Take a look at Bochym Manor Events on Facebook and Instagram for more information.

Please, if you can, share your love of this book by writing a short review on Amazon.

Thank you. Ann x

Printed in Great Britain
by Amazon